Peacocks of Pemberley

A Pride and Prejudice Variation

By Laraba Kendig

Table of Contents

Laraba's Regency Romance Newsletter

Sign up to get a FREE story just for members called *A Busy and Blessed Day*. You will also be among the first to hear when my next book is released, about special promotions, etc. Click here to get your free book.

Here is the link in case you need to manually type it in: www.subscribepage.com/s1p4z6

Chapter 1

Pemberley

June 3rd, 1812

"Mr. and Mrs. Bingley will occupy the blue suite at the west end of the guest wing, and Mr. and Mrs. Hurst will be in the yellow suite across the corridor. Miss Bennet will be in the green room and Miss Bingley, as usual, will be in the pink room."

Darcy nodded at his housekeeper and said, "Thank you, Mrs. Reynolds. I believe that will do very well. As always, I appreciate your diligent service."

"It is my pleasure, sir," the older woman returned. "Is there anything else?"

"I think that is all, thank you."

The lady bobbed her head and departed, leaving Fitzwilliam Darcy, master of the great estate of Pemberley, alone in his study. A quick glance at the clock showed it was but seven o'clock in the morning, and Mrs. Annesley would not be here for another thirty minutes. There were, of course, agricultural papers to read and letters to write, but nothing was of great urgency.

Darcy wandered over to the large window facing east, beyond which lay a well-manicured lawn and the paved path which led to the extensive stables of Pemberley. His friend, Charles Bingley, would arrive in a few hours along with his two sisters, his brother by marriage, Bingley's new wife, and the new wife's sister.

Darcy ran a weary hand down his face and released a soft sigh. He should have known that Bingley would get into trouble in Hertfordshire without his own guiding hand and direction. Last autumn, Bingley had leased Netherfield Park, located only four and twenty miles from Town, which seemed a perfect opportunity for Bingley to practice overseeing an estate.

When Bingley had first spoken of finding an estate a year previously, Darcy had offered to assist his friend for a few months as the younger man learned about the various responsibilities and challenges of managing an estate. Darcy was very fond of Bingley, and the two were great friends, despite the fact that Darcy was closely related to the Earl of Matlock and Bingley was merely the very wealthy son of a successful man of trade.

But then last summer came the catastrophe at Ramsgate. Darcy's sister Georgiana had been greatly distressed by both George Wickham's lies and treachery. Darcy had known, in his heart of hearts, that it would be unconscionable for him to leave Georgiana alone at

Pemberley, which forced him to bow out of his plan to join Bingley in Hertfordshire.

Thus, the two friends had not seen each other for a year, and in the interim, Charles Bingley had met a blonde angel in Hertfordshire by the name of Miss Jane Bennet and promptly married her.

Darcy groaned again, more loudly now. He knew very little about the new Mrs. Bingley except that she was (of course) exceptionally beautiful along with (of course) being celestial and pure. Bingley had fallen in love many a time with blonde beauties, but he had always fallen out of love in short order. Darcy was certain that if he had been at Netherfield with Bingley, he would have talked sense into his friend before Bingley took the fatal step of marriage.

But Darcy had been at Pemberley in Derbyshire, not at Netherfield Park in Hertfordshire, and now it was too late. For better or for worse, Bingley was married. Darcy was certain that the new Mrs. Bingley had married her husband for his wealth, but he hoped that the lady would treat Bingley well and be faithful to him. His friend was not the sort of man to marry for money or connections, which was just as well. The Bennets, while members of the minor gentry, could not boast of either advantage.

Well, he would find out soon how bad it was. Bingley had spent the early part of the Season in London with his new bride and two of her many sisters, and he now was traveling north on a protracted journey with yet another sister, which included visiting some of the great houses along the way. Darcy, informed of this plan, had naturally invited Bingley and his party to Pemberley for two weeks. He was looking forward to seeing his friend very much, as he had found the last year a lonely one. On the other hand, he was anxious about being faced with the reality of how poorly his friend had chosen without his wise oversight.

His gloomy thoughts were interrupted by the sudden sight of his sister, Georgiana Darcy, dressed in a sprig muslin dress, walking briskly across the lawn toward the walled garden near the southeast corner of the mansion. It was still very early and most young ladies of her age would still be abed, but Georgiana was not most young ladies.

Indeed, she was not like most young ladies.

Darcy lifted his hands and covered his face, swallowing hard in an attempt to retain control over his emotions. Of all the tasks which had been laid on his shoulders in the last seven years, the heaviest was his dear sister. He loved Georgiana more than his own life, but he was often at a loss as to how to care for her properly. Lady Anne Darcy, who had never been strong, had died when Georgiana was but five years of age. Their father, George Darcy had passed on through Heaven's gates when Darcy was one and twenty and Georgiana but nine. It fell to him, to a mere older brother, to guide an unusual young woman through her adolescence, to arrange for her welfare and her instruction so that when the time came, she could make her way, head held high, through the shoals of London society.

He knew he had failed in this, at least. Georgiana was still awkward around strangers and often unpleasantly blunt in her speech. She had made some progress in relating courteously to others in the last years, and then he, fool that he was, had sent her to Ramsgate with Mrs. Younge, who had proven entirely treacherous. The entire episode with George Wickham had been agonizing for both Darcys, and Georgiana had withdrawn even further into her shell. She was, he knew, happy here at Pemberley, but she could not stay here forever! There was a whole, beautiful world out there, and Georgiana, with her intelligence and her position as a Darcy, would be a pearl of great price to some lucky gentleman.

There was a rustle behind him, and Darcy turned to see that Mrs. Annesley, Georgiana's current companion, was standing in the doorway of the study.

"You wished to see me, sir?" she asked courteously.

"Yes," Darcy replied. "Please come in and close the door behind you."

1

Miss Elizabeth Bennet cast an experienced glance out of the window and bent her head over the desk. The sun on the eastern horizon glowed through a haze of pinks and purples, which meant it was still very early. She knew from long experience that once she was awake, there was no point in staying in bed, and she owed her friend, Charlotte Collins, a letter.

The Galloping Goose

Derbyshire

June 3rd, 1812

My dear Charlotte,

I write to you from the Galloping Goose, which is, I hope you agree, an absurd name for an inn. I have observed geese flying and fluttering and even running, but certainly never galloping. It matters not. The feather beds are comfortable, and the inn is not as noisy as many of the places in which we have stayed on our journey north. Oh, and the cook is marvelous! I am thankful we stayed here two nights as it gave us the opportunity to walk to a nearby waterfall yesterday morning. It was quite magnificent,

Charlotte, with the water falling into a deep basin and swirling ominously. Mrs. Hurst, who accompanied me and Charles on the walk to the falls, was in ecstasies over the wildflowers growing along the path. I confess to some surprise in Louisa; I found Charles's sisters proud and condescending at Netherfield last autumn, but now that Jane is married to Charles, Louisa has thawed toward both of us considerably. She also finds true joy in observing and sketching plant life, which gives us something to talk about during our times together.

We will drive today to Pemberley, the magnificent estate of Mr. Fitzwilliam Darcy himself. I concede to being most eager to meet the gentleman. Charles has said, more than once, that Mr. Darcy is the very best of friends, but then Charles, like Jane, looks for excellence in everyone. Lady Catherine de Bourgh also had nothing but good to say about her nephew, but I must confide that your husband's patroness and I do not agree about everything.

Against these cries of praise are the words of Lieutenant George Wickham in Meryton; he claims that the Mr. Darcy is jealous, resentful, and proud, and that he cruelly refused to bestow a valuable living on Mr. Wickham, his own father's godson.

I believe I can hear your very voice in my ears, my friend, and of course you are correct. I ought not to cast judgment until I meet the man. And I do promise you that I will be courteous and well-mannered during our time at

Pemberley. At the very least, the grounds should be a joy to observe.

I am glad to hear that the early peas grew well, and that Mr. Collins continues to enjoy working in the garden. I did enjoy my time in Hunsford this spring very much and often remember our pleasant hours of conversation together. I...

She broke off writing at a tap at her door and looked up in some surprise. The maid who brought her tea would not knock.

"Come in!" she called, and a moment later, the door swung open to reveal her beloved elder sister, Mrs. Jane Bingley.

"Jane! You are up early!"

"I am, Lizzy," Jane agreed, her handsome face drawn with weariness. "I woke up feeling quite ill and then could not get back to sleep."

"My poor Jane," Elizabeth said sympathetically. "Would you care for some tea?"

"I already had some, thank you," her sister responded, walking over to sink down on an overstuffed chair near the cold fireplace. "I wished to ask you a favor, but I do beg of you to say no if you cannot bear it."

Elizabeth lifted a dark eyebrow and smiled. "I cannot imagine a request of yours that I would deny, my dear sister."

"You might deny this one," Jane returned with a comical twist of her lips. "The Hursts' carriage has a broken lynchpin, you know, and it has taken longer than expected to fix it. Two of the servants can wait here and ride with it to Pemberley tomorrow, while Charles and I, Caroline, the Hursts, and you take the servants' carriage to Pemberley along with our own."

"That sounds reasonable."

"Yes, it is, but the servants' carriage is not well sprung, and Mrs. Hurst suffers greatly from motion sickness, so she wondered if..."

"If she could ride with you, and I could ride with Caroline," Elizabeth finished.

"Precisely."

Elizabeth considered for a few seconds and then shook a reproving finger, and responded dramatically, "I will do it, of course, but you will owe me a great favor in return."

"If it is really too much," Jane began worriedly, only for Elizabeth to interrupt her by saying, "I am teasing, my dear. I can manage a few hours of Caroline's company, I assure you. In fact, I daresay I will find our discussion most instructive. She knows all about the Darcys, of course."

Jane cast her eyes heavenward and said, "Yes, and is most eager to speak of her companionship with both Mr. and Miss Darcy. I do not know, Elizabeth; perhaps you should sit with the Hursts, and Charles and I should journey with Caroline."

"Nonsense," Elizabeth replied briskly. "It would not do for my beloved elder sister arriving at Pemberley wilting and nauseous. You are with child and ought not to be bumped around in a poorly sprung carriage."

"Thank you, Lizzy. I hope that Caroline will not be too exasperating."

"I do as well," Elizabeth returned with a smirk. "Now do go lie down again and try to get more sleep before we depart."

/

Pemberley

"Please sit, Mrs. Annesley," Darcy suggested.

His sister's companion, a pretty dark-haired woman of some five and thirty years, obediently walked over to a brown leather chair and sank into it, clasped her hands in her lap, and waited.

Darcy made his way slowly to his desk and sat down behind it, deep in thought, and then said, "You are aware that Mr. Bingley and his party will be arriving today."

"Yes, sir."

"I am concerned about Miss Darcy. Mr. Bingley is a kind gentleman, but his sisters, while eager to please, are overly talkative at times. Furthermore, Mr. Bingley's new wife and her sister are completely unknown quantities. I think that it would be unwise to bring Georgiana down to meet the party until I have the opportunity to meet and evaluate them."

"I agree, Mr. Darcy," Mrs. Annesley said composedly. "Miss Darcy is currently working diligently on her new piece of music, and of course she is devoted to her activities outside. I believe she would not be pleased to meet the new guests today, as she is intent on mastering a particularly difficult passage."

Darcy sighed. His sister did not especially like new people at the best of times and now was not the best of times.

"If I may say, Mr. Darcy?" Mrs. Annesley said hesitantly.

"Please, do go on," Darcy invited.

"I believe Miss Darcy would do better if she met the newcomers one at a time or, in the case of the couples, two at a time. I fear she would find an entire group to be overwhelming."

"That is a wise recommendation, Mrs. Annesley. I will consider how that can be arranged. Thank you."

Chapter 2

On the road to Pemberley

"I do beg of you not to concern yourself about your garments, Elizabeth," Miss Caroline Bingley said with false solicitude. "Mr. Darcy will not think the worse of you for being simply dressed, and it would be quite inappropriate, given your station, for you to wear the type of clothing which is common at Pemberley. Mr. and Miss Darcy, as close relations to an earl, wish for the distinction of rank to be preserved."

"Of course they do," Elizabeth returned, her eyes dancing.

Miss Bingley was not a perceptive woman, but she was well enough acquainted with Elizabeth to know that her companion was amused.

"You find my words diverting?" she demanded loftily.

"I do, a little," Elizabeth answered. "Pray forgive me; I am not laughing at you, of course. It is merely that when I visited my friend Charlotte Collins in Kent a few months ago, her husband told me exactly the same thing before I had dinner with Lady Catherine de Bourgh, aunt to Mr. Darcy. The Darcys and de Bourghs are fortunate to have such loyal and faithful connections. I am most appreciative, Caroline. It would be quite dreadful if I put myself forward in an unbecoming way while staying at Pemberley."

Caroline stared at her companion suspiciously, but Elizabeth merely peered back with limpid innocence, and Caroline was satisfied.

"I flatter myself that I *am* a close friend to the Darcys," the lady said complacently. "Mr. Darcy is my brother's closest friend, and I am confident that Miss Darcy enjoys my companionship very much. She is a truly remarkable young lady! I have never met a girl so accomplished for her age. She is but sixteen, you know, and already plays the pianoforte far better than I do, and I know myself to be quite a master at the instrument!"

"She sounds remarkable," Elizabeth replied, keeping her tone carefully neutral. She was quite certain she would dislike both Mr. and Miss Darcy profoundly. Mr. Darcy, of course, had deprived the charming Lieutenant George Wickham of a living intended for him, and Miss Darcy, according to the same Mr. Wickham, was excessively proud. Given their close familial relationship to the haughty Lady Catherine de Bourgh, it was no surprise that the Darcys were arrogant, though it was, perhaps, startling that Mr. Darcy was reputedly a close friend to Charles Bingley.

At least Pemberley was reputed to be beautiful, and she would have Jane by her side throughout the entire visit. Sweet Jane, now Mrs. Bingley, could render any social occasion a pleasure. Elizabeth was also very fond of Charles, her new brother by marriage. She was not the sort of person to be easily intimidated, and in spite of Mr. and Miss Darcy's pride, and Miss Bingley's sniping, she was certain she would have an agreeable time at Pemberley.

/

Pemberley

"Bingley!" Darcy exclaimed as his friend stepped out of his carriage and onto the gravel drive in front of Pemberley

"Darcy," his friend returned, reaching forward to shake his hand. "It is so good to see you again. It has been entirely too long!"

"I agree," Darcy replied, his soul lightening within him. It had been almost a year since he had enjoyed his friend's buoyant presence. It had been a difficult year, leaving him feeling emotionally dry and weary. Bingley had always been a source of good cheer, and Darcy had missed his friend more than he had realized.

"Darcy, I must introduce you to my bride," Bingley said, turning back toward the carriage. He held out his hand as a young woman, dressed in a dark blue gown, grasped his hand and stepped out beside him.

"Jane, my dear, Mr. Fitzwilliam Darcy, master of Pemberley and my good friend. Darcy, my wife, Mrs. Jane Bingley."

"Welcome, Mrs. Bingley," Darcy said, bowing as Jane curtsied. A moment later, Mr. and Mrs. Hurst emerged from the carriage, and in the midst of greetings and salutations, Darcy surreptitiously analyzed the new Mrs. Bingley.

His first thoughts were full of grim satisfaction. Mrs. Bingley was, as he expected, blonde and blue eyed. She was also, he admitted to himself, remarkably handsome; indeed, if she had come out in London society, she would have been one of the belles of the season. It was no surprise at all that the lady had captured Bingley's fickle heart, and based on the proud expression on Bingley's face, the marriage was a satisfactory one.

For now, at any rate. At least the new Mrs. Bingley was dressed with rather surprising restraint. Instead of wearing whites or yellows, which would show the dirt during the journey, she was wearing a patterned blue and green muslin gown. Her hat, too, was a simple straw hat trimmed only with a blue ribbon. Mrs. Bingley looked far more sedate than he expected for a woman who had married for money.

In the midst of his contemplation, another carriage had pulled up and a feminine voice cried out, "Mr. Darcy!"

Darcy slowly blew out a breath and turned to bow at Miss Caroline Bingley. The lady was, unlike her new sister, dressed in a light, diaphanous garment, and Darcy was startled to realize that the bodice was made out of silver muslin. It was a ridiculous gown to wear during travel but it was also an expensive dress; Miss Bingley had always flaunted her wealth, especially when she knew that Darcy would be present.

"Miss Bingley, welcome to Pemberley," he said courteously, taking her hand and bowing over it.

"Thank you, Mr. Darcy," Caroline gushed. "Oh, it has been far too long since we have seen one another! I do hope you and Miss Darcy are well?"

"We are," Darcy said calmly and was relieved when Bingley swam suddenly into view, his face wreathed with smiles, and said, "Darcy, I must make you known to my new sister. Elizabeth, Mr. Darcy, our gracious host. Darcy, Miss Bennet, Jane's next younger sister."

Again Darcy found himself bowing across from an unknown lady, and again he found himself reluctantly impressed. The girl standing in front of him was very pretty, if perhaps not quite as handsome as her older sister, with dark chestnut curls peeking out from her straw bonnet. Like Mrs. Bingley, she was sensibly dressed in a tan dress with a green bodice. She wore a necklace with a simple cross around her neck, and her dark eyes glowed with vitality and intelligence.

"Miss Bennet, welcome to Pemberley," he said courteously.

"Thank you, sir. We are most grateful for your invitation," the lady responded, then turned toward the lake which shimmered in front of the massive front façade of Pemberley. "You have an incredible view here, Mr. Darcy. Derbyshire is wilder than my home county of Hertfordshire, and I find the hills and rocks and streams to be remarkable."

"Thank you, Miss Bennet," Darcy replied, thawing a little. The lady was unusual in complimenting the landscape instead of the house itself.

"Of course, the scenery is nothing compared to the mansion!" Caroline Bingley simpered. "Pemberley is awe inspiring, and it is far greater than my brother's leased mansion of Netherfield Park. As for Longbourn, well, it is no doubt a charming little house, but nothing compared to the edifice before us. Do you not agree, Miss Bennet?"

There was a poorly concealed, venomous note in Miss Bingley's voice, but Elizabeth Bennet merely smiled and said, "Longbourn is much smaller, yes, but then my father's estate is far smaller than Pemberley. It seems reasonable that the size of the master's home ought to correlate with the size of the estate."

"That is true enough, Elizabeth," Mr. Bingley said, shooting an irritated look at his unmarried sister. "But come, the sun is hot and Jane should get out from the rays."

Jane Bingley blushed and said, "Oh, I am well enough, I assure you."

"Bingley is correct," Darcy said courteously. "Please, I beg you to come within. Mrs. Reynolds, our housekeeper, will show you to your rooms where you can refresh yourselves."

"Thank you, Mr. Darcy," Caroline exclaimed fulsomely. "You are too kind."

/

Twenty minutes later, Bingley, now dressed in buckskin breeches and an olive green coat, stepped into the study where Darcy was reading through a report on the wheat fields of Pemberley's home farm. Darcy set down the papers with a smile and said, "Do come in and have some brandy."

"Thank you," Bingley replied, wandering over to an open window which looked out over a large pond. "Ah, that breeze is most refreshing. I am sincerely grateful for your invitation, Darcy. Jane is not entirely well, and the London air is not salubrious this time of year, nor is she comfortable in a moving carriage."

"I hope it is nothing serious?"

"Well, no," Bingley said cautiously, and then grinned. "I can trust you, I know. The truth is that we are quite certain Jane is with child. We have not told my sisters but yes, it seems definite."

"Congratulations!" Darcy returned, and he meant it. Like most gentlemen, Bingley was eager to sire an heir. More than that, though, his friend had always been excellent with children. Indeed, Bingley had met Georgiana when the girl was only ten years of age and had managed to befriend her, which was not an easy task. Darcy had even entertained the hope that one day Bingley and his sister would make a match of it. Bingley was one of the few men who would be consistently patient with his sister's more unusual character traits. It was not obvious that Georgiana would ever make a suitable wife to anyone, but Bingley had been Darcy's best hope, now lost.

"I declare I am the happiest man in all of England," Bingley said, breaking into Darcy's gloomy thoughts. "I do pray that you find such a compatible wife, my friend.

Life is unquestionably better with a loyal, faithful, and loving companion at your side."

"You are fortunate to have found such a lady," Darcy said as he began pouring brandy into glasses. "What can you tell me about your bride? I know you wrote me several times while you were in Hertfordshire and London, but I confess that your letters were…"

He trailed off and Bingley laughed aloud. "Difficult to read? I know that I am often illegible, and given my courtship and marriage to Jane, I was probably even more confusing than usual. I would be delighted to tell you about my wife and her family if it is not too boring."

"Not at all, though I must ask, will Mrs. Bingley require your presence in the next hour?"

"No, she urged me to come and spend an hour or two with you while she rests. Elizabeth will make certain that Jane is well cared for; the two sisters are very close."

"That is good," Darcy replied, handing a glass to his friend and sitting down on a wingback chair near an open window.

"It is," Bingley said warmly, taking a sip of his own drink as he sank down into a chair near his friend. "Well, anyone with eyes can see that my wife is incredibly handsome. But more than that, she is kind, gentle, loving, and godly. I have never met anyone with such a tender heart. She has won the loyalty of the servants both at

Netherfield Park and in our London house through her good nature."

Darcy was impressed. Many a woman won admiration from nobles and gentry because of her beauty, but a servant often saw a different side of her mistress. In truth, one of the reasons that Darcy disliked Caroline Bingley was that she was often rude to servants, indicating that her natural tendency was to be arrogant and disdainful toward others. When she dealt with her social betters, she managed to conceal such propensities, but Darcy was more interested in a woman's true character as opposed to the façade she put on in elevated company.

"How many siblings does Mrs. Bingley have?" he asked.

"She has four younger sisters, with Elizabeth being second to Jane. Her father is master of a small estate which borders Netherfield Park, called Longbourn. Regrettably, the estate will pass to a distant relation when Mr. Bennet dies, as the estate is entailed to the male line."

"That is most unfortunate," Darcy agreed with a frown. "Do the daughters have reasonable dowries?"

"No. Mrs. Bennet, whose father was a solicitor, brought five thousand pounds into the marriage, and it has become clear that Mr. Bennet has not set any substantial sum for his daughters."

Darcy compressed his lips and said, "They must have been very pleased at your marriage, then."

Bingley's usually cheerful expression transformed into cold disapproval. "They were pleased because they wished for their daughter to be happy, nothing more. I expect such remarks from Caroline, but not you, Darcy."

"My apologies," Darcy said hastily. "Though there is no shame in a lady seeking a man of fortune, especially given the financial situation of Mrs. Bingley's family."

"That is true enough," Bingley allowed, his expression relaxing, "though Caroline, and to some degree Louisa, drove me nearly mad with similar remarks when I was courting Jane. My younger sister kept whining that the Bennets were merely interested in my fortune, and that my beloved would marry me for my money alone. Such absurdity! My dear bride is a most honorable woman, and she would not pretend an attachment which did not exist."

Darcy blinked and took another gulp of brandy. On this occasion, he was inclined to agree with Miss Bingley's assessment of the situation, but it would be foolish to say so, and would only serve to offend his friend. For better or for worse, Bingley was married to the former Miss Jane Bennet of Longbourn, and nothing could be done about it now.

Chapter 3

"Thank you, Lizzy," Jane murmured, taking a sip of cold lemonade and then setting it on a wooden side table near the bed. "Do not feel you must linger here; I expect that I will sleep for at least two hours."

Elizabeth cast a longing glance toward the window, which was covered in nearly-opaque shades so that she could only see light dimly filtering through it. "Are you quite certain?"

"Of course I am; indeed, I will find it difficult to sleep with you hovering over me. You should take a walk inside or outside the house, or perhaps prowl around in search of the library. Charles says it is most remarkable."

"Caroline Bingley said the very same," Elizabeth said with a roll of her eyes, "so it must be true."

Jane chuckled and lay back against her pillows. "I do thank you for being civil to Caroline, even when it is difficult."

"I am afraid I am often satirical when we speak together, though I am not certain she understands that."

"I am certain she does not," Jane murmured, closing her eyes. "You are being subtle, far more than Father ever is, and she does not realize when you are poking fun at her."

"That is probably for the best, as I don't wish to be too unkind to her," Elizabeth responded as she leaned over to kiss her sister on the forehead. She stepped back and regarded Jane's face for a moment, then relaxed and turned to leave the room. Poor Jane had been feeling very sickly most mornings, and hours in carriages, even well sprung ones, were hard on her. She was thankful they were at Pemberley, where Jane would no longer be jolted over good and bad roads.

She stepped out of the bedroom and shut it behind her. Jane relaxed as the sound of her sister's footfalls faded. She groaned and curled up in a ball, attempting to find a comfortable position. She was overjoyed that she had already conceived a child with her beloved Charles, but she felt truly terrible much of the time, not just physically, but in her emotional state as well. She was used to being a calm, collected woman, but now she grew frustrated easily and often fought tears over foolish things.

/

Elizabeth walked down the corridor a few yards and then entered her own room, which was adjacent to but not connected with Jane's bedchamber. That privilege was, of course, set aside for Charles Bingley. The guest quarters at Pemberley were as impressive as everything else, and thus Mr. and Mrs. Bingley were sharing a suite composed of two large bedchambers connected by a pleasant sitting room. Since Elizabeth knew that the Bingleys spent many nights together in the same bed, this was an ideal situation. For at least the hundredth time, Elizabeth thanked God for Jane's marriage; her sister was a charming, sweet gentlewoman, but she was also inclined to look for the best in everyone. Elizabeth, with a far more pessimistic view of mankind, had worried that Jane, whose beauty was truly remarkable, would fall in love and marry a man whose sole interest was in Jane's physical perfection. Instead, Charles Bingley had leased Netherfield Hall, and fallen in love with Jane, and she with him, and now they were happily married.

Elizabeth was less enamored with her new sisters by marriage, though Louisa Hurst had proven a far more amiable companion these last months. Caroline, on the other hand, had tried her hardest to keep Charles from wedding the eldest Miss Bennet. Now that Jane was the new Mrs. Bingley, Miss Bingley retained a veneer of courtesy around Jane and her family of birth, but often made subtle comments about their lack of education, their lack of fortune, and their lack of connections. It said a great deal that even Jane, who desired to see good in everyone, no longer thought highly of her new unmarried sister.

Elizabeth opened the door to her own chamber and sighed with pleasure as she entered the room, which was fitted up in greens and whites, with a charming seascape dominating the wall surrounding the unlit fireplace. Elizabeth had never seen the ocean, but she hoped it was as marvelous as the painting depicted with its white capped aqua waves and tiny painted figures.

The door opened behind her, and she turned as a young maid entered, her arms full of towels, and promptly squeaked in surprise. "Oh, I apologize, Miss Bennet. I did not mean to intrude!"

"Not at all," Elizabeth returned with a welcoming smile. "In fact, I have a question for you. I would like to stretch my legs outside, but naturally I do not wish to interfere with the smooth operation of the estate. Is there a garden where I could walk, perhaps?"

"Oh yes, Miss!" the maid replied eagerly. "If you will wait a few minutes while I finish my duties, I will guide you to the nearby door which leads to the rose garden. It is lovely!"

/

"It is just through that door, Miss," the servant said, pointing at a wooden door at the end of the corridor.

"Thank you," Elizabeth said. She walked down the corridor, opened the door, which was decorated with carved rose blossoms, and stepped out onto a paved walkway. She found herself alone in a large sunken garden, which was located along the south side of the guest wing of Pemberley. She pulled in a deep breath of clean air and felt her body relax with pleasure. She had enjoyed the trip north, with all its sights and sounds, but her current locale was both interesting and beautiful, and she looked forward to a time of relaxation.

She began wandering along the paved path, which twisted and turned its way through a variety of rose beds, some filled with bushes, others with trellises where roses had been trained to climb above her head. She had never seen such a profusion of rose blossoms, some red, some pink, some yellow, some white, some a mix of colors. The sizes varied as well, and the shapes, and the combined scent of so many blossoms was a true delight. Her mother, who loved roses, would be cooing with wonder at the very sight of this garden. There were definitely advantages to being very wealthy. This little piece of heaven must require the services of numerous gardeners!

After walking slowly for ten minutes, she crossed a small wooden bridge which was thrown across a tiny brook that wended its way from east to west in the garden. Elizabeth guessed that the water had been diverted from a large stream elsewhere. Pemberley seemed to be well watered, which was another point in its favor. It was, perhaps, not so surprising that Mr. Darcy was such a proud man. He was the extremely wealthy master of one of the largest, finest estates in all of Britain. Perhaps he had a right to be proud.

She paused to sniff a large yellow rose on a trellis, whose head was bobbing happily in the slight breeze, just as a strange sound emanated from beyond the wooden lattice. She straightened, her brow wrinkled in confusion. It was something between a trill, a warble, a hoot, and a squawk. What man or woman or child or animal could make such a noise?

She walked a few more feet and rounded the trellis, looking toward the source of the strange sound. A stone wall, at least ten feet high, loomed some distance away, a wall without a roof. It seemed that Pemberley, in addition to everything else, could boast of a walled garden. A paved path led from the rose garden, across a patch of well-trimmed grass, to a door in the wall.

A moment later, the same cry came again, obviously from within the walled area. Elizabeth started walking toward the door in a mixture of curiosity and concern. It seemed unlikely that a person could make such a noise, but suppose someone was injured within the walled plot? There were no servants in sight; surely it would do no harm to take a quick peek within?

Now that she was nearer the door, she could hear additional hoots and whistles. It seemed likely that there was an animal or animals within making the noise, but what animal?

She reached out to the knob of the door, hesitated briefly, opened it, and stepped within.

/

"Is it not marvelous to be back at Pemberley again?" Caroline Bingley asked, staring out the window of her sister's sitting room.

"Yes," Louisa Hurst agreed from her seated position on a leather settee, her attention on her knitting. "The air is fresh and fine after our weeks in London."

"I was quite pleased with our reception. I am entirely certain that Mr. Darcy missed me."

Louisa compressed her lips but said nothing. She knew perfectly well that Mr. Darcy would never offer for her sister. Why should he? The money Caroline would bring into marriage meant nothing to a man who earned ten thousand pounds a year in income. Darcy was nephew to an earl and a lady, and rumor had it that he was unofficially betrothed to his cousin Miss de Bourgh, heiress of the vast estate of Rosings in Kent.

But Louisa also knew that her sister was wholly unwilling to admit that she was unsuitable for the role of mistress of Pemberley. Ever since Charles had brought Darcy to visit the Bingleys' London home, Caroline had been enamored of Darcy's good looks, wealth, and connections to high society. Until Darcy was actually married, Caroline would flirt and boast of her own accomplishments. It was embarrassing and annoying.

"Of course, Mr. Darcy may no longer be willing to marry me now that Charles has been foolish enough to wed Jane. Really, what was our brother thinking? Men cannot be trusted to look out for their own interests. If only Mr. Darcy had been able to join us at Netherfield last fall! He would have pointed out the Bennets' unsuitability, and Charles always listens to Mr. Darcy."

Louisa frowned in irritation. Caroline had made similar statements at least one hundred times since their brother's marriage to the former Miss Bennet.

"Jane is charming, kind, and a gentleman's daughter," Louisa pointed out for at least the hundredth time. "No doubt Charles could have won a better connected bride, but he and Jane seem very happy together."

"Happiness," Caroline snorted inelegantly, and began pacing up and down the blue and scarlet carpet. "Happiness is for peasants. Our father did not struggle and strive and work so that his only son could be *happy* marrying a country girl with no dowry and poor connections, whose only asset is her considerable beauty."

Louisa lifted her eyes from her knitting and glared at her sister. "Jane is a pleasant, refined lady, and she and Charles are legally married. There is nothing to be done about it, Caroline. It would be best to accept the situation and turn your attention onto other matters."

Caroline harrumphed and sat down, and then admitted, "You are correct, of course. Nothing can be done about Charles. However, I will not give up hopes for my own ambitions. If nothing else, Jane and Elizabeth will prove a good contrast to my own accomplishments. It is shocking how little they are able to do. Jane cannot draw or sing or play the pianoforte ... and Elizabeth! Well, the people of backwards Meryton may think her an accomplished musician, but she plays and sings very poorly compared to us."

Louisa was of the opinion that Elizabeth, while not an expert, had a charming voice and played with reasonable skill. But again, there was no point in defending her. She went back to her knitting with a sigh, letting a moment of silence pass before she spoke again.

"Perhaps you and I should practice a duet?" she suggested, hoping to turn Caroline's thoughts in another direction. "I am certain the gentlemen would enjoy such an indulgence in the near future."

"That is an excellent idea," Caroline responded, her face suddenly cheerful. "I am certain Mr. Darcy will be particularly impressed. Miss Darcy is, of course, a remarkable player at the pianoforte, but she sings not at all."

She smiled to herself as she imagined this scene and said, "No doubt Mr. Darcy will find the contrast between Elizabeth's passable attempts and my lovely voice to be compelling indeed. Mr. Darcy will offer for me by the time it is ready for us to depart, Louisa. I am certain of it."

Chapter 4

Elizabeth pushed the door shut behind her and leaned up against the wood, overwhelmed with astonishment and wonder. She had expected the walled garden to be laid out with beds of flowers, perhaps with trees and fountains interspersed. Instead the entire area, which appeared to be close to an acre in size, seemed more like a scene in an exotic painting. In the center of the plot was a group of trees, each at least twenty feet high, under which numerous birds wandered to and fro, all large, some with blue bellies and a cornucopia of green, yellow, and blue iridescent feathers trailing behind them. Several of the winged creatures turned their heads toward her and began trilling and chirping, and the two birds closest to her retreated a few feet, obviously nervous about her presence.

"Who are you?" a voice demanded sharply from her left. Startled, Elizabeth turned and observed a girl of some fifteen or sixteen summers standing near her. The young woman was dressed in a simple blue gown which was rather too big for her, with an equally simple straw hat over her blonde locks, and she wore dirty half boots on her large feet.

"I am a guest at Pemberley as of a few hours ago," Elizabeth said coolly, arching one eyebrow in a challenging manner. She was not accustomed to peremptory challenges from the lower classes.

"Ah, are you Miss Bennet or Mrs. Bingley?" the girl asked, stepping closer, her blue eyes now focused on the cross pendant around Elizabeth's neck.

"I am Miss Bennet," Elizabeth answered in some confusion. It seemed unlikely that a servant girl who worked outside would know either her or her sister's name. Could this be an indigent cousin of the Darcys or something of the sort?

"Do you like birds, Miss Bennet?" the girl asked, gesturing toward the center of the garden.

Elizabeth turned back to view the strutting inhabitants of the garden and heaved a sigh of ecstasy. Birds hardly seemed the correct description for the wonderful creatures bobbing and trilling and murmuring within the stone walls of the garden.

"I am fond of doves and robins, and rather afraid of roosters because one pecked me as a child," Elizabeth said, "but I have never seen anything like this in all my life. Surely these are peacocks?"

"The *males* are peacocks," the young woman said reprovingly. "The females are known as peahens, and their young are peachicks. All together, they are known as peafowl."

"I suppose that makes sense," Elizabeth mused, her eyes focusing on a particularly handsome bird that was standing some yards away, its blue and green feathers rising high above its sleek, plump body. "Without a doubt, this is astonishing. I have seen pictures of peacocks in books, but to see them in real life! They are more beautiful than I imagined!"

"You truly like them?" the girl asked in a suspicious voice, causing Elizabeth to turn and regard her with surprise.

"I do," she said. "Truly, I cannot imagine anyone who would not like them. They are absolutely beautiful."

"My Aunt Catherine does not," the maiden responded with a scowl. "She says that they are noisy and useless, and that it is idiotic of me to spend so much time tending to my peafowl when I ought to be learning to speak French and design tables. I have no interest in other languages, and we have plenty of tables at Pemberley, but that does not seem to matter to my aunt."

Elizabeth's heart beat faster at these words and she asked, "Your aunt? Could you be referring to Lady Catherine de Bourgh?"

"Yes," the girl said, frowning even more hideously. "Do you know her?"

"I do not know her well, of course, but I met her when I was visiting a friend in Kent a few months ago. But if Lady Catherine is your aunt, you must be Miss Georgiana Darcy?"

This provoked a look of surprise and the girl said, "Yes, I am Miss Darcy."

Elizabeth took a startled step backwards and said hastily, "I must apologize for this intrusion. I regret that ... oh, this is terribly awkward!"

"Why?" Miss Darcy asked, now looking perturbed.

"I ought not to have come here without your permission, or Mr. Darcy's, and we have not been properly introduced by your brother."

"I find formal introductions most tedious," Miss Darcy stated, turning her face to peer at her birds. "Furthermore, you have my permission to observe the peafowl so long as I am here with you. Some of them are timid, and others are aggressive, and it would not be safe for you or the birds to be here without my oversight. Would you like to visit the peafowl again?"

"Very much," Elizabeth said warmly. "They are astonishing, Miss Darcy. How many peafowl live here?"

Georgiana Darcy grasped a gold chain around her neck and pulled it out from behind the bodice of her dress, revealing a delicate watch.

"I must return to the house in five minutes to change before my lesson with my music master," she announced, ignoring Elizabeth's query. "I will be here at noon tomorrow, if you wish to join me. You can ask questions then."

"Thank you, Miss Darcy," Elizabeth said, her brow crinkling at the girl's abrupt manner. "Perhaps I will see you in a few hours at dinner?"

Georgiana Darcy shook her head and declared, "I will probably have a headache."

Elizabeth blinked. "I am sorry. I hope you feel better soon."

"No," Georgiana explained, her gaze drifting down toward the hem of Elizabeth's dress. "I will not have a real headache. I do not like long dinners with people I do not know, and I am not fond of Miss Bingley. My brother says it is not polite to say that I do not like to be in the company of strangers and Miss Bingley, and that instead I should say that I have a headache."

Elizabeth found herself smiling. "Your brother is correct that it would be discourteous to be so blunt, but I will admit that I find Miss Bingley rather difficult at times as well."

"She is proud and conceited, and she flatters me," Georgiana said simply. "I must go and you are not allowed to be in here without me."

"Oh, I am sorry," Elizabeth said, opening the door and passing through.

Georgiana followed her and, to Elizabeth's surprise, produced a key from her pocket, which she used to lock the door.

"Well, I hope to see you tomorrow at noon," Elizabeth said.

"That will be nice," Georgiana Darcy said, and hurried away.

/

"Where is dear Miss Darcy?" Miss Bingley asked as Darcy entered the drawing room with Bingley at his heels.

"She has a headache," Darcy explained. "She sends her regrets that she is unable to join us this evening."

Elizabeth, along with Jane, had entered the drawing room some fifteen minutes previously, and she suppressed a smile at these words. After her curious interaction with her host's sister, Elizabeth had returned to her room and tried to read a book, though her mind inevitably wandered to the unusual Miss Darcy and her flock of incredible peafowl.

"Oh," Caroline said, looking disappointed, "well, I do hope she feels better soon!"

"As do I," Bingley said heartily as he walked over to stand by his bride. "My dear, how are you feeling?"

"I am much better, thank you," Jane answered, gazing fondly into her husband's face. "The air is so fresh and crisp here, especially compared to London."

"Yes, I quite agree."

The butler entered at this moment to announce dinner, and the gentlemen and ladies paired up to enter the dining room. Darcy took Jane's arm, Hurst took his wife's arm, and Charles gathered up both Caroline and Elizabeth and guided them into a small dining room with large windows. Elizabeth took her seat between Charles and Hurst, and found her eyes shifting to the window across from her. Some fifty yards away, a succession house, full of greenery, rose a full fifteen feet high from the ground. It was yet another indication of the vast wealth of Pemberley that Mr. Darcy owned such a fine greenhouse!

Servants began moving to and fro and moments later, and the party began serving food onto their plates. It was, of course, a lavish meal, though, to Elizabeth's relief, there was only one course. She was a hearty eater, but with such a profusion of dishes, she would need no additional sustenance once these were removed. Nor did she wish for Jane to sit overlong, since her sister, while generally better in the afternoons and evenings, was not feeling entirely well.

"My dear Charles," Miss Bingley said, "I do hope that during our time here you will ask Mr. Darcy his advice about managing an estate well, though Hertfordshire is far different from Derbyshire. Nonetheless, I am certain Mr. Darcy could provide much guidance, assuming you intend to keep the lease on the Netherfield estate. I believe you would do better to find an estate farther north, but I suppose Jane would not appreciate that."

Jane took a bite of potatoes, chewed, and swallowed before answering. "I believe Netherfield is a fine estate, but I would not be averse to moving elsewhere if Charles so desires it."

"My dear, I would never wish to remove you from your family in such a way," her husband protested.

"*You* are my family now," Jane said firmly. "A man is to leave his mother and father and cleave to his wife, and the reverse is true as well. If you decide that Netherfield is not ideal for your purposes, I will understand completely."

"And what of you, Elizabeth?" Caroline asked, turning a soulful look on her sister by marriage. "Would you protest if Jane and Charles moved away from Hertfordshire and your precious Longbourn?"

"I would not," Elizabeth said calmly, directing a smile at her sister. "Of course I would miss my Jane, but it is important that she be happy, and I cannot imagine that she would be happy if Charles was not."

"As to that," Charles said, "I believe I am a fortunate soul in that I find myself content in most situations. I find Netherfield a most convenient estate. I do hope you can visit someday, Darcy; I believe you will be pleased with it."

"Not that it compares in the least to Pemberley, of course!" Caroline exclaimed.

"Every estate is different," Elizabeth said. "Pemberley is certainly larger than Netherfield, and Netherfield is larger than Longbourn. There is more than size to consider, however; one advantage of Hertfordshire is that it is within easy distance of London, whereas it takes several days to reach Town from Derbyshire."

"I would argue, Miss Bennet, that such a distance is not necessarily a disadvantage," Darcy commented.

Elizabeth bent an arch look upon her host. "I quite understand, sir. If one is not particularly enamored of city life, it is convenient to be able to use distance as an excuse for declining invitations."

"Oh, Eliza," Miss Bingley exclaimed, "I am confident you misunderstand Mr. Darcy! As nephew of the Earl of Matlock, he has such wonderful opportunities for enjoying the very best of London society. Doubtless his experiences are far different than yours have been when you visit your uncle and aunt in Cheapside."

"That is true enough," Elizabeth agreed. "Certainly I enjoy parties and dancing, but in my mind, the real advantages of London lie in the museums and plays and the like, and our relations, the Gardiners, are kind enough to expose us to such amusements when we visit them."

"Mr. Gardiner is a man of trade like my father," Bingley explained to Darcy. "He and his wife are delightful people, and I am certain you would like them very much."

Darcy nodded but did not speak. While he was impressed with Mrs. Bingley's manners and affection toward her husband, he could only be dismayed at this further proof of her poor connections. Bingley, as a graduate of Cambridge, blessed with a great fortune and a winsome personality, could have easily found a wealthier bride with grander relations. If only Darcy had been able to join Bingley in Hertfordshire the previous autumn!

He took a bite of roast pheasant and found his gaze shifting to Miss Bennet, who was now engaged in a subtly antagonistic exchange with Miss Bingley.

She was a beautiful woman, Miss Bennet, and obviously intelligent. Miss Bingley obviously disliked her and took every opportunity to denigrate the Bennets, their connections, and their estate. It was to Miss Bennet's credit that she managed to be consistently courteous while also holding her own against Bingley's waspish sister.

At that moment, Miss Bennet's gaze shifted to his, and he felt his heart lurch within him. It was not the coquettish look that he generally received from single ladies. No, Miss Bennet was staring directly into his eyes, and her own eyes, a glorious mixture of greens and browns, were full of challenge. He was aware of a prevailing sense of discomfort in the room, and realized that he had missed part of the conversation. Given that Bingley was staring reprovingly at Miss Bingley, she had probably said something obnoxious.

"I apologize for my inattention," he said helplessly. "I was woolgathering. What did you say?"

"I said," Miss Bingley stated with relish, "that the customs here in Derbyshire are likely different than in Hertfordshire, and that Elizabeth should be certain of your approval before she traipses about the estate entirely alone."

Darcy coughed and repeated, "Alone?"

"Yes, Elizabeth is accustomed to wandering the paths of Longbourn and Netherfield entirely unaccompanied."

Darcy bent a surprised look on Miss Bennet, who said with a smile, "That is true enough. I enjoy walking very much, more than anyone else in my family."

"Furthermore," Bingley interposed, "Elizabeth walks so rapidly that there are few who can keep up with her."

"That is true," Caroline agreed brightly. "My new sister is such an excellent walker, and pays no heed to the weather."

"I do, of course," Elizabeth said calmly, "and when I walked to Netherfield last November, the storm was over."

This confused Darcy, naturally enough, and Bingley hastened to explain. "Last autumn, Jane came to visit my sisters and fell ill, which required her to spend the night at Netherfield. The next day, the carriage horses were not available at Longbourn, so Elizabeth walked to Netherfield so that she could nurse her sister."

"I was very grateful," Jane Bingley said.

"Nonetheless, it would be inappropriate for you to roam around Pemberley without your host's permission, Eliza," Caroline said smugly.

"Indeed. Mr. Darcy, do I have your permission to walk the estate alone?" Elizabeth asked, one dark brow raised.

Darcy blinked a few times to collect his thoughts. "The park is a full ten miles around, Miss Bennet," he said after a moment, "and I think that rather too far for you to walk alone. But of course there are numerous winding paths and you are certainly welcome to enjoy them."

Her expression relaxed and she smiled, which caused Darcy's throat to constrict oddly. She really was very beautiful, Elizabeth Bennet of Longbourn.

Chapter 5

"Would anyone care for cards?" Darcy asked when the gentlemen joined the ladies after dinner.

"Oh, yes, that would be delightful!" Miss Bingley exclaimed. "Do you not think so, Jane? Elizabeth?"

Jane, who had been steadily wilting throughout the evening, managed a smile but said, "I do beg you all play, but I am quite tired and believe I must retire."

"Shall I walk up with you to your bedchamber, my dear?" Charles asked immediately.

"Oh, pray do not!" Jane said. "You have not seen Mr. Darcy in a year, and in any case, I plan to go to sleep immediately. My maid can take care of me."

"Your maid is still back at the inn waiting for the Hursts' carriage to be repaired," Elizabeth reminded her sister as she rose to her feet. "But I will gladly look after you. I bid you good night, and thank you for a delightful dinner, Mr. Darcy."

"Until tomorrow," Darcy returned with a bow, which was mimicked by Bingley and Hurst.

Charles watched his bride leave, his brow wrinkled with concern, and Miss Bingley snapped impatiently, "She will be well enough, Charles. Elizabeth will no doubt take excellent care of her."

"She will," Louisa Hurst agreed gently. "You know the sisters are very close, and Elizabeth is accustomed to Jane's needs."

"Yes, of course, you are correct," Charles agreed, his expression lightening. "Well, Darcy, what do you think? There are five of us. Shall we play loo? Vingt-et-un?"

"I am confident that Mr. Darcy would prefer loo," Miss Bingley declared, and Darcy, who did not really care, could only acquiesce with a silent nod of his head.

/

"Sleep well, my dear," Elizabeth murmured, pressing a kiss on her sister's brow. Jane was already half asleep and merely smiled wearily as Elizabeth blew out the candle and glided out of the room and into her own chamber. She was pleased to have a good excuse for going above stairs early, and while usual etiquette would compel her to return to the drawing room, she felt it best to stay nearby in case Jane needed her. Molly, Jane's maid, was very competent, but with limited space in the two carriages, she had been left behind with Mr. Hurst's valet.

Elizabeth did not trust unknown servants to care for her sister appropriately, and thus enjoyed the pleasure of sitting by the window reading one of her favorite books as the sun sank toward the horizon. It was in every way delightful.

/

"Really," Caroline fumed angrily when she and Louisa retired to Louisa's sitting room later in the evening, "I cannot believe that Jane and Elizabeth could be so very rude! It is shocking that they retreated to their bedchambers within minutes of the gentlemen's arrival tonight!"

"I think it likely that Jane is pregnant and is both exhausted and ill," Louisa said baldly.

Caroline, who had been preparing her next batch of vitriol against her sisters by marriage, turned pale at these words and asked, "What?!"

"I think Jane is pregnant," Louisa repeated. "It should be no surprise, sister. Charles worships the ground she walks on, after all, and she is a most affectionate wife."

Caroline gulped and said, "What makes you think that she is increasing?"

"She has been exceptionally tired, and she was obviously uncomfortable with the motion of carriage. You know I am very sensitive to motion sickness, but while I felt reasonably well during our journey today, she looked very pale," Louisa said.

Miss Bingley pursed her lips in disapproval. "Even if you are correct, that is no reason for Jane to be discourteous to Mr. Darcy. Being pregnant is no great thing, after all."

Louisa huffed and stood up. "Nonsense, Caroline. Some women are entirely well during pregnancy, and others are terribly sick. Our mother was one of the latter, she was confined to bed for much of her time with you."

Caroline's mouth dropped open and she said, "Surely not! I never heard such a thing."

"Why would you?" her sister asked. "Mother died of fever when you were not yet six years of age, so she never told you, and I was not inclined to mention it previously. I was nine years old when she fell pregnant with you, and she was exhausted and in bed for weeks at a time. Now, I am weary and ready for my own bed. Good night, Caroline."

Caroline murmured her own good night and made her way out of the sitting room, into the corridor to her own bedchamber.

If Louisa was correct, and Jane was pregnant, well, that would only boost the bumptious pride of Charles's wife. On the other hand, if Jane was tired and ill, Elizabeth would be waiting on her sister more of the time. That was certainly to Caroline's advantage, as it would shield Mr. Darcy from the unladylike, country-bred Miss Bennet.

In any case, she would find some way to turn this to her advantage. She was Miss Caroline Bingley. She would not be dissuaded from her purpose. She *would* be mistress of Pemberley.

/

Elizabeth lay in her bed, a very comfortable one, and stared up at the ceiling. It had been an eventful day, and she ought to be tired, but her mind was too active for sleep.

Jane was her primary concern. Her dear sister was not inclined to complain, but Elizabeth knew that she was uncomfortable and fatigued. She would have to work with Charles to ensure that Jane was able to rest as much as she needed. Jane, whose awareness of cultural niceties was exquisite, would be reluctant to stay in her bedchamber when, by all rights, she ought to be providing good company to her host and his family. But whether Mr. Darcy liked it or not, Jane's health and unborn child were of primary concern, and Elizabeth would do everything in her power to protect both.

As for Mr. Darcy, well, the master of Pemberley was still a puzzle to her. He had been courteous to his guests today, but there was none of the ease of manner which drew men and women to Charles Bingley. Perhaps he was merely reserved.

Lastly, Elizabeth's thoughts turned to the most unusual Miss Darcy. She was certainly extraordinary in her speech, which was often discourteous, at least according to the mores of society. But it was obvious to Elizabeth that Georgiana Darcy merely spoke the truth as she saw it. Elizabeth frowned in the darkness. Lieutenant Wickham, who had known Miss Darcy from childhood, had said…

What *had* he said?

/

Longbourn

May 22nd, 1812

"My dear Miss Bennet," George Wickham exclaimed, striding over to her, his handsome face alight with pleasure. "I am pleased to be spending our last evening in Meryton here with my dear friends, the wonderful Bennet family."

"You know my mother enjoys entertaining, Mr. Wickham," Elizabeth said cheerfully, glancing around at the militia officers who were crowding into the drawing room of Longbourn. "Indeed, she would have been most distressed if Lady Lucas had prevailed in hosting the regiment for the last time."

"The last time, yes," Wickham responded, his blue eyes fixed sorrowfully on Elizabeth's fair countenance. "I am grieved that we will be parted soon and can only hope that someday our paths will cross again."

"That would be pleasant, sir, though I fear it is an unlikely happenstance. Your regiment is off to Brighton, and it seems unlikely that you will ever be stationed in Meryton again."

"That is true enough," the lieutenant agreed. "I understood from Miss Lydia that there is some chance that your family will travel to Brighton this summer. The sea air is supposed to be most salubrious."

Elizabeth shook her head and said, "Lydia is merely being foolishly optimistic. My father dislikes leaving Longbourn, and besides, both Kitty and Lydia just returned from London a few weeks ago. They were well entertained by Jane and Mr. Bingley, and my father is certainly not inclined to allow them to travel far from home again in the coming months."

Wickham sighed and inquired, "And what of you, Miss Bennet? Will you have the opportunity of traveling to London soon?"

"Well, as to that, no," Elizabeth answered, slightly uncomfortable. "Jane and her husband have invited me to join them on a journey north, and we will visit various great houses like Chatwood, Matlock, and Dovedale."

"How marvelous! Will you be journeying as far as Derbyshire, perhaps?"

Elizabeth took a deep breath and nodded, "Yes, Mr. Darcy is a close friend to Mr. Bingley, you know, and has invited our party to spend two weeks at Pemberley."

Mr. Wickham's smiling countenance shifted to one of profound melancholy. "Oh, how I envy you, I truly do! Pemberley is such a remarkable place; the woods, the streams, the mansion itself! It will always hold a special place in my heart, even though I can never return."

Elizabeth sighed sympathetically. In the course of her six month acquaintance with Mr. Wickham, she had heard much about his early life as the son of a former steward of Pemberley. The now deceased Mr. George Darcy had been Wickham's godfather and had set aside a valuable church in Derbyshire for the young man. Sadly, the current Mr. Darcy, apparently a jealous individual, had refused to bestow the living on Wickham, which had resulted in the lieutenant's current predicament. He was handsome and exceptionally charming, but he was also impoverished. Elizabeth had thought more than once that she might have considered marrying the lieutenant if he had been eligible, but alas, he was not. Wickham was poor, and Elizabeth's dowry was nearly nonexistent. No, there was no future for them.

"I am sorry for bringing up such a painful topic," she said.

"Oh, I beg you will not concern yourself," the gentleman said. "I am pleased that you will have the opportunity to delight yourself in the grounds, which are, I am certain, very much to your liking. As to Mr. Darcy, I expect that he will treat both you and your sister with reasonable courtesy now that Mrs. Bingley is wed to Darcy's friend. As for Miss Darcy, well, I confess to some pessimism there; she is a haughty young lady."

"How old is Miss Darcy?" Elizabeth asked curiously.

"She is some fifteen or sixteen years of age."

"Oh, she is yet still young! Is her character so very bad?"

Wickham sighed and shook his head. "She was a charming little girl, and I devoted many hours to her amusement when she was small, but now she is proud, very proud. I fear both Darcys are very much like their de Bourgh relations which, I am certain you agree, is no great thing."

Elizabeth cast her eyes heavenward and said, "Yes, though I would say only Lady Catherine is exceptionally insolent and dictatorial. Miss de Bourgh is merely quiet."

"Yes, that does not surprise me. Lady Catherine has such a forceful personality that all in her sphere are inclined to be silent, though I suppose that her manners did not discourage you from speaking, Miss Bennet."

Elizabeth chuckled and said, "I assure you that I was always perfectly polite in Lady Catherine's presence, for my friend Mrs. Collins's sake, if for no other reason."

"You are a most caring friend and sister," Mr. Wickham declared. "You will be a great comfort to Mrs. Bingley, who may find her reception rather discouraging, with Miss Darcy, at any rate. She is not very friendly to those she considers beneath her notice."

/

Elizabeth turned on her side and frowned into the darkness. Miss Darcy was certainly a peculiar young lady, but she did not seem unduly proud in the least. Perhaps Mr. Wickham had misinterpreted her blunt speech for pride?

She sighed and snuggled deeper into the feather mattress. It was late, and she was tired. She would learn more about the Darcys in the days to come. A few minutes later, she was fast asleep.

/

"Do go along, Lizzy," Jane ordered. "I appreciate your assistance last night and this morning, but Molly is here now, and she can look after me."

Elizabeth cast a questioning look at Jane's private maid who said, "I will look after Mrs. Bingley, Miss."

Elizabeth leaned over and kissed her sister on the forehead. "Very well. Now do promise me you will not drag yourself downstairs if you are feeling terrible."

"I will not," Jane answered wanly. "I do feel dreadful today."

"My poor dear. I will pray for you."

Elizabeth straightened and quietly walked out of the room. She was concerned about Jane, but there was no reason to hover over her, especially with Jane's loyal maid now in attendance.

She softly closed the door behind her and stood in the corridor. It was just eleven o'clock, and she had shared a small repast with Jane only an hour previously. Miss Darcy had invited her to the peacock ... no, peafowl enclosure at noon. There was a pianoforte in a room at the end of the corridor. She had not practiced her music for many weeks, and if she played softly, it would not bother Jane. Yes, that would be an excellent way to while away an hour.

The pianoforte in question was beautiful, both newer and more expensive than the one at Longbourn. Caroline had informed her that there was a special music room in the main part of the house, which held an even grander pianoforte along with a harp and even a lyre. It was a testament to the wealth of Pemberley that this instrument was relegated to a sitting room in the guest wing.

Elizabeth was pleased to find sheet music in the bench, including an old favorite, "Greensleeves". She placed it on the rack, sat down, limbered her fingers, and began to play. When she had finished the last few notes, she sighed and pulled her hands into her lap. Her playing was rusty after many months of neglect. Well, there was no time like the present to work on regaining her admittedly limited skill on the pianoforte.

She straightened her back, focused at the music, and played again, this time with better success. It was not perfect, of course, but…

"You made several mistakes," a female voice said from behind her.

Elizabeth turned on the seat and stared in astonishment at Miss Georgiana Darcy, who was standing ten feet away, dressed in an overly large green muslin dress.

"I know," Elizabeth said stiffly. "I fear I am somewhat out of practice."

Miss Darcy's mouth drooped miserably, and her gaze shifted to the parquetted floor. "I apologize. That was very rude of me to say."

Elizabeth, who had felt rather insulted, relaxed. "No, no, Miss Darcy, pray do not distress yourself. It is true that I have neglected my time at the pianoforte of late, and thus my skills have suffered."

"You are certainly welcome to use this instrument while you stay here," Georgiana said. "May I play "Greensleeves" properly?"

Elizabeth obediently withdrew from the bench and stationed herself such that she could watch Miss Darcy work her musical magic.

This provoked a grimace from the girl, who said, "Would you please look out the window? I do not like it when people look at me while I play."

Elizabeth found herself growing increasingly curious. Miss Darcy was certainly an unusual young lady!

"Of course I will," she agreed, and wandered over to stare out the window, through which stretched a pleasing landscape of wheat fields interspersed with copses of oak and elm trees. She heard Miss Darcy settle herself on the bench and begin playing "Greensleeves". The song began, and within a minute, Elizabeth found herself awed, delighted and, she realized with wonder, a little envious. The song was not especially difficult, but Miss Darcy played it masterfully. It was not just that she never missed a note or a pause – she imbued her playing with a special quality, a transcendent feeling, which wrenched Elizabeth's heart and brought tears to her eyes. Miss Bingley had not been in error. Miss Darcy was a clearly gifted player.

When the last note had died away, Elizabeth took a few moments to collect herself and asked, "May I turn around, Miss Darcy?"

"Yes, now you can, because I am finished," Georgiana said.

Elizabeth spun slowly and said warmly, "You play very well, Miss Darcy."

"Thank you, yes," Georgiana said, standing up and clasping her hands in front of her. "I am an excellent player of the pianoforte. Fitzwilliam says that some women are good at playing instruments, and others are gifted at drawing flowers. I do not draw flowers well at all. I am not interested in flowers."

Elizabeth lifted a rather surprised eyebrow. "Your brother is very wise, Miss Darcy."

"Yes, he is very kind to me, and also patient. Would you like to see the peafowl now?"

"Yes, very much."

Chapter 6

The June sun was hot, and Darcy sighed with relief as his black stallion, Phoenix, reached a stand of trees at the top of a hill. He pulled the horse to a halt, patting the great black neck fondly. Charles Bingley stopped his gray mare next to his friend's mount, and the two men gazed out over the vista stretching out below them. To the north reared the mansion, its great stone walls rising three stories high. The home farm of the estate stretched a full ten acres, filled with vegetable gardens and fruit orchards. Farther to the south and west, they could see the cottages of several tenant farmers, all dependent on Pemberley for their welfare.

It was, Darcy supposed, an indication of his own excessively serious nature that at times Pemberley seemed more burden than blessing. He knew that he was privileged to be master of such a fine estate, but the elder Mr. Darcy had died when his son was but one and twenty, and Darcy had wished, more than once, that he had not been required to carry such a heavy load at such a young age.

"You have a remarkable estate," Bingley said, breaking into his thoughts. "I have known that for many years, but now that I have attempted to manage Netherfield, I am far more aware of all the niggling details involved in keeping a large property running smoothly."

"That is true," Darcy said, turning to look at his friend. "Was Netherfield in good heart when you took the lease?"

Bingley sighed and absently brushed a fly off of his mare's neck. "It could have been worse, certainly, but it could have been better. The house itself is in excellent condition, but according to Mr. Brisby, the steward, the legal owner of Netherfield has not given him sufficient funds to keep the tenant houses in good repair."

"That is unfortunate," Darcy said heavily. "It is vital for the health of an estate that the tenants be well housed, and I believe that those of us who oversee estates have a moral imperative to look after those under our authority and care."

"I entirely agree with you, and so does Jane. She knows the tenant farmers well, of course, since Longbourn lies along Netherfield's western boundary. These past months, we have had many conversations, and I have authorized the outlay of considerable expenditures on behalf of the tenant farmers. There will be no tenants living with leaky roofs this winter! Why are you looking at me like that, Darcy?"

Darcy realized that he had indeed been staring in astonishment at his friend, and quickly turned his head so that he was once again looking toward the mansion. "I am ... merely pleased and, I confess, rather surprised. It is greatly to Mrs. Bingley's credit that she cares about your tenants."

"Oh yes! Jane is an angel! Elizabeth has been helpful as well. She is intelligent and a great reader, and she has far more knowledge of farming practices than many a gentleman of my acquaintance. You are staring at me again. Is that so shocking?"

Darcy flushed at his friend's amused gaze and said, "Shocking no, but it is surprising. I assume Mr. Bennet has also been of some use to you?"

Bingley blew out a breath and said, "In truth, my wife's father is an eccentric gentleman. He is a scholarly man and spends much of his time in his library, and he treasures Elizabeth as the only daughter able to keep up with his quick wit. Jane is always respectful of her father, but she has told me, quite privately you understand, that Bennet is an adequate, but not stellar, master of his lands and people. He is more interested in reading Greek tragedies than practical aspects of estate management."

"I suppose it must be discouraging that his estate will not pass on to his own children," Darcy mused.

"Yes, I suspect that is part of it, but he is also indolent. I like Mr. Bennet well enough, but he has abrogated his responsibilities toward his wife and daughters. He ought to have saved for their future, given that the estate will be lost to Mr. Collins."

"He is the heir?" Darcy asked, nudging Phoenix into motion.

Bingley tapped his mare with his heels to urge her into a walk and said, "Yes, and he has a rather odd connection to your family. Mr. Collins is a rector, and he holds the Hunsford living at Rosings."

Darcy jerked and turned a horrified look on his friend. "The heir is Lady Catherine's clergyman?"

Bingley grinned and said, "Yes. I met the man last autumn, and you will be pleased, but not surprised, to hear that he is absolutely devoted to Lady Catherine. He thinks her quite the most remarkable woman in all of England, I believe not excepting Queen Charlotte herself."

Darcy shuddered. His aunt, Lady Catherine de Bourgh, was mistress of Rosings, a large estate in Kent. She was autocratic, proud, arrogant, and insisted on obsequious servility from her underlings. Mr. Collins was probably a tedious man, and he would learn nothing of value about caring for an estate from his patroness, who was not inclined to spend money on the tenants who lived off of her own lands.

/

For the second time, Elizabeth found herself walking through the rose garden to the south of Pemberley. When she had first laid eyes on the beds of roses, she had found it difficult to step more than three paces without feeling compelled to stop, observe, admire, and smell the beautiful blossoms.

Now she found herself pumping her arms to keep up with Miss Darcy, who did not spare a glance at the flowers as she marched along the paths to the southeast corner of the rose garden, whereupon she led Elizabeth across the grass to the wooden door. With practiced ease, the daughter of Pemberley withdrew a key from the pocket of her simple dress, opened the door, and swept inside with Elizabeth at her heels.

For the second time in as many days, Elizabeth was filled with wonder at the sight before her, a little slice of Paradise.

"How many birds do you have, Miss Darcy?" she asked, following the younger woman toward the far corner of the walled enclosure.

"We have six peacocks and twenty peahens, plus twelve peachicks," Georgiana answered.

"Is it normal to have more peahens than peacocks?"

Georgiana nodded but did not look at Elizabeth; the latter had, by now, grasped that Miss Darcy did not find it easy to look into her eyes and thus she did not take offense.

"Yes," Georgiana said. "The males generally collect several peahens as a harem of sorts. If the ratio between the males and females is imbalanced, the peacocks will fight."

"How many eggs do the peahens usually lay?"

"Between three and twelve in a clutch," Georgiana answered, turning to look at Elizabeth's chin. "The peahens do not lay their first year, and only a few eggs their second year. They are fully mature by..."

"Oh!" Elizabeth exclaimed, interrupting her hostess's explanation. Later that evening, she would berate herself for her incivility, but at this moment, the sight before her startled eyes overwhelmed all rational thought.

"This is Rainbow," Georgiana said, a smile filling her usually serious face.

Elizabeth gazed in wonder at the sight before her. A few feet away stood a peacock facing the two ladies. The bird had lifted its long feathers vertically into a fan and now stood, tall and stately, in front of the young women. The feathers varied in length from one to three feet, and the green wisps along the white stalk shimmered in the noonday sun. Each feather boasted a sort of eye near the end, composed of concentric circles of purple, yellow, brown, and bluish-green, all of which sparkled and dazzled in the bright light.

"He is beyond anything I have ever imagined," Elizabeth breathed.

"Yes, he is," Georgiana agreed fondly.

/

"I need to check on Jane," Bingley said to his friend. The pair had finished their ride and were now enjoying the welcome cool of the Pemberley stables. "Are you ready to return to the house?"

"Go ahead, Bingley," Darcy suggested. "I need to speak to my stable master as one of my best mares foaled yesterday. I wish to be certain her filly is doing well."

Bingley nodded and strode rapidly out of the stable toward the mansion, while Darcy made his way along the corridor that led to the foaling boxes at the north end of the stable. He found his stable master, Barstow, standing at the gate of the foaling box, watching the mare and filly within. Darcy took his place next to the man, and for a few minutes both men watched with silent pleasure as the filly, a chestnut with white stockings, nursed enthusiastically at her mother's teats. The mare, a five year old chestnut thoroughbred, nuzzled her infant's hindquarters and cast occasional threatening glances toward the men. She was, Darcy knew, a high tempered beast.

"They both look well," Darcy finally said.

Barstow, a grizzled man of some fifty years, nodded. "Yes, sir, the mare foaled with ease, and the filly is active and eating well."

"Thank you for your care," Darcy said sincerely. Barstow had served most of his life in the Darcy stables, first as a stable boy, then as a groom, and was now overseeing the numerous horses that belonged to Pemberley.

"It is my honor, sir," the older man said with a mixture of respect and affection. He had known his master since the boy was in short coats, and he was devoted to the Darcy family.

The church bell chimed once and Darcy, somewhat reluctantly, turned away. He had several letters to read and respond to, and he intended, if possible, to introduce Georgiana to Mrs. Bingley and Miss Bennet sometime this afternoon. He marched out of the cool of the stable and into the sunlight. The bright rays briefly blinded him, and he tilted his hat forward to shade his eyes, which allowed him to observe the woman standing by the path under a tree, dressed in an expensive silk dress, her eyes avaricious, her teeth gleaming in her smiling mouth.

"Mr. Darcy, how good to see you this beautiful day!" Caroline Bingley trilled.

Chapter 7

"Miss Bingley," Darcy said, bowing slightly and casting an unhappy look toward the house. Bingley was not in sight, but two gardeners were working in the flower garden. He need not worry about a compromise in such a public place, but he did not enjoy a tête-à-tête with his friend's sister. There was nothing to be done without gross discourtesy, however, so he unhappily held out his arm and Caroline took it, her mouth curved in a satisfied smile.

"It is wonderful to be here at Pemberley again, Mr. Darcy," she declared, gazing with admiration at the mansion. "I suppose Netherfield is respectable enough, but it is nothing compared to your marvelous estate."

There was nothing that Darcy could say to this, so he chose to remain silent.

Miss Bingley waited a few seconds until it was obvious that her companion had no intention of speaking, and said, "I confess that I am pleased to have the opportunity to speak to you alone, Mr. Darcy, and to warn you."

"Warn me?" Darcy returned, his brows lowered. "About what, may I ask?"

Miss Bingley glanced around and lowered her voice dramatically, which was absurd, as they were well away from any listening ears. "I wished to give you more information about the Bennets. It is a great pity that you were not able to join us at Netherfield last autumn. Louisa and I tried to convince Charles that his attraction to Jane was merely infatuation, but he would not listen."

She sighed deeply and said, "My brother was meant for so much more, but he has always had a soft spot for pretty blondes."

'Pretty', Darcy thought, was far too subdued a word to describe Mrs. Bingley. She was, in fact, quite one of the most handsome women he had ever met.

"Am I to understand that you do not approve of Mrs. Bingley?" he asked, bending a frowning look on his companion.

"Oh, it quite depends on what you mean by approve!" Caroline answered with a wry twist of her lips. "I like her well enough; Jane has excellent manners and is kindness itself. But I certainly do not approve of her family! Her father spends all his time in his library, and her mother is a most vulgar person, a mere solicitor's daughter, and I have no doubt that she ordered Jane to accept my brother's offer, for I cannot believe that Jane actually cares for Charles! As for the younger girls, Elizabeth is arch and pert, Mary, the middle girl, is a bluestocking, and as for Jane's youngest two sisters ... well, they are hoydens who chase after officers and gentlemen's sons. Are you aware that Longbourn, the Bennet estate, is entailed away to a distant relative?"

"I am," Darcy said stiffly. He did not care to discuss this matter with Miss Bingley, but he did not know how to cut her off without being openly rude.

Miss Bingley shook her head in exasperation. "Jane has no prospects and her only connections in Town are her uncle and aunt Gardiner, who live in Cheapside. We met them at the wedding, of course; Mr. Gardiner is a tradesman who lives within view of his own warehouses! When I think of my brother's amiable temper, his fortune, and his education – oh, I know he could have found a much better wife."

Darcy blew out a breath. "It is too late for that, Miss Bingley. In any case, you can rejoice that your brother has chosen a charming wife with excellent manners. We must hope that they are happy together."

Based on Miss Bingley's expression, Darcy was certain that Bingley's happiness was not her primary concern. No, it would not do to accept too much of what Miss Bingley was saying about her new relations by marriage. The lady had always been ambitious and...

"Miss Darcy!" Miss Bingley suddenly exclaimed, her face wreathed with smiles.

"Which are the females and which are the males?" Elizabeth asked, leaning over the fence of the pen where two peahens and eight peachicks were rustling about on a layer of straw.

"These hatched in the last three weeks," Georgiana explained, "and thus I cannot tell. The hatchlings only begin showing dissimilarities when they are about five months of age."

"It is remarkable that they look so plain as babies," Elizabeth mused.

"It is," Georgiana agreed, glancing at the watch suspended around her neck. "We need to return to the house."

"Of course," Elizabeth said, and the two girls walked rapidly toward the door which led outside the walled garden.

"Something positively ghastly just occurred to me," Elizabeth said a moment later. "I know many ladies in society decorate their hats with peacock feathers. Are these beautiful birds killed to reap their feathers?"

Georgiana looked startled and shook her head, "No, the peacocks molt all their glorious plumage every year, and grow a new train of feathers for the next mating season."

"Truly?" Elizabeth marveled. "The feathers must grow very quickly then!"

"They do," Georgiana agreed, reaching the door, opening it, passing through, waiting for Elizabeth to join her, and then locking the door securely behind them.

"I am most relieved that the birds do not have to die for us to enjoy their plumage," Elizabeth said as the two women began walking across the grass toward the rose garden. "I will try to obtain some peacock feathers soon to show Jane."

"I will give you some," Georgiana promised. "I have stored many of them."

"Thank you very much," her companion said, and stopped at the edge of the rose garden. "Oh, how beautiful these roses are! Such a variety of colors and the fragrance is divine! I confess I envy you your grounds, Miss Darcy. Both the peacocks and the roses belong in paradise."

"I love the birds, of course," Georgiana said seriously, "but I do not care a great deal about the roses. I find them dull."

"Dull?"

"Yes. I agree they are beautiful, but they are not like my peacocks. They just sit there and grow, after all. All the same, I am thankful my father and brother have spent considerable sums to keep the roses in good order for so many years. My mother, Lady Anne, passed on when I was a young child, and she designed this garden herself. She adored roses even as I adore peacocks."

"She was very gifted," Elizabeth marveled, and then turned as a familiar feminine voice cried out, "Miss Darcy!"

/

Darcy hurried after Miss Bingley as she strode rapidly toward his sister, who was standing next to the rose garden with Miss Bennet. What were Georgiana and his guest doing together, when they had not yet been introduced?

"Miss Darcy," Caroline repeated when she had reached the pair. "How wonderful to see you again after all these months!"

Georgiana, to Darcy's considerable surprise, shifted a little closer to Elizabeth Bennet and recited, "Good morning, Miss Bingley. It is good to see you again."

"I hope you are well, Miss Darcy," Caroline continued brightly.

"I am well," Georgiana responded woodenly, shifting even closer to Elizabeth.

"Miss Bennet," Darcy said frigidly, "I was not aware you had been introduced to my sister."

Elizabeth lifted a dark eyebrow and smiled, "In truth, we met by chance and were forced to introduce ourselves to one another. Miss Darcy and I were just speaking of the rose garden. It is absolutely breathtaking, sir."

"Indeed it is," Caroline chirped eagerly. "Netherfield's formal gardens are nothing compared to the grandness of Pemberley, nor, I am certain you would agree, is Longbourn anything like either of those larger estates."

"I agree entirely, Miss Bingley," Elizabeth said cheerfully. "Now, if you will excuse me, I must see how Jane is feeling. Miss Darcy, it was a pleasure speaking with you."

"I enjoyed speaking with you too," Georgiana said, provoking a surge of surprise in Darcy's mind. He knew Georgiana as well as anyone, and her tone was genuine. He had thought his sister would be distressed at encountering a stranger, but based on their brief interaction, it seemed that Georgiana was comfortable in Miss Bennet's presence, which was a near miracle.

"Now, Miss Darcy," Caroline Bingley said, moving a little closer to the girl, "I do hope you are still playing the pianoforte?"

"Yes, I am," Georgiana answered, shifting backwards a little, her posture unhappy.

Darcy stepped forward and held out both arms so that Miss Bingley was forced to take his arm. Georgiana thankfully took his other arm, eager to be separated from Miss Bingley.

"Georgiana plays very constantly," Darcy said. "In fact, I believe you have a lesson soon, dear sister?"

"Yes," Georgiana agreed thankfully. "I do."

"Then we should return to the house," Darcy declared.

/

"Are you quite certain you are well enough to go down for dinner?" Elizabeth fretted.

Jane, who was sitting on a green wingback chair near the window of her bedchamber, bent an amused look on her sister and said, "Yes, I promise I am well enough. I do feel quite a bit better than I did this morning. All the same, Charles made me promise to wait until he arrives before I join everyone in the drawing room before dinner. Caroline is fatiguing at the best of times, and I wish to have all my energy for dinner."

"Very reasonable. And I, as your heroic sister, will stay with you until your equally heroic husband arrives," Elizabeth concluded with a smile.

"That is truly courageous," Jane said, her blue eyes twinkling. "Now do tell me about your day, Lizzy. I assume, since you have Mr. Darcy's permission, that you took the opportunity to walk some of the lovely grounds?"

"Yes, though I did not venture far, as I found much of interest within easy walking distance of the house," Elizabeth answered, and proceeded to tell her wondering sister of her introduction to Miss Darcy and the girl's magnificent peafowl.

"That is marvelous and astonishing!" Jane declared.

"It is," her sister agreed, walking over to her reticule, which she had placed on a small writing desk. "Miss Darcy gave me these feathers only an hour ago. Are they not incredible? Miss Darcy says that every year, the peacocks molt and release their plumage onto the ground, and every year they grow a new train of feathers."

Jane took the feathers in her hand and eyed them with wonder, tilting them back and forth in the light from the window. "Oh Elizabeth, I have seen peacock feathers on hats and the like but to hold them in my hand! Do you see how the colors seem to change as you turn them in the light?"

"I do. Peacocks are a remarkable example of God's creative glory."

"Tell me about Miss Darcy," Jane requested, her eyes fixed on the feathers.

Elizabeth sat down on a green settee across from her sister and said, "In all honesty, I find her a puzzling individual. Mr. Wickham said that she was proud and imperious, but I quite disagree. Her manners are certainly unusual; she is very blunt, for example, and speaks boldly of her own feelings in a manner which could be construed as discourteous. All the same, I do not think she is proud at all. However, I can imagine someone thinking she is haughty if they misinterpret her plain words as arrogance."

"Do you like her?" Jane asked curiously.

Elizabeth nodded immediately. "I do, very much. She is a genuine person, very unlike Miss Bingley, for example. When Miss Darcy says something, she means it, whereas Caroline, as you know, often says something but her tone indicates quite the opposite."

"Yes, I know," Jane agreed with a sigh. "It is remarkable how different Charles is from Caroline. He is all that is amiable and looks for the good in others, whereas Caroline thrives on disparaging and mocking those she considers below her in an effort to elevate herself."

"We five sisters are very different," Elizabeth pointed out. "Not only in looks, but in character. Nor can we boast of our younger siblings; Mary is overly studious and pedantic, Lydia is a reckless menace, and Kitty follows her younger sister in her foolishness."

"They are not so very bad," Jane protested. "Charles and I quite enjoyed having them in London in March and April. You have not spent much time with them since we were married, Elizabeth. I contend that they have all improved, and perhaps Kitty most of all. She relished the opportunity to work with a drawing master in London, and even Lydia seemed quite cheerful when she was with us, though there were no officers in sight. They were even quite at peace with our decision to keep them away from parties and assemblies due to their youth, though we did entertain them at Astley's and the opera."

"You are such a good sister," Elizabeth said warmly. "And Charles is an excellent brother. You are correct, of course; I was in Kent with Charlotte Collins while you were hosting Lydia and Kitty, and then within a few weeks of their return to Longbourn, you collected me for our trip north. I am relieved that they have improved. I suspect that your marriage has helped. Mother no longer needs to worry about being thrown into the hedgerows when Father dies, and she is not nearly as frantic about marrying us all off as quickly as possible."

"I am so thankful to have brought such happiness to my family," Jane said, her cheeks glowing with pleasure, "especially as I have found such joy myself. Charles is wonderful."

"He is, and I do believe that is him out in the corridor. I had best return to my bedchamber and change for dinner."

"Of course," Jane said, standing up to walk her sister toward the door.

"Oh, Jane!"

"Yes?"

"Pray do not mention the peafowl to anyone. I believe it is Miss Darcy's own private domain, and she would not care for Miss Bingley to know about it."

"Of course I will not mention it."

Chapter 8

"Georgiana?" Darcy asked from outside his sister's sitting room.

Georgiana, who was writing a list of necessary supplies for her birds, finished a line of script and then called out, "Come in!"

Darcy opened the door and found his sister at her desk, a quill pen in her hand and a piece of foolscap paper covered in words in front of her. He shut the door behind him and looked at her with concern. "Are you well?"

Georgiana, who was now wearing a yellow muslin gown, looked startled and said, "Yes? Is something wrong?"

"No, nothing at all," Darcy returned hastily, sitting down near, but not too near, his sister. "I merely was concerned that you might be distressed over your unexpected meeting with Miss Bennet this morning."

"We met yesterday morning," Georgiana stated, placing her quill pen on the desk. "I am not upset because I like her. She is a pleasant person."

Darcy squinted in confusion. "What do you mean, you met yesterday?"

"She was outside, heard the peafowl being noisy, and investigated. We met inside the walled garden."

Darcy frowned. "It was not entirely courteous of her to introduce herself to you."

"She was concerned about the impropriety of our meeting without you," his sister said calmly. "I told her I had no interest in such formalities. We talked about the peafowl, and then I had to leave the enclosure to change for my music lesson, and of course she was not allowed to be in the garden without me. We met again this morning when she was playing on the guest wing's pianoforte, and then we visited the peafowl together."

Darcy blinked in astonishment. "And you like her?"

"I like her very much," Georgiana said, shifting her gaze to stare out the window at the blue sky, which was interspersed with bright, fluffy clouds. "She is very kind, and did not make me feel awkward in the least, even though I know my manners are often not appropriate in company…"

She trailed off, gulped, and tears filled her eyes. Darcy immediately left his chair and fell to his knees in front of his sister, whereupon he reached over and pulled her close to him. Georgiana had always been a sensitive girl, and he had discovered, long ago, that she relished a firm embrace when she was distressed.

"You are a wonderful young lady," Darcy said passionately.

"I know I am not," Georgiana sobbed into his shoulder, leaning harder into his caress. "I know that I am rude, though I do not intend to be, and I cannot be at peace when Miss Bingley flatters me. I know I am a disappointment to you, Brother."

"You are not, and never will be, a disappointment," Darcy declared fervently. "Now come, dry your eyes, and when you are ready, tell me more about Miss Bennet."

Georgiana obediently retrieved her handkerchief and dried her eyes. Two minutes later, she leaned back from her brother who was quite relieved, as his knees were numb from kneeling on the hard floor. Not, of course, that he truly minded any discomfort when it was for his sister's sake.

"She plays the pianoforte, but not terribly well," Georgiana stated. "She says she has not practiced enough. I know not everyone wishes to practice as much as I do. She had good questions about the peafowl. So many people merely exclaim over their beauty, but she was interested in how they grow feathers, and how similar the peachicks are to one another. She is a comfortable person."

Darcy smiled at her in relief, not unmixed with surprise, and said, "I am delighted that you feel at ease in

Miss Bennet's presence. Now, do you feel able to come to dinner tonight? I will not press you if..."

"May I sit between you and Miss Bennet?" Georgiana interrupted.

"Yes."

"Then yes, I will come."

/

"My dear Eliza," Miss Bingley said, "I hope you will tell us of your rambles about the estate today. I know you find great pleasure in walking, and your ability to roam on foot put those of us who are town bred to shame. Please, where did you wander today?"

Elizabeth saw Georgiana stiffen next to her and bestowed a reassuring smile on the girl.

"I confess that I did not walk far today," Elizabeth said. "I was so taken by the rose garden that I was not inclined to strike out any further. I do wish to follow the windings of the stream in the next few days."

"Oh, the rose beds are breathtaking, as are all the lands of Pemberley," Miss Bingley declared.

"I understand that Rosings has quite an impressive park as well, Elizabeth," Louisa Hurst said. "How do they compare?"

"You have been to Rosings?" Georgiana asked, speaking for the first time since the party had sat down at the table.

"I have," Elizabeth said. "My father's heir is a distant cousin by the name of Mr. Collins. He is a clergyman who was so fortunate as to be awarded the Hunsford living by your aunt, Lady Catherine de Bourgh. Mr. Collins married a dear friend of mine, and only a few months ago, I enjoyed a six week visit to Kent, where I had the honor of meeting Lady Catherine and Miss de Bourgh."

"I find it astonishing that Mr. Collins journeyed all the way to Hertfordshire to meet your family and came away with your friend as a wife," Caroline mused. "Indeed, I thought I heard a rumor, no doubt false, that you were intended to marry Mr. Collins, Elizabeth!"

"There is no reason to speak of such hearsay, Caroline," Bingley said reprovingly.

"Oh, my apologies, Eliza. I did not mean to be discourteous," Caroline said, opening her eyes dramatically.

"I am not disturbed in the least," Elizabeth responded calmly. "Mr. Collins was desirous of marrying a thrifty, sensible woman who would serve competently at his side in Hunsford. My friend Charlotte is wise, intelligent, and hard working. She is far more suited to be clergyman's wife than I am, and I am confident that Mr. Collins chose well."

"Were you pleased with Kent, Miss Bennet?" Darcy asked.

"I was," Elizabeth said. "The grounds of Rosings are beautiful and I spent many happy hours walking the trails. As for the gardens of Rosings, they are beautiful but rather more elaborate than I prefer. That is, of course, all according to personal preference. I find Lady Anne's arrangements to be elegant and tasteful, but others prefer more formality."

"I too prefer that the landscape and gardens conform to the natural contours and character of the land," Darcy said, taking a sip of dinner wine. "As you say, Miss Bennet, it is merely a matter of preference."

"Certainly," Elizabeth agreed, bestowing an approving look on the master of Pemberley.

"Charles, have you told Mr. Darcy about our meeting with Colonel Fitzwilliam in London?" Caroline asked, determined to wrest the conversation away from Elizabeth.

"I do not believe I have," Charles said amiably. "Yes, we met your cousin at Lady Mostyn's ball one evening, and his sister, Lady Rebekah, was with him. I understand he is settled in England for the present, which must be a comfort to his family."

"It is," Darcy agreed, and Georgiana, at Elizabeth's side, gave a soft sigh of relief. Their beloved cousin had been injured during the siege of Badajoz, and the entire family was most relieved that the colonel had largely recovered.

The conversation grew general as the ladies and gentlemen discussed the war in France until it was time for the ladies to withdraw after dinner.

/

"Miss Darcy," Caroline Bingley cooed, "I know that your skill on the pianoforte is unparalleled. Do promise us that you will play a song or two when the gentlemen join us tonight!"

Georgiana Darcy, stared at Miss Bingley, her mien that of a startled deer, and said, "Oh no, Miss Bingley, I do not wish to play tonight."

"Come, come!" Miss Bingley urged with a coquettish smirk. "We are all friends, after all. You would not be so cruel as to deprive us of the pleasure of hearing you play, I am certain!"

Georgiana cringed in terror, and Elizabeth said quickly, "I have no doubt that Miss Darcy is an excellent performer, but surely her brother has heard her many times before. I understand that you and Mrs. Hurst recently practiced a duet, and have no doubt that the gentlemen would enjoy your performance."

"I am certain they would," Caroline agreed complacently. "Very well, we will play first, but I promise that I will not forget that we have a truly remarkable musician in our midst, Miss Darcy."

Jane and Elizabeth exchanged glances and Jane said, "Caroline, I have been trying to remember the curtains in the east sitting room. Louisa mentioned that they are rather faded and worn, and I confess I do not remember them at all. Are they green?"

"No, of course not," Caroline said reprovingly. "They are royal blue, and Louisa is correct; they really ought to be replaced. I am surprised you have not already done so…"

Under cover of the ensuing discussion, Elizabeth murmured to Georgiana, "When your brother arrives with the gentlemen, I suggest that you tell him you have a headache and need to retire. You have no obligation to play if you do not wish to, but I fear Miss Bingley is unduly inclined to have you perform."

Georgiana sighed and said, "She is and I will do that. Truthfully, I *do* have a headache now. Miss Bingley gives me a headache."

"I understand completely," Elizabeth assured her.

"Will you join me at the peafowl enclosure tomorrow?" Georgiana asked.

"If you do not mind me joining you, yes, I would like that very much. Nonetheless, I beg you will tell me if you wish for private time alone with your birds, Miss Darcy."

"I like having you there," Miss Darcy said simply, "and the peafowl like you too. I will see you at eleven, as I have a music lesson at noon."

"I look forward to it," Elizabeth said, and turned as the gentlemen entered the room.

Darcy watched his sister glide over to him and murmur into his ear that she had a headache. He kissed her on the cheek and sent her on her way, and he was startled when Georgiana paused by the door to bestow a grateful smile on Miss Bennet, who was watching her go. He hesitated and then walked over to the young lady, who said, "Mr. Darcy, we have a treat in store for us, as Mrs. Hurst and Miss Bingley plan to perform a duet for us this evening."

"That sounds delightful," he responded politely.

"They are very accomplished," Elizabeth declared, "though neither is as gifted as Miss Darcy. She is an incredibly skilled pianist, Mr. Darcy. You must be proud of her."

Darcy could not prevent his start of surprise. "Did my sister actually play for you?"

"She played Greensleeves, yes," Elizabeth murmured, "and I do not think I have ever heard anything like it. Her fingering, her timing, her presence, is absolutely astounding. I feel privileged to have listened to her perform."

"She trusts you very much," Darcy said in wonder. Georgiana was, as Miss Bennet said, incredibly skilled. She was also painfully shy and disliked playing for an audience.

"I am honored by her trust, sir, and will do my best to be a good friend to Miss Darcy. She is a remarkable and wonderful young lady. She did me the honor of introducing me to her peafowl, and I quite adore them."

Darcy looked directly into Miss Bennet's eyes and was pleased by what he saw; there was no hint of mere flattery in either the lady's tone or expression. It seemed she genuinely enjoyed Georgiana's company.

"Yes," he agreed, "they are a remarkable, if very unusual, diversion."

"I think it is delightful, and most impressive. It is obvious that Miss Darcy has studied the care of her birds with great intensity, ensuring her success. I have my own areas of interest, but I confess that I do not spend my time to grow truly skilled in any way."

"What do you enjoy?" Darcy asked curiously.

"Oh, I like walking and observing nature, and reading books – so many books, and my father's library is quite extensive! I like to sing and play, and dance, and I am a reasonably competent chess player. Yes, I enjoy many things, but have mastered nothing."

"I enjoy chess as well, though I do not pretend to be an expert. Perhaps we could play a game some day?"

"I would enjoy that," Elizabeth agreed.

Chapter 9

"I will be well, Elizabeth," Jane insisted. "Do go along. Molly will care for me, you know."

"I know she will, and very well," Elizabeth said, smiling gratefully at her sister's maid. "I am grieved you continue to feel so unwell in the mornings."

"It is definitely not pleasant," Jane said with a grimace, "but at least it is for a good reason. Now as your older sister, I order you to go enjoy yourself."

"As you wish," Elizabeth returned and kissed her sister's forehead and exiting the room. A few minutes later, she had changed into a pair of stout leather boots. Yesterday, she had foolishly worn more delicate shoes, and thus had been required to walk very carefully to prevent them from being soiled. The peacocks, while lovely, were also quite messy.

When it was time for her to leave her room, she did so quietly, in part because she did not wish to disturb Jane with a slamming door, but more because she did not wish to encounter Caroline Bingley. Both of Bingley's sisters were late risers and thus were likely still either in bed or pottering about in their bedchambers, but Elizabeth was still eager to keep Miss Darcy safe from Miss Bingley's curiosity.

Elizabeth walked softly to the stairway which led downstairs, then along the corridor to the rose garden. As usual, she was filled with wonder and was inclined to amble slowly, the better to enjoy the flowers. However, it was nearly eleven o'clock, and Miss Darcy seemed to appreciate timeliness. She would have plenty of time to enjoy the roses later.

When she reached the edge of the rose garden, she paused again and looked around, feeling rather like a spy in a hostile land. Based on his words the previous day, Mr. Darcy was protective of his sister, and Elizabeth could not blame him for that. She hoped that Miss Darcy had told her brother of Elizabeth's incursion into the walled garden. Indeed, she needed to be certain of it, and would ask Miss Darcy today.

Worse than Mr. Darcy observing her would be Miss Bingley. Caroline would bray questions, and Elizabeth would be forced to go elsewhere to protect Miss Darcy from Caroline's irritating presence.

Elizabeth was a quick walker, and she crossed the greenery in record time. The door was open, and she scuttled through and closed it, then laughed as she felt her heart beating rapidly in her chest. It was not as if there was any real danger, after all!

Once her heart had settled, she walked toward the trees, beyond which she could hear a strange sound mixed in with two voices. When she had passed between the trees, she observed Georgiana standing across from a man dressed in the simple garb of an outdoor servant. The man had a large male peacock wrapped in a sheet of burlap, and was pinioning the body and tail feathers with his own strong, muscular arms.

"I have him, Miss Darcy," the man said as Elizabeth looked on curiously.

"Hold him very still, Abel," Georgiana directed, pulling out the bird's left wing and carefully, cautiously, cutting the feathers of the wing along a line. Elizabeth watched in breathless silence until Miss Darcy said, "There, that should be enough. You can release him."

The peacock, who had held surprisingly still for the delicate operation, flounced off squawking, and Georgiana turned and jumped as she observed Elizabeth standing nearby.

"I am sorry, Miss Darcy," Elizabeth said remorsefully. "I did not mean to startle you."

"Is it eleven o'clock?" Georgiana asked, brushing her gloved hands together.

"It is two minutes after the hour," Elizabeth said after peeking at the watch dangling around her neck.

"Then you have no reason to apologize, because I told you to be here at eleven."

"Thank you. May I ask what you did to that peacock?"

Georgiana wandered over to sit on a wooden bench placed on a patch of grass and explained, "Abel and I clipped Neptune's wings because he kept trying to fly over the wall. He would not be safe outside, since there are numerous predators, like foxes and dogs."

Neptune, Elizabeth presumed, was the peacock in question. "It does not hurt him?"

"No, not at all," Georgian assured her. "It is entirely safe to cut the flight feathers of peafowl, chickens, ducks, and geese, and it is advisable if flying will put them in danger. Do sit down, Miss Bennet."

Elizabeth obediently took her place next to Georgiana and said, "In truth, I find it remarkable that peacocks can fly. They are beautiful, of course, but seem quite ungainly."

"They do not generally fly far," Miss Darcy agreed. "Most of our peacocks were hatched here at Pemberley or were brought here when still very young, and this garden is their home. My brother gave me Neptune as a birthday present a month ago. He has not adjusted to his surroundings and thus keeps flying up and over the wall. Abel has had to retrieve him several times, and it is only a matter of time before he encounters a dog or other predator if he keeps escaping."

Privately, Elizabeth wondered why Miss Darcy wished for a peacock when she had the ability to hatch out new ones, but she merely said, "He seems a fine specimen."

Georgiana's eyes lit up and she said, "He is very special. Abel!"

"Yes, Miss Darcy?" the man answered from his place over by the peachick pen, where he was throwing grain to the babies.

"Can you capture Neptune again? I wish to show Miss Bennet his tail feathers."

The servant, a man of some forty years, smiled tolerantly and said, "Of course, Miss Darcy."

Elizabeth stood up and watched curiously as the man approached Neptune, confidently grabbed the bird's large body, and walked back to the two women.

"Look at this," Georgiana directed, gently shifting Neptune's train of feathers.

"Oh!" Elizabeth exclaimed. "Two of the feathers are white! Is that common?"

"Not at all," her hostess said excitedly. "That is why I was so pleased when my brother bought him for me. Very few peafowl are piebald. I am hopeful that Neptune will breed soon and that some of his babies will have white feathers too. Is it not marvelous?"

She nodded to Abel, who carefully lowered the peacock onto the ground. The bird, apparently irritated with being handled so much, tried to take flight but instead lurched to one side, obviously out of balance because of his recently shortened wing. Abel watched with a smile until Neptune strutted over to a nearby tree, and then, with a tip of his hat, the man strode to another door in the rear wall and exited the garden, leaving Elizabeth and Miss Darcy alone.

"Neptune is incredible," Elizabeth agreed, her eyes fixed on the large bird. "I have never heard of peacocks with any white coloring."

"Oh, there is a painting in the library of a piebald peacock," Georgiana explained eagerly. "That is how I learned that such birds exist. My brother is always so very kind to me, and he arranged to buy one for a surprise."

"You are fortunate to have such a caring brother," Elizabeth said, and she meant it. Whatever else could be said about the man, it was obvious that Mr. Darcy cared deeply about his sister. It was odd, really, that the man had apparently treated Mr. Wickham, a most charming, amiable man, with such cruelty in the manner of the promised church living. Of course, she had only known Mr. Wickham for a few months; people *did* change over time, and perhaps Mr. Wickham had, in his younger years, grievously offended Mr. Darcy in some way.

"Would you like to see my books about peacocks in the library?" Miss Darcy asked.

"Very much," Elizabeth responded. "Truthfully, I have longed to see the library at Pemberley ever since Mr. Bingley told me of it. He says that it has been the work of many generations."

"My brother is very proud of it," Georgiana said, though not with any great enthusiasm. "I am grateful that the library contains books on animals and birds, but I find most of the books to be boring, irritating, or confusing."

"What books do you consider irritating?" Elizabeth inquired as her companion stood up. She rose to her feet as well and followed Miss Darcy as the she began walking toward the door of the walled garden.

"I find some of Shakespeare's work to be exasperating," Georgiana said. "My governesses forced me to read a number of his tragedies and comedies, and even some of his poetry. The tragedies, in particular, were ridiculous and frustrating. *Romeo and Juliet*, for example, has an entirely absurd plot! Juliet drinks a potion that mimics death, and Romeo foolishly believes she is dead, and kills himself by drinking poison, and then, just as he dies, Juliet wakes up and discovers he is dead, and kills herself. It is entirely unrealistic!"

"I do not believe it is meant to be realistic," Elizabeth said in amusement.

Georgiana passed through the gateway onto the outer lawn and, after locking the door behind Elizabeth, said reasonably, "I do not understand why I should enjoy a sad story that is ridiculous. Why should I mourn over a character who died due to his or her own stupidity?"

"I do not have an answer to that," Elizabeth admitted. "Do you like Shakespeare's comedies?"

Georgiana walked halfway across the lawn before saying, "I saw *The Tempest* in London some years ago. I enjoyed it, largely because the scenery and costumes were interesting. I did not mind the confusing aspects of the story, because the entire affair, with sorcerers and magicians and magical spirits, is fantastical. *Romeo and Juliet* is supposed to be about normal people, and I do not think a normal person would act in such an idiotic way."

"Nor are there potions which can make one appear dead," Elizabeth mused as the women entered a door into a side hall of Pemberley. She had never been in this part of the house before and found herself looking around curiously.

"This way, Miss Bennet," Georgiana said impatiently, and Elizabeth hurried after her young hostess, who was walking rapidly toward the front of the house.

Georgiana opened a door and stepped inside, and Elizabeth followed her, only to stop and gasp in wonder.

Pemberley's library was awe inspiring. Her father's library at Longbourn was a fine room, but this vast chamber was at least five times larger. Gleaming wooden shelves stretched from floor to ceiling, and nearly every inch of space on those shelves was filled with books. Comfortable leather chairs were in each corner, and a settee and wingback chair flanked the currently cold fireplace. Last of all, large windows let in plenty of light from the glowing sun outside.

"Oh, how incredibly marvelous!" Elizabeth exclaimed.

"In the winter, my brother spends much of his time here," Georgiana said.

"My father would love it as well," Elizabeth commented. "He is a great reader."

"Come here, Miss Bennet. The painting is in the northeast of the room," Georgiana said imperiously, striding toward the far corner of the library.

"Do give me a minute to recover," Elizabeth returned playfully. "Otherwise I might faint in astonishment. This library is truly spectacular."

Georgiana halted with a frown and waited impatiently as Elizabeth spun around, her eyes taking in the multitude of tomes with covers of brown, blue, red, and green. She had never seen so many books in a private residence. A soft huff pulled her attention to her companion, and Elizabeth smiled and walked over to the younger woman.

"Please, do show me the portrait of the peacock," she invited.

/

Darcy was writing a letter to his banker in London when he heard feminine voices emanating from the room next to his study. He puckered his brow in confusion and looked at his watch. It lacked fifteen minutes until the noon hour, and the ladies of the house were generally doing needlework and practicing their music at this time of day. Georgiana, of course, tried to visit her peafowl every morning, and Miss Bennet might be with her. But why would they be in the library? Georgiana was not a great reader; not because she found it difficult, but because her interests were narrow, and she found most books to be dull. She often joined him in the library on winter evenings, but that was because she enjoyed his companionship, not because she wished to delight herself in the multitude of rare volumes on the shelves.

He set aside his letter, stood up, and walked over to the side door which led into a corner of the library, which was partially obscured from the rest of the book room by a small table holding a porcelain Chinese vase. He opened the door in time to hear Georgiana say, "The painting is in the northeast of the room."

"Do give me a minute to recover," her companion, Miss Bennet, said cheerfully. "Otherwise I might faint in astonishment. This library is truly spectacular."

Darcy watched as Miss Bennet began spinning around slowly, her lips curved upward, her eyes dancing, her yellow skirt swaying, as she gazed at the multitude of books. The lady was blessed with a beautiful face but now, with the joy on her face, she was equal to her elder sister, which was saying a great deal. What an exquisite woman!

Georgiana, now openly impatient, finally made an irritated noise, which caused Miss Bennet to stop and look toward her with a cheerful countenance.

"Please do show me the portrait of the peacock," Miss Bennet said, walking over to Georgiana, who quickly made her way to the Cradock painting in the corner of the room. Darcy, realizing that neither woman had noticed his presence, found himself standing in place, his heart beating with strange rapidity. He almost never observed single ladies when they were not aware of his presence, and those of marriageable age always postured before him in the hopes of drawing his attention and, perhaps, an offer.

But, he suddenly recognized, Miss Bennet was an exception to that rule. She was well-mannered and polite, but she never flattered him. Perhaps that was why Georgiana had taken to the woman so quickly; as the sister of the wealthy, unattached Mr. Darcy, the girl had been the focus of many fulsome compliments in the hopes that if Georgiana was drawn to a woman, her wealthy brother might be as well. But Miss Bennet, it seemed, liked Georgiana for Georgiana, not because she was attempting to ensnare Darcy.

By this time, Elizabeth had joined Georgiana in the corner of the room and was leaning toward the painting.

"Where is the…? Oh, I see, yes, some of the neck and flight feathers look white. The white feathers can appear anywhere on the body, then?"

"Yes," Georgiana said. "After Fitzwilliam acquired this painting and I noticed the white feathers, he wrote to a gentleman friend who has a flock of peacocks, and he confirmed that some of the birds have white feathers. My brother purchased Neptune from his friend."

"And now you will see if Neptune will sire sons and daughters with white feathers," Elizabeth commented.

"Yes, exactly. Are you familiar with Sir Robert Bakewell, Miss Bennet?"

"The agriculturist? Yes, indeed. My father has some literature regarding his work in selective breeding."

"We probably have the same texts!" Georgiana said excitedly, hurrying over to a shelf. "Look here. I have read all these many times, and I am quite certain that I can do similar work with my peacocks, not to the extent of Sir Thomas or Coke of Norfolk, of course, but I can breed Neptune, and breed those of his progeny who have white feathers…"

"I wonder if someday, there will be an entirely white peacock," Elizabeth said dreamily.

"Oh, that would be the most wonderful thing in all the world!" Georgiana exclaimed, clasping her hands together, her face beaming.

Darcy, uncomfortably aware that he was effectively spying on his sister and her friend, withdrew quietly into his study, closed the door gently, and wandered over to the window. He had just observed a scene which surprised him greatly. Could it be that Georgiana had found a genuine friend, a friend who was kind and generous, but who also did not always submit to Georgiana's immediate demands? A friend who was intelligent and interested in the things that Miss Darcy was? If Miss Bennet was truly the woman she appeared to be, she was a great gift to the unusual, vulnerable daughter of Pemberley.

Nonetheless, he must be cautious, as he could not afford to make a mistake in this matter as he had with Georgiana's previous companion, Mrs. Younge. Miss Bennet seemed a truly exemplary individual, and not on the hunt for a wealthy husband. Nonetheless, he owed it to Georgiana to be careful about those whom he allowed in her orbit. He determined to learn more about Miss Elizabeth Bennet of Longbourn. He would keep his precious sister safe.

Chapter 10

Darcy guided Mrs. Bingley into the dining room and helped her into her seat, then proceeded to the head of the table. Georgiana had pleaded a headache and was above stairs, but everyone else was present. He had chosen to place Miss Bennet next to himself today in the hopes of learning more about her. In retrospect, that was a dubious decision, as Miss Bingley was now eyeing Miss Bennet with envy in her predatory eye. He hoped that there would be no unpleasant scenes at the table tonight.

"Have any of you had the opportunity to read Lord Byron's recent poem?" Caroline Bingley asked as the servants placed dishes around the table and poured the dinner wine.

"I have," Elizabeth said, spooning potatoes onto her plate.

"I have not," Darcy said, and then added, more to be provoking than anything else, "I am not inclined to waste my time reading a poem written by a dissolute spendthrift. I can only imagine that the poem is absurdly pretentious."

"Oh, Mr. Darcy, I could not agree with you more!" Miss Bingley exclaimed. "It is such a pity that the bourgeois have taken so much to his lordship's puerile writings."

"I have read it, and found it captivating," Elizabeth declared. "Mr. Darcy, while I may not approve of Lord Byron – and I confess that I do not know a great deal about his lifestyle – I think it unreasonable to avoid what might be an excellent piece of literature merely because you disapprove of the author."

"Oh Elizabeth!" Caroline cried out, "I am certain you would agree that Mr. Darcy knows far more about literature than you do. He is, as Charles has told us many a time, a most gifted scholar."

"That may be," Elizabeth answered, "but that does not mean that Mr. Darcy is an expert on every type of literature. He says he has not read Byron's work, so how could he know much about it?"

"Elizabeth is correct, Darcy," Bingley said with a grin. "If you are to truly lambaste the man's work, you ought to at least read some of it."

Darcy fought a smile and said, "I suppose that is true enough. I cannot suppose you brought a copy of *Childe Harold's Pilgrimage* with you, Miss Bennet?"

"I fear not, sir. My father was fortunate enough to obtain one of the quartos of the second printing, but he would not entrust such a treasure to his wandering daughter."

"I never had much use for poetry myself," Mr. Hurst grunted, startling the entire table, as he was usually too busy eating at dinner to bother with talking.

"I enjoy good poetry, and I consider Lord Byron an excellent poet," Elizabeth said, and then added slyly, "I fear that Jane is responsible for my exposure to bad poetry."

"Now Lizzy," Mrs. Bingley said, turning pink and smiling at her sister, "it was not my fault that Mother read Mr. Dowding's poetry to the entire family."

"It was not, of course, but oh my, the poor man certainly admired you, but he was not gifted with words."

"A former admirer, Jane?" Louisa asked curiously.

"Yes, a friend of my uncle Gardiner's, who was much taken with Jane when she was but fifteen," Elizabeth said with a chuckle. "She was far too young for marriage, of course, and I am thankful that business concerns drew him away before he felt it necessary to produce any more verses to my sister's blue eyes."

"Perhaps Mr. Dowding has improved with time," Jane said charitably. "I will say that I read only a few pages of the *Childe Harold* and gave it up. I enjoy novels more than poetry."

"What novels do you like, Mrs. Bingley?" Darcy asked.

"Oh, I am very fond of *Robinson Crusoe*," Jane answered, "though of course I would be horrified if I was actually shipwrecked on a deserted island and was fearful of being attacked by wild animals or starving to death. I enjoy reading about it, though."

"I am very fond of that book as well," Darcy admitted. "I daresay I have read it in full at least twenty times."

"And do you approve of its author, Daniel DeFoe?" Elizabeth inquired archly. "He was certainly as much a spendthrift as Lord Byron, and I would argue that he was a most reprehensible husband and father."

Darcy leaned back in his seat and allowed his lips to curve up in a smile. "Do you think so, Miss Bennet?"

"I do, why…"

Darcy found himself listening intently to the young lady's arguments, which were cogent and well informed, even as his heart rejoiced within him. Unlike Caroline Bingley, Miss Elizabeth Bennet showed no inclination to pander to his remarks or venerate him unduly. These were not the actions of a woman anxious to capture a husband by fair means or foul. It seemed that Georgiana had found a truly honorable friend.

"Georgiana?"

"Yes, Fitzwilliam?" Georgiana asked as Darcy stepped into his sister's private sitting room. The girl had a book in her hand and Darcy recognized it as a book on agricultural techniques, no doubt one his sister had read many times before.

"How are you feeling?" he asked.

"Oh, I am well enough," Georgiana answered, carefully placing a marker in her book and setting it aside. "I did not really have a headache, but I was nervous about being with Miss Bingley tonight after dinner. She keeps provoking me to play for you and the others, and I despise playing in front of numerous people."

"I know," Darcy said, walking over to sit near his sister. "I am sorry, my dear, and it is entirely appropriate for you to use a headache as an excuse."

"I do not like it because it is not true, but I understand that sometimes we say something is true, and everyone knows that it is not true, so it is not really a lie."

Darcy tilted his head and said, "Yes, I think that is an accurate description of the matter."

"It is like when we are here and someone comes to call, and the butler says that you are not at home. It is not that you are truly absent, it is that it is not polite to say that you do not want to see the person, so instead Thompson says you are not at home. That way, no one's feelings are hurt."

"Precisely," Darcy said with relief. He had had similar conversation with Georgiana many times before, and this was the first time his sister had truly seemed to understand such social niceties.

"Miss Bennet and I talked about this today," his sister explained, her gaze shifting to the window, beyond which the sun was sinking in the west. "I did not want to come to dinner tonight because of Miss Bingley, and Miss Bennet explained that it is kinder to say I am ill than to argue with Miss Bingley openly."

"That is true," Darcy said in wonder. It seemed that Miss Bennet was truly a miracle worker. "It seems you are fond of Miss Bennet, Georgiana."

"Oh, I am, Brother, very much! I will be very sad when she leaves."

Darcy sighed. Naturally Miss Bennet would return home in time, and yes, that would be extremely painful to Georgiana. His precious sister did not love easily, but when she did, her attachment was fierce and unwavering.

"They will be here for more than another week," he said finally, "and perhaps we will see them in London or Pemberley again someday. Bingley is a valued friend, and I hope we will see him, his wife, and her sister in time."

Georgiana, who had been looking woebegone, cheered up at these words. "That is true, and while I dislike London, I will gladly go if I could see Miss Bennet."

"What of Mrs. Bingley?" he asked curiously. "Do you find her pleasant?"

"Oh, yes, she is very kind, though rather quiet. Miss Bennet says she has been ill lately and is spending much time in her bedchamber. Is that because she does not want to be in our company?"

Darcy suppressed a groan. What was he to say to that? He (and Miss Bennet) had finally managed to convince Georgiana that it was reasonable to claim illness to avoid discourtesy. Now would his sister think that every time someone claimed to be ill, they were actually disinclined for company?

He made a sudden decision and turned toward his sister, his expression grave. "Georgiana, I have a secret to tell you, but you must not speak of it to anyone but to me, Mr. and Mrs. Bingley, and Miss Bennet. If you do talk to them about this, you must do it privately."

Georgiana looked alarmed. "Very well, what is it?"

"Mrs. Bingley is expecting a child, and is feeling unwell because of her pregnancy. She is genuinely feeling sickly."

Georgiana blinked. "Is it not a good thing to bear a child?"

"A very good thing! It is merely … well, there are times when a husband and wife choose to keep such a thing private for a season."

"Why?"

Darcy felt an urge to pull at his hair, but instead said, "Sometimes a pregnant lady loses her baby during early pregnancy, and if such a thing comes to pass, she and her husband do not always want everyone to know about it."

"Oh, because people might say hurtful things?"

"Yes."

Georgiana stared at him, her brow puckered, and then her forehead smoothed and she nodded. "I understand."

"Good," he said with relief. "Now, I will leave you alone. Good night, my dear."

"Fitzwilliam?" she said, holding out a staying hand. "When are we going to Ramsgate this summer?"

Darcy gulped and stared at his sister, berating himself inwardly. Once again, he had assumed that Georgiana would grasp something which, to him, was obvious.

119

"I … I did not think we would go to Ramsgate this year," he finally said in a halting voice.

Now her blue eyes grew wide with bewildered unhappiness. "Not go to Ramsgate? We always go to Ramsgate, Brother! Why would we not go this year?"

Darcy blew out a quick breath as he prayed for guidance. He reached out to clasp his sister's hands in his own. "I … I assumed you would not wish to return because of what happened last summer."

"Because of Mr. Wickham? He will not be in Ramsgate, will he?"

"No, certainly not," Darcy said harshly, and then winced as his sister flinched. "No, I promise you that he will never be permitted to get near you again, Georgiana."

"Then I do not understand. I wish to go. My birds are there!"

"You have birds here too, Georgie," Darcy answered rather helplessly.

"Not wild birds," his sister said. Her blue eyes were pools of grief, and Darcy felt his own heart breaking. "This is all my fault. I did not know … I did not imagine…"

"Of course you did not," Darcy said swiftly. Indeed, he knew it was not Georgiana's fault in the least. It was his; he had allowed his sister to trust Mrs. Younge, who proved traitorous. And George Wickham – well, Georgiana had only fond memories of their times together when she was but a child.

"Perhaps we can go to Ramsgate," he found himself saying. "I thought that last summer's painful experience would give you a distaste for the town and even the birds, but I see that I was wrong. Let me see what I can do."

"Thank you," Georgiana said, lowering her eyes. "I would like to go, but I understand if it is not possible because of my actions.

He lurched forward and pulled his sister to his strong chest. "I love you, Georgiana. I will always love you."

She lifted slender hands and caught onto his arms. "I love you too, Brother."

Chapter 11

Elizabeth woke up, stretched luxuriously, and opened her eyes. Based on the dim light glowing through the drapery over the windows, it was not yet daybreak. Why had she woken so early?

A moment later, she heard a loud trill, followed by an indignant squawk, and she smiled. The peafowl were being noisier than usual this morning, which had interrupted her slumber. She hoped that the birds had not disturbed Jane. It was unlikely that they had, as Jane slept heavily now due to her pregnancy.

She could try to go back to sleep but no, she knew from experience that she would merely toss and turn. She might as well rise and dress. Perhaps she could find an interesting book in the library to read. Well, she could find a hundred interesting books. It would be difficult to pick just one!

Twenty minutes later, she was dressed and, preparatory to leaving the room, pulled the curtains aside to stare at the newborn dawn. She peered out and narrowed her eyes, attempting to make out the form of the figure hurrying past her window. A minute later, she reached for her boots, put them on, and rushed out the door.

Georgiana Darcy, only daughter of George and Lady Anne Darcy, walked across the lawn toward the north of the great mansion, where a creek meandered down a gentle hill before spilling into a large pond across from the impressive frontage of her home. She took deep breaths of cool morning air and stepped onto the stone bridge which spanned the narrowest part of the stream. It was very early, hardly past sunrise, and morning mists were still swirling and roiling over the waters. Here, above the surface of the brook, she could see well enough, not that she truly needed her eyes. The walkways along the creeks, and around the ponds, and through the woods of her beloved Pemberley were engraved in her memory and her heart. How she loved her home! There was much she did not understand about the world and her place in it, but she was safe and comfortable at Pemberley.

"Miss Darcy!" a voice cried out from behind her, and Georgiana turned uneasily, only to smile in pleasure.

"Miss Bennet!" she answered. "Why are you up so early?"

"As to that, your charming peafowl awoke me," Elizabeth said cheerfully, "but I assure you that it matters not as I enjoy waking up early. Now do tell me honestly – am I interrupting you? I have not made the time to wander this lovely area, but if you wish for solitude, I can retreat to the house and explore the library."

"Oh, not at all," Georgiana said. "I would enjoy your company very much."

"Thank you," Elizabeth said, stepping next to the taller girl, leaning her arms on the stone parapet, and looking down into the rushing waters below. "I think I see a fish down there!"

"A trout," Georgiana confirmed. "My brother has stocked the pond and stream, and he often fishes here."

"Oh, how lovely! I have an uncle who enjoys angling very much, though he lives in London, so rarely has the opportunity to do so."

"I do not like fishing," Georgiana said seriously. "The fish are so wet and slimy when I catch them, and I hate how they flop in my hands."

This startled a laugh out of Elizabeth, who said, "I am impressed that you have even tried fishing, Miss Darcy. I confess that the very thought of a wriggling, squirming trout in my hands is extremely unpleasant."

"A few years ago, I begged Fitzwilliam to allow me to accompany him on an angling expedition. He was kind enough to set aside an afternoon of fishing for me, and one experience was quite enough."

"I understand completely."

Silence fell for a few minutes, punctured only by the whistle of crickets, the croak of frogs, the sounds of the leaves rustling gently in the trees, the gurgle of the stream and the cries of nearby birds.

This provoked Elizabeth to ask, "Tell me, Miss Darcy, do you find other birds interesting, or only peacocks?"

Georgiana tilted her head up to enjoy the light from the sun, which had crept slightly above the horizon and said, "I like all birds, though my brother does not wish me to acquire numerous geese and ducks and hens and quail. He says that the peafowl take enough of my time, and I suppose he is correct, because I also need to practice my music."

"I presume there are some interesting birds in the woods here at Pemberley," Elizabeth commented, lifting her eyes toward the woods beyond the stream. "Doves and blackbirds perhaps?"

"Yes, both," Georgiana responded, her face growing animated. "There are also wrens and robins in Derbyshire. As for other wild birds – well, for the last six summers, we have journeyed to Ramsgate on the sea in Kent. We have always taken the same red brick house there on the beach and I visit the salt marshes and mudflats nearby, where there are numerous birds! It is not easy to see them, of course, but I have spied nightingales, cuckoos, warblers, and redshanks."

"It sounds spectacular," Elizabeth said, genuinely envious. "I have never seen the ocean, and I long to do so someday."

Georgiana blew out a slow breath and said sadly, "Well, as to that, I just remembered that we may not go to Ramsgate this year, but Fitzwilliam is thinking about making arrangements so that I can go. I hope we can. We always go."

"Oh!" Elizabeth answered. "I am sorry, though of course gentlemen often have business concerns and the like which prevent them from leaving their estates."

"It is not that," Georgiana said, her expression mournful. "Last year, my brother had business in London and sent me ahead to Ramsgate. I fear I caused a dreadful amount of trouble while I was there."

Elizabeth stopped and stared at her in wonder. "My dear Miss Darcy, I am certain you were no trouble at all."

To her surprise and distress, Miss Darcy's eyes filled with tears, and her head lowered despondently. "I *am* trouble, and I know it," she said in a choked voice. "You see, I do not understand why people act the way they do. I think people should always tell the truth, but sometimes they lie. I do not understand why people tell falsehoods."

Elizabeth put out a hand and touched her companion's arm gently. "People ought not to lie, of course, but the Bible warns that some people will speak falsely for their own gain. It is a sad thing, certainly."

"It is *terrible*," the girl said disconsolately. "Last summer, while Fitzwilliam was in London, an old friend from my childhood visited me at Ramsgate. He said he was in love with me, that we should marry and I would not have to enter society, which I do not want to do. I do not like strangers, and dancing, and excessive noise. My friend promised that he would buy an estate with my dowry, and I could have as many peafowl, geese, ducks, doves, and chickens as I wanted. I told him that I would marry him. We were planning to go to Gretna Greene when my brother arrived unexpectedly, having by chance put his trip forward a few days. Fitzwilliam was so angry, Miss Bennet, more at my friend than me, but I know he was also angry with me."

Elizabeth, who had been listening to this recitation with mounting horror, asked, "How old was your gentleman friend?"

"He is a year younger than my brother," Georgiana said, turning her head and focusing her gaze on Elizabeth's chin. "He is so handsome and charming, and even now I wonder if I was at fault for his offer. Perhaps I was flirting with him and did not know it. I do not know how to flirt, but I have read of it. Perhaps he merely was being kind…"

"Miss Darcy," Elizabeth interrupted, reaching out her gloved hands to grasp the younger woman's in her own. "I promise you that this was not your fault. No gentleman of any honor would make an offer to a girl of sixteen…"

"I was only fifteen then, actually."

"Fifteen?! It is an utter outrage, Miss Darcy, to do such a thing and to suggest that you abscond to Gretna Greene to be married over the anvil? No, my dear, no! This old friend was no friend at all, I promise you that! There are good reasons for the laws which prevent a girl under one and twenty from marrying without the permission of her guardian, and especially a girl with a substantial dowry, which I presume you have."

"Thirty thousand pounds," Georgiana said, pulling her hands away and turning to clutch the balustrade of the bridge. "Yes, Fitzwilliam said that all Mr. Wickham cared about was gaining control over my money."

Elizabeth, who had been overflowing with outrage on behalf of her young friend, felt as if she had suddenly been stabbed in the heart.

"Mr. *Wickham*?" she repeated in horror.

Georgiana nodded miserably. "Yes, Mr. Wickham. He was my father's godson, and I thought him a faithful and good friend. But Fitzwilliam says that he was lying to me, that all he wanted was money, as he is a spendthrift and a gambler. It still seems hard for me to believe; I remember him so fondly from when I was a child. He was always kind to me and played games with me, and he is very good looking, too."

She cast a fearful look at Elizabeth and said, "Have I ruined your good opinion of me forever, Miss Bennet? I know I acted very poorly, with a horrifying lack of propriety, and perhaps you despise me now."

Elizabeth had a strong inclination to scream, so stricken was she at this newfound knowledge, but she needed to stay calm for Miss Darcy's sake. She reached out a hand, took Georgiana's arm gently in her own, and guided her off the bridge and down the path, which passed under a leafy archway of trees.

"I do not despise you in the least," Elizabeth said as soon as she was able to speak. "Oh Miss Darcy, if you were foolish to trust Mr. Wickham, so was I!"

"You … you *know* Mr. Wickham?" Miss Darcy gasped.

"I do, because until recently, he was a lieutenant in a militia regiment stationed in my home town of Meryton," Elizabeth said, her spare hand tightening into an angry fist. "Oh, you are correct, Mr. Wickham is good looking and charming, with exquisite manners and gentle speech. I thought him one of the very best men in the world, and it seems he is, instead, the worst!"

"Do you really think so?" Georgiana asked shyly.

"I know so," Elizabeth declared, her pace increasing slightly in her anger, both at Wickham for deceiving her, and herself for having listened so credulously to the man. "He flattered and charmed me and I ... oh, fool that I am ... I was honored by his attentions and believed his slanderous words about your brother."

"My brother? What did Mr. Wickham say about my brother?" Georgiana asked sharply.

Elizabeth looked at the girl, her expression contrite. "Mr. Wickham said that he grew up at Pemberley as the son of your father's steward, that your father was Mr. Wickham's godfather, and that the elder Mr. Darcy set aside a valuable church living for Mr. Wickham, which your brother refused to give him. Mr. Wickham ascribed your brother's actions to pride and jealousy, and I, depending on his outward façade as a likable and attractive gentleman, believed his story. I am a fool."

"My father did set aside a church living for his godson, Mr. Wickham," Georgiana said, her gaze now fixed on the path in front of them. "Fitzwilliam did not think he would be a good clergyman, so my brother was happy when Mr. Wickham suggested he give up all rights to the living in exchange for three thousand pounds."

"Three thousand pounds!" Elizabeth repeated, and her pace increased still more in her agitation.

"You are walking too fast," Georgiana protested, and her companion immediately stopped.

"I do apologize," Elizabeth said, bestowing a rueful look on the younger woman. "When I am upset I often walk very quickly. I did not mean to drag you along."

"I am sorry that I upset you," Georgiana said meekly.

"No, I am so glad that you told me about Mr. Wickham's disgusting behavior. I have long prided myself in my ability to understand the characters of my fellow man, and I am humbled to discover how poorly I comprehended Mr. Wickham's true character. In any case, let me reassure you that the fault lies completely with Mr. Wickham. He has a strange magnetism to him, and you, who knew and trusted him as a child, had no reason to doubt his good faith."

"I did not doubt him at all," Georgiana agreed, a few more tears dripping down her cheeks. "I have thought much of it, and part of the reason I was so eager to wed immediately was that Mr. Wickham spent hours telling me about London high society and all the people and noise and rigid etiquette. Do you think that he said those things because he knew that I would hate London society?"

"I am certain that is exactly what he did," Elizabeth responded grimly. She shook her head and said, "I think he is something of a chameleon, Mr. Wickham, and easily adjusts his speech and topics based on what he wants from someone else. He is such a despicable man!"

"Why did you believe bad things about Fitzwilliam when you had never met him?" Georgiana asked.

Elizabeth swallowed hard and again pulled her companion into a walk, though a slow one.

"There was no good reason at all," she confessed. "I trusted Mr. Wickham because he seemed affable and honorable. I also, well, I spent a number of weeks in Kent, as you know, and your aunt, Lady Catherine is..."

"Proud, arrogant, and rude," Georgiana finished, and then added indignantly, "Fitzwilliam is nothing like Lady Catherine!"

"I know he is not," Elizabeth said miserably. "I apologize profusely, Miss Darcy. I have no excuse for my assumptions about you or your brother which were based entirely on the lies of a winsome, vile man. Can you forgive me?"

"Of course I forgive you," Georgiana said immediately. "We all sin and fall short of the glory of God. Besides, you know the truth now."

"I do," Elizabeth agreed, greatly relieved. Miss Darcy, while unusual, was a compassionate and generous girl. "I hope you do not mind me asking a further question. I am confident you were not at Ramsgate alone. Surely you had a companion?"

"Yes, Mrs. Younge," the girl said softly. "She was an excellent performer on the pianoforte and the harp. My brother told me that she had a prior acquaintance with Mr. Wickham and invited him to come to Ramsgate to see me."

"Oh, Miss Darcy," Elizabeth exclaimed, shaking her head in distress. "So the woman who was looking after you was in league with Mr. Wickham!"

"Yes," Georgiana agreed and pulled the watch on her neck away from her so that she could read the time. "It is getting late, Miss Bennet. We should return to the house."

Elizabeth could only nod in agreement as Georgiana directed their steps towards another bridge, this one constructed of wood, and set a brisk pace toward the great mansion rising into the morning skies. She felt faint, not with hunger, but with horror. She, who had so long prided herself on her acuity, stood revealed as a featherhead who had accepted the slanderous accusations of an unrighteous man toward the honorable Mr. Darcy.

"Miss Darcy?" she asked.

"Yes?"

"It might be well to speak to your brother about our conversation this morning. As your guardian, he ought to know."

Georgiana frowned and then said, "You are correct, Miss Bennet. I will tell him as soon as possible."

"In a private setting, of course," Elizabeth cautioned. "It would be dangerous if you were to speak openly in front of the servants or, far worse, Miss Bingley."

"Yes, I ought to speak to him alone. Thank you."

Chapter 12

"I practiced billiards throughout the winter, Darcy," Bingley said as the two gentlemen climbed the steps leading to the main door of Pemberley. "I flatter myself that I have improved greatly."

Darcy cast a skeptical look at his friend and said, "I thought you were far too busy courting Mrs. Bingley to bother with games."

"Nonsense," Bingley retorted with good humor. "I did devote many of my daylight hours to Jane, but my evening hours were my own."

"Whom did you play with?" Darcy asked as he stepped into the front door of the mansion. The butler and a liveried footman waited within and relieved Darcy and Bingley of their hats.

"I played with Hurst," Bingley explained, grinning, "and make no mistake, the man is remarkably skilled at the game."

"Is he?" Darcy asked. He had thought that Hurst's only great skills were for eating and cards, though the man also seemed to enjoy shooting pheasants.

"Yes. Now I hope you will excuse me, but I must see how Jane is doing this morning."

"Of course," Darcy agreed. "I enjoyed our morning ride very much, and I will see you later."

Bingley nodded, turned, and bounded up the stairs, his face alight with excitement. Darcy, watching him go, was aware of an unaccustomed twinge of envy. He was still uncertain of the wisdom of Bingley's choice of wife in terms of her wealth and connections, but without a doubt, the younger man was madly in love with his wife and she, in turn, was openly affectionate toward her husband.

Would he ever be fortunate enough to find such a wife? As master of the grand estate of Pemberley, Darcy was expected by the upper crust of society to marry a woman of fashion, accomplishments, connections, and wealth. But while his mind knew and accepted such demands from the Ton, his heart misgave him.

He did not want a marriage of convenience. He did not want to share a bed with a woman whose only interest in him was his affluence and good birth. He did not wish to stare across the table, day after day, month after month, year after year, at a woman with no similarity of mind.

Perhaps that was why he had never seriously considered offering for a woman, even though he was eight and twenty. He must marry, of course; Pemberley needed an heir. But he had attended numerous assemblies, routs, dances, and Venetian breakfasts in London, and been the focus of flirtatious glances, vapid speeches, and pursuit by matchmaking mothers and their eligible daughters, and he had never felt an iota of the love which Charles Bingley so obviously felt toward his handsome wife.

"Is there anything you need, sir?"

Darcy turned in surprise toward Reynolds, his butler, who had served the Darcys for some thirty years now. He realized he had been standing stock still, staring as Bingley disappeared up the stairwell, which was unusual behavior on his part.

"Erm, do you know where Miss Darcy is?" he asked Reynolds.

"Yes, sir. Miss Darcy is in the music room."

"Thank you."

It would be pleasant to spend a few minutes with Georgiana, so long as Mrs. Hurst and Miss Bingley were not hovering over her. Furthermore, if they *were* present, he owed it his young sister to be certain that her guests were not making her uncomfortable.

He walked down the main corridor toward the music room, the polished wooden floor clicking under his booted feet, the white plastered walls decorated elegantly with beautiful and expensive paintings.

Pemberley was glorious, he knew that. It was natural enough that eligible young women were more interested in his possessions than his person, though certainly he had received plenty of compliments about his tall figure and handsome face.

He wanted a woman to love him for himself, not for his money, his lands, his position in society, or his looks. He wanted a woman who would engage him intellectually, but who was also kind, diligent, loving and yes, amusing. He knew himself to be a dour fellow and would do better with a cheerful wife.

But where could he find such a woman? Certainly not at Rosings in Kent, where his cousin Anne de Bourgh, heiress to Rosings, dwelled with her autocratic mother. Lady Catherine was absolutely determined that her daughter marry Darcy in order to combine the two great estates. Darcy had only a cousinly affection for Anne, who was frail and quiet. No, he would not marry Anne.

He sighed. It seemed an insoluble problem. He had prayed for many years that the Lord on High would send him a compatible wife. So far, He had not. Perhaps Darcy needed to lower his sights and marry a high born woman whom he believed he could tolerate.

Either that or he needed to be patient and wait on God. After all, David had waited years to be crowned King of Israel, and the Israelites had waited forty years in the desert to enter the Promised Land.

He stopped in front of the door to the music room, opened it, and stepped in. To his relief, the only people present were Georgiana, who was playing the pianoforte, and Mrs. Annesley, who was seated comfortably nearby knitting something blue. The older lady looked up and smiled at him, and he quietly took a seat next to her, though there was no actual reason to be noiseless. He knew the expression on Georgiana's face well; the girl was in her own world now, one full of harmony and melody. Darcy closed his eyes and allowed both body and mind to relax as the complex chords rippled through the air.

Under his closed eyelids, he felt liquid form. He worried about Georgiana – oh how he worried about her! She was so fragile and uncertain in some areas of life that came easily to most, yet so incredibly gifted in others. Musically, she was a near genius. The notes flowing from the instrument were perfect, the timing exquisite, the fingering difficult but exact. How could someone so adept, so brilliant in some areas, struggle so much in relating to others, in understanding that some people, like George Wickham, were treacherous?

He opened his eyes and released a soft sigh. He had forgotten perhaps the most important thing of all in his contemplation of the perfect wife; she must love Georgiana and be patient with her.

The song came to its magnificent end, and both Mrs. Annesley and Darcy clapped a few time, causing

Georgiana to turn in surprise, which shifted to pleasure when she saw who had joined her companion on the couch.

"Brother, I did not know you were here!" she said, standing up and shaking out her skirts.

"I entered only a few minutes ago, my dear," Darcy said, "and I enjoyed the end of…"

"The third movement of Beethoven's Sonata No. 14 in C sharp minor," Georgiana said. "I am still playing it a little too slowly, but I am making progress."

"Indeed you are," Mrs. Annesley agreed, bestowing an approving look on her charge. "You played it beautifully, Miss Darcy."

"Thank you," Georgiana said with a slight smile, then turned her clear eyed gaze on her brother. "Fitzwilliam, I would like to speak to you in private."

Darcy felt a distinct surge of anxiety, which he firmly beat down. Georgiana, who trusted too easily, had learned the wisdom of coming to him alone when faced with a question or problem. Her desire to see him alone did not mean anything catastrophic had occurred; she might well be interested in acquiring a guinea hen for all he knew!

"Of course," he said heartily. "Please join me in my study, Georgiana. Mrs. Annesley, we will see you shortly."

"Of course, sir," the lady answered, gathering up her knitting and departing through the main door. Darcy took a few steps after her, then halted and said, "Perhaps we ought to walk through the library into my study."

"Why?" Georgiana asked.

"Because we have less chance of coming across someone who wishes to speak to us."

"And whom we do not wish to speak to, like Miss Bingley?" his sister asked with a grimace.

"Precisely."

The twosome thus made their way to the side door of the music room, which led into the library which, in turn, led into the study, whereupon Darcy released his sister's arm and looked down upon her expectantly, only to be distracted.

"You look lovely today, Georgiana!" he said approvingly.

"Thank you, Brother," the girl responded, looking down on her yellow muslin, which was fitted perfectly for her tall, slender form. "I feel peaceful today, and this dress suits me well enough."

"I am glad," her brother answered with satisfaction. From her earliest days, Georgiana had been very sensitive to the feeling of fabric and tight clothing. As a small child, she had screamed and howled until her nurse discovered that she could not bear the lace in contact with her tender skin, nor could she, then or now, wear woolen clothing. Even now, she preferred to wear overly large dresses, though Mrs. Annesley had gently coaxed her to don more form fitting clothing when she was in company. It said much for Georgiana's state of mind that she had willingly adorned herself in a well-fitting dress many hours before dinner.

"I spoke to Miss Bennet at length this morning," Georgiana said, breaking into his musings. "She was very encouraging, but I told her about what happened at Ramsgate last summer, and she said that I should tell you all about it."

Satisfaction gave way to horror. "*What?*"

/

"It is heavenly, is it not, Charles?" Jane Bingley asked her husband, drawing in a long, full breath of scented air.

"It is," Bingley agreed, though his eyes were on his wife's exquisite countenance such that he hardly noticed the roses surrounding them.

"It is wondrous," Elizabeth declared, looking around her with satisfaction. "Longbourn's rose garden is pleasant enough, but compared to Pemberley's – well, it is like comparing a pond to an ocean."

"I agree," Jane said, her face glowing. "It smells delightful, and whether coincidence or not, I feel less queasy when surrounded by so many fragrant blossoms."

"Perhaps we ought to plant a rose garden at Netherfield?" Charles suggested, eager to please his darling wife.

Jane tilted her head and considered, then said, "I think we should wait until we are certain we wish to live at Netherfield for many years. It takes time and money for roses to grow, and if we choose to move farther north…"

"You would truly be at peace with such a move?" Charles asked.

Jane chuckled and said, "I think it quite likely that we would both enjoy living farther from Longbourn. I love my family, of course, but my mother can be intrusive, and she might well grow more so when we have a child."

"That is true," Elizabeth agreed, wandering over to stand in the shade of a rose trellis, "especially if you have a son."

"Son or daughter, I care not," Bingley said stoutly, "just so long as you and the child are safe. I only hope…"

He trailed off and his countenance darkened. Childbirth was a chancy business, and many a woman died in the process. He loved Jane to the very depths of his soul, and such a thought was terrifying. How could he live without her?

"I am the very image of my mother," Jane said into his ear, "and she birthed all her children with ease. Do not worry, my love."

He kissed her gently on the lips and then turned an embarrassed look at Elizabeth who was staring intently at a particularly large red blossom, though the smirk on her face indicated she was quite aware of what was going on behind her.

"Jane," she said casually, "we have been outside for some time. Perhaps you should go inside and rest? The sun is very hot today."

"Yes, my dear, you must not overheat," Bingley agreed hastily.

Jane nodded and said, "I confess to being rather warm and tired, though it is difficult to withdraw from such a lovely place. All the same, I am ready for a nap."

"You should eat a small nuncheon as well, as that helps you feel better," Bingley said. "Elizabeth, I hope you do not mind if we leave you?"

"Of course not," his sister by marriage replied. "I will see you both later."

The couple smiled and returned to the house, leaving Elizabeth alone, surrounded by flowerets bobbing in the soft breeze. She glanced at her watch and noted it was still an hour before noon, and Miss Darcy had said that she would not be visiting the peafowl for an hour. She could walk elsewhere, or visit the library in search of a book, or...

"Miss Bennet."

She turned in surprise to discover Mr. Darcy standing some five yards away, his expression even more serious than usual, which was saying something.

"Mr. Darcy! How you startled me!"

"My apologies, Miss Bennet," the man said stiffly, walked a little closer, and then said quietly, "I sought you out so that we could speak of your conversation with my sister this morning."

"Of course," Elizabeth said, glancing around, "Perhaps we could find a private, but not confined place, where we are certain not to be interrupted but where there is no suggestion of impropriety?"

Darcy relaxed at these sensible words, considered, and said, "Do you like horses, Miss Bennet?"

"I like to watch them, though I am not a horsewoman."

"Would you care to observe one of my finest mares with her new filly?"

"Very much, Mr. Darcy."

Chapter 13

"They are both lovely," Elizabeth said truthfully, her eyes on the mare and her daughter who were standing in a shady part of the pasture north of the stables.

"Yes, they are," Darcy agreed, looking around carefully. The gentleman and lady were seated on a wooden bench within easy sight of several gardeners who were working on trimming some shrubbery. There was no one in earshot, but plenty of witnesses to testify that nothing indecent was happening between the master of Pemberley and one of his female guests.

Elizabeth turned to look directly into her companion's face and said, "Before we begin discussing specifics, Mr. Darcy, I wish to assure you that I will not share so much as a word of what Miss Darcy confided to me to anyone, not even my sister Jane, without your permission."

Darcy stared back to her, his eyes boring into hers. Miss Bennet's expression was grave and her dark eyes shone with sincerity.

He relaxed still more and said, "Thank you, Miss Bennet. I confess that I am concerned, and yes, uncomfortable that Georgiana chose to share such private details about her life."

"In retrospect, I likely should have stopped her from confiding in me," Elizabeth said contritely, "though I cannot, for personal reasons, regret the information. I know that I am entirely reliable and will not give away any of Miss Darcy's secrets, and now I know the truth about Mr. Wickham."

Darcy swallowed hard. "Georgiana told me that you are personally acquainted with him, though she did not provide details. How do you know the gentleman?"

"Well, he is hardly a gentleman, is he, Mr. Darcy?" Elizabeth asked, fixing her gaze on the mare, who was now nuzzling her filly's fuzzy head. Her own hands clenched in outrage, and she continued, "I met him last November when a militia regiment was stationed in our nearby village of Meryton. He took a commission as a lieutenant, and along with his fellows enjoyed the favor of our rather restricted society of families, and thus we met many times at assemblies and gatherings. I am ashamed to admit that I liked him very much and accepted his description of his previous life without question, including the claim that you deprived him of a church living. I am disgusted with myself, sir. I ought never to have believed such a thing without any sort of proof, and the man was extremely discourteous to slander you to me."

"Did he say anything about my sister?" Darcy demanded harshly.

Elizabeth turned her beautiful eyes on him and shook her head, "Nothing in particular, no. He did say she was proud and arrogant, but he said the same about you. He did not so much as hint of his attempt to convince Miss Darcy to elope with him, but of course he would not – I would have despised him if he had confessed to such a thing."

"Would you have?" Darcy asked grimly. "Does it not speak more to the disgraceful character and upbringing of my sister that she would agree, at the tender age of fifteen, to run away to Gretna Greene with a steward's son?"

Elizabeth's brows lowered into a reproving glower. "Mr. Darcy, I must speak honestly. Mr. Wickham is exceedingly handsome, his manners are captivating, and his speech enchanting. Your sister knew him as a child, and at that time, he appeared to be an honorable friend. You sent her to Ramsgate with Mrs. Younge, who was in league with Mr. Wickham, and together they convinced her to elope. I would argue that you, sir, are far more at fault than your sister. Wickham is capable of turning the head of many women; I am ashamed to say that I was attracted to him myself, though I knew he was too poor to be a proper husband to me. Nor, given my current knowledge of his character, was I of any interest to him except as a source of flirtation, since my dowry is small. No, it is not Miss Darcy's fault. She is an unusual young woman who speaks truth and expects others to speak truth in return."

Darcy bit his lip and turned his gaze toward the pasture. "You are correct," he admitted. "I am entirely at fault, and my sister is extraordinary."

"You worry about her," Elizabeth said gently.

"I do," Darcy agreed heavily. "I love her with all my heart, but she does not look on the world as most women do. I fear for her entrance into society and her marrying well. She has such a tender heart..."

He trailed off and turned in some surprise toward Miss Bennet, who was regarding him compassionately.

"I suppose I cannot reprove Georgiana for confiding in you, Miss Bennet," he said. "You are a very sympathetic listener."

"Well, I am one of five daughters, and I assure you that I grew up both talking and listening a great deal!" Elizabeth said, rising to her feet and taking a couple of steps toward the fence. "I see Miss Bingley walking here briskly so we have but little time to speak further. I hope you will continue to allow me the honor of being Miss Darcy's friend?"

"You wish to be?" Darcy asked quietly, keeping a wary eye on Miss Bingley, who was now close enough that he could see her smiling face, which was at odds with the jealous look in her eyes.

"Very much. Miss Darcy is a marvelous young lady. Miss Bingley, good morning! I hope you are well?"

"I am very well, Miss Bennet. Mr. Darcy, good morning!"

"Good morning, Miss Bingley," Darcy said, rising to his feet and bowing slightly.

"It is such a surprise to see you both here this morning, together!" Caroline continued brightly.

"I find horses beautiful," Elizabeth said truthfully. "Are they not lovely, Miss Bingley?"

Caroline cast a quick glance toward the mare and her filly and nodded. "Yes, they are charming. Mr. Darcy, Louisa and I were speaking only last night about your folly behind the copse of trees to the north of the lake. I expect Charles will wish to build something similar; please, do tell me, how long has it stood on Pemberley grounds? Is the architect still living, perhaps?"

Darcy tightened his lips but managed to say courteously, "It was built by my grandfather, Miss Bingley, so no, I fear the architect has long passed on."

"What a pity," Caroline said, her eyes limpid pools of regret. "Perhaps you know of a present day architect in London?"

"Mr. Darcy, Caroline, I fear I must return to the house," Elizabeth interposed. "Please excuse me."

"Good day, Miss Bennet."

"We will see you at dinner, Elizabeth," Caroline said in a satisfied tone, taking Darcy's arm and turning toward the pool, which currently showed fractured reflections of the blue skies and puffy clouds as the wind rippled the surface of the waters. "Now, I do hope you will be willing to advise Charles regarding a folly like your own."

Darcy suppressed a huff and glanced at Elizabeth, who bestowed a mischievous look on him before striding rapidly toward the mansion. The folly in question was designed to look like a small, derelict Roman temple, and he despised it for the pretentious waste of space that it was. The only reason he had not had it pulled down was that his father, George Darcy, had altered the landscaping considerably during his lifetime such that the folly was no longer visible from the main house. From his current position, he was able to observe the structure in all its extravagant glory. It was a ridiculous thing, a true folly, for it had no purpose. Nonetheless, it was considered a valuable addition to any gentleman's property to have such a building. He supposed that was another reason to allow it to stand.

"If Bingley is interested, I can certainly suggest a reliable architect for such a purpose," he told his companion stiffly, glancing toward the house as Miss Bennet disappeared through the side door. She was such a vigorous, energetic woman, and a very fast walker.

"Wonderful!" Caroline said eagerly. "I suppose it must wait until my brother decides whether to stay in Hertfordshire or not. I do hope that you and I can convince him to move northward, Mr. Darcy. The air here in Derbyshire is far more salubrious than that of the southern counties, not to mention that the landscape is far more interesting."

Darcy grunted in what could be construed as agreement, or disagreement, depending on one's point of view, but Miss Bingley, naturally enough, assumed her host was in complete accord with her own wishes. She continued to prattle on as the twosome made their way along the verge toward the small lake, from there to the main steps, and finally to the front door where Darcy was able to bid his guest a courteous farewell before striding hastily to his office on the score of having business letters to write. Early this morning, he had walked from the stables with Charles Bingley and found the experience pleasurable. The short walk with Miss Bingley had felt three times longer and very annoying. He relished and honored Bingley, but his friend's younger sister was entirely tedious.

/

"We should go on a picnic," Georgiana Darcy said suddenly.

Elizabeth was watching Neptune, who had lifted his fan of vibrant, waving feathers and was displaying them for the benefit of a nearby peahen. The female in question seemed quite disinterested in the display and pecked away at something in the dirt. An insect, perhaps? A bit of corn? Perhaps a pebble? Much as Elizabeth admired the peafowl, she did not think them especially intelligent birds.

"I apologize, Miss Darcy, what did you say?" she asked.

"We should go on a picnic," the girl repeated. "There is a hunting lodge some three miles from here on Pemberley land, and a well maintained road leads to it. The cottage stands adjacent to a charming lake, which boasts a small waterfall from another pond slightly higher up. The view is remarkable and I have seen kites flying overhead a few times."

"I adore picnics," Elizabeth said warmly. "If your brother approves, I would be delighted."

"Miss Bennet?"

"Yes?"

"Would you be willing to call me Georgiana?"

Elizabeth turned in startled pleasure. "I would be overjoyed, so long as you call me Elizabeth."

"Very well, Elizabeth," the younger woman said shyly. "I am glad that you are my friend."

"I am honored and delighted to be your friend, Georgiana. I do suggest that we act more formally when we are among others."

"Why?"

"I fear that Miss Bingley might be envious of our friendship. I am not afraid of her pouting and indignation, but she could make the situation uncomfortable for Mr. Darcy, Jane, and Mr. Bingley."

Georgiana's expression cleared. "I understand, Elizabeth. That is very wise."

/

"Caroline, Louisa, I hope you are well?"

His two sisters had taken refuge from the late morning heat in the Hursts' private sitting room, where the open windows provided a welcome breath of fresh air.

"We are, Charles," Louisa said, lifting her head from her knitting.

"Where have you been all morning?" Caroline asked sharply. She was working on a complex piece of embroidery and had just made a mistake, which always made her more fractious than usual.

Charles shut the door of the room behind him and advanced a few feet before saying, "I rode with Darcy earlier this morning, and then Jane and I wandered the rose garden for some time. I also wrote a few business letters before seeking you out. I wished to tell you that we are quite certain that Jane is expecting a child."

"That is wonderful news!" Louisa exclaimed, casting a smug look at her younger sister. "Congratulations, brother! I am very happy for you, and Hurst will be as well!"

"Thank you, Louisa," Charles said gratefully, and turned an expectant look on Caroline.

"Yes, congratulations!" the lady said with a saccharine smile. "Do convey my felicitations to Jane if you see her before I do."

"I will," Charles said enthusiastically. "I expect you will see her at dinner, but it is not a definite thing. You have both likely observed that she has been excessively fatigued; the child is making her both tired and ill, and there are times when she is not well enough to be in company."

"When will the little one be born?" Louisa asked curiously.

"It will likely be after the New Year."

"Oh, you have plenty of time to think up a good name," Caroline exclaimed. "Perhaps you can name her Cecilia, after our mother."

Charles blinked and said, "Perhaps, though of course the child might well be a son."

"Oh, nonsense," Caroline said with a roll of her eyes. "Given that Mrs. Bennet birthed five daughters, it is almost impossible that Jane will bear a son with her first pregnancy. Perhaps if you are very fortunate, you will one day produce an heir."

Her brother's cheerful expression shifted to one of disapproval. "As to that, the Bingley fortune is not entailed away from the female line."

"Nor does it hold that merely because Mrs. Bennet had only daughters, Jane will as well," Louisa said impatiently. "Do not be ridiculous, Caroline."

"I am not being ridiculous in the least! If Charles had married Miss Winton, or Miss Clarissa Yardley, both of whom have three or four brothers, it is far more likely that the first child would have been a son."

"Caroline, really, the things you say! You are being completely absurd!"

"I most certainly am not!"

Charles, forgotten in the sudden quarrel between his sisters, hastily slipped out of the room and crossed the corridor to the sitting room he shared with Jane. His beautiful wife was sleeping at the moment, and he picked up an agricultural book and prepared to learn more about Tullian drills and raising turnips to feed sheep.

After reading a few, admittedly dull paragraphs, he put the book down and stared out the window toward the western horizon, his fingers tapping absently on the arms of the chair.

He felt disturbed for some reason, and he knew not why. Before his marriage, he would dismiss such feelings and busy himself with something else. But when Jane had discovered how Caroline, and to a lesser extent Louisa, had fought against their marriage, she had confided that she finally understood Elizabeth's warnings against assuming the good intentions of those around her.

Bingley knew that he, like Jane, was overly prone to believe the best of everyone. Certainly that was preferable to always assuming the worst about his fellow members of mankind, but it was unwise. There were villains in his world, and he, Charles Bingley, now a husband, soon to be a father, had best learn to accept reality, not an overly optimistic fantasy.

He leaned back in his chair, closed his eyes, and allowed his thoughts to drift here and there, seeking the source of his distress. Two minutes later, he sat up straight. He was upset by Caroline's response to Jane's pregnancy! He had spoken the truth to both his wife and sisters that he cared not whether the child was male or female. His greatest prayer and hope was that Jane and the babe would both survive the birth in good health. But it was equally obvious that Caroline meant to be deliberately insulting in her prediction that Jane would bear only daughters.

Bingley's frowned as he mulled over his younger sister's behavior and words in the last days, weeks, and months. He had, he decided, grown far too accustomed to his sister's cutting words toward Jane, Elizabeth, and the entire Bennet family. He was generally an easygoing soul, which had served him well at Cambridge while he made his way socially amongst the sons of gentlemen and nobles. His dear wife was also blessed with the sweetest of dispositions, and had treated both her new sisters with great kindness in spite of their earlier attempts to cut her out of their lives.

Louisa, to her credit, had embraced Jane as a true sister as soon as the new Mrs. Bingley had signed the wedding register. Caroline, on the other hand…

Charles Bingley grimaced and shook his head. It was not fair to Jane that he continually ignored Caroline's insolent remarks toward and about his wife, nor was it fair to Elizabeth who, to her credit, had always behaved with outward courtesy toward Caroline, though there were times when Miss Bennet used her sardonic wit at Miss Bingley's expense.

Darcy, too, must dread the sight of his sister, not because Caroline was ever rude to the host of Pemberley, but because the lady longed, above all things, to be mistress of this great estate, and thus pursued and flattered him with unremitting enthusiasm. It had to be exasperating.

He was master of an estate now, and the head of his household. If he could not manage his younger sister, he would doubtless struggle to be a good overseer of his tenants and a wise father to his children. He needed to do something about Caroline.

His first impulse was to consult Jane, but then he discarded that idea. Ordinarily, he would go to her for advice, but given that Jane was pregnant and struggling, it would be unkind to talk at length about Caroline's attacks on the Bennet family. Nor did he wish to discuss the matter with Elizabeth; the second Bennet daughter could be fiery in defense of her elder sister, and he did not wish to ignite that fire when the whole party was cooped together at Pemberley.

He would speak to Darcy; his friend had a powerful intellect and was sensible, along with being more cynical about the true motivations of those around him.

Chapter 14

Rosings

Kent

Lady Catherine de Bourgh, mistress of Rosings in Kent, leaned back in her favorite wingback chair and read her nephew Darcy's letter for a second time.

June 3rd, 1812

Lady Catherine,

Thank you for your inquiries in your recent letter, and I am pleased to report that Georgiana and I are well. The crops are growing apace, and if the weather continues to favor us, the harvests will be good this year. I purchased a farm from a neighboring estate a year ago and discovered that two of the fields require the installment of extensive drainage. That process required much expenditure and labor, but the yields should be excellent this season.

I regret exceedingly that I was unable to travel to Rosings last March, but my duties at Pemberley required that I stay in Derbyshire. Possibly next spring I will be able to spend a few weeks at Rosings, perhaps with Colonel Fitzwilliam. Regrettably, I will not be able to visit this year; at the moment, we have visitors in the form of my old friend Mr. Bingley, his new wife and a variety of relations. This winter, I intend to spend some time in London. Perhaps you and Anne will journey to London, and we will be able to meet there.

Please give my respects to Anne, and I pray that this letter finds you well.

God bless you,

Fitzwilliam Darcy

Lady Catherine stared down at the letter and huffed indignantly.

"Is Darcy coming to Rosings soon?" a voice inquired timidly from her right.

Lady Catherine turned and glowered at her daughter, Miss Anne de Bourgh, who was, in spite of the warm weather, well wrapped in shawls. The young woman shrank a little at her mother's fearsome gaze and looked down at the floor.

"Gracious, Anne, how you startled me!" the lady exclaimed indignantly. "What did you mean by creeping in so quietly?"

Anne winced and said apologetically, "I am sorry, Mother. I did not mean to surprise you. I did not wish to disturb you while you were reading Darcy's letter."

"That was courteous of you, at any rate," Lady Catherine said, mollified. "As to your question – no, Darcy declares that he will not visit Rosings until next spring at the earliest, as he is far too absorbed entertaining his friend, Mr. Bingley, and the man's numerous plebian relations. Really, my nephew is far too congenial with the lower classes! One would think that he prefers the company of a tradesman's son over his own relations!"

Anne thought, privately, that Darcy certainly did prefer Mr. Bingley's companionship to that of her mother, who was autocratic, imperious, and often rude, but naturally she did not say so.

"Mr. Bingley is married to Miss Elizabeth Bennet's sister, is he not?"

"That is correct," Lady Catherine agreed, turning back to read the letter. "I have not met Mrs. Bingley, but I understand her to be a remarkably handsome woman. I suppose a man like Bingley would require nothing else in a bride; certainly the new Mrs. Bingley brings neither fortune nor connections into the marriage!"

"She is, at least, a gentleman's daughter," Anne pointed out meekly.

"Yes, a gentleman whose estate is entailed to my own parson!" her mother said. "I have been informed that the girls will bring less than one hundred pounds a year into marriage, which is quite absurd. Well, it is hardly my concern whom Mr. Bingley decided to marry, though if I had been able to advise him, I would have strongly suggested that he look for more than a mere pretty face."

Anne had no doubt of that; her mother adored giving advice to everyone about everything under the sun, regardless of whether she was asked for her opinion or even had any knowledge of the situation in question.

Lady Catherine read through the letter for a third time, and when she was finished, she put down the foolscap paper and turned to peer at her daughter. "Anne, it is imperative that you and Darcy see one another before next spring. You will be five and twenty soon, and Darcy is nearly thirty! It is long past time for you to marry. If your cousin refuses to come to Kent, we must go to Derbyshire in either July or August."

Anne was always pale, but her face grew even whiter at this announcement. "Oh, Mother, no! You know how much I dislike traveling, and Pemberley is so far away!"

Lady Catherine compressed her lips and said, "Nonsense! You know that our carriage is the very best that money can buy, and everything will be done to make the journey as comfortable as possible. Indeed, Derbyshire will be cooler than Kent, and Pemberley is a lovely estate."

Anne opened her mouth to protest, then closed it. Her mother never listened to her; there was no point in additional argument on the matter.

"I will determine when would be most convenient for us to be away from Rosings," Lady Catherine continued, "and inform Darcy soon of our plans."

"Yes, Mother."

/

Pemberley

"That is why I feel the need to address my younger sister's behavior," Bingley explained. "It is not fair to my wife or her sister to overlook Caroline's reprehensible conduct toward them both. I know this is a great deal to ask, but do you have any suggestions about how best to manage her condescending remarks and sneering outbursts?"

Not for the first time in the last week, Darcy found himself astonished and impressed by the changes in his friend. He had long valued Bingley, but the man had always been an affable soul with a profound antipathy for any kind of conflict. Bingley had ignored both Miss Bingley's haughty speeches and her relentless, inappropriate pursuit of the master of Pemberley. It seemed that Bingley had acquired a spine along with a wife.

"Allow me a minute to think," Darcy requested, looking around to be certain that no one was in earshot. It was as overly cautious movement since the two gentlemen were out on the morning ride, this time through the Home Farm, and the only individuals in sight were two servant girls hunting for eggs some fifty yards away.

After the requisite cogitation, he turned to look directly at Bingley and asked, "Are you truly serious about this, my friend? Miss Bingley will not be inclined to alter her ways after so many years of acting as she wishes."

"I am determined," Bingley pledged.

"Very well, firstly, what is the situation regarding Miss Bingley's money?"

"She has a dowry of twenty thousand pounds, and has a yearly allowance based off the interest of that money."

"So eight hundred pounds, which is a significant sum given that she lives with you. Is she able to access the principal?"

"No. She is but two and twenty, and my father's will dictates that the money will be released to her when she turns five and twenty, or to her husband after she marries, whichever comes first."

"Does she stay within her income?"

Bingley shook his head unhappily. "No, she often overspends, and I cover her extra bills."

Darcy tightened his lips at these words and Bingley threw up a hand. "I know, Darcy, I know. I have been too lenient with Caroline and, to a lesser degree, Louisa. I dislike conflict, as you well know, but I had an epiphany last night. My primary loyalty must be to Jane and our future children. Jane herself is too gentle a soul to combat my waspish sister, so it falls to me, especially since I, as husband and brother, have the responsibility."

"Am I correct that Miss Bennet has a more impassioned character?"

Bingley laughed and said, "You are entirely correct! Elizabeth combines great intelligence with an acerbic wit and passionate love for her family in general and Jane in particular."

"I have observed how close Mrs. Bingley and Miss Bennet are. It is a beautiful thing."

"It is," Bingley agreed fervently. "Nor has Elizabeth ever so much as hinted at any resentment over our marriage. Jane is her dearest friend, and it could be argued that I took her away, but Elizabeth has always been supportive of our relationship."

Darcy thought, cynically, that Miss Bennet was far too intelligent a woman to regret her elder sister's marriage to a rich man. A moment later, he took himself to task for such unkind thoughts. Miss Bennet was an affectionate woman who obviously adored her sister. For all that the Bennets had benefited from the marriage, they no doubt missed the presence of the beautiful, charming Jane at Longbourn.

What would it be like when Georgiana married and left Pemberley? He had never thought about it before; indeed, his primary fear was that she would never be normal enough to marry anyone. But he would miss her. Oh, how he would miss his dear Georgiana.

"Darcy?" Bingley asked in a puzzled tone.

His friend shook his head and said, "My apologies, I was woolgathering. Regarding your sister – it is very much your decision on how to proceed, but I do have an idea…"

/

Brighton

Sussex

George Wickham, militia lieutenant, felt entirely satisfied with the world as he strode briskly along North Street. In spite of the sun beating down upon him, the temperature was comfortable due to the cool breezes flowing in from the endless ocean. It was an hour before noon and the road was not extremely busy, but he was satisfied at the nods and smiles of the various women walking in the opposite direction. He knew he cut a very fine figure in his red coat; in fact, he had it on the authority of more than one young woman that he was the most handsome lieutenant in all of Brighton!

The shopkeepers and pub owners had also easily fallen under the spell of his charm and apparent respectability, and had happily permitted him to purchase food, drink, clothing, and trinkets on account. He had no intention of paying them, of course, but he hoped that by the time they grew anxious about how much he owed them, the regiment would have moved onward to another town. If not, well – he would figure something out. He was far too handsome and charming a gentleman to go hungry, or to miss out on female companionship, for that matter…

He smiled broadly as he turned the corner onto a less traveled street. A few minutes of brisk walking later, he turned into a narrow alley, which led to a wooden building, which led to a staircase, which led to…

"Oh! Are they real?" Alice Brown squealed, gazing raptly at the necklace in George Wickham's hand.

"My dear!" Wickham protested, bestowing a charming smile on the only daughter of one of the local tavern keepers. The girl was a true beauty with dark hair and blue eyes, and her father was a fool to allow such a handsome creature to stay home alone in the morning. He had every intention of taking advantage of that foolishness. "My dear Alice, would I give the most beautiful girl in all of Brighton anything but real pearls?"

He gently pushed the girl over to her dressing table, upon which sat a mirror. He turned her toward the mirror and carefully placed the fake pearl necklace, made of fish scales and paste, around her slender neck. The dark haired girl smiled tremulously into the mirror and said, "Oh, Wickham!"

"Now you are absolutely perfect," he murmured, leaning over to kiss her on her neck.

"Oh, Wickham!" Alice repeated, turning around and leaping into his arms and lifting her face to his. "I love you so very much!"

/

"Miss Bingley is waiting under the tree in front of the stable, Mr. Darcy," Mr. Barstow said from his position at the main door of the stable.

Darcy sighed in exasperation and squared his shoulders, ready to face the dragoness, only to stop at the sight of his stable master's expression. "Do you have a suggestion, Barstow?"

"As to that, sir," the man said in a neutral tone, "I do believe that you might wish to examine the new fencing south of the walled garden. It was just replaced two days ago, and perhaps you should make certain that it was done to your liking."

Darcy fought a grin and lost. His workers were hard working and competent, and there was no chance that the fencing had been built incorrectly. However, if he exited through the back entrance of the stable to study the fencing, he would be concealed from Miss Bingley by a row of trees, and then the walled garden.

"Thank you, Barstow," he said genuinely.

"It is my pleasure, sir."

/

Inside the walled garden

"Oh Georgiana, it is so … so…"

"Ugly?" Georgiana Darcy inquired.

Elizabeth chuckled and said, "I was planning to say, peculiar, but yes, it is ugly. I hope you are not offended."

"Why would I be?" her companion returned, reaching down with a gloved hand to carefully inspect the chick which had just flopped out of its egg. "The newborn peafowl are all scrawny bodies and yellow down and grotesque feet when they are born, but then I have heard that human babies are often ill favored at birth. In time, this little male, or female, will be far more attractive."

"Does it seem healthy?" Elizabeth asked, squinting down at the yellow ball of fuzz.

"It does," Georgiana said, "though I will know better in a day or two. The babies are quite fragile and sometimes one born healthy dies in short order.'"

"That is sad."

"It is, but it is the way of life, I fear. This one is, I believe, one of Neptune's progeny, and I look forward to seeing whether he or she will form unusual white feathers. I ... oh, Fitzwilliam!"

Elizabeth turned and straightened up at the sight of Mr. Darcy, who was standing framed in the east doorway of the garden.

"Good morning, Miss Bennet, Georgiana," he said, bowing to both of the ladies. "I hope I am not intruding. I overheard your voices in the garden and gave way to a surge of curiosity."

"You are always welcome, of course," Georgiana said happily. "Elizabeth and I were fortunate enough to observe one of the peachicks hatching just now."

"How wonderful," Darcy said, striding over next to Georgiana and looking down at the peachick, which was now standing on wobbly legs with its mother hovering nearby. Elizabeth, to her considerable surprise, felt her breathing quicken and her face flush at the gentleman's close proximity. Mr. Darcy was a very handsome gentleman, but he generally seemed distant, dressed as he typically was in austere elegance, with a remote expression on his face. Now, with his hair tousled under this hat and his clothing smelling slightly of horse, with his arm around his sister, he seemed far more approachable and along with that, exceptionally attractive.

She took a deep breath in an attempt to control her racing heart. Really, this would never do! She thoroughly admired Mr. Darcy, but she understood him to be promised in marriage to his cousin, Anne de Bourgh. Even if he was inclined to look elsewhere for a bride, he could look very high in society, as the nephew of an earl and the master of a great estate. No, it would do no good at all to lose her heart to him.

"I do believe another chick is hatching," Darcy observed. "Am I right?"

"You are," Georgiana agreed, squinting down at the egg which was now showing a crack in the shell. The threesome leaned a little closer, and all could hear the soft peeping of a peachick struggling to escape the confines of its small world.

Elizabeth exhaled in delight. It was a glorious thing to be in a beautiful garden on a lovely summer day watching a new life breaking free.

Darcy found his gaze drifting from the small bird to the happy countenance of Miss Bennet, and when the little creature had finished hatching, he felt a sudden desire to spend additional time with the lady and his sister.

"Miss Bennet?"

"Yes?"

"I recollect that you are a chess player; would you and Georgiana care to join me in the library for a game or two?"

"I would enjoy that very much," Elizabeth said, feeling another unaccustomed surge of attraction toward the handsome gentleman. Yes, she would like to spend more time with Mr. Darcy.

Chapter 15

The Parsonage

Hunsford

Kent

"I will return by dinner unless, of course, Lady Catherine requires me for some special purpose. If so, I will arrange for a message to be sent to you by one of her ladyship's servants."

"Thank you, Mr. Collins," Charlotte said with a smile at the rector. Her husband was not romantic, handsome, charming, or even sensible, but he was a kindly husband, and that, along with his good income and position as heir of Longbourn, made him a most acceptable partner to her, at least. Her friend, Miss Elizabeth Bennet, was a romantic, along with being young and handsome, and had refused Mr. Collins's offer of marriage in no uncertain terms. Charlotte could only be grateful; she had been a single lady on the shelf one day, engaged a week later, and now was mistress of her own home.

Collins glanced at the timepiece on the mantle and squeaked, "Oh, I must hurry if I am not to be late, and Lady Catherine is always most displeased when I am tardy!"

An instant later, he jammed his hat on his head and rushed out the door, letting it slam rather loudly behind him. Charlotte waited two minutes to be certain he would not return before reaching for her knitting basket and pulling out a half made baby sock. She was quite certain now that she was expecting a child, but she did not care to share that knowledge with her husband yet, as the man would undoubtedly inform Lady Catherine immediately. The mistress of Rosings believed that she knew everything there was to know about everything under the sun, and Charlotte had no desire at all to be harangued with endless advice about how to enjoy, or endure, a pregnancy.

So far she was enjoying it. Her latest letter from Elizabeth Bennet, which had arrived only the day before, informed her that Jane Bingley was having a difficult time with her own pregnancy. Perhaps Charlotte too would succumb to nausea and exhaustion, but for now, she felt well enough to manage her household, her husband, and her knitting.

She bent over and added a few more rows when the door to the sitting room opened and a maid entered and announced, "Miss Anne de Bourgh."

Charlotte cast the knitting aside hastily and stood up in surprise. "Miss de Bourgh, good morning!"

"Good morning, Mrs. Collins," Anne said. "I do apologize for disturbing you, but I have a favor to ask."

"I am honored by your visit," Charlotte declaimed because, of course, she could say nothing else. "Susanna, bring tea for us."

"Yes, Madam," the maid answered, retreating from the room and closing the door.

"Do sit down and tell me how I may serve you," Charlotte suggested, waiting until her guest had taken her place on the settee before resuming her own position.

Anne blew out a breath and managed a shaky smile. "Mrs. Collins, this is forward of me, but I have little time, so I will be direct. I have written a letter to my cousin Mr. Darcy at Pemberley, but I do not wish my mother to know, and our butler always informs her of all my correspondence going out. I was hoping that you could send a letter to Mrs. Bingley at Pemberley and enclose my missive with it? I believe you and Mrs. Bingley are friends."

"We are," Charlotte agreed, suppressing her surprise. "However, I am closer to Elizabeth Bennet and owe her a letter. She is currently at Pemberley and will be for at least ten days, which should be plenty of time for your letter to reach her, if you are not in a hurry, that is."

Anne considered and then nodded, "That would do very well, for my mother will not send her letter express. They should arrive at about the same time, if you can write to Miss Bennet soon, that is."

"I can send my letter out by tomorrow morning," Charlotte promised.

"Thank you, Mrs. Collins," Anne said, her face turning pink with relief as she reached into her reticule. "Here is my letter to Darcy, and may I ask for another favor? Perhaps you could arrange that Mr. Collins is not aware of my visit today? My mother thinks that I am resting in my bedchamber at the moment."

"I will speak with the maid, and assuming that no one else saw you..."

"Oh, I was careful that I was entirely unobserved," Anne declared, standing up. "Now I must go."

"You do not wish to stay for tea?"

"No, I must return before anyone discovers I am gone. Thank you again, Mrs. Collins. I am most grateful for your assistance in this matter."

/

"Oh, Miss Darcy, we are all friends here!" Caroline Bingley enthused. "I am certain you would not wish to deprive us of the pleasure of hearing you play the pianoforte when you are so very accomplished?"

Georgiana stared with wide eyes at Miss Bingley before turning a piteous look on Elizabeth. Darcy, along with the other gentlemen, had entered the music room only a few seconds before and was thoroughly startled. Georgiana must think very highly of Miss Bennet if she thought that the young lady would be able to protect her from Miss Bingley!

"Oh, Miss Darcy!" Elizabeth exclaimed. "Pray do not think me discourteous, but I hope you will allow me to play instead? I have been working hard on "Greensleeves" and believe I have finally conquered it!"

Georgiana's distress gave way to obvious relief. "Of course, Miss Bennet."

"My dear Elizabeth," Caroline said haughtily, "I do beg you to give way to a far more accomplished player. I venture to say that all of the ladies here, excluding Jane, are better players than you are. That is, of course, no reflection on you, dear sister; it is merely that Louisa, Miss Darcy, and I all have had the opportunity of studying with true masters of the instrument."

Bingley, who had walked over to his wife, turned an angry face on his younger sister, but before he could speak, Elizabeth said, "Oh, Caroline, but surely it is helpful for a less gifted player to practice before an audience? I would not dream of doing so amongst strangers but we are all friends and family, are we not?"

"Indeed we are," Charles agreed, glaring at Caroline. Elizabeth had, by this time, sat down on the bench and, after finding the score, began playing a rousing, if not entirely accurate, rendition of the song.

Darcy, filled with admiration at Miss Bennet's bold words and actions, which were undoubtedly meant to protect Georgiana from Miss Bingley's harassment, quickly made his way over to his sister and murmured, "I believe, my dear, that you should retire to your bedchamber. I will inform the company…"

"That I have a headache," Georgiana whispered back. "Thank you, Brother."

"Of course. I love you, my dear."

/

"I do wish that Charles would speak to Elizabeth, though I suppose it is too much to hope for!" Caroline fumed, pacing up and down the Hursts' sitting room. "I cannot fathom her discourtesy in her insistence of playing "Greensleeves", of all things, when Miss Darcy was waiting to perform!"

Louisa gritted her teeth and said, "I do not believe that Miss Darcy wishes to play in company."

Her sister turned an astonished look upon her. "Do not be absurd, Louisa! Miss Darcy is so truly gifted and she must long to display her skills! Really, Charles is too amiable. It is bad enough that he married Jane, but at least she does not put herself forward unbecomingly. Elizabeth is like her younger sisters; always eager to show off and make a spectacle of herself!"

Louisa bit her lip at these words but did not speak. She knew, from past experience, that her sister was not inclined to listen to anyone whose viewpoint was different than her own. She also knew that Caroline's dislike was based on envy; Elizabeth was more beautiful and charming than Caroline, along with being witty and clever. Caroline Bingley, aged two and twenty, blessed with an expensive education and a dowry of twenty thousand pounds, had not won Mr. Darcy as a husband and had garnered no offers of marriage during her three London seasons. That was partially because Caroline was only interested in Darcy and had never encouraged any other gentlemen, but part of it was due to the woman's abrasive personality.

"Caroline, I am fatigued and will bid you good night," she said, standing up slowly.

"It is not yet nine o'clock! It is still light outside!" her sister said in exasperation.

"Yes, but I am tired, nonetheless," Louisa said wearily and marched toward her bedroom. She was now a full three weeks past her normal courses and was strangely exhausted and yes, on occasion, nauseous. It seemed that at last, her prayers had been answered and she was with child. She would not tell Caroline, or even Mr. Hurst yet; the former because she would be irritating, the latter because he had longed for a child for two years, and she did not want her husband's hopes to rise, only to be dashed if she miscarried.

Louisa smiled at her maid and allowed the woman to assist her in removing her dress. A few minutes later, she was comfortably tucked up in bed, and within a short time, she drifted off to sleep.

/

Caroline marched down the hall in a miasma of indignation at her sister's selfishness in going to bed so early. She needed to complain more about Elizabeth, and now she had no audience.

She opened the door to her bedchamber and jerked in surprise. Her brother was seated next to the writing desk, reading a book in the light of several candles.

"Charles, what are you doing here?" she demanded.

Her brother deliberately placed a bookmark to keep his place, set the volume onto the table next to him, and turned toward her. "I wish to speak to you."

Caroline frowned. "Does not Mr. Darcy require your presence this evening?"

"He is spending some time with Miss Darcy," Charles said, "largely because…"

"Oh, I am certain he is!" Caroline huffed, stalking over and planting herself in an armchair near the cold fireplace. "You simply must do something about Elizabeth, Brother! Her discourtesy to Miss Darcy this evening…"

"Caroline!"

"It is bad enough that you married Jane given her poor connections and lack of dowry," the lady continued angrily, "but to be related by marriage to Elizabeth and her gauche sisters and mother…"

"Caroline!!"

"You really must send her back to Longbourn, Charles, as soon as possible, or she will disgrace us with Mr. Darcy and…"

"That will be ten pounds!" Charles bellowed, turning and reaching for paper and pen on the writing table.

Caroline Bingley froze, mid rant, and turned toward her brother in confusion. "Ten pounds? What are you speaking of?"

Her brother carefully wrote one line on the foolscap and then glowered at his younger sister. "Are you willing to listen, or are you merely going to interrupt me again?"

The lady swallowed hard. There was a peculiar expression on her brother's usually cheerful face, which provoked an uneasy sensation in her chest.

"Of course I will listen," she said carefully. "What do you mean, ten pounds?"

Charles leaned forward and said, "I realize that I have been greatly at fault for allowing you to speak so rudely to and about Jane and Elizabeth. I should have confronted you long ago, but as I cannot go back in time, I will begin now. You will speak courteously in company with them, and cease complaining about and insulting them when conversing with me. Every time you say anything malevolent, every time you are unpleasant, every time you use a mocking or disrespectful tone toward my family by marriage, I will deduct ten pounds from your income for the year."

Caroline's lips were parted in outrage now, and she sat up straight. "What are you speaking of? I have not been rude, not at all! I know what this is; Elizabeth has complained to you, or Jane perhaps! I suppose given their plebian origins, they are overly sensitive to my words of advice and…"

"That is another ten pounds," Charles interrupted, turning to write another line on the paper.

Caroline froze in horror for a moment before exclaiming, "Charles, you cannot be serious. I am merely saying what everyone is thinking, I assure you."

"Oh, I am serious about deducting the money from your income," the gentleman said. "Furthermore, you are entirely in error. Both Mr. and Miss Darcy like Elizabeth and Jane very much. It is you who have exasperated and annoyed them with your insistence that Miss Darcy play in company, when it is plain to all but you that she does not wish to do so!"

The lady gaped and then blurted, "Charles, you must be mad! Miss Darcy is so gifted, so accomplished, especially compared to Elizabeth, who plays very ill indeed…"

"Thirty pounds total now," Charles said, turning to add another line to the paper.

Caroline jerked in confusion. "What did I say?"

"You said Elizabeth plays very ill, which is rude, Caroline."

"But she…" the woman began, and then shut her mouth. This entire situation was preposterous and absurd, but given her brother's demeanor, she had best stop arguing for now. Charles had always been easy going, and she had, in the past, been certain of having her way, but – well, she had best retreat verbally until she determined how best to manage this unusual situation.

"Let me say it another way," she said finally. "Miss Darcy is very skilled, and she must long to have the opportunity to show off her skills…"

"She does not!" Charles interrupted in exasperation. "Have you even looked at her face when you plague her to play, Caroline? Have you seen the distress in her expression? Have you seen how she cringes away and protests? How is it not entirely obvious to you that she is very shy and does not wish to play for us?"

"But … but we are all friends, Charles! Why would she…?"

"She is not your friend! Why would you imagine that you are her friend! You have, after all, spent far more time with Elizabeth than with Miss Darcy, and I am certain you would not say that she is your friend!"

Caroline opened her mouth, ready to unleash a torrent of invective, then slammed it shut before she lost even more money, before beginning again, much more cautiously.

"Elizabeth is my sister by marriage, which is a different relationship compared to my acquaintance with Miss Darcy who, well, perhaps she is a little shy, but I am certain Mr. Darcy agrees with me that she needs to learn to play in company. She will be entering society in the next few years, after all…"

"And who are you, Sister, to decide how to prepare Miss Darcy for society? That is Darcy's role, not yours! Has it not occurred to you that every time you harass and pressure Miss Darcy to play the pianoforte, she immediately retreats with a headache? Really, Caroline, for someone who prides herself on her educational accomplishments and awareness of social niceties, you are truly dense! Now I must depart to see how Jane is feeling, but mark my words, I am determined to hold the line regarding your treatment of Jane, Elizabeth, and the Darcys. I am entirely ready to inform your milliner and dressmaker that I will not be covering any excess bills, so do not push me!"

Caroline could only stare in dazed horror as her brother rose to his feet and stalked out of the room.

Chapter 16

"Georgiana, are you well?"

The girl was seated by the window staring at two peacock feathers in her hand, and it took her a few seconds to emerge from her reverie, whereupon she looked up in confusion at her brother. "Yes, Fitzwilliam, I am well. Why do you ask?"

Darcy walked over to take a seat next to her and said, "I was concerned you might be distressed by Miss Bingley's insistence that you play in company."

"Oh, no, I am quite at ease because Elizabeth took my place, though…"

Here the young lady's face clouded, and she said, "I hope I am not being a bad friend by making Elizabeth protect me in this way. It did not occur to me before; she must have hated playing "Greensleeves" when she has not yet mastered it. Should I apologize to her?"

Darcy reached out to take her hand in his own, even as he smiled upon her reassuringly. "I do beg you not to concern yourself. Miss Bennet has a very different disposition compared to both of us. She manages Miss Bingley's barbs with rare wit and was entirely at ease after you left the music room."

"I am so glad," the girl said, her shoulders sagging with relief.

"I am as well," Darcy returned. "It is a difficult situation for both of us, of course. Miss Bingley is a guest, and we cannot be openly discourteous, but I am not adept at turning the conversation gracefully when she speaks out of turn. I will share this, though I beg you not to mention to anyone else. Mr. Bingley intends to speak to his sister about her incivility toward Miss Bennet and, to some extent, Mrs. Bingley. I hope that Miss Bingley will mend her ways."

"I hope so too, because she is very exhausting and irritating and annoying."

"She is," Darcy agreed with a sigh.

Silence fell for a minute and then Georgiana said, "Do you like Miss Bennet, Brother?"

"I do, very much. I believe her to be most worthy of your friendship in every way."

"I think you should marry her," Georgiana said bluntly.

Darcy jerked and turned incredulous eyes on his sister. "What?"

"I think you should marry Elizabeth. She is kind, intelligent, outgoing, honorable, and godly. She loves books like you do, and is appreciative of nature. She is well liked by the servants and knows about how to care for an estate. She does not play the pianoforte well, but many people do not. She would be a good wife."

Darcy's surprise gave way to affectionate amusement as he gazed upon his sister's earnest face. Georgiana's view of the world was delightfully different from most of the ladies who inhabited their sphere of society. She looked upon character traits and interests as opposed to wealth and connections. She was correct, too – Miss Bennet was the sort of woman he would like to marry. It was a pity that it was impossible.

"She is a charming woman," Darcy agreed, "but I fear she is not an eligible bride."

Georgiana straightened her spine and stared directly into his eyes, her forehead creased in her perplexity. "Why is she not eligible? You are a gentleman, and she is a gentleman's daughter. Furthermore, her elder sister is married to Mr. Bingley."

As usual, what was obvious to Darcy was not remotely obvious to Georgiana.

"She is a gentleman's daughter, yes," he explained patiently, "but her mother's father was a solicitor, and Miss Bennet has relations in trade. It is not a great concern for Bingley. As the son of a tradesman himself, he is not so greatly affected by the want of connection. But for me, the master of Pemberley, grandson and nephew of an earl? No, my dear, I fear it is quite impossible. I admire Miss Bennet and am grateful that you and she are friends, but I must find a high born bride to fill the role of mistress of Pemberley."

Georgiana carefully removed her hand from her brother's and said, "You mean that you must find a woman like Miss Bennet, but with statelier relations?"

"Yes, precisely," her brother said approvingly. He was pleased that Georgiana was beginning to understand such things.

"You are eight and twenty, Fitzwilliam. Why have you not married such a woman already?"

Darcy blinked and said, "I have not had the pleasure of meeting such a lady yet, I fear."

"You entered society at one and twenty," Georgiana said. "You have been master of Pemberley for seven years now. You have attended routs and assemblies and balls and house parties. If you have not met a woman like that by now, what makes you think you will ever discover such a lady?"

Darcy's feeling of contentment gave way to surprise and yes, dismay. "I … well, I am not yet thirty and…"

He took a deep breath, blew it out, and said, "Georgiana, I realize you do not understand all the subtleties of the society in which we live, but I assure you that for your sake, and that of the estate, I must marry well. After all, you will eventually enter society yourself, and since our mother is gone, you will benefit from a sister who can help you with your introduction to the haut ton."

"It seems quite stupid to me," his sister said baldly, standing up and peering down at him. "I would far rather have a sister who is kind and loving, even if she is poor and a solicitor's granddaughter, than to be forced to live with a woman like Miss Bingley who cares only about clothing and gossip and the like. If you truly were happy with such a woman, you would have married long ago; there are certainly plenty of women like Miss Bingley who are well born. Besides, I do not wish to enter society ever, and you know that!"

Darcy found that he, too, was on his feet now, and he looked down on his sister in distress. "Georgiana, I…"

"I am tired and wish to go to bed," the girl said, and now her eyes were bright with tears. "Good night."

He was tempted to continue speaking, to reassure her, but he knew from experience that she was too upset to listen to him. He would tell Mrs. Annesley, and he hoped that she would be able to calm his darling sister down. It was difficult when Georgie was being completely unreasonable, but he could only trust that his sister's companion, a widow with a remarkable ease of manner, would be able to do so.

Or *was* Georgiana being unreasonable?

He fetched Mrs. Annesley to his sister, retired to his bedchamber, and wandered over to the window to stare out toward the Home Farm, which stretched out toward the west where the golden sun was now disappearing below the horizon.

He sighed deeply and leaned his head against the window, suddenly exhausted to the bone. Georgiana was correct; he had met every debutante of note for the last seven years. He had danced and talked and even rode the Promenade in the hopes of finding some woman with whom he could be, if not happy, at least content. And he had not, in all those years, found anyone he found remotely attractive. He was not thinking, of course, of physical beauty. Many of the young ladies of the ton were exquisite. But their interests, their conversation, their passions – they left him entirely cold. That was not, he knew, the fault of the young women. He was not as peculiar a person as Georgiana, but he knew himself to be unusual.

He could, of course, marry his cousin, Anne de Bourgh. She interested him as little as all the other ladies of the ton, but he would acquire Rosings if he married her and, while he did not need, or even want, an additional estate, he would be able to take over the management of the de Bourgh holdings, which were currently suffering under the care of a foolish mistress in the form of his aunt, Lady Catherine.

But he did not want to marry Anne, who was sickly and quiet, and would be no use at all in helping Georgiana launch into society. He wanted to marry a woman he truly admired, a woman he truly loved. But how could he, when he owed it to his sister, to his estate, to his name, to marry a woman of standing?

/

"It is just beyond the trees," Georgiana explained, striding rapidly along the path which led away from the hunting lodge of Pemberley.

Elizabeth, whose legs were shorter than her friend's, found herself hurrying to keep up, which was enjoyably unusual. So often she found herself needing to walk slowly when in company with women, and even some men were inclined to dawdle.

She glanced behind her and was amused to observe Owen, the manservant assigned to watch over them, puffing a little at their rapid pace. A moment later, the path broke out through a stand of ash trees, and Elizabeth found herself crying out with delight at the entrancing sight. A forest of birch, ash, and oak trees flanked the grove to the north and south, while to the east, the ground rose precipitously. Within the grove was a pond of some forty by thirty feet in size, surrounded by watercress and a variety of colorful wildflowers. In spite of the June sun shining above them, there was a pleasant breeze blowing from the west, cooling Elizabeth's heated face.

"Georgiana, it is lovely!" she exclaimed, walking closer to the pond and peering into the waters. A moment later, she saw a flash of gold and turned wide eyes on her companion. "What is that?"

"Goldfish," Miss Darcy explained, stepping a little closer to the water and gazing at the small school of fish congregating beneath the surface. "My father introduced goldfish to this pond some years ago and they have grown substantially. That one there looks to be at least six inches long!"

"It is marvelous," Elizabeth enthused, turning to inspect the rest of the pond. On one side of the pool, a rocky cliff, some ten feet high, rose to some other source of water, because two streams of liquid were flowing down the stones, striking the surface of the pool, causing the surface to ripple coyly in the light. On the other end of the pool, a stream flowed out of one corner and made its way, splashing and rippling and gurgling, down a gentle slope toward the west.

"Look over there!" Georgiana said, pointing toward the small waterfall.

"Oh," Elizabeth gasped, "is that a rainbow?"

Her companion grasped her arm and pulled her forward a few feet closer to the pool and said, "Yes, the sun often strikes the waterfall at this hour and makes a rainbow. It is not as beautiful as my peacock named Rainbow, but it is still charming."

Elizabeth laughed and said, "One pleasant thing about the bird it is that he is solid, not ephemeral. Look, it is gone already."

Georgiana peered skyward and said, "It will return soon. There is a cloud covering the sun at the moment, but it will pass within minutes."

Elizabeth squinted upward as well and then looked back at the waterfall. "Even without a rainbow, it is pleasant. The sound of falling water is soothing."

"It is! I think you would love the seashore on that account too, Elizabeth. The sound of the waves breaking rhythmically against the beach is calming."

"I would like to go someday," Elizabeth agreed wistfully, and then shook herself. "But I cannot complain. I have been blessed to visit both Hunsford in Kent and Pemberley in Derbyshire this year. I am grateful for such opportunities to travel, to see new places and meet new people."

"Which have you enjoyed more?" Georgiana asked, turning her clear eyed gaze on her friend.

Elizabeth smiled at this question, knowing that Miss Darcy would far prefer truth than courteous falsehood. In this case, she could speak the truth without hesitation.

"I enjoyed walking the paths of Rosings very much, but I far prefer Pemberley's gardens, peafowl, landscape and geography. As for the companionship – well, I find the company here at Pemberley to be far more pleasurable than in Hunsford. My friend Charlotte Collins is delightful, but her husband and I have little in common, and Lady Catherine is, frankly, quite exhausting in company. Here I have the pleasure of spending time with Jane and Charles, and I am very fond of you, Georgiana, and I find your brother a most interesting gentleman. I am honored to be your friend and will always have fond memories of my time here at Pemberley."

"You must endure Miss Bingley, however, and she is often obnoxious to you. I do not know how you can bear it."

Elizabeth snorted at this blunt assessment but said quickly, "Believe me when I say she does not distress me in the least, my dear friend. Caroline does not like me, and I do not particularly like her. I hope that I am always at least outwardly courteous, and as for her veiled insults, I assure you that I am entirely indifferent."

"Miss Darcy?" a male voice called.

Both women turned toward the manservant, who had remained under the shade of several trees some fifty feet away.

"Is it time to return?" Georgiana inquired, pulling out her watch to consult it. "Oh, yes, it is! Elizabeth, Fitzwilliam said that we would enjoy our picnic at two o'clock, and it is fifteen minutes until two. We must return to the lodge and the others."

"Of course," Elizabeth agreed, though she took a last moment to enjoy the view before turning away. It was likely a forlorn hope, but she would like to return to this place one day.

Chapter 17

"Are you quite comfortable, Jane?" Bingley asked, looking down on his precious wife who was seated on a plain wooden chair in the shade of a convenient oak tree.

"I am, Charles. Pray do not worry," Jane answered, smiling reassuringly. In fact, she felt reasonably well at the moment, and the pleasant shade and cool breeze were invigorating.

"Is it not lovely?" Louisa Hurst asked from her own chair under a neighboring oak tree.

"It is," Jane agreed, looking around. The hunting lodge was a charming, half-timbered building composed of one main block with an additional wing built off the southwest side. It was not large, but it was, like everything else on the estate, well built and maintained.

"The servants will bring out the food for the picnic in about five minutes," Darcy announced, walking up to the party reclining under the trees.

"Good," Hurst grunted, speaking for the first time since they had left the mansion.

"Where are Miss Darcy and Elizabeth?" Miss Bingley asked. She, along with Jane, Louisa, and Mr. Hurst, had traveled in a carriage, whereas Elizabeth and Georgiana had arrived in a phaeton.

"They went to observe a pond situated half a mile from the lodge," Darcy explained. "It is one of Georgiana's favorite locales, and I am confident Miss Bennet will enjoy it as well."

"I am certain she will," Jane agreed warmly. "Lizzy greatly enjoys observing nature, especially when the sights are new to her."

"Oh yes," Caroline said with a dramatic grimace, "it was apparent on our recent visits to Chatworth and Dovedale that Elizabeth was quite indifferent to the beauty of those great houses, but cared only for the grounds, and the wilder the better."

"There they are!" Jane said hastily, standing up as Georgiana and Elizabeth appeared from behind the lodge. She and Darcy stepped forward to greet the two young ladies, which allowed Charles to rush over to Caroline.

"That will be ten pounds," he hissed into her ear.

Caroline's eyes widened in surprise. "What are you speaking of? I said nothing that was untrue!"

"You sneered when you spoke of Elizabeth's delight in wilderness areas. Do not prevaricate, sister. It was obvious to everyone here that you meant to denigrate her."

Caroline opened her mouth in protest, only to shut it. She had hoped that Charles would think better of his idiotic championship of Elizabeth Bennet, but his determination had lasted two days now, and she was down eighty pounds already!

Heedless of the drama between Charles and Caroline, Elizabeth reached out impulsive hands toward her elder sister and said, "Oh Jane, you would love the little lake up there. There are goldfish!"

"Are there?" Jane exclaimed with more exuberance than was common for the generally placid Mrs. Bingley. "Oh, how marvelous! I love goldfish!"

"Do you?" Georgiana asked, peering doubtfully at Mrs. Bingley.

"I do! When I was a child of six, my dear uncle Gardiner gifted three goldfish to my aunt Gardiner to celebrate their first anniversary. I spent literally hours sitting in the parlor watching them swim around in their bowl. They seemed magical!"

"Did you also enjoy your aunt's goldfish?" Georgiana asked, regarding Elizabeth gravely.

Elizabeth laughed and shook her head. "No, for I was but four when Jane was six, and I confess to being an overly active, even unruly, child. Jane was always far more sensible and sedate. If I had been permitted in the parlor, I am certain the bowl, and its poor goldfish, would have found themselves on the floor in no time!"

"How far is the pond?" Jane asked eagerly. "Perhaps Charles and I can walk there after we dine!"

Elizabeth pursed her lips in thought and said reluctantly, "I fear it might well be too much for you, at least for now. It is … I do not know. How far is it?"

"I am not certain," Georgiana said. "Brother, how far is the pond from here?"

Darcy found himself struggling to speak, having been strangely affected by the sight of Miss Bennet, her handsome face flushed with exercise, her eyes bright with enthusiasm, a few of her chestnut curls escaping her white bonnet. She was glorious!

"It is a full half mile," he finally managed to say, "and the path is moderately steep in one place."

"Oh, I should not attempt it then," Jane said, obviously disappointed.

"Perhaps you can visit Pemberley in the future," Georgiana suggested with a smile, provoking a surge of amazement in her brother's heart. Georgiana had obviously decided that Mrs. Bingley, too, was a safe friend.

"Perhaps we will," Bingley agreed, coming up and beaming down at his bride. "However, I would be delighted to buy you some goldfish for Netherfield if you would like it."

Jane flushed with pleasure and said, "Oh I would, very much, Charles, though not at the expense of the Millers' house…"

"Darling, we are entirely capable of rebuilding a tenant house *and* buying some goldfish," Charles said fondly, then glanced at Darcy and explained, "I received a letter this morning that one of our tenant families lost their house in a fire."

"Was anyone harmed?" Elizabeth asked worriedly.

"They escaped without injury," Jane said, "but lost everything but the clothes on their backs. Charles sent an express letter to our steward this morning instructing him to provide temporary shelter in the back stable, but that will not do for long."

Caroline, bored with this talk of tenants and their tiresome needs, chose this moment to approach the group and interject, "Oh, how delightful this is, Mr. Darcy! I declare there is nothing as enjoyable as eating out in nature under the blue skies of heaven!"

Darcy, noting that the servants had finished placing platters of food on a simple trestle table, said, "I believe it is time for us to sit down and dine. Shall we?"

The meal was an unqualified success for everyone but Darcy.

Mr. Hurst, who considered himself something of a connoisseur of fine food and drink, was pleased by the cheese pastries, sausage rolls, mushroom pies, apple tarts, and cold lemonade.

Jane Bingley and Louisa Hurst, both of whom felt queasy, were delighted with the fresh strawberries and clotted cream.

Bingley, Georgiana, and Elizabeth ate heartily of the various dishes while they discussed *Robinson Crusoe,* with a particular focus on the more absurd aspects of the plot. Jane, who adored the book, argued cheerfully with her sister over certain points, which Georgiana found inspiring. She had never observed two people debating vigorously but not antagonistically. She had not even known such a thing was even possible.

Caroline Bingley, smarting from her recent argument with her brother, was elated to snatch the seat next to Darcy, and she used the opportunity to monopolize and flatter that gentleman ceaselessly through dinner.

His companion's simpering compliments were, of course, why Darcy did not enjoy the meal as much as he had hoped. He was thankful, however, to observe Georgiana's contentment. He had never seen his sister so comfortable nor so ready to speak with anyone outside her immediate circle.

It was only after the meal was over and the ladies and Mr. Hurst had returned to the carriages, and Bingley and Darcy to their horses, that Darcy realized that he had watched Miss Bennet as much as he had Georgiana. The lady's piquant countenance and verbal repartee with her elder sister had caused him, more than once, to lose the thread of his conversation with Miss Bingley. That was no great loss on his part, but he prided himself that he always behaved in a gentleman-like manner. Based on Miss Bingley's smiling face as she climbed into the carriage, she was not distressed, so he ought not to concern himself.

Nonetheless, he was unsettled – not about Miss Bingley, but about Miss Bennet. All day yesterday, his sister's words had rung in his ears. Elizabeth Bennet was a most remarkable lady, and Georgiana seemed well on her way to adoring her. He himself was strongly attracted to and even entranced by Miss Bennet's unusual vigor and views and by her intelligence, graciousness, and kindness. But could he, *should he*, marry a woman with relations in trade, a woman totally unknown by the ton in London? Was that fair to Georgiana, to his estate, to the Darcy name?

He sighed as he directed his favorite stallion, Phoenix, to fall in behind the carriages as they began rolling back toward Pemberley. He suddenly wished that

Richard Fitzwilliam was here. His cousin, as the son of an earl, was born into the cream of society; however, as a second son and an army colonel, Richard had respect for those of supposedly lower birth. Indeed, Colonel Fitzwilliam had often railed at the idiocy of upper class officers while also applauding the courage and diligence of simple privates.

Yes, he would very much like to speak to Richard, who perhaps could advise him on his conundrum.

Chapter 18

"I must see how Jane is," Bingley said to Darcy.

"Of course," Darcy agreed. The two men had made a habit of going for an early morning ride, and Bingley always rushed to his wife's side when they were done. "I have letters to write and will see you later."

"Until then," Bingley concurred and then raced up the staircase which led to the guest suite, his heart thumping. Six months of marriage had not diminished his love for his Jane, and he could hardly wait to see her and discover how she felt today.

He opened the door and looked around eagerly, only to feel his chest constrict at the sight of Jane, seated on a chair by the window, sobbing softly.

"Jane? Jane, what is wrong?" Bingley asked, hurrying forward to embrace her. "Is … is it the baby?"

"No, no!" Jane exclaimed, turning tear stained cheeks toward her husband. "I am well, I assure you, and the babe as well."

He was on his knees now, his hands cupping her beautiful cheeks. "What is it then, my darling?"

"I am upset about … about the Millers!" she choked out, and burst into tears.

He reached forward and pulled her close to him, rocking her as if she were a child, her beautiful tresses, still unbound, cascading around them both. She cried for a few minutes before sitting back and accepting Bingley's handkerchief.

"I am so very sorry, my love," she said, her cheeks flushed with weeping and embarrassment. "I do not know what has gotten into me."

"I believe a child has gotten into you," Charles said fondly, slipping onto a chair next to her, though he retained his hold on her hands. "I well remember my aunt Barbara who, along with her husband and family, lived with us for the six years before I went to Cambridge. She always grew moody and easily distressed when expecting a child. I believe it to be quite normal."

"It does not feel normal," Jane said, her lips trembling. "I despise feeling this way, and have been working very hard to not give into my feelings of sorrow. I fear it all caught up with me this morning."

"Which is entirely reasonable," Bingley said soothingly. "But do tell me, why are you anxious about the Millers?"

Jane gulped and wiped her eyes again. "I was thinking last night about how terrible it must be for them, to have lost their entire home and all their possessions. They have four children, you know, and the youngest an infant. I cannot imagine how upset Mrs. Miller must be right now. Just think how we would feel if our own children were threatened by a fire, and then we found ourselves homeless, with all our belongings destroyed by the flames!"

"We sent an express to Netherfield," Bingley reminded her. "Mr. Brisby will ensure they are well cared for until their new home is built."

Jane bit her lip and said, "I am worried about the details. We spent significant money on other tenant houses earlier this year, not to mention the drainage on the southwestern field. Mr. Brisby will not have the funds easily in hand to rebuild, and many of the other tenant families are busy with their own fields. If you are not there to approve specific expenditures, I fear that the steward will not push forward on the rebuilding."

Bingley peered at her for a moment and then said, "Do you wish to return to Netherfield, Jane?"

His wife compressed her lips and nodded. "Yes, I would, but oh, Charles, if you wish to stay, I understand completely. I am sorry. I feel so peculiar, quite unlike myself, and Mr. and Miss Darcy have been so welcoming, but I just wish to be home at Netherfield. But I assure you that if that is inconvenient to you..."

"My dear, I understand completely," he interrupted her, standing up and planting a loving kiss on her forehead.

"Let me think and pray about it. Does that give you peace, my love?"

"It does," Jane agreed, smiling mistily at him. "Thank you."

/

"I think Fitzwilliam is in here," Georgiana said to Elizabeth, knocking on the door of her brother's study. She heard her brother's familiar voice respond and opened the door. "Brother? May we talk to you for a moment?"

Darcy, who was staring uneasily at a letter in his hand, promptly shoved the offending missive into a drawer, stood up, bowed, and said, "Of course, Georgiana, Miss Bennet, good morning! I hope you are both well?"

"We are," Elizabeth said, advancing into the room and pushing the door closed behind her with one foot. "I do apologize for interrupting you, sir, but I have a mission, and I will not be swayed from it."

"A mission?" he asked in amused surprise. "What kind of mission?"

"A very important one, I am certain," Elizabeth answered solemnly, reaching into a pocket and withdrawing a letter. "This is for you, Mr. Darcy, from your cousin, Miss Anne de Bourgh. It was enclosed in a letter from Mrs. Charlotte Collins in Kent. Miss de Bourgh wished the letter to reach you without any possibility of interference and asked Charlotte to enclose her note in my friend's letter to me. Now I am handing it to you, and I have fulfilled my task."

Darcy was both perplexed and disturbed at the sight of the blue note, but he could only smile at Miss Bennet's speech.

"Do you suppose something is wrong at Rosings? Perhaps my aunt or cousin is ill!" Georgiana said anxiously.

"Oh, surely Miss de Bourgh's letter would have been sent by express if there were any urgent concerns," Elizabeth said reassuringly. "Now, it appears to me that Mr. Darcy has paperwork to see to, and I believe Neptune and Rainbow are waiting for us."

"They are!" Georgiana agreed. "Come along, Elizabeth."

Darcy found his eyes fixed on Elizabeth's slender form, clad in charming blue, as she departed the room with Georgiana at her heels. He blew out a breath, sat down, broke open the seal, and read Anne's letter.

June 7th, 1812

Rosings

Darcy,

I hope this letter makes it to you safely, and I apologize for the roundabout method of getting it into your hands. Naturally I could not write you directly, given Lady Catherine's insistence that we are destined to wed, and our butler makes a point of telling my mother about all my correspondence.

My mother informed me that she plans to write you and invite herself and me to Pemberley in July or August. I beg you to put her off in some way, Cousin. My health is uncertain, and I know that a four day journey in a carriage along jolting roads in the very heat of summer would be an utter misery, regardless of how well sprung our coach is! I would arrive only fit for bed, but Lady Catherine would not allow me to hide away when she has the opportunity to throw me at you.

Mother will not, of course, listen to me. I therefore implore you to fend her off somehow.

Sincerely,

Anne de Bourgh

Darcy felt a mixture of relief and dismay. On the one hand, he was glad that nothing dire had happened at Rosings. On the other, the thought of Lady Catherine descending upon Pemberley, with Anne in tow, was disconcerting.

He now opened up a drawer in his desk and pulled out the unopened letter from Lady Catherine that he had been considering only a few minutes ago.

June 7th, 1812

Darcy,

Anne and I will be journeying to Pemberley and will arrive on the twenty-ninth of July. It is quite tedious that we are required to travel so far, but given your refusal to visit Rosings, you have given me no choice in the matter.

Anne will soon be five and twenty, and it is time that you and she are wed. You can purchase a common license and be married at the chapel in Pemberley. If your mother were still alive, she would be most pleased to have the heir of Pemberley and the heiress of Rosings joined together in marriage on the grounds of the estate where she herself lived for many happy years.

Sincerely,

Lady Catherine de Bourgh

Darcy groaned softly just as there was another tap on the door. He called for his latest visitor to come in and shoved both letters into a drawer as Bingley, his face uncharacteristically grave, entered the study.

"Bingley," he said, rising to his feet, "I hope your wife is well?"

"She is no worse, anyway," Bingley said, wandering over to the window to look out toward the west, "but I fear she is feeling quite distraught today."

"I am sorry."

Bingley shrugged and turned toward his friend. "It is not unusual for a woman in a delicate condition to feel poorly. However, Jane is worried about the Netherfield tenant family whose cottage burned down and expressed a longing to return soon to the estate. I spent the last hour seeking God's wisdom, and I believe that it would be best for us to journey back to Hertfordshire in two days. You have been a wonderful host, and I know we intended to stay longer at Pemberley, but it will be easier to oversee and expedite the rebuilding of the cottage from Netherfield. I also think Jane would be more comfortable in her own home during this challenging time."

"Certainly," Darcy responded, though he felt his heart sink at these words. "I understand completely,

Bingley, and can only applaud you for your devotion to both your wife and your tenants.

"Perhaps you can visit us at Netherfield soon!" Bingley said eagerly. "We would gladly welcome you and Miss Darcy if you can tear yourself away from your duties here."

Darcy glanced briefly at the drawer, which held the letters from his aunt and cousin, and he narrowed his eyes thoughtfully. "I may well take you up on that offer, my friend; in the meantime, would you allow me to break the news to Georgiana before you tell the others? She will be most disappointed, as she has grown very fond of both your wife and Miss Bennet."

"Of course," Bingley promised and strode out of the study.

Darcy watched his friend leave before lowering himself into his chair again, his eyes fixed on an ormolu paperweight crafted in the shape of a rearing stallion. It had been a gift from his father a decade ago, and he reached out to run his fingers over the smooth back and legs of the figure. How was he going to tell Georgiana? She would be bitterly unhappy.

For that matter…

He leaned back and closed his eyes. He was fooling himself if he thought Georgiana was the only one affected by the Bingleys' decision. A good night's sleep had not erased the confusion swirling in his mind. He had come to realize that he was greatly drawn to Miss Bennet, but was that merely infatuation, or true passion? He had looked forward to having her under his roof for at least another week and had, in fact, intended to urge Bingley's party to stay longer.

He groaned and massaged his forehead before reaching for his cousin and aunt's letters again. He must find a way to stave off Lady Catherine's intended visit in a few short weeks, and he must find a way to keep Georgiana reasonably happy, and he must consult with Richard regarding Miss Bennet, and...

Five minutes later, he pulled out paper and pen and began writing. He had a plan.

Chapter 19

"Brother, no!" Georgiana cried out, her blue eyes dark with distress. "Mr. Bingley and his party are to stay for at least another week!"

"I fear it is necessary that they depart for Hertfordshire in two days," Darcy said and then continued hastily, "but pray do not disturb yourself, my dear. I have a plan which will, I hope, bring you great pleasure."

Georgiana swallowed hard and struggled to calm herself. She despised unexpected changes in plans, and the loss of her first true female friend was devastating. Nonetheless, she knew it was not her brother's fault.

She tried to form a smile, which came out looking like a pathetic grimace, and said, "A plan?"

"Yes," Darcy answered. "I presume you still wish to visit Ramsgate?"

"Yes?" Georgiana said hesitantly.

"I believe we should plan to travel to Ramsgate at the end of July, but I would like to invite Miss Bennet to accompany us there. I understand she has never seen the ocean before, and I know she values your companionship."

His sister's expression shifted from a miserable smirk to blank astonishment. "Invite Miss Bennet to Ramsgate?"

"Yes? Would you like that, or…"

"Oh, Brother!" Georgiana shrieked, rushing forward to embrace him, and now her smile was real. "Oh, that would be wonderful! I could show her the wild birds, and she would love the waves, and the shells, and…"

"It is possible that she will not be able to come," Darcy cautioned. "It is also conceivable that she will not wish to leave her home again so soon. But even if she cannot come now, I promise we will arrange to see her again. She is a very good friend."

"Yes," Georgiana agreed fervently. "She is."

/

"You cannot be serious, Charles!" Caroline snapped, leaping to her feet as if stung by a hornet. "We are to stay here at Pemberley for at least another week!"

"No, Caroline," Charles said calmly, though his jaw flexed ominously. "We will depart Pemberley for Hertfordshire two days hence."

"But why?" Caroline demanded and then turned an angry glare on Jane, who was sitting in the corner of the music room in the guest wing, her eyes downcast. "Is this your doing, Jane? Are you so enamored of your vulgar mother and sisters that you are forcing my brother to…"

"Silence!" Bingley thundered, so angrily that all the ladies present jumped. "You will not insult my wife, do you hear?"

"Charles," Jane said softly, "I understand Caroline's unhappiness. Perhaps…"

"It would be horribly rude to Mr. Darcy to leave on such short notice!" Caroline exclaimed. "Surely even *you* must see that, Elizabeth!"

"Twenty pounds!" Charles snarled, walking over to glare down at his unmarried sister. "We will continue this conversation in my sitting room, Caroline. Elizabeth, Louisa, will you stay with Jane?"

"Of course," Elizabeth assured him, her brow crinkled in confusion. What did 'twenty pounds' mean?

Charles grasped Caroline's arm and nearly dragged her out of the room, shutting the door behind them. Jane immediately burst into tears, causing both Elizabeth and Louisa to rush over to her.

"My dear Jane," Louisa said, reaching out to take Jane's hands in her own, "I do beg you not to concern yourself over Caroline's behavior. She has always been a selfish creature who wants her own way."

"I do feel guilty," Jane sobbed. "I know Caroline was looking forward to our time here at Pemberley, and Elizabeth, you are enjoying yourself very much…"

"I am, but you must not concern yourself about me," Elizabeth said. "I agree that Charles is needed to oversee the situation with the Millers, and you should be wherever you feel most comfortable."

"What of you, Louisa?" Jane said, turning her tear stained face toward her sister by marriage. "Are you greatly disappointed?"

"I am not," Louisa said softly. "In truth, well, I do beg you not to tell Caroline yet, but I am quite certain now that I too am with child."

Jane's distress gave way to immediate delight. "Oh, Louisa, truly?"

Now Louisa's eyes were wet, her expression joyful. "Yes, truly, at long last. I am exceptionally fatigued and am feeling nauseous in the mornings. I am only a few weeks along and suspect I will feel worse before I feel better. I would prefer to return to Netherfield now."

"I presume Mr. Hurst knows?" Jane asked. Elizabeth's stomach twisted oddly at the sight. Jane and Louisa had something in common that Elizabeth knew nothing about, the knowledge of intimacy with a husband and the resulting conception of new life within the womb.

To her astonishment, her wayward mind shifted immediately onto Mr. Darcy, which in turn provoked her face to flame with heat. What was she thinking? Yes, the master of Pemberley was handsome, kind and intelligent, but there was no indication that he was interested in her as a possible wife!

Louisa, heedless of Elizabeth's thoughts, smiled and said, "I intended to wait to tell him, but he suggested the possibility to me this morning. He is well aware that my courses should have started weeks ago."

"I am so happy for you," Jane declared, kissing Mrs. Hurst on the cheek, "and I do feel better about wishing to return to Netherfield. I am sorry about Caroline, but it cannot be helped."

"Nor should it be," Louisa said stoutly. "Caroline has been spoiled since she was a child, and it is best that she learn now that she cannot always have her way."

"Perhaps that is the purview of youngest daughters," Elizabeth suggested with a smirk. "Certainly our sister, Lydia, believes that the universe should revolve around her person."

"Lizzy!" Jane protested, but she could not help but smile as well.

Outside the great walls of Pemberley, blue skies had given way to banks of dark clouds which had, in turn, released torrents of rain to water the extensive fields of the estate. Inside the peafowl garden, the birds were trilling or complaining, depending on each bird's particular disposition. The young peachicks huddled under the cover of their coop, their mother guarding them jealously from the water.

In his office, Darcy spent a few minutes staring dreamily out of the window, his mind envisioning a pair of bright eyes in the face of a pretty woman. Finally, he forced himself back to his desk, dipped his quill into ink, and began to write.

June 10th, 1812

Pemberley

Richard,

I hope this letter finds you well. I am planning to escort Georgiana to Ramsgate in the latter part of July. I can almost hear you crying out in dismay at the very thought, but I have my reasons, which are as follows.

Firstly, and most importantly, Georgiana is eager to return to the sea in spite of the trauma of last year's visit. You know that she relishes her routine, and we have been to Ramsgate the last six years. She is very fond of the birds found in the salt marshes and in the sea, and the ocean is a peaceful place for her.

Secondly, and nearly as importantly, Lady Catherine informed me by letter that she intends to descend on Pemberley in late July, with Anne reluctantly in tow. I do not wish to host my aunt and cousin, and escaping to Ramsgate will prevent such a thing.

Thirdly, well, I cannot mention the third point in a letter. Suffice it to say that I very much wish for your advice, Richard, which brings me to a request; can you join us on our trip to Ramsgate? I intend to spend a few days with my friend, Bingley, in Hertfordshire, and then we will proceed onward to London and spend a day or two there, with a planned arrival at Ramsgate on the 29th of July. We intend to spend three weeks there. Please inform me as soon as possible whether you can join us.

God bless you,

Fitzwilliam Darcy

Darcy read the letter to be certain the salient points had been covered, folded it, sealed it with wax, and placed it on the tray.

There was a knock on the door. He called out a welcome and the door swung open to reveal Georgiana, looking excited, and Miss Bennet, looking uneasy.

He quickly rose and bowed to both of them, but before he could say a word, Georgiana blurted, "Brother, pray tell Elizabeth that you truly wish for her to join us at Ramsgate. I do not think she believes me!"

"I do believe you," Elizabeth said hastily. "I merely wish to be entirely certain that Mr. Darcy would not find me in the way. I am aware that he has many responsibilities when overseeing Pemberley and would not want to interfere with his desire to spend more time with you while you are on holiday by the sea, dear Georgiana."

Darcy looked down on the lady with respect, not unmixed with awe. He often found it difficult to speak to Georgiana directly without distressing the girl, but Miss Bennet always seemed to be able to weave her words in such a way that she was both firm and encouraging.

He was suddenly aware that both women were staring at him expectantly, and he said hastily, "Miss Bennet, I do look forward to spending more time with Georgiana, but I also would be honored and delighted if you would join our little party. I will still have business letters to write, and I hope that my cousin, Colonel Richard Fitzwilliam, will be joining us..."

"Richard is coming?" Georgiana interrupted excitedly.

"I hope he is," Darcy said, and then cautioned, "but of course his military duties may prevent him."

He turned his dark eyes on Elizabeth and said, "In any case, Miss Bennet, I do hope you will join us at Ramsgate. It would give me great pleasure to know that my sister is well entertained with a good friend while I am required to fulfill other obligations."

Elizabeth found herself blushing at the gentleman's intense gaze upon her face. Was it her imagination, or was there something more than mere courtesy in that deep voice?

"I would be delighted to come," she said, turning toward her younger friend. "I will need to be certain that such a journey is convenient for my family, but yes, I would very much like to visit the sea with you."

"I am so happy!" Georgiana exclaimed. "Now come, Elizabeth, there is not a great deal of time before you must leave, and since it is pouring outside, we should take this opportunity to look in the library for information regarding goldfish."

"Goldfish?" Darcy repeated in surprise.

"Yes, for Mrs. Bingley wishes to have goldfish," Georgiana explained, "but she does not know much about fish. Miss Bennet and I will read about fish and take notes so that when Mrs. Bingley acquires hers, she will know how to take care of them."

Darcy looked at Elizabeth Bennet uneasily. Georgiana wanted to be helpful, but her desire to gain and then impart information to others often came across as pretentious and overbearing.

Elizabeth smiled reassuringly at him and said, "Jane will be very pleased to have more information about goldfish. As you know, she is not feeling well, and it would certainly grieve her if her fish did not survive due to her lack of knowledge."

Darcy relaxed and said, "Well, in that case, perhaps I can be of help?"

"Oh, that would be wonderful, Brother!"

Chapter 20

Caroline Bingley stomped down the stairs from the guest wing of Pemberley and began marching through the corridor which ran parallel to the façade of the great mansion.

She was angry, nay, furious, but she dared not express her ire toward Jane or Elizabeth, else she would lose even more money from her annual allowance. As for Louisa, well, her sister had pleaded exhaustion and taken to her bed, which was absurd. Who needed a nap in the middle of the morning? It was just like Louisa, was it not? Caroline's elder sister pretended to be certain of her own mind, and yet, with Charles's idiotic championing of Jane and Elizabeth, now seemed bent on worming herself into their good graces.

It was terrifying how much had changed in the last months; indeed, Caroline cursed the very day her brother had heard of Netherfield Hall! Presently she was saddled with five new sisters with relatives in trade, and Charles, who had been the most amiable and agreeable of brothers, was now behaving in a thoroughly obnoxious way!

Caroline's pace increased still more, her shoes thumping on the wooden floor. She needed to find a way to expel her anger without losing more money, and given the rain outside, she could hardly go outside to walk away her outrage.

The sound of familiar feminine voices drew her attention, and she halted in front of an open door of the library on her left.

She stepped within and looked around, marveling at the sight before her, though she had, of course, seen it before. She was no great reader, but this library of Pemberley was magnificent, with tens, maybe hundreds, of thousands of pounds worth of books within sight. Oh, to be mistress of an estate with such wealth in the written word!

"Hertfordshire is significantly south of Derbyshire," Miss Darcy's voice remarked. A moment later, her host's sister appeared from around the corner of the freestanding shelves which separated the main library from the area with the rarer volumes. "Our own goldfish survive the winters nicely so it should not be a problem."

"That is good," Elizabeth answered, following Georgiana into view. "I would think that the waterfall would limit how much ice forms ... oh, Miss Bingley!"

Georgiana, who had been focusing on the floor as she walked, lifted her face and blanched at the unaccustomed sight of one of her least favorite people.

"Elizabeth," Caroline returned sharply, before adding politely, "Miss Darcy. What are you doing?"

"We are learning about goldfish," Elizabeth explained cheerfully, shifting to block Georgiana from Caroline's curious gaze. "Jane wishes to obtain goldfish at Netherfield, and Miss Darcy offered to see if there are any books here which might provide information on how best to care for them."

"Goldfish!" Caroline responded in complete exasperation. "I cannot fathom why Jane would desire goldfish!"

A moment later, she flinched and glanced around, then relaxed in relief. Charles was not in sight and could not take away ten pounds for her *honest* remark.

"Well, as to that, Caroline," Elizabeth said gravely, "Pemberley has goldfish in its ponds. It is, I think, the mark of a truly sophisticated estate when the ponds have goldfish."

Caroline blinked at these absurd words just as a deep voice announced, "I do believe that to be true, Miss Bennet. My father introduced goldfish some twenty years ago to the pools here, and I am delighted that they have thrived."

Miss Bingley turned in horror as Mr. Darcy stepped into view from the hidden part of the library, his arms filled with books.

"Georgiana," he said, walking over to place his burdens on a nearby table, "There may be useful information in these books, though I cannot be certain. Miss Bingley, good morning."

"Good morning," Caroline answered, curtseying as the gentleman bowed slightly. "I did not realize you were here, Mr. Darcy."

"Yes, I wished to assist my sister and Miss Bennet," Darcy responded. "There is a reproduction of a Marguerite Gerard painting of goldfish in a bowl in the book on the top, Georgiana. You might enjoy looking at it, though I daresay it will not help you care for the fish."

"Thank you, Brother," Georgiana exclaimed, grasping the tome in her slender hands and opening it.

Elizabeth shot a quick glance at Caroline, then a meaningful one at Darcy, and the gentleman said, "I need to speak to Mrs. Reynolds, as we should have an exceptional meal tomorrow night before you all depart for Hertfordshire. Is there anything you ladies particularly would enjoy?"

"Oh, Mr. Darcy!" Caroline trilled. "I am certain anything your wonderful cook prepares will be excellent."

"I quite agree with Caroline," Elizabeth said, "but I know Jane and I would particularly relish some of the marvelous strawberries that were served at the picnic. They are delicious."

"That can be arranged," Darcy said, bowing to the ladies and striding out of the door. Miss Bingley, seeing her quarry disappearing, abandoned Elizabeth and Georgiana without compunction, eager to take this opportunity to speak with the man she wished to make her husband.

Elizabeth waited until both had disappeared before walking over to the door and closing it. She turned around to observe Georgiana staring ahead with a troubled expression, an open book lying in front of her.

"I think that Miss Bingley wishes to marry my brother," she said, her brow wrinkled.

Elizabeth walked over to take a seat at the table and gently pulled Georgiana down next to her.

"I am certain she does," she agreed calmly, looking down at the reproduction of a painting with, yes, three goldfish swimming happily in a bowl. "It is no surprise, Georgiana. Mr. Darcy is handsome, wealthy, intelligent, and master of a great estate. No doubt that there are scores, or even hundreds of women who wish to be mistress of Pemberley. It does not mean that your brother will ask for Miss Bingley's hand in marriage, however."

Silence fell for a full minute while Elizabeth stared down at the painting. To her surprised distress, she felt her face flush, and she had to fight to keep from crying.

"Elizabeth?" Georgiana asked timidly.

"Yes?" Elizabeth returned, forcing herself to look up and smile.

"Do you admire my brother?"

"Oh yes, very much," Elizabeth said with determined cheer. "He is a wonderful man, Mr. Darcy."

"Yes, but do you *like* him?" Georgiana said with emphasis.

Elizabeth swallowed hard and said, "I know you appreciate honesty, so I will say that yes, I *like* Mr. Darcy very much. I hope, oh my dear friend, I do hope you realize that your brother can look very high for a bride, and while I am content with my person and my family, I know that I was not born into the haut ton."

"If Fitzwilliam wished to marry into the cream of society, he could have done so long ago," Georgiana stated. "I want him to marry you."

Elizabeth could not help but laugh at this and then, at the hurt look on her companion's face, pulled her into a firm embrace.

"You are marvelous, Georgiana, you truly are," she said fervently. "Now do listen to me, dear one. Your brother and I have known one another for only a week which is, I contend, far too short a time to truly fall in love. I admire him very much as master of this estate, an intellectual, a very kind brother to you and a generous overseer of his tenants and servants. But Mr. Darcy is far too sensible a man to offer for a woman within a week of her acquaintance, even if he is so inclined, and I daresay he is not. Nor am I willing to accept an offer on so short an association."

Georgiana untangled this speech with some difficulty and then said, "We will see you again, and soon, at Ramsgate. You will have time to know one another better then."

Elizabeth could not help the surge of hope which accompanied this comment. A faraway look transformed her face, and she said "We will, and I am looking forward to it."

/

"Mr. Darcy!" Caroline exclaimed, struggling not to puff in an unbecoming way as she hurried to catch up with the master of Pemberley.

"Yes?" Darcy inquired, halting in the great vestibule at the front door of the estate. He had succeeded in drawing Miss Bingley away from Georgiana and now wished to be completely certain that the Bingley's sister did not try anything foolish in the way of an attempted compromise. With two footmen present, he should be safe enough.

"I merely wished to say that I must apologize for my brother's decision to leave Pemberley on such short notice," Caroline said earnestly, gazing into Darcy's eyes. "It was very ill done, I fear."

"On the contrary," Darcy retorted, stepping back a few inches. "It is greatly to your brother's credit that he is devoting himself to the needs of his estate."

Caroline felt as if someone had thrown cold water on her face. "Come now, sir," she protested, quite heedless of the listening ears of the nearby footmen. "I cannot believe that if you were in London, you would rush back to Pemberley if some tenant farmer's cottage burned down."

"I would not," Darcy agreed in a measured tone, "but Pemberley has been under the care and oversight of the Darcys for more than a hundred years. My steward is familiar with my ways and can manage such events without my direct oversight. Netherfield has been neglected for five years, and Bingley's steward does not know entirely how his master wishes to proceed regarding such a catastrophe as a fire. Thus, Bingley is wise to return to Netherfield to provide the appropriate direction."

Caroline forced herself not to wrinkle her nose at the thought of money and time directed toward caring for mere peasants. "I had not thought of it that way," she said with becoming meekness. "I understand now. I regret leaving Pemberley so soon, which is one of the most remarkable estates in all of England. That is, of course, entirely due to your wise administration, Mr. Darcy."

"Thank you," Darcy said drily. "Now I must meet with Mrs. Reynolds. I will see you at dinner, Miss Bingley."

/

"Elizabeth said that she likes you, but that she does not know you well enough to marry you," Georgiana said.

Darcy, who had joined his sister in her private sitting room before dinner, blinked in astonishment.

"You spoke of a possible marriage between Miss Bennet and me?" he asked, caught between amusement and horror. Ordinarily, such a bold speech would be a catastrophe, but Darcy thought very well of Miss Bennet's sense. She would not take such a question amiss.

"I asked Elizabeth if she *liked* you and she said yes, but that you have known one another but a week, and it would be foolish for you to offer, or her to accept, after such a short acquaintance," Georgiana explained. "That makes sense to me. A person might well present a winsome facade on short acquaintance, only to reveal different, less amiable, traits later. Mr. Wickham is always charming initially, only to reveal his repugnant nature in time. I do not think Elizabeth is like that, but it is wise to be certain of the disposition of one's future mate before embarking on a lifelong commitment in marriage."

Darcy stared at his sister in wonder. Once again, Miss Bennet had managed to explain something to his sister in a gentle but direct way. The lady was a miracle worker.

He was also impressed that Miss Bennet had not leapt at the suggestion of a marriage between herself and the wealthy master of Pemberley. The more Darcy knew her, the more he understood that Miss Bennet was not overly swayed by connections, status or money. She was a most singular woman. He felt his heart swell within him; Miss Elizabeth Bennet was remarkable, and his attraction, far from fading away, was growing by the day.

He was extremely thankful that she was going to Ramsgate with them.

Chapter 21

"Lizzy?"

"Yes, Jane?" Elizabeth asked, pouring lemonade from a pitcher into a glass for her sister. She and Jane had gone above stairs earlier than usual, as Jane was feeling exhausted and ill after a long day.

"Do you think ... is there any chance that Mr. Darcy admires you?"

Elizabeth made rather a show of lowering the pitcher and wiping a few drops of lemonade off the table with her handkerchief before turning around and carrying the glass over to her sister.

"I am not aware that he does," she said calmly, "nor do I have any expectation of winning the gentleman's affection. It is enough that he is pleased that Georgiana and I are friends."

Jane took a long sip of lemonade and then narrowed her eyes, focusing on Elizabeth's cheeks.

"You are blushing, Lizzy!" she accused, her smile animating her already lovely face. "My dear sister, do you care for him?"

"Dearest Jane," Elizabeth answered, as she plumped down on the bed and rubbed her temples with her fingers,

"I do like Mr. Darcy very much, but I do not love him. How could I, after only a week's acquaintance? As for me, well, he has behaved very kindly to me, and is openly encouraging of my friendship with his sister, but I do not think that means – oh, how confused I am! My own heart pulls me toward the gentleman, and first Miss Darcy, and now you, are speaking of marriage…"

"Miss Darcy?" Jane asked in astonishment.

"Yes," Elizabeth returned, blowing out a long breath. "She is, you know, a wonderfully direct girl, and she said that she wants me to marry her brother."

"How did you answer?"

"I told her what I just said to you, that we have not known one another long, and of course that means it would be unwise to consider marriage…"

Elizabeth trailed off at the smug look on her sister's face and, to her own surprise, grabbed a convenient cushion lying on the bed and threw it at her sister.

Jane caught it with one hand, her mouth open in a startled 'o', and then chuckled. Elizabeth rushed over and embraced her sister, who returned the hug fervently as they laughed for a full minute.

Finally Jane leaned back and wiped tears of amusement from her eyes and said, "At this particular moment, I am not feeling sick. You should throw cushions at me more often!"

"I will keep that in mind. But come now, you do need to go to bed, for I know you are exhausted. I promise you that if Mr. Darcy proposes to me, I will tell you as quickly as I can."

Jane, suddenly solemn, reached out her hand and caught Elizabeth's arm. "Charles thinks very highly of Mr. Darcy, and based on my own understanding of that gentleman's character, I believe you and he would do very well together."

Elizabeth's eyes tingled. "Yes, Jane, I think so as well."

/

The rains of the previous day had given way to sunny skies, and Elizabeth, thankful for her stout boots, squelched her way across the grass to the door of the walled garden in pursuit of Miss Darcy.

She followed Georgiana inside and then halted beside her friend, her eyes lighting up at the performance playing out before them. Two peacocks, one of whom she recognized as Neptune because of his white feathers, were facing one another, cooing and trilling, their glorious trains raised, their feathers opalescent in the morning sun, their bodies shaking, their feet dancing. Elizabeth laughed in delight as yet another peacock approached and lifted his magnificent fan, wiggling the feathers with exuberance.

"What are they doing?" she asked, enchanted.

"They are showing off for the peahens," Georgiana said, gesturing at four hens who were wandering around in the vicinity, apparently far more interested in pebbles and bugs than their prospective suitors.

"How can they ignore such a marvelous display?" Elizabeth asked in wonder.

"Peahens are not very intelligent."

"They are not. Oh, Georgiana, the birds are so lovely! I will miss them."

"The peafowl will miss you too," Georgiana said sadly, "and I will as well. Even if you do not marry my brother, I hope you will visit us here in Derbyshire again. You are my friend, and my brother is very fond of Mr. Bingley."

"I relish the thought of returning here in time, but I am also ecstatic over our upcoming visit to the ocean. I keep trying to imagine water reaching to the horizon, but it is beyond even my imagination."

"If all proceeds as planned, it will only be eight and forty days until we arrive at Ramsgate," Georgiana pointed out. "That is not very long."

"No," Elizabeth agreed, smiling at her friend's precision, "it will pass in no time."

/

Darcy, looking over the dinner table, found himself torn between pleasure and sorrow. His French cook, spurred on by his request for a magnificent banquet, had outdone himself with a lavish array of dishes which would tempt even the most capricious appetite. Darcy was thankful to observe that Mrs. Bingley, while a little pale, was eating with apparent pleasure.

The conversation around the table was lively, with Bingley and Georgiana and Miss Bennet speaking of the care and feeding of goldfish, Mrs. Bingley and Mrs. Hurst discussing knitting, and Miss Bingley asking him intrusive questions about his upcoming trip south.

"I do hope to spend a few days at Netherfield at the end of next month," Darcy said to Miss Bingley. "Your brother has offered to host us in Hertfordshire, and Georgiana and I would relish a few days before traveling onward to London."

"Oh, of course, you are welcome at Netherfield any time!" Caroline gushed, ignoring the reality that Jane Bingley, as mistress of the establishment, had the right to bar the door of her home to anyone she chose. Not that she would, of course; Mrs. Bingley was a most hospitable woman.

"The only barrier to our visit would be if some problem here at Pemberley delayed our journey," Darcy said politely, his gaze shifting to Miss Bennet. The young lady's eyes were sparkling, and she suddenly laughed aloud in a most entrancing way.

There was an irritable harrumph from Darcy's left and he turned to observe Caroline Bingley staring at him reprovingly, her lips compressed, her brown eyes glittering with jealousy. Ordinarily, he would not care in the least about the lady's possessive behavior, but given that Georgiana was at the table, he had best keep Miss Bingley moderately calm.

He wracked his brain for a minute in search of a safe question and finally said, "Do you intend to take part in next year's Season, Miss Bingley?"

Caroline's sour glare shifted to one of pleasure. "Of course, Mr. Darcy, of course! Dare I hope that you and Miss Darcy will be traveling to London in the new year as well?"

Darcy returned a vague answer just as Elizabeth Bennet happened to lift her head and look into his eyes. He felt a strange thrill course through his body, and based on the lady's sudden stillness, she felt something as well.

"I daresay Jane will not feel strong enough to host a party in London during next year's season," Caroline droned on, thankfully unaware of the interplay between her host and Miss Bennet. "But I will be available as a hostess, and will ensure that the Bingley name is not disgraced…"

/

"Thank you for your hospitality, Mr. Darcy," Jane said and then turned to Georgiana, who was looking woebegone. "Miss Darcy, I look forward to the day we meet again."

"Thank you, Mrs. Bingley," Georgiana murmured, struggling to hide her tears. A week ago, she had been fearful of Mr. Bingley and his party arriving and disrupting her typical routine. Now she was miserable because Elizabeth was leaving her.

"Be certain to attach my trunk carefully so that there is no chance it will fall off," Miss Bingley sharply ordered one of Darcy's servants before turning a beaming smile on the master of the estate. "Oh, Mr. Darcy, thank you again for your kindness in hosting us. I will remember this all too short visit for the rest of my life!"

Darcy replied with careful courtesy while Charles assisted Jane into the first carriage drawn up along the main drive on front of the mansion. Mr. Hurst helped his own wife into the second carriage, and in the midst of Miss Bingley's chattering, and the sound of servants running to and fro, and the horses shifting and whickering, Elizabeth took the time to murmur into Georgiana's ear, "Do not be downhearted, dear friend. We will meet very soon, and I promise to write frequently."

"Thank you, Elizabeth," Georgiana answered. "I look forward to your letters, and I will even write back to you, though I generally dislike writing letters."

"My father does as well," Elizabeth with a chuckle. "Until we meet again, Georgiana."

She turned toward toward Darcy with a smile and said, "Mr. Darcy, I have had a truly wonderful time here at Pemberley. Thank you very much for your kind invitation."

"It has been a pleasure making your acquaintance, Miss Bennet," Darcy said, then hesitated. He longed to say something more personal to this lovely lady, but with the eyes of the party on him, along with several servants, he had better not.

"I look forward to seeing you again," he said with a heartfelt smile.

"Until then," Elizabeth said, turning to allow Charles to hand her into the carriage, where she took the rear facing seat across from Jane. Elizabeth looked out the window and smiled at Georgiana, then shifted her gaze to Mr. Darcy, who chose this moment to look toward her.

To her surprise, she felt her scalp prickle and her entire body flood with heat at the intensity in Mr. Darcy's dark eyes, and she found herself beaming back at him. A moment later, she lurched back in her seat just as Caroline Bingley turned a suspicious gaze toward her. Elizabeth did not know if Mr. Darcy admired her in the least, but she certainly did not want to give Miss Bingley any additional reason to dislike her.

Jane, who had observed the entire exchange, grinned at her, and said, "We will see Mr. and Miss Darcy soon, Lizzy."

Elizabeth could only be thankful.

/

"Farewell, Mr. Darcy, Miss Darcy!" Caroline called out the window of her carriage as the horses began walking, and then trotting, along the road which would lead to the highway. "I look forward to seeing you in Hertfordshire next month!"

Mr. Darcy lifted a hand of goodbye toward the departing carriages and then turned to climb the stairs to the main door of Pemberley with Miss Darcy at his side.

Caroline craned her head and watched until the twosome disappeared through the massive front door, then leaned back against the scarlet squabs of her seat and allowed her face to relax from its frenzied smile.

"Oh, it is truly dreadful that Jane insisted that we leave prematurely!" she complained. "I am certain that if we had stayed even a few days longer, Mr. Darcy would have offered for me!"

Louisa, seated across from her on the forward facing seat, merely compressed her lips and said nothing, but Mr. Hurst, who always fell asleep as quickly as possible on carriage rides, said, "You are living in a fantasy if you believe Darcy will ever offer for you, Caroline."

Miss Bingley gawked, gasped, and even drooled before croaking, "*What* did you say?"

"I said Darcy will never marry you," Hurst repeated, shifting closer to his wife to avoid the sun shining in his eyes. "You should lower your sights, Sister, or you will find yourself on the shelf!"

"Patrick, really," Louisa protested weakly. She was not feeling well today, and the thought of Caroline having a tantrum while they were trapped together in a carriage was unappealing.

Caroline glared at her brother-in-law and declared, "I am certain that Mr. Darcy admires me exceedingly. I am beautiful, accomplished, and wealthy. I would be the perfect mistress of Pemberley."

"Nonsense," Hurst returned irritably. "Darcy could marry any one of literally dozens of women with similar wealth and accomplishments to your own, and they are the daughters of nobles and gentlemen, not the children of tradesmen."

Miss Bingley snorted like a bull, and her fingers curled into tight fists. "You did not mind marrying a tradesman's daughter, Brother!"

"Of course I did not; I love and appreciate Louisa, but my situation is different than Darcy's. My estate is a small one, and my father still lives. Thus, I am dependent on a mere allowance which makes Louisa's dowry vitally important. Darcy is nephew of an earl, and his estate earns some ten thousand pounds a year. It exasperates me to see you wasting your life trying to win a man who has no interest in you."

"How dare you?" Caroline snarled in fury, and Louisa flinched at the loud noise and put a hand to her head.

"Oh, pray do not argue," she begged, and Hurst, who had been preparing his next words of attack, immediately turned toward her.

"I am sorry, my dear," he said contritely, lovingly patting his wife's hand. "I apologize for my words, Caroline."

"As well you should," Miss Bingley said, tilting her nose into the air. "Mark my words, I will be Mrs. Darcy by Christmas!"

Hurst cast his eyes heavenward in exasperation and turned toward his wife. "Louisa, I know you slept poorly last night. You should take a nap if at all possible."

Louisa cast a nervous glance at her sister, only to relax when Caroline, jaw clenched, turned to glare out at the passing countryside. It appeared that Miss Bingley intended to sulk instead of snarl, which she appreciated.

"Thank you, Patrick," Louisa said, leaning against his comforting bulk. A few minutes later, she was fast asleep.

Once he was confident that his wife was truly slumbering, Hurst leaned back carefully and closed his own eyes. He was skilled at drowsing without falling over, which was a blessing given that he found life dull much of the time. Far better to sleep to hasten the hours of a boring afternoon or evening.

He smiled as he drifted off to a light sleep. If all went well, a child would be born early next year, the baby that he and Louisa had desired since they had married five years previous.

Caroline heard the soft snore of her brother by marriage and harrumphed in exasperation. Mr. Darcy never fell asleep in company, and she was certain that her chosen partner in life would never be so rude as to snore, whether privately or publicly.

To her distress, she felt tears prickle in her eyes, tears of anger, and yes, fear. For as long as she could remember, she had been confident of her ability to prevail in getting exactly what she wanted. Her father, her brother, her relations – all had eventually succumbed to her determination. She was confident that with time and work, she would win what she wanted most of all, the position of mistress of Pemberley.

And yet…

Charles was being so ridiculous, with his absurd decision to defend Elizabeth Bennet against her own, well-reasoned remarks. As if Elizabeth, sly thing that she was, needed anyone to protect her. Caroline was certain that even if her own words were a little sharp, Elizabeth was not distressed in the least.

As for Miss Darcy – well, Caroline had known her these five years now! Surely they were friends. There was no reason for Georgiana to fear playing in front of her. None at all!

It was all absurd. She was handsome, well educated, accomplished, wealthy. She was the perfect wife for Mr. Darcy.

She stole a careful glance at Hurst, who was now leaning back against the seat cushion with Louisa sleeping against his shoulder. What would Hurst know? It should not matter that such an undistinguished gentleman thought that Darcy would never offer for a tradesman's daughter.

But somehow … somehow it did matter.

Chapter 22

June 17th, 1812

London

Darcy,

It would be my pleasure to join you and Georgiana at the seaside. I spoke to my commanding officer, and he has given me leave. My duties have been heavy of late, but by the end of July, I should have my current recruits whipped into some semblance of shape. I have a good captain under me who can continue the work.

I am both thankful and relieved that Georgiana is doing well, and I confess to great curiosity about the third point in your letter. It speaks of a mystery, and you, Cousin, are rarely mysterious! In any case, you know how I love giving advice, and I look forward to blessing you with my mature analysis of whatever situation you find yourself in.

Colonel Richard Fitzwilliam

/

Pemberley

June 27th, 1812

Lady Catherine,

I hope this letter finds you and Anne healthy and well.

Regrettably, Georgiana and I will not be at Pemberley at the end of July. My dear sister longs to visit the ocean, and we intend to make our way to one of the seaside towns for a few weeks. I apologize for the inconvenience.

We have plans of a tentative nature to visit London early next year. Perhaps we can meet then.

Respectfully,

Fitzwilliam Darcy

/

June 28th, 1812

Longbourn

Dear Charlotte,

I am delighted that your hens are doing so nicely and that the pig is fattening well. It will be pleasant to have good stores of ham during the winter. Pray congratulate Mr. Collins on his fine vegetable marrows. He is definitely a most skilled gardener.

Everyone at Longbourn is well, thank you, as are the inhabitants of Netherfield. Jane is with child, you know. She has been most uncomfortable, but my mother says that she was horribly ill with all her pregnancies, so that is to be expected. Mama admits, somewhat reluctantly, that she felt better by the time the baby quickened, so we are hoping and praying that Jane will experience the same.

You asked whether I will be bored at home after so much travel. I do not bore easily, dear friend, but in actual fact I will be journeying to Ramsgate at the end of July. I have been so fortunate as to receive an invitation from Miss Georgiana Darcy, whom I met while visiting Pemberley last month. She is a delightful young lady, and I accepted her invitation with alacrity. I have never seen the ocean and find it somewhat difficult to wait!

You also asked about my three youngest sisters. Mary is far more content than she was last year. She is *currently living at Netherfield in order to assist Jane during her more difficult hours, and she has a music master who is assisting her. Her playing is much improved. I too am sitting in on the lessons on occasion. Unfortunately, given that I keep gallivanting here and there across England's fair acres, I am not improving nearly as quickly as Mary.*

Kitty also is seeing a master regularly, though her interests are in sketching and painting. She has grown quite adept of late.

Lydia is, well, she is Lydia. However, she is a bit less rambunctious now that the militia is no longer in Meryton.

With much love,

Elizabeth

/

Longbourn

June 28th, 1812

Dear Georgiana,

Mary is working on Mozart's Sonata No. 16. She learned it some years ago, but her music master is encouraging her to work on simpler scores while imparting more feeling and movement into her pieces. I think she is doing very well.

The master tells me that my style is good, but my fingering poor. I have been working on a section of Beethoven's Piano Sonata No. 14. It is difficult but I believe I am improving.

I am counting the days until you and Mr. Darcy arrive at Netherfield. I very much look forward to spending time with you, my friend. I will warn you that my two youngest sisters, whom I love very much, can be rather noisy. If you find them overwhelming, you can claim a headache. Are the peafowl well?

With both friendship and love,

Elizabeth

/

Netherfield

July 4th, 1812

My dear Amelia,

I accept your invitation most gratefully! I understand that London in August is hot and rather dull at this time of year, but it must be better than being positively buried here in the countryside. I know you admired my brother Charles when you last met, but most regrettably, his character has deteriorated significantly in the wake of his marriage. He is now completely under the domination of his wife, my new sister Jane. Well, perhaps that is not entirely true; it is more accurate to say that he is under the thumb of Elizabeth, Jane's next younger sister. There are five daughters in the family, you know, and no sons! Furthermore, the estate is entailed away to an idiotic cousin!

Elizabeth is an impertinent woman with no beauty and even fewer accomplishments, though she does plink away at the pianoforte on occasion, though not well. She is a dominating, imperious sort of girl, and Charles, always far too amiable, does not see the truth of her truly regrettable character. I have done my best to open his eyes, only to win disapprobation from my own brother, who should always have my best interests at heart. Louisa, too, has quite fallen under the spell of both Jane and Elizabeth. Is there something in the waters here that makes formerly sensible individuals lose their minds?

I would travel to London earlier except that I will be needed here at Netherfield in three weeks' time. Mr. Darcy, Charles's closest friend, along with his sister Miss Darcy, intends to stay here for a few days before proceeding on to London. Jane is with child and making an enormous fuss about it; thus, I feel it my duty to be present while the Darcys are in residence. Someone must be certain that the meals are adequate. Mr. Darcy is nephew to the Earl of Matlock, you know, and master of a great estate!

Once the Darcys have gone on to London, I will no doubt be quite desperate for time away from my various relations. I would be honored to provide some financial assistance to your family; well do I know the expense of a London House!

Gratefully,

Caroline Bingley

/

Hunsford

July 8th, 1812

Dear Lizzy,

I feel I must apologize. I told Mr. Collins of your planned trip to Ramsgate with the Darcys, entirely in innocence, and naturally he told Lady Catherine. Our patroness was most exasperated, though I do not know why. I know you do not find Lady Catherine particularly intimidating, but I thought I should mention it.

As for me, I am well enough, though I have been sickly in the mornings. I am hopeful that my malady is the same as that of Jane.

With friendship and love,

Charlotte Collins

/

Pemberley

July 8th, 1812

Dear Elizabeth,

Two of the eight young peachicks died last week. I am not certain why, but sadly such a thing is not uncommon. The remaining six are doing well. We do not truly need quite so many peafowl, but Fitzwilliam's friend, the one who sold us Neptune, has a larger area for his birds than I have and has agreed to take any unneeded peafowl, so long as they are healthy, of course.

We begin our journey to Netherfield in twelve days. I look forward to seeing you very much, my friend. The journey itself will be tedious, as I find it difficult to read while in a moving carriage. However, I will have Fitzwilliam in the carriage with me, and he is a good conversationalist.

Sincerely,

Georgiana Darcy

/

July 8th, 1812

Rosings

Nephew,

I have discovered that you and Georgiana are journeying to Ramsgate in Kent, and that you have invited Miss Elizabeth Bennet to accompany you. Such a thing is not to be borne, nor can I fathom why you would take such a foolish step. I grant you the girl is pretty enough, but during her visit to Mrs. Collins, she showed herself to be quite impertinent on occasion. Miss Bennet is therefore in no way a suitable companion to my niece. Furthermore, only a fool would be unaware of the potential dangers of such an invitation. Miss Bennet's elder sister has married well to your tradesman friend, Mr. Bingley, but given that Longbourn is entailed to my own rector, I have no doubt that Miss Bennet is eager to wed most advantageously. She will undoubtedly assume a degree of familiarity with the Darcy family which is most unseemly!

I insist that you inform Miss Bennet that she is not permitted to join you at Ramsgate, do you understand?

You will be driving within a few miles of Rosings, and I will expect you to stop here and spend a few days before continuing onward. Indeed, given the relatively short distance from Rosings to Ramsgate, Anne and I may well join you at the seashore.

Lady Catherine de Bourgh

/

July 10th, 1812

Edward Street

London

Wickham,

I daresay you are enjoying yourself in Brighton, surrounded by cool breezes, tolerant shopkeepers, and pretty servant girls who are eager to swoon over your handsome face. I am certain the weather is far more propitious on the seashore than here in the middle of London, where the very timbers of my boarding house groan and shift because of the heat.

You asked that I write if I learned anything of Darcy. As you know, he has been at Pemberley since our failure at Ramsgate, with young, foolish Georgiana there as well.

My cousin Mildred's cook's daughter works at Pemberley as a maid, and the girl informed her mother, who in turn told Mildred, who informed me, that the Darcys plan to journey to Ramsgate at the end of July and will be staying in the same red brick house as usual. I find that rather peculiar given the dramatics of last year's visit to that town, but Georgiana no doubt wishes to drool over the wild birds in the salt marshes.

I think you will be safe enough; Brighton is some eighty miles from Ramsgate, and Darcy generally adheres to his plans except when he does not. I still wake up at night on occasion and think about the 'if onlies', my dear Wickham. If only the three of us had fled for Gretna Greene a few days earlier. You would be master of Georgiana Darcy's dowry, and we would be happy together.

If you are ever in London, I beg you to visit. My bedroom door is always open for you.

With much love,

Mrs. Henrietta Younge

/

July 14th, 1812

Longbourn

Dearest Charlotte,

I will wait on my congratulations until you are entirely certain, but I do pray that the Lord will bless you with a healthy child, and soon.

I forbid you from concerning yourself about Lady Catherine. She is far away and totally unconnected from me, so her disapprobation concerns me not a whit.

My greater concern is to keep Caroline Bingley unaware of my plans. Somehow, miraculously, she has not yet learned that I will be accompanying the Darcys to Ramsgate. I do not care about her tantrums, but poor Jane does not need such disruption during this delicate time of her life.

I do remember my time in Kent very fondly, Charlotte. Please greet Mr. Collins for me, or do not, if you think it would cause trouble.

With much love,

Lizzy

/

July 14th, 1812

Rosings

Richard,

Do you know where Darcy is? Do you know what his plans are? I sent him a vitally important letter by express more than a week ago and have received nothing in return. If you hear from or speak to him, inform your cousin that I am most displeased by his tardiness and expect him to respond to my letter immediately.

Lady Catherine de Bourgh

/

London

July 16th, 1812

Darcy,

Just a warning that I received an enraged letter from Lady Catherine, asking about your location and plans. She is on the warpath, though I know not why.

I apologize for forcing you to pay for the express, but I thought you were willing to disburse a little extra

266

money to be aware of our formidable aunt's latest activities.

In haste,

Richard Fitzwilliam

/

July 19th, 1812

Pemberley

Richard,

Many thanks for sending me the warning about Lady Catherine. Simply put, she is displeased that Georgiana is bringing along a friend to Ramsgate, a delightful young woman named Miss Elizabeth Bennet, who is younger sister to my friend Bingley's new wife. Our aunt wishes me to disinvite Miss Bennet, whom she knows a little, and bring Anne to Ramsgate. I intend to do neither, and thus have ignored her latest letter entirely.

We will leave for Hertfordshire tomorrow, arrive at Bingley's home of Netherfield in three days, spend two or three days there, then go on to London for a day or two, where you can join our party, and finally we will make our way to Ramsgate, though not with a halt at Rosings. I have no intention of marrying Anne and the sooner Lady Catherine accepts that, the better!

Georgiana and I both look forward to seeing you soon.

God bless,

Fitzwilliam Darcy

Chapter 23

She stood on the stone bridge facing east, her back toward him, her head bent toward the turbulent waters of the stream. The sun's setting rays shone against her luxurious dark hair, a tantalizing mix of browns and reds.

"Elizabeth…"

She turned toward him now, her fine eyes a mesmerizing amalgam of golds and browns, her unbound hair cascading down her shoulders. She was wearing her favorite green gown, and her skirt swayed gracefully with her movements.

"Fitzwilliam, my love…"

He moved toward her, his hungry gaze fixed on her beautiful face, and she was in his arms, and he pressed a kiss on those enchanting pink lips, and…

The whole world shifted abruptly, and Fitzwilliam Darcy, master of Pemberley, jerked in astonishment and nearly fell off the seat of his carriage. He woke up with a start and looked around in confusion. What was happening?

"Fitzwilliam!" Georgiana exclaimed, peering worriedly at her brother. "Is something wrong?"

Darcy looked around rather wildly, then relaxed as his mind caught up with his surroundings. He was in his carriage traveling on the road to Hertfordshire. His sister and her companion were with him and lovely, glorious, enchanting Elizabeth Bennet was some thirty miles farther down the road.

"I am well," he said hastily, noting the look of concern in his sister's eyes. "I fell over while drowsing, that is all. I apologize to you both."

"I am certain we are all a little weary after last night," Mrs. Annesley said, returning her attention to her knitting. "The inn was rather a noisy one."

"It was," Georgiana agreed somberly. "I find it odd that some people enjoy staying up so late. I like the mornings better."

"I do too," Darcy said, recovering his poise, "but of course different individuals enjoy different things, my dear. During the Season, balls often last into the wee hours of the morning."

Georgiana shuddered and sighed. "I will not like that in the least. It is bad enough to be up so late, but the thought of being around all those people makes my stomach hurt."

"You still have several years before your presentation," Mrs. Annesley said comfortingly. "Moreover, there are some remarkable experiences in

London which are available only at night. Vauxhall Gardens, for example, is a fairyland of lights after dusk. There is also an orchestra which plays under a large pavilion."

Georgiana had been eyeing her companion doubtfully, but she smiled at these last words. "Do the musicians play well?"

"Oh yes, very well. They are well trained, and..."

Darcy, confident that Georgiana was properly distracted, leaned back in his seat and allowed his thoughts to drift back to his dream. It was not the first time that he had dreamed of lovely Miss Bennet, but this was by far the most detailed, most ... romantic, vision yet. It seemed that with the closer he drew to the enticing Elizabeth, the more his mind focused on the lady.

He blew out a breath as he turned to stare out the window at the passing countryside, which was full of fields, cottages, and groves of trees. In the few weeks since Bingley's party had left Pemberley, Darcy had missed Miss Bennet more than he thought possible. His mind told him that he was being absurd; he had only known Miss Bennet for a little more than a week, and he was far too jaded and intellectual a man to fall for a maiden in such a short time. And yet, it appeared that he had done exactly that, tumbling into love like a mooncalf rather than a sensible man of almost thirty summers.

He felt his mouth curve into a smile at this thought. At least his wayward heart had chosen a truly remarkable woman. Elizabeth was handsome, most definitely, but she was far more than that – she was intelligent, well read, vigorous, godly, and kind. She had also won the admiration and devotion of Georgiana, and Darcy's little sister did not love easily.

He forced himself to breathe deeply in an attempt to think logically. Miss Bennet was exceptional, but her connections were poor and her dowry nonexistent. He was inclined to believe now that such things did not matter in the least, but he was eager to consult with Richard. Would his marriage to Elizabeth harm Georgiana's chances in society? Would it affect their children? Furthermore, was it possible he had put Elizabeth on a pedestal in the last weeks since they had parted? Would she disappoint him when they met again? Would she seem a different woman amongst her family and in her place of birth? The wisps of the dream nibbled at the edge of his consciousness. His mind yearned for her; his chest ached as he thought of her.

And if she was the woman of his dreams, would he in turn disappoint her? He was not entirely certain that if he offered, she would accept. She was no society miss, to marry only for money and connections, of that he *was* confident.

His breath came more quickly, his heart beating faster as the turning wheels brought him inexorably closer to Netherfield.

/

Elizabeth Bennet looked out the window of the library, her eyes fixed on the graveled road which led to Netherfield. The sun had not yet reached its zenith and she knew that the party from Pemberley would probably not arrive for at least two hours. Nonetheless, she found herself quite unable to read the book in her lap, in spite of the fact that it was an old favorite, Ann Radcliffe's *Romance of the Forest.* Her mind was, instead, distracted by the thought of a well sprung carriage rolling toward Netherfield carrying Mr. Darcy, Miss Darcy, and Mrs. Annesley.

In the weeks since she had returned to Hertfordshire, Elizabeth, usually a sanguine soul, had been seized by occasional bouts of melancholy, all of which centered around Fitzwilliam Darcy of Pemberley. She had always considered herself a practical woman with a gift for understanding the characters of those in her sphere. Well, she had learned better this summer! She had championed George Wickham, who was in fact a dissolute rake. She had first met Mr. Darcy with an arch certainty that the man would be proud and arrogant, only to determine that he was a most admirable gentleman. There were few young men of his birth and connections who, burdened with the oversight of a large estate at a young age, managed to fulfill their duties with diligence and sense. In addition, Darcy was a remarkable older brother to Miss Darcy who was, while wonderful, also unusual.

Elizabeth let out a sigh, and her lips curled into a smile. Mr. Darcy was also exceptionally handsome, with his tall, fine figure, his dark eyes, his perfectly straight nose, his dark hair which curled around his temples. She had dreamed of him only last night, a prosaic dream, to be sure, in which they had argued over the meaning of a plot point of Shakespeare's *Macbeth*, but it was obvious that her own subconscious was spending a good deal of time contemplating Mr. Fitzwilliam Darcy.

She wondered if perhaps she was in love with him. She had no experience at all in love – the closest she had felt before this was toward George Wickham, but she knew now, with the benefit of hindsight, that her attraction had been all for Wickham's handsome countenance, fine figure, and pleasing speech. Behind that façade lay the soul and character of a snake. But with Mr. Darcy it was quite different. She had initially been impressed by his looks and unimpressed by his reputation, but it was in his kindness toward Georgiana, his diligence as master of a great estate, and his powerful intellect, which had initially drawn her to him.

Georgiana had spoken openly of a possible marriage to her brother. But that was Georgiana; she cut through such trifling concerns as connections and money with regal indifference. Mr. Darcy, as master of his house, might well consider the second daughter of a country gentleman not worthy as a possible bride.

Elizabeth felt a tear form in her eye and quickly wiped it away. There was no reason to mourn. She would find out soon enough whether there was hope for such a match.

/

Brighton

Sussex

"Wickham!"

George Wickham cringed inwardly, but he turned a confident stare toward Lieutenant Pratt, who was puffing slightly, obviously having hurried down the street to catch up with him. "Pratt! How are you this fine morning?"

Pratt glowered at him, obviously indifferent to the blue skies and fair winds. "I would be far better if you would pay me. Come now, Wickham; it has been three weeks since you lost thirty pounds to me. It is time to pay up!"

Wickham produced his usual charming smile and said, "It is, without a doubt, and I apologize for the delay. In truth, I am in the same situation as you are; Captain Oakley from Dorset owes me fifty pounds, but I intend to find him today. I assure you that I will pay you as soon as I receive those funds."

Pratt, a tall, well-built young man, puffed his chest up, the better to look more menacing, and said, "See that you do, Wickham."

The man stalked away, and Wickham heaved a soft sigh of relief as he turned to enter the barracks where he was staying. He found himself hurrying a little to attain the relative safety of his small room; Pratt was not the only fellow officer to whom he owed money, and several of them were growing restive with his continued delays.

Wickham walked over to open the top drawer of his wooden bureau and pulled out a small pile of correspondence. A few were bills, which he tossed aside indifferently, and most of the rest were letters from female admirers. The one on the top, from his old paramour, Mrs. Younge, was the most intriguing. He opened and scanned it in search of the paragraph of interest. Ah, there it was:

My cousin Mildred's cook's daughter works at Pemberley as a maid, and the girl informed her mother, who in turn told Mildred, who informed me, that the Darcys plan to journey to Ramsgate at the end of July and will be staying in the same red brick house as usual. I find that rather peculiar given the dramatics of last year's visit to that town, but Georgiana no doubt wishes to drool over the wild birds in the salt marshes.

Wickham wandered over to stare out of the small window, which opened out toward an odiferous stable yard. It was not an attractive view, but at least the window opened to allow the ocean breezes to dissipate some of the heat.

He wrinkled his nose as he pondered his next move. Regrettably, he would need to leave Brighton within the next few days. Gaming debts were not legally enforceable, but it would be impossible for him to coexist with his fellow officers if he did not pay them off. Naturally he would pay them if he could, but the dice and cards had been cruel to him of late. Captain Oakley from Dorset had left the regiment the previous day on leave, and thus Wickham felt safe claiming that the man owed him money, when in fact he did not.

No one owed Wickham money. He owed many officers substantial sums, along with numerous shopkeepers, pub owners, and the like. He would have to flee. The question was, where could he go? As confirmed in her recent letter, Mrs. Younge's boarding house and bedchamber were open to him, but that was a short term solution to his difficulties. He would have to find another source of income from somewhere.

He looked down at the letter in his hand and read it again, his eyes now gleaming rapaciously. It seemed curious that Miss Darcy was returning to Ramsgate, but he would be a fool if he did not take advantage of the situation. Georgiana, with her singular temperament and thirty thousand pound dowry, had slipped between his fingers the previous year. This time, with Darcy in Ramsgate as well, Wickham would need to use a more *firm* approach to successfully carry Miss Darcy away if he hoped to succeed.

Did he dare do so? Abduction was a capital offense. But even if he were caught, there was no true danger. Darcy would be forced to accede to the situation; Wickham would take care that Georgiana's precious reputation was entirely ruined unless Darcy either permitted the marriage, or paid him off well.

It was a risky, without a doubt – Colonel Fitzwilliam, Georgiana's other guardian, had threatened to shoot him down when last they met. But truly, Wickham had no choice. Ever since Darcy had refused to give him the church living, he had been living on borrowed time. He was the godson of the deceased George Darcy, raised as a gentleman, and he was as deserving of good things as his former friend!

Furthermore, Georgiana loved him, or at least she loved him inasmuch as was possible in such an unusual girl. At an early age, Wickham had discovered that he had a gift for making himself agreeable to women, for understanding their dreams and hopes, and their yearning desires. Sometimes this took the form of physical passion, sometimes delicate compliments, and in Georgiana's case, a promise of a farm with limitless birds. He had no intention of wasting his money in such a way, of course, but Georgiana would not understand that. She was a naïve maiden and all too inclined to believe what others told her, especially her old playmate, George Wickham, godson of her father. No, he would spend Georgiana's dowry in whatever way he saw fit, and Darcy would doubtless provide well for his only sister. It was a perfect situation for all of them; he would get his money, and Georgiana would attain a husband. Given her bizarre passions and predilections, Miss Darcy would find it difficult to find a man to wed. Really, he would be doing Georgiana a favor in taking her off the Marriage Mart.

Darcy had undoubtedly done his best to poison Georgiana against him, but Wickham knew the girl well. It would not take long before she was once again under his spell. He would have to act cautiously. He was confident of his own ability to prevail, and he had no intention of accepting failure. He nodded with determination. He would flee Brighton and go to Ramsgate in pursuit of his fortune.

Chapter 24

Netherfield Hall

The footman opened the door to the carriage, and Darcy stepped out with a courteous word of thanks. A moment later, he turned and held out his hand for Georgiana, who leaped lightly down onto the ground, her eyes scanning those assembled to welcome her.

"Elizabeth!" she exclaimed, rushing forward to embrace her friend.

"My dear Georgiana," Elizabeth returned happily, though inwardly she was a trifle dismayed. It was obvious that in the excitement of their reunion, Miss Darcy had forgotten that their friendship was a secret to Miss Bingley, who was standing a few feet away looking rather as if she had just stepped on a cow patty.

"Darcy, Miss Darcy, Mrs. Annesley," Bingley said, "welcome to Netherfield Hall!"

"Thank you, Bingley," Darcy said, stepping up next to Georgiana, who had disengaged from Elizabeth. He too was aware of his sister's minor *faux pas*, but he found himself largely indifferent as he looked upon Elizabeth Bennet's lovely face and exquisite form. She was even more beautiful than he remembered, which was saying a great deal!

"Please do come in," Mrs. Bingley urged. Darcy found a few seconds to look upon his friend's wife and was pleased, for Bingley's sake, to observe that the lady seemed in good health again. It appeared that the worst of her sickness had passed, which was a relief.

"Yes, do come in and refresh yourselves," Caroline Bingley cooed, though her eyes were fixed angrily on Elizabeth. "Jane, my dear, I would not dream of having you climb the stairs in your condition. Mr. Darcy, Miss Darcy, Mrs. Annesley, allow me to show you your rooms."

"I will come too," Elizabeth declared, casting a reassuring look at Jane.

"Thank you both," Darcy said, hiding his disappointment. He wished to speak to Elizabeth, but that would have to wait until a more private time.

"Darcy, I do hope you and Miss Darcy will join us in the drawing room shortly?" Bingley requested.

"Certainly."

/

"Mama, make Kitty give me her pink lace!" Lydia Bennet exclaimed.

"Kitty, give Lydia the pink lace," Mrs. Bennet ordered.

Kitty cast her eyes heavenward and exclaimed, "Why should I when Lydia has plenty of lace of her own? Why should she take mine?"

"Because my new dress requires it," Lydia snapped. "Come now, Kitty, everyone knows that I am more beautiful than you are. It would be a waste for you to use your lace tonight, especially since your dress is old!"

Kitty opened her mouth in protest, only to shut it. A year ago, she would have argued and fussed and perhaps even wept at this juncture, but she had learned wisdom. Mrs. Bennet would always take Lydia's side in an argument like this, and Kitty was required to obey her mother. It was certainly frustrating, but not worth crying over. At least in a few hours, the family would gather with the Darcys and Bingleys at Netherfield Hall, and Kitty, who often felt out of place and unsettled at Longbourn, adored being at Netherfield Hall. She, Elizabeth, and Mary were taking turns living with Jane to assist their married sister during her pregnancy, and Kitty's turn would start a few days from now. There was no reason to be overly distressed about the lace. No one at Netherfield would likely even notice Lydia's new dress except, perhaps, Caroline Bingley. That lady always made a point of denigrating the Bennets' dresses and would probably make subtly disparaging remarks about Lydia's gown, which was in fact quite attractive.

"Very well," Kitty said calmly, turning back to her sketch book. Her last lesson with her art master had focused on how to draw someone's eyes. Her mother and Lydia both had beautiful eyes; her mother's were, like Jane's, clear blue, and Lydia's were so dark as to be almost black.

"Mama?" she asked.

"Yes, Kitty?" Mrs. Bennet returned, her brow lowering suspiciously. She hated it when her children quarreled over ribbons and hoped that Kitty was not about to bring that up again.

"Would you be willing to sit for me so that I can practice drawing your eyes? They are such a glorious blue."

Mrs. Bennet's expression shifted from ominous to gratified. "Why of course, Kitty, I would be delighted!"

"I have beautiful eyes too!" Lydia insisted.

"Yes, but you are so very active that I think it would be more difficult for you to sit still for as long as Mama," Kitty said diplomatically.

Lydia tossed her head and boasted, "That is true enough. All the officers used to say that I was the most energetic of all the ladies here in Meryton. Oh, how I miss them all, especially Mr. Wickham!"

Kitty pulled out a piece of fresh paper and turned toward her mother, her pencil at the ready. In truth, she was now far more interested in art than officers, but there was no reason to say such a thing to Lydia. Her youngest sister was, regrettably, not very wise and cared more about looks than fortune or character. Kitty, observing the adoration between her eldest sister and Mr. Bingley, wished for a similar marriage in time.

/

"Checkmate," Mary said, moving her bishop two squares.

Mr. Bennet blinked, leaned forward, considered, frowned, and then grinned. "You are entirely correct. What a clever series of moves, my dear!"

"Thank you, Father," Mary replied, blushing with pleasure. A year previously, she had not even known how to play the game, nor had she considered it important to learn, since chess was neither spiritual nor considered a useful accomplishment for a lady. After Jane's marriage, Elizabeth had asked Mary to learn how to play as a way to honor their father, since Elizabeth suspected, correctly, that she would often be gone from Longbourn. Mary had discovered that she had a remarkable ability to visualize the way a match would play out, and in a few short months of study and practice had matured from rank beginner to skilled journeyman.

"Yes, very clever," Mr. Bennet repeated, staring down at the board. He was both astonished and impressed at his third daughter's play. Even Elizabeth, who enjoyed the game, rarely beat her father.

"Do you have time for another game, Mary?" he asked hopefully.

"Of course, Father."

/

Netherfield

"Mrs. Annesley, your room is here, and Georgiana, my dear, I have set aside the green room for you. I hope it is…"

"You ought not to call me Georgiana," Miss Darcy interrupted, sounding more bewildered than angry. "We have not given one another permission to call each other by our first names."

Caroline Bingley found herself flushing uncomfortably at these words. It was true that no such permission had been given, but…

"Oh, as you wish, Miss Darcy, of course," she said with nervous cheer. "I merely thought that since you and Elizabeth are on such close terms, you would be on equally informal terms with me, as we have known one another far longer."

Georgiana cast a confused look at Elizabeth, who promptly stepped into the breach. "Georgiana and I discovered a mutual interest in domestic fowl while we were in Derbyshire, which resulted in our friendship blossoming with surprising haste. My friend, I was wondering if you would care to look over Jane's poultry yard? Something keeps infiltrating the coop at night and killing the layers, and the poultry maids are quite at their wits' end!"

"Oh yes, I would be delighted!" Georgiana exclaimed, hurrying over to the door of her bedchamber. "I will, erm, refresh myself and be available in ten minutes!"

"The poultry yard is rather muddy," Elizabeth warned, "so I recommend you wear boots!"

"You should change out of your traveling clothes as well, Miss Darcy," Mrs. Annesley suggested. "You might want to wear your brown dress. I am certain the servants' carriage is here by now, and I will arrange for Selina to assist you in changing."

"Thank you, Mrs. Annesley," Georgiana said. "Elizabeth, I will see you in fifteen minutes, perhaps?"

"I am not in any great hurry; I will be waiting on the chair in the alcove down there, reading *The Romance of the Forest* again, and you can find me when you are ready."

Georgiana nodded and disappeared into her room, pushing the door closed behind her. Mrs. Annesley nodded toward Elizabeth and Caroline and also retreated to her room, leaving the two sisters by marriage alone.

"I had no idea that you were so interested in poultry," Caroline said unpleasantly.

"I must go find my book, which I left in the drawing room," Elizabeth said, turning and beginning to walk toward the stairs. "Regarding poultry, my friend Charlotte is very fond of her hens, which inspired my interest. They are quite fascinating creatures, as are ducks and geese."

"I confess to finding livestock of any sort tedious," her companion said loftily. "Certainly, I find it astonishing that a member of the Darcy family could possibly find any interest in such things, but then Miss Darcy is the soul of tact. I do hope you will not force her to stay out of doors for too long, Elizabeth."

Elizabeth's lips thinned, but she remained silent until the two ladies had entered the drawing room, where Bingley, Hurst, and Darcy were standing near the large picture window with brandies in hand. Upon observing the ladies, all three gentlemen bowed, and Elizabeth said archly, "Miss Bingley and I were discussing livestock, specifically poultry. Do be truthful, do you not find geese, ducks, and hens to be thoroughly fascinating?"

Darcy blinked, but he was a quick-witted man. "I am far fonder of horses and dogs," he said, "but my sister is undeniably interested in poultry."

"I suppose that birds are more practical," Bingley admitted, "but I am like you, Darcy; I can spend countless hours and a great deal of money on horses, but birds? Their eggs are useful, but they seem to be very foolish creatures."

"That was my meaning exactly," Caroline Bingley said, advancing upon Mr. Darcy and smiling up at him. "Horses are so marvelous, are they not? Indeed, I know you intend to purchase a new pair of horses at Tattersall's soon, Charles, and I do hope you will ask Mr. Darcy's advice before you do so!"

"Oh, Bingley is entirely capable of picking out his own horses," Darcy said absently. His own eyes were fixed on Miss Elizabeth Bennet, who had backed away from the group, picked up a book from a small wooden table, and after bestowing a saucy smile on him, retreated out of the room. He suppressed a groan. He wished to spend time with her, of course, but given Caroline Bingley's hovering, he would have to wait. He turned back toward Bingley and his relations, and winced at the sight of Caroline's jealous expression. Was his interest in Miss Bennet obvious, and if so, would Miss Bingley be even more exasperating than usual?

Bingley, oblivious to his friend's concerns, said, "Thank you, Darcy. Speaking of that, one of my best mares birthed a colt a few days ago, and I hope you will give me your opinion on him."

"I would be honored," Darcy answered and then added eagerly, "Perhaps we might have time now to go to the stables? I would enjoy a walk after our time in the carriage."

"Of course! Caroline, Hurst, I hope you will excuse us?"

"I must see how Louisa is feeling," Hurst said, setting down his tumbler.

"And I will check with the cook to discuss dinner," Caroline declared crisply. "I would not wish for you to find Netherfield's kitchens wanting in any way, Mr. Darcy!"

"I believe that Jane already spoke to Laurent on the subject," Bingley said with a frown.

"Oh, of course!" his sister responded hastily. "I meant no disrespect toward Jane. It is merely that she is resting, and if Laurent has any questions, I would be happy to assist."

She waited with bated breath as Bingley peered at her intently. Weeks had passed since Charles had taken her to task regarding her treatment of Jane and Elizabeth, and he had still not relaxed his irritating oversight. She had not lost any part of her allowance in a full eight days, but that was only because she had been *very* careful about what she said. As for her thoughts – well, thankfully, her brother could not listen to her very mind.

"Thank you, Caroline," Bingley finally said. "Shall we, Darcy?"

/

"Do you like Kent?" Elizabeth asked.

Georgiana, who was striding briskly toward the poultry house arm in arm with her friend, cogitated for a moment before saying, "I prefer the more hilly landscapes of Pemberley, but from an agricultural point of view, the flat fields are advantageous."

"That is true enough," Elizabeth agreed. A moment passed and then she continued, "Georgiana?"

"Yes, Elizabeth?"

"My family will be coming to Netherfield for dinner tonight. I know you appreciate when I speak plainly, so I will say that I doubt you will enjoy spending time with my mother and youngest sister."

Georgiana tightened her grip on Elizabeth's arm and asked, "Why not?"

Elizabeth patted her friend's hand reassuringly as the two girls turned a corner to walk along the back of the stables. "My mother and Lydia are both garrulous, and my mother is regrettably often vulgar."

"Unrefined and lacking sophistication and good taste?" Georgiana recited.

"Precisely," her friend said ruefully.

"Is Mrs. Bennet like me?"

"Like you? No, not at all! Why do you ask?"

Georgiana's face drooped sadly, and she said, "I know that I am sometimes vulgar as well, because I do not understand the rules of society."

"Oh, my dear!" Elizabeth exclaimed. "No, no, you are not like my mother at all. Now mind you, I love her very much, but my mother was born the daughter of a solicitor and was not educated for her role as mistress of a gentleman's estate. She speaks of money and the beauty of her daughters in a very forward way. It puts new acquaintances off, though that is not her intention."

"In that case, perhaps I will like her well enough," Georgiana declared. "I too say things with good intentions, only to insult people inadvertently."

Elizabeth opened her mouth, and then shut it again. She did not think that her mother or sisters were quite the same as Georgiana; the latter had a singular personality, whereas Mrs. Bennet and Lydia were poorly trained and, sadly, rather selfish. Nonetheless…

"You are correct!" she said in wonder. "I mean, you may not like her, but it is true that my mother genuinely does not know better and given that she was never taught properly, it is not her fault. I fear I have grown rather impatient with her and my two youngest sisters these last years, which is unkind of me. In any case, I wished to say that if you find them overly talkative, you can wink at me, and I will know that you would appreciate my assistance in escaping them."

"Very well," Georgiana said after a long moment of consideration. "Thank you. What about your next younger sister?"

"Mary? She plays the pianoforte, though not as well as you do. You are remarkable. All the same, she is far more diligent about practicing than I am. She is…"

Elizabeth trailed off and said carefully, "My mother was a great beauty in her youth, and all of us but Mary inherited that beauty. It has been a hard thing for my dear sister. Her physical form has often been compared to the rest of us and found wanting."

"That is sad," Georgiana stated. "I know I am not as beautiful as you are, but my brother has never said such a thing about me."

Elizabeth glanced over uneasily and said, "You are lovely, Georgiana."

"I am pretty, not lovely," Georgiana answered precisely. "I do not worry about my face and figure, Elizabeth – I did nothing to earn my looks, nor did you. My brother and friends love me the way I am, so why should I long to be as beautiful as you and Mrs. Bingley?"

Not for the first time, Elizabeth was struck with wonder. Miss Darcy's remarkable view of the world enabled the young woman to see a reality that was often lost in the confusion of societal expectations.

"You are right, of course," Elizabeth agreed, stopping near the poultry yard. "You are absolutely right."

Chapter 25

Darcy leaned against the wooden fence and took off his hat. It was a hot summer day, and he was thankful to stand under a spreading elm tree with a brisk breeze rustling his dark hair.

"He looks very well, Bingley," Darcy commented, peering into the small pasture beyond the fence. A bay colt on exquisitely slender legs stared back with large eyes, with his chestnut mother hovering over him. The mare, in turn, eyed Darcy uneasily, obviously concerned about this unknown man so close to her baby.

"Yes, he has excellent proportions, and I am hopeful that he will be a fine stallion in time," Bingley said with satisfaction. A moment later, he looked over to his friend, only to observe that the gentleman's eyes were no longer fixed on the horses, but on the two ladies marching briskly toward the poultry yard. He did not know why Miss Darcy and Elizabeth were wandering around outside, but he was more confused by his friend's peculiar expression.

Miss Darcy and Elizabeth disappeared around the corner of the henhouse, and Darcy turned back to his friend. "I am sorry, Bingley. What did you say?"

"I said that I hope the colt will be a fine stallion in time," Bingley repeated, regarding Darcy thoughtfully. "Is something wrong, Darcy? You were staring at Miss Bennet and your sister rather oddly."

"Wrong?" Darcy asked, looking uncomfortable. "No, of course not. Nothing is wrong."

Bingley raised his brows, and a slow smile formed on his lips. "Is it possible, my friend, that you have some interest in my sister-in-law?"

Darcy promptly flushed and looked away, which provoked a pleased grin from his friend. "It seems that you do! I promise I will not plague you with questions, but I would be remiss if I did not say that Elizabeth is a truly excellent young woman, and I believe you would suit one another well. She is, frankly, too quick for me; there are times when she and Mr. Bennet speak of some complicated topic, and I find myself completely lost."

"I remember you telling me that Mr. Bennet is a scholar," Darcy mused. "What of Elizabeth's mother?"

He knew, of course, that Miss Bingley thought Mrs. Bennet a vulgar woman, but Caroline Bingley's opinions could not be trusted in the least.

Bingley leaned against the wooden fence and sighed, "My mother by marriage is not an intellectual in the least. Indeed, I am not sharing any secrets when I say that my wife's parents are not well suited to one another. I understand that Mrs. Bennet was a great beauty in her youth, very much like my Jane, but she is a silly woman, and the entail has made her both nervous and shrill. Jane and Elizabeth assure me that with my marriage to Jane, she has settled somewhat, as she no longer fears being thrown into the hedgerows when Mr. Bennet dies. However, she is still not compatible with my bride's eccentric father."

"I believe Mrs. Bennet has near relations in trade?" Darcy asked, trying to sound casual.

His friend swung to face him directly, the man's usually cheerful face now unwontedly stern. "She does, indeed; her father was a solicitor, and her only brother is in trade in London. But then, my father was a business man also, Darcy. You have never seemed to mind."

Darcy looked away and ran a hand through his dark hair, causing it to ruffle up in a most unaccustomed fashion. "No, no, I do not mind, of course. We have been friends for many years, and I do not regret your antecedents in the least. Quite the contrary – you are a most amiable and sympathetic companion, and I can only regret when our separation is too long.

"I do confess to an internal struggle, though, when it comes to Miss Bennet. On the one hand, I am full of admiration for the lady, as she is truly remarkable. Not only is she handsome enough to tempt me, but her wit and character are like no other woman I have met. And yet, I have my sister to launch into society, and Georgiana would benefit if I married a woman with extensive connections to the very height of society, which Miss Bennet does not have."

Bingley wrinkled his brow as he considered his friend's startling confession; it was obvious that Darcy had been considering Elizabeth for some time now. "Could not your aunt assist with Miss Darcy's introduction to Society? Not Lady Catherine de Bourgh, of course, who is reputed to be rather difficult, but Lady Matlock?"

Darcy rubbed his head even more such that his hair stood up nearly straight. "My uncle has long hinted that he wishes me to marry either my cousin Anne, or failing that, into the nobility, and my aunt is a rather proud lady herself. Neither will be pleased if I wed the second daughter of a country gentleman."

"I see," Bingley said. "Well, in that case I suppose you need to decide whether you should set aside your own happiness for the possible pleasures of societal success for Miss Darcy. I would not wish to do so, of course, but you are not me. I would add, however, that it seems Elizabeth and Miss Darcy are on excellent terms, which is an additional point in my sister-in-law's favor."

Darcy's face lit up at these words. "Indeed, they are! Georgiana has not formed many strong friendships in her life, but she quite adores Miss Bennet."

"I would suggest that a sympathetic sister-in-law is far more beneficial than a fashionable one, but again, you must do as you think best."

Darcy stared at his friend, then turned to look at the poultry house. He smiled as Georgiana, with Miss Bennet close behind her, wandered into sight. Georgiana was staring up at the roof of the chicken coop and saying something, though Darcy could not quite make out the words, while Elizabeth listened with obvious interest. "You are correct, Bingley, that is an additional point greatly in Miss Bennet's favor."

/

Elizabeth had proposed a trip to the poultry yard so that she and Georgiana could enjoy a comfortable chat away from Caroline's jealous ears, but once again, she had forgotten Miss Darcy's unique view of the world. Georgiana had no time for casual conversation when chickens were in danger, and the girl was now wandering around the poultry yard, peering up, peering down, and tilting her head on occasion, obviously deep in thought. Elizabeth thought it unlikely that her friend would succeed where experienced poultry maids had not, but there was no harm in it so long as Georgiana was not too cast down when she failed.

"I see how it is being done," Georgiana said suddenly, her gaze fixed on a tree branch of a tall oak tree near the poultry house.

"What do you mean?" Elizabeth asked in confusion, staring at the same branch. It was a large one and stretched across the roof of the coop, but it was at least three feet above it. Surely...

"The predators are entering the chicken coop at night by climbing that tree there, walking along the long branch, dropping onto the coop roof, then climbing in through that small hole under the roof there. The poor hens have no chance at all."

Elizabeth had been following her friend's pointing finger in surprise, not unmixed with skepticism, but when her eyes focused on the supposed hole, she saw something.

"Is that brown fur?" she demanded, squinting and taking a few steps closer.

"I think so," Georgiana said. "If we had access to a ladder, someone could go up and check to be certain."

"I can fetch a ladder from the stable!" an enthusiastic stable boy piped up. He, along with two goggling poultry maids, had been watching Miss Darcy's investigation with great interest.

"Go on," Georgiana ordered, continuing to wander to and fro, her forehead creased with thought.

Elizabeth, both interested and amused, continued watching her friend until the sounds of boots caused her to turn.

"Mr. Darcy, Charles!" she exclaimed, beaming at both the gentlemen. "Georgiana thinks she has determined how the predators are getting into the henhouse."

Darcy smiled back at her and hoped that his hair, now safely confined under his hat, was not in too much disarray. "I am not surprised," he said with a warm look at Georgiana. "My sister is remarkably adept at discovering how predators are entering enclosed spaces."

The stable boy appeared at this juncture with a short ladder, which he happily pushed up against one wall of the chicken coop. A minute later, he had climbed nimbly to the top, reached over, grasped a clump of brown fur, and brought it down for his master's consideration.

"Is that the fur of a fox?" Bingley asked curiously.

"Not a fox, a weasel, or two weasels, or three," Georgiana corrected. "Foxes are strong jumpers, but they do not climb particularly well. Weasels are excellent climbers, and their fur is brown as opposed to red. It appears the animal had to push its way through the hole and left some fur behind. I advise that you have someone close that hole up immediately, Mr. Bingley, before another poor hen dies."

Bingley stared at her in amazement and said, "Of course, Miss Darcy, of course! I am both impressed and grateful, and Jane will be delighted that her poultry are safe again. How did you determine the access point so rapidly?"

Georgiana ducked her head shyly and said, "I am not quite certain, Mr. Bingley. I seem to be able to imagine the thought processes of animals at times, which I am certain sounds most peculiar."

"On the contrary, it is marvelous," Elizabeth assured her. "It is a most useful gift, and Charles is correct, Jane will be most relieved!"

"Darcy!" a voice suddenly called out from behind them, and the foursome turned as a red coated gentleman on a trotting white horse appeared on the path leading to the stables.

"Richard!?" Darcy and Georgiana exclaimed together.

Colonel Richard Fitzwilliam pulled his horse to a halt, handed the reins to a stable boy, and said, "I need to talk to you, Darcy, at once!"

"Is someone ill?" Georgiana asked fearfully, grasping Elizabeth's arm and clinging to it.

The colonel's eyes opened wide at the sight of his shy cousin looking to an unknown lady for comfort but said hastily, "No. No one is ill! It is merely that…"

Here he glanced around and glowered at the nearby servants, who all promptly retreated in pursuit of their own duties.

"It is merely that Lady Catherine is causing trouble," he said quietly, which provoked a deep sigh from Darcy, who retorted, "Of course she is!"

/

"It is my fault," Colonel Fitzwilliam said gloomily, pacing up and down Bingley's office. He and Darcy had requested some privacy for the ensuing conversation, and Georgiana had begged to come along, so anxious was she to learn the worst about her imperious and intrusive aunt.

"What is your fault?" Darcy demanded from his seat on a settee near the cold fireplace. Georgiana was positioned next to him, clinging to his arm.

"It is my fault that Lady Catherine learned of our specific plans regarding the journey to Ramsgate," Richard explained, turning toward his cousins. "I wrote you that she was on the warpath …"

"You did," Darcy agreed, "not that I care particularly so long as I do not have to interact with her directly."

"The problem is that you may be forced to do exactly that. I have been staying at Matlock House while stationed in London and was fool enough to leave one of your letters in a sitting room. My father read it and took it upon himself to inform Lady Catherine of your plans to stay here for a few days, journey to London for a short stay, and then travel directly on to Ramsgate."

"Is that not incredibly rude?" Georgiana asked, staring at her brother in bewilderment. "I thought it impolite to read another person's mail without permission."

"It is very discourteous," Darcy said, placing a long arm around his sister's shoulders. "I fear that your uncle Matlock, as master of his house, has a domineering streak and probably considers it his right to read the correspondence of all those dwelling in his house."

"Very much like Lady Catherine," Richard concurred, wrinkling his nose with distaste. "I do not remember your mother, Lady Anne, all that well, but she was a charming and delightful lady. I fear both her siblings are far more dictatorial and inclined to rule, or attempt to rule, all those in their orbit."

"Why would Lord Matlock wish to have Lady Catherine bother us?" Georgiana asked timidly.

"Probably because he wishes Darcy to marry Cousin Anne," Richard said grimly. "He has spoken on the topic more than once of late. He is eager for Anne to marry one of her cousins so that Rosings stays within the family."

"If that is all he cares about, he ought to encourage *you* to marry Anne, not me," Darcy returned in frustration.

"Ah, my father would be very pleased if I married the heiress of Rosings," Richard said, "but Lady Catherine would not. Her precious daughter to marry a mere second son? She would consider that a degradation."

"It seems very stupid to me," Georgiana said plainly. "Fitzwilliam, you do not wish to marry Cousin Anne, do you?"

"I do not," Darcy said, and his mind quickly shifted to a lively face with dancing eyes, framed by glorious chestnut curls.

"Does Anne wish to marry you?" Georgiana asked.

"No, I am confident that she does not," Darcy said.

"Then Lady Catherine is being ridiculous!" the girl protested. "She cannot force even one of you to marry, much less both of you!"

"She *is* ridiculous," Darcy said heavily, and stalked over to stare gloomily out the window. "Nonetheless, our aunt does not see it that way. I can only hope that Lady Catherine does not decide to come to Netherfield to harass me on the subject. It would be uncomfortable for the Bingleys."

"Again, I am sorry," Richard said remorsefully.

"Would it not be simpler to change our plans so that our aunt cannot find us?" Georgiana asked. "We could leave tomorrow directly for Ramsgate, avoiding London entirely."

The two gentlemen stared at her, then at each other, and Darcy said, "That is an excellent idea."

"So long as Elizabeth is able to leave so quickly," Georgiana said. "I do not want to go to Ramsgate without her."

"Of course," Darcy agreed fervently, which provoked a curious look from his cousin. He needed to speak to Richard about Miss Bennet, soon, but not in front of Georgiana. His sister would not understand the complexities of the lady's family situation.

"I do feel sorry for Anne," Georgiana commented suddenly. "It must be very hard to live under such a rude and despotic mother."

"It is hard," Darcy agreed, "but unhappily there is not anything we can do about it, since every time I so much as speak to Anne, Lady Catherine speaks of calling the banns."

"*You* cannot do anything about it," Richard said, his forehead creased in thought, "but perhaps I can."

Darcy quirked an inquiring eyebrow at this, but Georgiana said with urgency, "We must ask Elizabeth if she can come tomorrow."

Chapter 26

"Oh, my dear Jane, how well you look!" Mrs. Bennet exclaimed as she stepped into the vestibule of Netherfield, her husband and younger daughters in her wake. "Mr. Bingley, is your wife not particularly beautiful?"

"She is always beautiful, Mrs. Bennet," Bingley answered with an easy smile. "I hope you and the rest of the family are well today?"

"We are very well!" Mrs. Bennet fluted and then turned toward Darcy, Georgiana, and Richard, who were standing a few feet away. "Jane, will you not introduce us to your guests?"

"Miss Darcy, Mr. Darcy, Colonel Fitzwilliam," Jane said, "may I please introduce you to my mother, Mrs. Bennet, my sisters, Miss Mary, Miss Kitty, and Miss Lydia, and my father, Mr. Bennet. Mama, Papa, Sisters, Miss Darcy, Mr. Darcy, and Colonel Fitzwilliam."

The various ladies and gentlemen curtsied and bowed as appropriate, and Mrs. Bennet, her eyes bright with hopeful curiosity, said, "I have heard much of Mr. and Miss Darcy, but I do not believe my daughters have mentioned you at all, Colonel Fitzwilliam. Are you a member of the militia?"

"The Regulars, Madam," Colonel Fitzwilliam said with a bow, and Lydia, who had been twitching impatiently throughout the introductions, immediately cried out, "The Regulars, Colonel? How wonderful! We had a militia regiment here in Meryton all last winter, and we had such wonderful times with the officers. Have you ever been to Brighton? The regiment moved there recently, which was terribly disappointing!"

The colonel glanced at Mrs. Bingley, and observing the discomfort on her face, said quickly, "I *have* been to Brighton, Miss Lydia, though only for a few weeks before my regiment was shipped to the Continent."

"We are most grateful to you for your service to the Crown," Mary said seriously.

Bingley interjected, "Shall we all go into the drawing room? Dinner will be ready shortly."

/

"Tomorrow?" Mr. Bennet repeated, lowering himself onto a divan in the corner of the drawing room. "I understood Mr. and Miss Darcy would be staying here a few days before driving on to London with you."

"Yes, Father," Elizabeth agreed, taking a seat next to him, "but unfortunately, Lady Catherine de Bourgh, who is aunt to the Darcys and Colonel Fitzwilliam, learned of our plans and is most displeased that I have been invited to Ramsgate. There is a good chance that she will shortly descend either on the Darcys' London House, or here at Netherfield. Jane does not need a family argument in her drawing room, and Mr. Darcy does not wish for me to be exposed to Lady Catherine's vituperation."

Bennet's usual sardonic expression shifted to one of genuine anger. "Was Lady Catherine insulting to you when you were visiting Charlotte Collins in Kent, Lizzy? You did not tell me that."

"No, not at all," his daughter assured him. "She was haughty, demanding, and domineering, but she did not single me out for any particular abuse, nor am I in the least afraid of her. But according to Mr. Darcy, Lady Catherine has taken exception to my being invited to accompany Georgiana to Ramsgate. She thinks that I might put on airs and become overly proud, which is a clear case of the pot calling the kettle black. In any case, I do not wish for Jane, in her delicate condition, to be present for a shouting match here at Netherfield."

Bennet sighed and said, "Yes, Jane has more sensibility and would not enjoy such a quarrel in the least. Indeed, ever since we first met Mr. Collins, I have known that his patroness was a fool, but it seems she is even more foolish than I imagined. Yes, of course you can go tomorrow, my dear. I will miss you, but Mary and Kitty have grown far more sensible of late. Mary even beat me at chess this morning, which was both remarkable and enjoyable!"

"She beats me most of the time now," Elizabeth admitted. "Mary has a wonderful ability to think through possible future moves, which I find astonishing."

"It is both surprising and satisfying," Bennet said as he considered his third daughter, whom he had long disdained for her addiction to Fordyce's sermons and moral treatises. The last few months, Mary had displayed additional talents which had flowered under instruction and encouragement. For all his pride in his own intellect, it was clear that where his family was concerned, he had been both lazy and foolish.

/

"Of course, London is very quiet in summer compared to during the Season," Caroline Bingley declared, "but the little Theater is open, and there will be some good families in town. I do hope that my friend, Miss Amelia Fawnthorpe, and I will have the opportunity to call on you in London next week, Miss Darcy."

Georgiana cast a confused look at her brother, who came to the rescue, "Regrettably, Miss Bingley, our plans changed only today due to some family business. While we had intended to spend a few days in London before proceeding on to Ramsgate, we now will leave tomorrow directly for the seaside."

Caroline's mouth gaped open with astonishment at these words, and Louisa, eager to head off any incivility, said, "I am certain you will have a delightful time there. I have heard that the beach is captivating."

"The birds are even more so," Georgiana stated, shifting a little closer to her brother on the couch. "There are such lovely warblers, plovers, falcons, loons, and nightingales on the beaches and in the nearby marshes, though it is rather late in the year for us to hear nightingalcs."

"Dinner is served," Jane said to the assemblage, and all rose to enter the dining room.

/

"Why did you not tell me that the Darcys are going to Ramsgate?" Caroline hissed to her brother. The meal was underway and conversation flourished, which made it easy for her to speak quietly so that only Charles could hear her.

Charles, who was congratulating himself for his forethought in having his irritating sister placed at his left, murmured back, "Their plans are of no concern to you; you have no right at all to be informed of Darcy's travels."

"You know perfectly well that I accepted Miss Amelia's invitation to London in the hopes that I would see more of the Darcys!" Caroline seethed, tapping her soup spoon on her empty bowl in agitation.

"That was a mistake on your part," Bingley returned blandly. "Now, dear sister, do calm yourself. Would you care for a drink of madeira?"

"I want claret," Caroline said sullenly.

"As you wish. Jane, what would you like?"

"May I please have lemonade?"

Charles bestowed a loving smile on his wife. She was feeling much better these days, but still found most alcoholic beverages entirely unpalatable. "As you wish, my love."

/

"My music master wishes for me to practice simpler scores for now while I learn to imbue my playing with more character," Mary explained, her eyes downcast. "I know that you are a truly excellent player, Miss Darcy, and would no doubt laugh at my dabbling on the pianoforte."

"I would never laugh at someone in such a way," Georgiana said seriously. "It is true that I am an excellent performer on the pianoforte, but I perform poorly on the harp. No one is good at everything."

"That is true enough," Mary said in obvious relief. "Please do tell me, which composer do you like the best?"

/

"I am thankful that your father is willing to allow you to leave on such short notice, Miss Bennet," Darcy said.

"I am too," Elizabeth replied, putting a bite of fish into her mouth. When she had chewed and swallowed, she said, "I would have been most disappointed to miss out on this trip to the sea with Georgiana. She has grown to be a very dear friend."

"I am aware," Darcy said and then added hesitantly, "I hope it is not too bold to say that we both count you a friend, Miss Bennet."

Elizabeth, startled by his words, blushed pink and found her eyes lowering in her confusion. After a long moment, she managed to look into the gentleman's concerned face and said, "Indeed, I am honored to be counted a friend of both you and your sister."

"I expect that during our time at Ramsgate, we will be able to spend more time together," Darcy said, smiling openly now.

"I am certain we will," Elizabeth returned, struggling to regain her composure. "How far is it to Ramsgate?"

"It is about one hundred miles from here, and during our journey, we will be obliged to stop for the night, but there is an excellent inn in Kent which caters to the gentry."

"Yes, but are there any birds at the inn in question?" Elizabeth inquired archly.

Darcy laughed. "I am not certain that there are, but the hostelry is called The Eagle's Nest, which will, I hope, propitiate Georgiana."

"I do not think I would care to live in a tent," Lydia declared, wrinkling her nose. "Is it not rather small?"

"Oh yes, Miss Lydia," Colonel Fitzwilliam concurred. "It is small, and in spite of the noble efforts of my batman, often dirty due to men coming in and out."

"How do you manage to dine in such conditions?" Kitty asked, her blue eyes large in her heart shaped face.

"Well, we rarely enjoyed such wonderful food as this, Miss Kitty, though we used to eat paella, which was a sort of stew made of this and that. The commissary provided for our basic needs, but some of the officers hunted as well. I was stationed outside the city of Badajoz earlier this year, and the hares ran thickly in the warrens. Many an officer's pot was filled with rabbits during the siege."

"It sounds marvelously exciting," Lydia cooed. "I was hoping to go to Brighton this summer with the militia regiment, but my father refused. It must be heaven there, with rows upon rows of tents, all filled with dashing officers in their red coats."

Colonel Fitzwilliam looked down on the girl's pretty, vacuous face and sighed inwardly. He still woke with nightmares of the storming of Badajoz, when nearly five thousand Allied soldiers were killed or wounded during the taking of the city. He himself had taken a ball in his side. Thankfully it had not lodged deeply, and the surgeons removed it with relative ease. However, it still ached at night sometimes.

But naturally Miss Lydia knew nothing of the fighting in the muddy breaches, of the frantic whinnying of injured horses, of the men falling and dying as their companions climbed over them in an effort to take the town. It had been a victory, but an incredibly costly one, and the day after the city was taken, the Earl of Wellington had cried openly at the sight of the mounds of dead.

And yet it was for pretty, ignorant girls like Lydia Bennet that he and his fellow men suffered and died, so that they could live in an England independent of the Corsican tyrant and free to remain naïve to such horrors.

"I suppose it was really quite dreadful," Kitty Bennet said solemnly from his left, and Richard turned to regard the girl gazing at him sympathetically.

"It was, rather," he admitted, and shook his head a little. A glance to his right showed that Lydia was now speaking with her father, so he felt free to focus his attention on his more agreeable partner. "Please do tell me about yourself, Miss Kitty. Are you fond of music?"

"I enjoy listening to music, but am not a performer like Elizabeth and Mary. I like to draw and paint," Kitty said. "I think I would enjoy sculpture as well, but that is not really practical at the moment."

"Have you had the opportunity to visit the British Museum? They have some remarkable artifacts from Egypt. Oh, and the Elgin Marbles in Piccadilly are also incredible."

"I have not, though I would enjoy seeing the Marbles very much," Kitty said, her face growing animated.

Richard responded cheerfully, and the conversation proceeded smoothly through the next course.

In the midst of good food and pleasant exchanges, Colonel Fitzwilliam found himself glancing frequently at Darcy, who was seated between Mrs. Hurst and Miss Bennet. His cousin was far too much a gentleman to entirely ignore Mrs. Hurst, but it was obvious from Darcy's cheerful countenance that he was far more interested in Miss Bennet. Richard had never seen Darcy so comfortable in the presence of a young lady outside of his own family. It was interesting. It was very, very interesting.

Chapter 27

"Darcy, do you not mind stopping at Longbourn tomorrow morning to collect Elizabeth?" Bingley asked his friend.

Darcy, whose eyes were naturally enough fixed on Elizabeth's face, promptly said, "That will be no problem at all. Miss Bennet, would it be possible for you to be ready to begin our journey by ten o'clock, or is that too early?"

"No, that is no difficulty at all," Elizabeth said, smiling warmly up into the gentleman's face. "I am always an early riser. Indeed, if it would be more convenient, I could probably come over by carriage an hour earlier so you do not need to stop at Longbourn."

"That is hardly necessary," Darcy protested, "and I would not care for you to go to such extra effort."

"Thank you, sir," Elizabeth said gratefully. "Jane, Charles, I will see you when we return in a few weeks. Caroline, I hope you have a *lovely* time in London. Jane, do give my regards to Louisa and Mr. Hurst."

"Come along, Lizzy!" Lydia exclaimed through the open front door. "Father wishes to return home before it is too dark."

Elizabeth obediently rushed out the front door of Netherfield accompanied by cries of farewell from Jane and Charles Bingley. Darcy watched until the door closed behind the object of his admiration and turned toward the stairwell, only to stop at the sight of Caroline Bingley, whose brown eyes were a mixture of shock and fury.

"What is this all about?" she gasped, quite heedless of normal etiquette. "You cannot … surely Elizabeth is not…"

"She is joining us for our trip to Ramsgate," Darcy said simply and turned toward his host. "Bingley, I hope you do not mind if I follow Georgiana and Colonel Fitzwilliam upstairs? We will need to make an early start tomorrow morning."

"Certainly," Charles said, glowering at Caroline menacingly. He waited until Darcy had disappeared upstairs before turning to his unwed sister. "Caroline, my study. Now."

/

"How could you not tell me that the Darcys are going to Ramsgate and that Elizabeth with them?" Caroline snarled as soon as the office door closed behind her brother. "Did you want me to look like a complete fool?"

Charles regarded his sister with exasperation. "How do you feel about Elizabeth accompanying the Darcys to the seaside, Caroline?"

"Feel about it? Feel about it?" his sister retorted, her angry hands pulling at her carefully coiffed hair. "I am irate. No, I am furious! And …. and I am completely and utterly bewildered. Elizabeth Bennet, of all people! Why on earth would Mr. Darcy choose to bring *her* over *me*. She is impertinent and not even very pretty, and …"

"Ten pounds," Charles interrupted, reaching into his desk to pull out a ledger. "Do go on, Sister. I have plenty of space in my ledger for your additional insults towards our mutual sister-in-law."

Caroline stared at her brother for an outraged minute and then, to the astonishment of both of them, burst into noisy tears. Charles watched in silence and, when the storm showed no signs of abating, walked over to push her gently into a nearby chair. He pulled out his handkerchief, fortunately clean, and handed it to her. She took it and held it to her face, her pent up misery exhibiting itself in wrenching sobs, while her brother patted her clumsily on the shoulder.

Bingley found his younger sister thoroughly infuriating much of the time, but he also pitied her. For reasons he had never quite understood, his sister had decided at an early age that she was destined for the first circles of society, in spite of her position as the daughter of a tradesmen. When she had met Darcy some seven years previously, Caroline had resolved that the master of Pemberley was her ticket to her societal dreams and had set her sights on him with the rapacious enthusiasm of a boa constrictor for a hapless rat. Unfortunately, she had misread Darcy quite profoundly, and in spite of various warnings, had refused to give up.

"Mr. Darcy is never going to marry me, is he?" Caroline sobbed, sitting up and mopping her face.

"No, he is not," Bingley said gently. "It is no particular reflection on you, Caroline. He merely wishes for a different bride."

"Like Elizabeth Bennet?" Caroline asked, rubbing her forehead with trembling fingers. "Unbelievable. And do not dare take ten more pounds away, Charles; I am only saying what everyone will think. He can reach very high for a bride, and while Elizabeth is intelligent, lively, and even beautiful, she is not wealthy, nor is her family part of the ton."

"It is Miss Darcy who specifically invited Elizabeth to Ramsgate," Charles said, standing up and pouring his sister a cup of water, which he then handed to her. "At Pemberley, they discovered a shared interest in birds, and Miss Darcy is eager to show off some of the feathered creatures which make their homes along the shores and marshes of Ramsgate."

"Birds," Caroline said bitterly, drinking the water and setting the empty cup down such that it clanked loudly against her brother's wooden desk. "I did everything in my power to make Miss Darcy like me, and it turns out that she wanted me to talk about birds."

Bingley lowered himself onto his chair and said gently, "Caroline, I have a suggestion. Instead of trying to make someone like you, why do you not search for friends with similar interests to your own? You and Darcy are not well suited, you know. He does not enjoy society and is happiest in the country, whereas you thoroughly enjoy the pleasures of Town. Surely you will enjoy your marriage more if you have something in common with your husband?"

Caroline stared at him, her eyes blank with misery, and she shrugged. "I do not know what I truly enjoy. All I ever wanted was to rise above my circumstances as the daughter of a tradesman."

She passed her hand over her face, stood up, and shook out her skirts. "I am going to bed, Charles, and will stay in my bedchamber until after our guests leave. Then I will arrange to go to London as soon as possible to stay with Miss Fawnthorpe. Perhaps I cannot capture Mr. Darcy, but I am determined to wed a gentleman with good connections."

"As you wish," Charles said sadly, feeling a pang in his heart. Caroline was often annoying, but he loved her and wished that she could find joy and contentment as he had.

She took a few steps toward the door and then turned around suddenly, her expression anxious. "Charles?"

"Yes?" he returned warily.

"I will need to purchase some new gowns and hats and I am a little short of money because of … well, you know why. I know you care about me and my future. I will need you to write letters to my milliner and dressmaker assuring them that you will cover any extra costs for my wardrobe."

Bingley gazed back at his sister and felt his heart waver within him. He did care about Caroline and he wanted her happily married, and the sooner the better. If a few extra gowns would smooth the way toward her wedding, perhaps...

A moment later, reason asserted itself. His sister had countless gowns and hats and scarves and pelisses and even a riding habit, in spite of the fact that she rarely rode horses.

"No, Caroline," he said, assuming a stern face. "You lost considerable money from your allowance because you repeatedly insulted my wife and sister and their family. You have plenty of dresses and other accessories. If you cannot afford additional items due to your behavior, you will not suffer unduly."

Caroline stared at him and her eyes flashed with fury. "Everyone is against me, everyone!"

"I am sorry you think that, Sister."

/

"Tell me about Miss Elizabeth Bennet," Colonel Fitzwilliam suggested.

Darcy glanced at his cousin, who was riding beside him. He had not been prepared for such a blunt question and said, "Erm, what do you mean?"

"Come now, Darcy," Richard said, gesturing toward the carriage in front of him, which carried Elizabeth, Georgiana, Mrs. Annesley, and a maid. "I have known you for nearly thirty years, and I have never seen you behave in such a way toward a beautiful young lady. Am I correct that Miss Bennet is the 'third point' of the letter you sent me some weeks ago?"

Darcy patted his stallion's neck and his mouth widened into a besotted grin. "You are correct indeed, Richard. I think … I think perhaps I am in love."

"In love?" the colonel responded. "It is truly as serious as that?"

"Without a doubt, it is," Darcy said, his gaze now fixed in a lovelorn way on the carriage rolling ahead of them on the road. "I … I need to talk to you, Richard, desperately. She is a marvelous person, Miss Bennet. She is intelligent, kind, honorable, and Georgiana adores her. But you met her family last night, and you now know that Mrs. Bennet and at least the youngest Miss Bennet are rather loud and vulgar. They have relations in trade. Can I truly marry into a family with poor connections? Though truly I do not think it matters, but I am responsible for Georgiana, and…"

"Wait, wait, wait just a minute," the military man ordered, struggling to suppress his amusement over the frantic mutterings of his usually stoic cousin. "Start at the beginning. When did you first meet her?"

"At Pemberley," Darcy said, his mind shifting back to the day when he first laid eyes on Elizabeth. "She was with Bingley and her sister, Bingley's bride, you know, and…"

Elizabeth felt the carriage begin to turn on the road and leaned over to stare eagerly out the window. She was sitting on the rear facing squabs of the vehicle and thus enjoyed occasional glimpses of Mr. Darcy perched atop the great stallion Phoenix. Yes, there he was now, his posture both easy and elegant, his face turned toward Colonel Fitzwilliam. She leaned back as the road straightened out and felt her lips curl upwards. There could be no question about Mr. Darcy's meaning only yesterday; he was interested in her as a possible wife, and she found herself looking forward to spending more time with the fascinating master of Pemberley.

/

"You should marry Miss Bennet," Richard Fitzwilliam said decidedly.

Although he was somewhat taken aback by the straight forward statement, Darcy's expression transformed from worried to joyful. "You truly think so?"

"I do," Richard answered, obviously amused. "Really, Cousin, it is so patently obvious that I cannot imagine why you are even asking! She is charming, beautiful, lively, honorable, intelligent, and obviously not a fortune hunter. She and Georgiana are on the very best of terms. She is a woman in a million, and if I were wealthy, I might try to cut you out!"

"You met her mother and youngest sister last night," Darcy reminded him anxiously. "Mrs. Bennet is rather vulgar and Miss Lydia is overly noisy…"

Richard waved an impatient hand, cutting him off. "It matters not, Darcy, not in the least. They will not be living with you, after all."

"What of Georgiana's coming out into society? Elizabeth does not have connections among the haut ton. Will Lady Matlock still sponsor my sister if I marry the daughter of a country gentleman?"

Fitzwilliam cast his eyes forward at the carriage and then looked over at his cousin. "Darcy?"

"Yes?"

"How is Georgiana? She seems happy, but has she changed substantially in the last year in terms of her … more unusual character traits?"

Darcy also looked ahead and then turned back toward his sister's other guardian. "She is, I think, a bit easier in company, at least when Miss Bennet or I is with her. She is also able to bear tight clothing more often, though there are days when she still insists on baggy garments. She still adores her music and her peacocks, but she struggles to understand the conventions of society."

The two men rode silently for a full five minutes, and then Richard said, "Darcy, I know this is difficult for you to accept, but I think it quite likely that Georgiana will never be able to enter society in a traditional manner."

Darcy swallowed hard and felt his eyes grow wet. "That is what I am afraid of."

Another silence fell, a shorter one, before the colonel said, "Why does that distress you so much? You have never had much use for high society, after all."

Darcy sighed heavily and said, "It is true I do not, but Georgiana is a Darcy, and if she is never presented and never does her bow to the queen, people will talk about her. I hate the thought of that. She is already fragile; how will she bear it if people gossip about her in such a way. I also wonder..."

He trailed off and Richard, after waiting a minute, prompted, "Wonder what?"

Darcy turned a sorrowful countenance toward his cousin, hesitated, and then said, "I wonder if this is all my fault. Georgiana was only nine years old when our father died, leaving me as her primary guardian. Your parents urged me to send her away to school, but I refused. I thought that after such a shattering loss, she would be absolutely miserable away from Pemberley and me."

"If you remember, I agreed with you entirely," the military man said. "More than that, as her other guardian,

I argued that she absolutely should *not* be sent away. You know that boarding school can be a difficult transition for even a typical child. But Georgiana, with her love of birds and her hatred of tight clothing – Darcy, she would have been entirely wretched!"

"I agreed then and I agree now, but when she was twelve, you were away on the Continent and your parents urged me again to send her away to boarding school. Again I refused, as Georgiana was devastated at the thought of leaving me and Pemberley, but now I wonder if she would have grown more able to manage society if I had forced her to face up to her fears by sending her away."

"I do not think so," Richard said without hesitation. "You were very unhappy in boarding school, were you not?"

Darcy grimaced and nodded. "I was, but I did feel better able to manage societal expectations after my years at Eton."

"And perhaps if you had been privately educated at Pemberley, with periodic trips to London, you would have learned similar lessons entirely due to maturity," his cousin retorted. "You know that I have no great love of boarding schools, Darcy."

Darcy winced and nodded. "I know, but what happened to Anthony might have happened anywhere."

Richard Fitzwilliam gritted his teeth and said, "Boarding schools are notorious for just the kind of epidemic which nearly killed my older brother, not to mention the often foul interactions amongst the children. You know that even now, Anthony is somewhat delicate after his bout with smallpox. If I ever marry, I assure you that I will not send my children into such an environment. No, Darcy, Georgiana would never have thrived at boarding school. She is a delightful, gifted, very unusual young woman who may well never marry, and if she does not, the best thing in the world is for you to wed a woman whom she loves, like Miss Elizabeth Bennet."

/

London

"You must be mad!" Mrs. Younge cried out, jerking to a sitting position. She had been delighted to welcome George Wickham into her house and her bed, but this plan of his was insane!

Wickham reached out a long arm and pulled her down to nestle in his embrace. She resisted briefly before succumbing and curling up next to him. Her companion, with his handsome figure and charming face, was quite the most remarkable man to ever enter her life, and she could no more resist him than a compass needle could resist turning to the north.

"Henrietta," Wickham murmured into her ear. "Do you not understand? Georgiana Darcy is an unsophisticated girl, and in spite of last year's … difficulties, she is certainly still attached to me from all those hours I spent amusing her when she was young. I will not pretend that it will be *easy,* but we do have this in our favor; we know the usual haunts where she likes to look for her ridiculous birds. If we can find her alone, we can…"

"She will scream the moment she catches sight of you, or me for that matter," Mrs. Younge said irritably. "Darcy is no fool. He will have warned her against us both."

"Warned her, yes, but he will not expect us at Ramsgate, nor will she. As for screaming – I am confident she will be too stunned by my sudden appearance to so much as squeak, or at least not before I can cover her mouth with my hand."

Mrs. Younge rolled over and stared at her lover incredulously. "Are you speaking of abduction?"

"And if I am?" Wickham asked, running an affectionate hand through her red ringlets. "The Darcys owe me, and they owe you. I will not physically harm

Georgiana, but I intend to obtain her dowry by fair means or foul."

"Abduction is a hanging matter, George! If we are caught…"

"If we are caught, Darcy will do everything in his power to hush it up, and you know it! Do you imagine he will allow polite society to know his dear sister nearly ran off with a steward's son last year, and then was *supposedly* abducted by the same man when she returned to Ramsgate a year later? Everyone in society will assume that she deliberately arranged to meet me at Ramsgate. It is quite safe, my love. Either I will marry the girl and gain control over her dowry, or I will blackmail Darcy into paying us off so that we do not spread rumors about his sister throughout society. Either way, you and I can finally be happy."

Mrs. Younge stared intently into Wickham's winsome face, her heart thumping wildly within her. He was so attractive, and her life here as mistress of a boarding house was dull and difficult. She would need to ask her cousin Martha to take over her duties for a few days, but if they succeeded at Ramsgate, she could run away with Wickham and leave this foul existence forever.

"Very well," she said.

Chapter 28

Darcy House

London

"The master is not here, Lady Catherine," the butler said calmly.

"He will be," Catherine de Bourgh returned with an arrogant tilt of her nose. "I have it on excellent authority that he will be arriving this very day from Netherfield, and I will wait for him in the blue salon. Have one of your maids bring me tea and crumpets."

"As you wish," the man replied with a courteous bob of his head. He led his master's aunt to the blue salon, bowed her in, and retreated to the kitchen to order the requisite refreshments. The lady would, he knew, be waiting a very long time; in his own pocket, he held a letter, sent express, from his master. Mr. Darcy would not be stopping at London today but would be proceeding directly to Ramsgate. In the quiet of the corridor, Mr. Campbell allowed himself an unprofessional, very satisfied smile.

/

Matlock House

London

"Hello, Mother!"

Lady Matlock, dressed in a rose pink morning gown, had been gazing drowsily out the window at a particularly fine rosebush. At the sound of her second son's voice, she leaped to her feet and exclaimed, "Richard!"

Richard strode forward to kiss his mother on the cheek and said, "I hope you are well this fine day?"

"I am, my dear, I am!" the countess declared, thoroughly awakened at the sight of her military son. "Do sit down and have some tea! Where have you been, Richard? I thought you were planning to join us for dinner last night. We hosted the Lord Solphington and his family, and Lady Phoebe was most disappointed at your absence."

Richard suppressed a cringe at these words. Lady Phoebe Asbury, only daughter of the Earl of Solphington, had been pursuing him for the last year, and regrettably both Lord and Lady Matlock were promoting the woman as a suitable bride for their second son. Lady Phoebe was reasonably pretty with a dowry of twenty thousand pounds, but she was also vain and voluble, and her mother,

Countess Solphington, was well known for combining a shrewish disposition with a deep and abiding delight in interfering in the marriages of her children. Richard had decided long ago that he was not interested in taking the young woman as a bride, but no one else in the family was inclined to respect his decision.

"I fear that duty called, Mama," Richard explained with a casual wave of his hand. "I hope it was a pleasant dinner party, anyway."

The countess huffed as she prepared a cup of tea with milk for her son. "In truth, it was quite exasperating, because your aunt appeared in the middle of it."

Richard successfully managed to hide the glint of interest in his eyes and said, as he accepted the tea, "Which aunt? Lady Catherine?"

"Yes, of course Lady Catherine! If it had been one of my sisters, I would have been pleased but you know Catherine. She is so demanding and irritable much of the time."

"What was she doing here?"

"Oh, Matlock did not tell me much. She was closeted with your father for a full hour after the guests departed. It has something to do with Darcy. She is growing more and more anxious that he marry Anne and wishes for your father to exercise his avuncular authority, such as it is, in the matter. I think the whole thing is quite foolish; Darcy is well able to manage his own affairs and has never shown the least inclination to bow meekly before the dictates of his elders."

"That is true enough," her son agreed, taking a sip of tea. "Is Anne here as well?"

"No, no, Lady Catherine left her at Rosings. The poor girl really is not a good traveler, and there is no reason to drag her here to London until the matter is settled."

Richard, having obtained the information he sought, leaned back and said, "That is sensible, at any rate. However, I fear my aunt will be disappointed, as Darcy received an urgent message and has changed his plans. He departed Bingley's estate this morning as intended, but he is not coming to London."

"Oh dear, she will be quite enraged!" Lady Matlock exclaimed. "How very tiresome of Darcy, though he does have the right to go where he wishes. He is his own man."

"I quite agree, Mother. Now, how are my sisters?"

"They are very well! I just learned yesterday that Rebekah is increasing with another child, and Vivian is hopeful of an offer from Lord Rosewood in the near future…"

/

The Eagle's Nest

Kent

"But where are the eagles?" Georgiana demanded, looking around eagerly.

"I am not certain there are eagles, my dear," Darcy said meekly.

"Then why call this inn ~~called~~ The Eagle's Nest?" his sister asked indignantly, following her brother into the open door, where the owner of the inn was waiting to welcome his wealthy, well born, guests.

"Perhaps there once were eagles in the area," Elizabeth suggested from behind her. "We should refresh ourselves, and later we can see if the host can tell us more about bird life in the area."

"Very well," Georgiana replied reluctantly.

/

Darcy House

London

"Where can my nephew be??" Lady Catherine demanded, biting angrily into a macaroon.

"I fear that I am unable to tell you, my lady," the butler returned stolidly.

/

Rosings

Kent

Anne de Bourgh, heiress of the grand estate of Rosings, frowned down at the folio in her hands, and then deliberately placed it on the painted table next to her.

"Have you had quite enough of Lord Byron?" her companion, Mrs. Jenkinson, inquired.

Anne chuckled and said, "Yes, I confess to great disappointment. I know that his lordship's poems are supposed to be the very epitome of culture, but I find I cannot enjoy them. Indeed, I would far prefer a novel!"

"I have several Gothic novels in my room, and with Lady Catherine in London, you can read them without fear of reproach. Would you like me to fetch one for you?"

Anne shook her head. "Thank you very much, Mrs. Jenkinson, but no. My head is starting to ache, and I do not think I can concentrate."

"Do you wish for some laudanum?"

"No, I think not. It always makes me even sleepier than usual, and I do not want to sleep this day away."

"I understand completely," Mrs. Jenkinson said fervently. Both ladies thoroughly enjoyed those rare times when Lady Catherine absented herself from Rosings; Anne because she disliked her mother's penchant for controlling every aspect of her life, and Mrs. Jenkinson because her employer wanted her to hover over Anne in a way that annoyed them both.

The door to the sitting room opened, and the women looked up as the butler, Mr. Lawton, entered with a red coated military gentleman at his heels.

"Colonel Richard Fitzwilliam," Lawton announced.

Anne lurched to her feet. "Richard! What a surprise!"

"A pleasant one, I hope?" Richard returned, bowing to his cousin and Mrs. Jenkinson. The butler retreated and shut the door behind him, leaving them alone.

"Oh yes, I am very pleased to see you!" Anne exclaimed. "But what brings you here to Rosings? I fear you have missed Lady Catherine, who went away to London only this morning."

Richard grinned roguishly and said, "That is quite all right, Cousin, because I came to speak to *you*. What would you think about taking a trip to the seaside for your health?"

Anne blinked at her cousin in bewilderment and then cast an uncertain look at Mrs. Jenkinson, who asked, "What do you mean by that, Colonel Fitzwilliam?"

"The Darcys are on their way to Ramsgate even now, and they are eager to have you come along, Anne. They are spending the night at The Eagle's Nest, which is only twelve miles from here, and we can join them this evening if you are willing. The journey tomorrow will only be some thirty-five miles, which should not be exceptionally exhausting. Not that I mean to press you to come, Cousin; it is entirely up to you. But the sea is delightfully cool in the latter part of summer, and I am confident it would do you good."

Anne frowned in confusion. "I do not understand. Mama sent a letter to Darcy telling him to stop here at

Rosings, but she did not receive a letter back from him. Mother was most displeased and indeed, that is why she went to London, to speak with Darcy."

"Oh!" Richard said, opening his eyes wide. "Well, that is *most* unfortunate, as Darcy's party came directly from Hertfordshire today, bypassing London entirely. He and Georgiana were visiting Darcy's friend, Mr. Bingley, and Miss Elizabeth Bennet, whom you know, is accompanying them to the sea. Both ladies indicated they would very much enjoy getting to know you better, Anne."

Anne hesitated and said, with obvious embarrassment, "Do you know … is Darcy thinking about...? I do not truly wish to … to..."

Richard grinned and said, "I assure you that our mutual cousin is interested in nothing more than a friendship between the two of you. You need have no concern on that account."

Anne looked at Mrs. Jenkinson, who smiled and said, "I believe Colonel Fitzwilliam's suggestion is an excellent one, Miss de Bourgh. You have been suffering from the heat, and your mother did wish for you to accompany Mr. Darcy to Ramsgate."

Anne's eyes lit up, her face full of excitement at the thought of departing without her mother. "Very well, thank you! I would be delighted to join you!"

/

Matlock House

London

"Where is that boy?" Lady Catherine shrilled. "Matlock, you told me yourself that Darcy would return to London today!"

"How would I know?" her noble brother demanded irritably. "Perhaps they were delayed in Hertfordshire! Carriages do break, and horses go lame on occasion."

Lady Catherine huffed indignantly and took a few turns up and down the drawing room. "I do dislike tardiness, Brother. It is quite exasperating. Very well, I will return to Darcy House and wait, but if he does not arrive by tomorrow, I will journey to Hertfordshire. I will not permit Darcy to delay any longer in marrying my daughter!"

Lady Matlock, who had been hovering outside the door of the drawing room, heaved a soft sigh and decided to intervene. She did not know Darcy's friend, Bingley, but as a Christian and a lady, she would be most unkind to allow Lady Catherine to descend on the hapless man if she could prevent it.

"Catherine, my dear," she said, strolling into the room and gazing at her fulminating sister-in-law, "I could not help overhear your last remark, and fear that I have some discouraging news. Richard stopped by a few hours ago and mentioned that Darcy is not coming to London; apparently something came up, and he changed his plans."

Lady Catherine's face changed from pink to purple, and her eyes bulged with indignation. "What?!"

/

The Eagle's Nest

Kent

"I have never gone ice skating," Elizabeth admitted. "Is it very difficult?"

"No," Georgiana said baldly.

"Yes," Darcy said at exactly the same time, and then laughed at the sight of his sister's surprised face. "I know it is easy for you, dear one, but you have remarkable balance. When I was first learning, I fell down repeatedly. I do not remember skating well until I had practiced it a dozen times!"

"Truly? I had no idea, Brother! I thought you..."

Georgiana trailed off, looking uncomfortable, and Darcy immediately put his arm around her and said, "That I learned as easily as you did? No, but there is no shame in struggling with such things. I persevered and learned to skate well, and it is indeed enjoyable."

Miss Darcy relaxed and turned a beaming smile on her friend. "It is delightful, Elizabeth! There is a pond about a quarter mile beyond the peacock garden, and the servants brush off the snow, and we skate for hours! Then when we are thoroughly chilled, we rush back and drink hot chocolate in front of the fire. It is great fun."

"It sounds like it," Elizabeth agreed, then turned as the door to the private parlor opened, and the innkeeper entered with three people at his heels.

"Mr. Darcy, your guests have arrived," the man said with a low bow and retreated, shutting the door gently behind him.

"Anne, Mrs. Jenkinson, thank you for joining us on such short notice," Darcy said enthusiastically as he and the ladies rose to their feet. "Richard, thank you for escorting them."

"It was my pleasure, of course," the colonel said cheerfully. "Georgiana, you know your cousin Anne, certainly, but may I please introduce you to Anne's companion, Mrs. Jenkinson? Mrs. Jenkinson, Miss Georgiana Darcy and her companion, Mrs. Annesley."

Anne was staring at Georgiana and said, "I know that you must be my cousin, but I can hardly believe it! When I last saw you, you were shorter than I am and look at you now! You are all grown up, Georgiana!"

"I have grown five inches in the last two years," Georgiana said, ducking her head shyly. "I fear I do not remember you well, Cousin Anne. It has been six years since you were last at Pemberley."

"Yes, that was a long journey, and I spent the first week in bed recovering" Anne said with a sigh. "I fear I am not a good traveler, especially during the summer."

"Please do sit down near the window, Miss de Bourgh," Elizabeth suggested, gesturing to a padded seat. "There is a fine breeze which is most refreshing. Would you care for some iced lemonade, perhaps, or would you like some tea?"

"Thank you, Miss Bennet, I would enjoy some lemonade," Anne responded gratefully, sinking into the padded chair and letting the cool winds wash over her. She was vaguely puzzled as to why Miss Bennet was acting the hostess instead of Georgiana, but she dimly remembered that her young cousin was very shy.

Darcy smiled at Elizabeth and said, "I will arrange to have a maid bring lemonade as quickly as possible."

"Thank you, Mr. Darcy," Elizabeth returned warmly.

Anne, who had not had time to think much in the last hours, caught her breath in amazement. Her only knowledge of romance was from the pages of the novels that she hid in her bedroom. Lady Catherine was so determined that her only daughter marry the master of Pemberley that Anne had never been permitted a London season, and eligible men crossed the doors of Rosings only once or twice a year. However, she thought she knew Darcy moderately well, and she had never seen such an expression of affection on his face toward anyone but his sister. So that was the way the wind blew!

Anne de Bourgh leaned back in her chair and exhaled in relief. In spite of Richard's assurances, she had been a trifle worried that Darcy was still considering her as a possible wife. Now she knew better – if Darcy's loving looks were any indication, Miss Elizabeth Bennet would become Mrs. Darcy.

Lady Catherine would be furious. Upon consideration, Anne looked forward to her mother's disappointment. It was about time that Catherine de Bourgh learned that she was not mistress of everyone in her orbit.

Chapter 29

"Are you well, Anne?" Colonel Fitzwilliam asked in some concern. He was seated in the Rosings' carriage across from Anne and her companion, while a vigorous summer rain fell on the surrounding fields and forests. As a member of His Majesty's army, Fitzwilliam had often been forced to ride many weary miles in the middle of poor weather. It was a delight to be in an expensive vehicle, completely dry, though he spared a moment of compassion toward the footmen and postilions who were getting wet. His horse, too, was wet, but Pineapple had always enjoyed the rain and was no doubt happy enough.

"I am well," Anne assured her military cousin, forcing her lips to tilt upwards at Richard's worried gaze. "I am pleased that the weather is not overly hot, and this carriage is sufficiently well sprung that I am not ill in the least. I confess that I am rather fearful of Lady Catherine's response to this journey, but there is no point dwelling on it. I made my decision and must deal with the consequences."

"It is difficult for you, I know," Richard agreed compassionately. "You have every reason and right to come to Ramsgate with us, but I fear Lady Catherine will likely disapprove because she was not part of the decision. Your mother is at fault for treating you like a child when you are a woman."

"A woman with poor health and a weak will," Anne said drearily, turning to stare out at the sodden countryside.

"If I may say," Mrs. Jenkinson said in a stern voice, "you are doing yourself a disservice. You know your mind as well as anyone, but you choose not to battle with Lady Catherine, which would turn Rosings into a war zone."

Anne sighed and said, "That is true enough. Mother will not tolerate disagreement from anyone except, perhaps, Lord Matlock. She respects him as head of the family, but no one else."

"Anne?" Richard asked impulsively.

"Yes?"

"You do not need to answer this, but I wonder why you do not wish to marry Darcy. He is quite able to maintain a firm position with Lady Catherine, and he is a good man who would not try to control your life as your mother does."

Anne grimaced. "I agree that Darcy is a good man. However, his character is too much like mine; we are both quiet and taciturn. I believe that he would do well with a livelier partner, and based on his interactions with Miss Bennet ... am I reading too much into his obvious delight in the lady's presence?"

The Colonel chuckled and said, "Not at all, Anne. You are entirely correct that Darcy admires Miss Bennet, and Georgiana quite adores her as well."

"I am happy for them," Anne said. "In any case, even if Darcy were interested in marrying me, I have no desire to wed a man who owns a large estate of his own. Our mutual cousin is a very diligent man and would doubtless wish to travel between the two estates, and I hate long trips by carriage. I always feel sick and bored and weary. I really would like to spend the rest of my life at, or within easy distance of, Rosings, but without my mother in residence."

"You need to marry a man without an estate, who has sufficient force of will to manage Lady Catherine," Mrs. Jenkinson said decidedly.

Richard cast a startled look at his cousin's companion and Anne, observing his surprise, said, "Mrs. Jenkinson is a dear friend, and I find her advice invaluable. Due to my mother's dictates, she is required to play the part of the hovering companion in company, while displaying her true character in more private settings."

"Away from your mother, you mean," Richard said heavily. "It is an exasperating and frustrating situation, Cousin. However, in two short months, you will turn five and twenty, and Rosings will legally revert to you at which point you can, if you wish, require Lady Catherine to live at the Dower House."

Anne shook her head sadly. "Realistically, I will not be able to do so. I have been under my mother's thumb for too long, and I know I cannot stand up to her fury."

The colonel sighed and patted his cousin's hand sympathetically. "I understand completely."

/

"I thought all ladies knew how to ride a horse!" Georgiana said in astonishment.

Darcy winced at his sister's rather strident tone, but Elizabeth only smiled and said, "Well, I do not. Jane is an accomplished horsewoman, as is my sister Lydia, but I prefer walking to riding."

"But you cannot walk nearly as far as you can ride!" her friend pointed out.

"No, but then Longbourn is not nearly as large as Pemberley. There is another factor at play as well. My father has not devoted much of the income of Longbourn to horseflesh. We have carriage horses that are also used for the farm, and only three mares for riding, none of which are appropriate for a beginner. There was a more sedate horse available for Jane when she was learning to ride, but it died and was not replaced. Lydia is such a bold soul that she learned on a difficult beast, but I, after being thrown once, decided that walking was preferable."

"That is sensible," Darcy said. "Many men and women have been gravely injured, and some even killed, while attempting to ride an unruly horse."

"Is your family so poor that you cannot afford more horses?" Georgiana asked unhappily. "That is sad."

This time, both Darcy and Mrs. Annesley, who was seated next to Georgiana, cringed openly, but Elizabeth merely said, "No, not at all! My dear friend, it is all a matter of priorities! My father loves books far more than horses, and he will always choose a folio over a foal. I approve, since I too love to read."

"Fitzwilliam can buy both horses and as many books as he likes," Georgiana said in a troubled tone. "It seems unfair."

"Your brother has a very substantial income," Elizabeth said, looking at Darcy. "Furthermore, given how large Pemberley is, I daresay it is vital that there are plenty of horses so that he and others can make their way quickly to tenant farms. Of course, even Mr. Darcy cannot buy everything. Everyone makes choices about how they spend their money, and anyone can go into debt even with a vast income."

"The Regent has shown us that," Darcy agreed grimly, grasping Georgiana's hand in his own. "I do not think Miss Bennet minds that she does not have a horse to ride, my dear."

"Indeed, I do not," Elizabeth assured her friend. "Now I presume you are an excellent rider?"

"I am a good but not excellent rider. Fitzwilliam bought me a golden mare that I named Sunbeam, and I often ride her around the estate. Oh!"

"Oh?" Darcy repeated, puzzled.

"Do you smell that?" his sister exclaimed, her blue eyes suddenly alight with excitement.

"I do!" Elizabeth answered in wonder, turning her head toward the open carriage window. "What is that wonderful scent?"

"It is the ocean, Elizabeth. That is the fragrance of the salt air. Is it not delightful?"

Elizabeth felt her nostrils quiver at the smell drifting in the window. "It is glorious."

/

"Here you are, Mr. and Mrs. Smythe," Mrs. Albert said to her guests. "It is quite a large room, and you can just see the ocean from the northwest window. Breakfast is served at nine o'clock, and dinner at six. Now, I will leave you both, and I hope that you have a very pleasant stay in Ramsgate."

The landlady hurried out of the door and shut it behind her, leaving George Wickham and Henrietta Younge to curiously survey their surroundings.

"It is quite decent," Mrs. Younge said grudgingly. "I see no dust on the floors and the room is a reasonable size."

"So is the bed," Wickham commented lasciviously.

Mrs. Younge slapped him gently on the arm. "We have no time for such nonsense now, George. I hope that we can see the back of Darcy's rental house from here."

Wickham strode over to the corner window and peered out, then nodded with satisfaction. "We have an excellent view of the courtyard behind the house. Do look!"

The woman joined him and said, "Yes, you are quite right. We can take turns watching to determine when their carriage is being readied for departure. Of course, last year Miss Darcy and I often walked to the beach from the front door, and if she and her party depart through that door, we will not be able to see them from here."

"It matters not," Wickham said. "I know Georgiana – she will insist on visiting the birds in the marshes at least twice, and we can follow with our horses and snatch her. We can hardly abduct her on the road or the beach, but the marshes are lonely places."

Henrietta Younge stared at her companion and said, "So it is openly abduction now, is it?"

"Certainly," Wickham returned, lifting the woman's right hand and pressing a kiss on it. "I am hoping Georgiana comes willingly, but it is still an abduction since she is not yet of age. Do not worry, my dear Henrietta. All will be well."

"I hope so. Now get some sleep. I will watch for the Darcys and will wake you up in time for dinner."

"Very well, love," Wickham responded, and promptly threw himself onto the bed, where he drifted off to sleep in a few short minutes.

Mrs. Younge quietly approached a mirror hanging on the wall and stared into it, considering her reflection. Both Mr. and Miss Darcy knew her well, and thus she had chosen to wear a black wig over her usual red tresses, and she was wearing a sturdy blue gown which made her look like the wife of a publican or something of the sort. Wickham, too, had taken care to disguise his appearance by setting aside his red military coat, allowing his beard to grow, and putting on (rather to his disgust) a loose fitting white shirt covered by a rough hunting jacket, and a pair of brown trousers. It was likely that they would be recognized if they came within twenty feet of the Darcys, but they had no intention of doing so until they were ready to capture Georgiana.

Mrs. Younge opened her valise, pulled out a fashion periodical and walked over to sit on the chair which looked down upon the Darcy's courtyard. So far, there was no sign of Darcy's party, though they might have arrived earlier in the day or, if they were delayed, they might not arrive for a few days yet. All she knew was that they were to arrive by the end of July, and that time had come.

She chewed on her lip and frowned worriedly. They had enough money to stay for a week here at Ramsgate, but the cost of their room would make a severe dent on their savings. At least Wickham had provided both horses for their ride from London to Ramsgate. They were surprisingly good horses, and Henrietta guessed that Wickham had stolen them, not that she really wanted to know.

An hour went by as Wickham slept and Henrietta read *The Ladies' Monthly Museum*, with occasional glances at the still quiet courtyard behind the red brick house where the Darcys would be staying. A gentle huff caught her attention at this point, and she turned to regard her beloved George who had turned over and was now facing her, though his eyes were closed in repose. Even with his face partially covered by a nascent beard, he was an incredibly handsome man.

She smiled, her thoughts going back to her first meeting with the handsome godson of George Darcy. She had been born Henrietta Mason, eldest daughter of a country gentleman of moderate wealth and expensive habits. At the age of nineteen, she had married a neighbor, Mr. Stephen Younge, a military man with his own predilection for the gaming tables. Within a year, Mr. Younge had spent all of her dowry. A year after that, he had fallen in battle. Her father had died only two months afterwards, and Henrietta's eldest brother had succeeded to an impoverished estate and a mountain of debts. She, Mrs. Henrietta Younge, had been well educated and found herself having to earn her daily bread by serving as governess of three spoiled children in the family of a baronet who lived near London.

She had met George Wickham there. He was studying at Cambridge and came home with the eldest son of the house. It had been, for Henrietta at least, lust at first sight. Her own husband had not been a handsome man, and George Wickham, with his effortless charm and elegant features, had provided excitement and pleasure in a drab and dull life. She had been disappointed that Wickham had only visited his friend once more, and then disappeared from her life for several years.

Nearly two years ago, he had found her working for another family and proposed that she seek a position with the Darcys. She had leaped at the chance; one girl in her teens, even a peculiar one, would be far less exhausting and irritating than the four noisy, ill-mannered boys in her care!

It was only after she won the position that Wickham had approached her again, in secret, urging her to help him convince Miss Georgiana Darcy to elope with him. She had agreed, of course. She could hardly deny Wickham anything, and if they had succeeded, she would have obtained a large sum for her part of the plot, not to mention more time in Wickham's arms.

And then Darcy had shown up early at Ramsgate, and it had all fallen apart. Well, this time would be different. She hoped.

To her considerable surprise, tears suddenly sprang to her eyes, tears of anxiety and anger. This entire plot was, she knew, reckless in the extreme. If they succeeded, she and George would be wealthy beyond anything they had ever known. If they failed, well, it could mean that they could both end their lives at the end of a jerking rope. On the other hand, it was entirely unfair that the Darcys were able to live such easy, comfortable, indulgent lives while she had to work so hard to make her own way. She and George deserved good things as much as anyone else.

And George was correct about another thing; Darcy, a haughty, proud gentleman, would do anything in his power to suppress a hint of scandal surrounding his only sister. Even if they failed, they would be well enough.

A sound from outside prompted her to set aside her musings and turn to the window. A moment later, she let out a sigh of pleasure; two carriages had pulled up in the courtyard behind the red brick house, and a number of men and women alighted. She recognized Mr. Darcy and Miss Darcy among them. Excellent.

Chapter 30

"Elizabeth, are you ready?"

Elizabeth, having already changed out of her traveling dress into a blue day dress, quickly tied the blue ribbons of her straw bonnet under her chin and opened the door of her bedchamber where Georgiana was standing impatiently.

"Yes!" she declared, linking her arm in her friend's. "I am truly excited!"

The two girls made their way down the wooden steps into the vestibule of the house, where Darcy was waiting for them.

"Shall we go down to the beach?" the gentleman asked, gesturing toward the door.

"Miss de Bourgh and Colonel Fitzwilliam are not coming?" Elizabeth asked, looking around curiously. The house they were staying in was a large, handsome structure built of red brick, with clean lines and well-polished floors. It was pleasant.

"Anne wishes to rest," Darcy explained, "and Richard has promised to stay with her so that if by any chance Lady Catherine appears unexpectedly, she will have someone at her side."

"That is sensible," Elizabeth said, following the Darcys out the door, down the stone steps, and onto the cobbled street. Once the threesome had descended to the pavement, both ladies took a proffered arm from Darcy, who was surprised at the surge of happiness which filled him to have those two slender hands on his arms.

"It is well that you are wearing a bonnet with ribbons, Miss Bennet," Darcy said, casting an admiring glance at the lady to his left. "The sea breezes can be rather strong, and more than one lady has lost a hat."

"Like me," Georgiana said with a chuckle. "Do you remember, Brother? It was three years ago. I was looking up at a flying falcon and the wind caught my favorite hat and swirled it into the ocean!"

"You did not leap into the water after it, Mr. Darcy?" Elizabeth asked, her eyes sparkling mischievously.

"I did not," Darcy admitted with a grin. "I considered it, but I waited too long, and by the time I was ready to leap, it was already fifteen feet away and quickly heading out to sea."

"I have plenty of hats," Georgiana said seriously. "It does not matter."

"I wonder if any passing ships saw your hat," Elizabeth mused, her eyes fixed on the water stretching out before her. "If so, I daresay it surprised them."

"I think that unlikely," Georgiana responded. "It is true that it was a straw hat and would likely float for some time, and Ramsgate is a military port, but still, there are not that many ships sailing about."

"That is true enough," Elizabeth agreed and found herself speeding up, so eager was she to reach the waters. As usual her companions easily kept pace with her, which she enjoyed. Elizabeth, a vigorous walker, often found herself dawdling when walking with others, but both Darcys were as quick as she.

Ten minutes of brisk striding brought them to a set of wooden stairs, which they descended until they halted on a wooden boardwalk next to an expanse of sand, which dropped gracefully, gently, into the vast ocean.

Elizabeth was vaguely aware of tears filling her eyes at the sight before her. She had, of course, seen paintings of the sea, and she had read of the great expanse of waters which stretched to the horizon, but even with her own fertile imagination, nothing compared to the actual sight before her.

The August sky was blue, though numerous puffy clouds floated overhead like so many docile sheep. The sun shone down exuberantly, but the pleasant sea wind kept her delightfully cool. She watched in awe as distant waves tumbled toward her, their white caps dancing along the surface of the blue waters as they gradually turned aqua, then transparent, until finally the foaming crest crashed onto the shore.

"Oh, it is marvelous!" she finally managed.

"Is it not?" Georgiana cried out. "The motion of the waters, and the sea birds circling and diving?"

Elizabeth lifted her hand to shade her eyes as she tipped her face upwards towards three white and gray birds floating above her. "Oh yes, I see! What kinds of birds are those? Do you know?"

"Those are gulls," Georgiana said authoritatively. "They are very common birds, but graceful nonetheless."

"They also are notorious for stealing food from picnickers," Darcy commented. He had, of course, taken a few moments to enjoy the view, but he was more interested in watching Elizabeth's expressions. It occurred to him that one of Miss Bennet's attributes was that she did not disguise her enthusiasm about new experiences, which stood in sharp contrast to most ladies of the upper classes, who put on airs of weary indifference about even the most exciting of adventures. Darcy much preferred Elizabeth's openness.

"That is true enough," Georgiana said. "We often picnic near the marshes, and Fitzwilliam has had to scare off gulls more than once."

"It seems impossible that the marshlands could be better than this," Elizabeth murmured.

"There are more birds in the marshlands," Georgiana explained.

Elizabeth turned a happy face on her friend and said, "I look forward to seeing the marshlands, but for now can we walk down to the edge of the water?"

"Of course," Darcy agreed. Once again the two ladies each took an arm, and the small group made their way across the bright sands to where the waves flowed up over the sand before withdrawing coyly, leaving the wet beach behind.

Elizabeth sighed in exasperation. "I wish I had worn mitts, not gloves. I very much wish to touch the water."

"I am not wearing gloves," Georgiana said calmly. "I find them rather unpleasant, and my brother generally does not mind if I do not wear them."

Elizabeth had indeed noticed her friend's dislike for gloves, but Georgiana could behave at Pemberley in a way that would be quite inappropriate for Elizabeth, and the only male present was Georgiana's brother.

"Miss Bennet, I beg you not to concern yourself about propriety if you wish to take your gloves off," Darcy said bravely, if awkwardly. "I believe that when on the very beach itself, it is quite appropriate to touch the waters."

Elizabeth hesitated, blushed, then quickly pulled off her gloves and knelt by the water, allowing the ripples to wash over her hand. "What an amazing feeling! It is cooler than I thought it would be, though."

"I have never bathed in the sea," Georgiana said, "but I understand that after a few minutes, cool water feels quite warm."

Elizabeth felt herself redden even further, and she turned her head away from Darcy toward the sands to the south. "I have read of bathing machines before; do they have them here at Ramsgate?"

"They do," her younger friend said. "I hope some day to try one, but my brother is not yet ready to trust one of the dippers to do her job properly."

"I suppose it is safe enough," Darcy said in what he hoped was a natural tone. Many a physician touted the benefit of being dipped (if one were a woman) or bathed (if one were a man) in the salt seas, but Georgiana was not a strong swimmer, and if she were to panic out in the waters, it would be dangerous indeed. Bathing was considered a quite risqué activity given that ladies often wore bathing costumes, and gentlemen nothing at all; thus it was of doubtful taste to discuss the topic in mixed company.

"The sand is soft, yet different than normal mud," Elizabeth commented, digging her fingers into the wet sand.

"The particles are bigger than normal dirt particles, so they behave differently," Georgiana explained. She too was crouching down, and she pushed her fist into a moist patch, then watched as it filled up with water.

Elizabeth stood up now, brushed off her hands, and carefully pulled her gloves back on. "It is phenomenal."

"Wait until you see the beach near the marshlands!" Georgiana declared.

/

Rosings

"Where is Miss de Bourgh?" Lady Catherine demanded, handing her gloves to a waiting footman and turning toward her butler. "Has she come down for dinner yet?"

Lawton plastered on his most remote expression and said, "No, Madam, Miss de Bourgh has left the estate in the company of Colonel Fitzwilliam. The colonel left this letter for you."

"What?" the lady exclaimed, grabbing the paper from the man's hand.

Her butler, correctly assuming that his mistress was asking a rhetorical question, said, "Dinner will be served in an hour, if that is agreeable, Madam."

"Yes, yes," the lady answered, breaking the seal and spreading it open.

Rosings

August 25th, 1812

Lady Catherine,

Anne has agreed to accompany me to the seaside to join Darcy and Georgiana. We will use the second best carriage along with the bay horses. With Mrs. Jenkinson and Anne's maid accompanying us, you need have no concern. Your daughter will be in the very best of hands.

We plan to stay some three weeks and Anne will no doubt send you letters of her progress. The sea is most salubrious at this time of year, and I have every hope that my cousin will return to Rosings in the best of health.

Sincerely,

Colonel Richard Fitzwilliam

Lady Catherine read the note twice more and then lifted her face to aim a displeased look at her butler, who was waiting silently nearby.

"Colonel Fitzwilliam does not report where exactly the party is going. Do you know their final destination, Lawton?"

Her butler coughed discreetly and said, "As to that, my lady, I did happen to overhear their conversation. They are going to Ramsgate."

Catherine narrowed her eyes in consideration. "Very good, Lawson. You have done well."

/

Ramsgate

"Can it be five o'clock already?" Anne asked, staring at the clock on the mantelpiece.

"It is," Colonel Fitzwilliam answered, rising to his feet and smiling at his cousin, who had just descended from her bedchamber. "I hope that means you had a pleasant rest?"

"Oh yes, I slept for two full hours and did not even stir. I have been sleeping poorly of late, though I do not know why."

"It is much cooler here on the coast," Richard commented, "and the sea breeze is very pleasant."

"Yes, I daresay that is much of it," Anne mused, wandering over to stare out the large picture window toward the cobblestoned street. "Are the others resting upstairs?"

"No, Darcy, Georgiana, and Miss Bennet left some time ago to visit the beach."

"Oh Richard, I apologize! I did not mean to keep you trapped here in the house while I slept!"

"Nonsense," the colonel said. "I have seen the beach at Ramsgate, and while it is charming, I would far rather sit in a very comfortable chair enjoying a newspaper."

"I did not realize you had been to Ramsgate before," Anne said, taking a seat across from her cousin. "Have you joined the Darcys during previous sojourns here?"

"No, when I last embarked for the Continent, I did so from here. The harbor here sees many a military ship setting sail."

"Oh!" Anne exclaimed. "I did not know…"

She trailed off and said nervously, "I heard you were injured in battle, Richard. Are you entirely recovered?"

The colonel set aside his newspaper and put a hand to his left side. "I took a ball to the hip, Anne, but thankfully it was not terribly deep. I am largely recovered, though I still am in some pain after a long day of riding."

"I am sorry."

"It could have been a great deal worse," Richard Fitzwilliam said, his face suddenly grim. He had lost countless soldiers under his command, and more than a few friends, in the vicious fighting of the Peninsular War.

"Do you intend to return to active fighting?" Anne asked worriedly.

The colonel shrugged and said, "For the moment, I am settled here in England training raw recruits, but I could easily be sent overseas again."

"Do you wish to go?"

Richard sighed deeply and ran a hand down his face. "Truthfully, I do not wish to go, but naturally I must obey orders. "

"Surely you could sell out?"

"Not without being dependent on my father, and I refuse to do that, Anne."

"You could marry an heiress," Anne suggested daringly.

Richard grinned and said, "That is true, but I would need to find an heiress interested in a slightly damaged second son of an earl, which is not a trivial matter."

The door to the drawing room opened, and Elizabeth, Georgiana, and Darcy entered. Anne turned toward the threesome with a smile, even as her own brain worked busily. She knew of one heiress, at least, who would delight in marrying a second son of an earl. But was Richard at all interested in marrying a sickly cousin?

/

"Are you certain you do not wish me to accompany you, Miss de Bourgh?" Mrs. Jenkinson asked.

"I am certain," Anne assured her companion, turning toward the mirror on the dressing table and putting her hat on. "You and Mrs. Annesley should relax and play draughts or nap or enjoy a good gossip, certain that your charges are in safe hands."

373

In the reflection, Anne saw Mrs. Jenkinson fight a smile, causing her to turn in confusion. "What is amusing?"

"Your dress, Miss de Bourgh, or more accurately, Miss Bennet's dress. Lady Catherine would be horrified."

Anne grinned as she looked down on the green muslin dress draping her thin form. "Indeed she would," she agreed with satisfaction. "I hope that someday I can purchase simpler garments like this dress. I find it much more comfortable than my usual elaborate gowns."

"Yes, I fear Lady Catherine is far more interested in showing off her wealth and rank than being comfortable," her companion said. "Now I do believe it is time for you to depart for the marshlands. I hope you have a marvelous time."

"I am certain I will," Anne said, opening the door, walking down the corridor, and then halting at the top of the staircase which led to the main foyer.

The rest of her party was waiting below, and she stared in wonder at Darcy's joyful face as he looked down on the countenance of Miss Bennet. Anne could not hear what they were saying to one another, but even as she watched, Elizabeth released a silvery laugh, which provoked Darcy to laugh as well. Anne could not remember ever seeing her wealthy cousin so happy!

"There you are, Anne," Colonel Fitzwilliam said, looking up at her.

She smiled at him, hastened down the stairs, and said, "I am sorry that I am late."

"You are not in the least late," Richard assured her. "How are you feeling today?"

"I feel very well! I slept peacefully and continue to enjoy the cool temperatures."

"I do not like your hat, Cousin," Georgiana said suddenly, frowning.

Anne reached a hand up to touch her elaborate straw hat, confused. "What is wrong with it?"

"I fear you will lose it," her younger cousin explained. "The wind may be strong on the beach, and it will likely fly away from you. You should wear a bonnet with strings."

"Oh," Anne said blankly. "Oh dear, I do not own any such bonnets as I rarely go outside at Rosings except when I am in the phaeton."

"I will lend you one," Georgiana said and, without another word, rushed up the stairs toward her bedchamber.

"I am sorry to be such a bother," Anne said nervously. "First I had to borrow a dress from you, Miss Bennct, and now a hat from Georgiana."

"Nonsense," Elizabeth said firmly. "We are pleased to have you here with us, and you had very little time to prepare for your journey here, after all."

"Miss Bennet is correct, Anne," Darcy assured his cousin. "Furthermore, Georgiana has plenty of bonnets."

"And I have plenty of dresses which are appropriate for wandering around in marshy areas," Elizabeth added cheerfully.

Georgiana ran lightly down the stairs and handed a bonnet to Anne, who looked down at it, then at Georgiana's head. "This looks the same as yours, Georgiana!"

"I have six essentially identical bonnets because they are comfortable. Now, shall we go?"

Darcy gestured for the ladies to walk toward the back door, which led to the courtyard. "We shall indeed."

Chapter 31

"George! George!" Mrs. Younge exclaimed from her position near the window.

Wickham, who was flopped on the bed nursing a hangover, lifted one weary eyelid. "What is it?"

"Darcy and his company just appeared … there they are! They are getting into the carriage!"

Headache forgotten, Wickham leaped to his feet and rushed over to stare out at the courtyard behind the red brick house. He could see the tall form of Fitzwilliam Darcy helping a feminine figure wearing a familiar bonnet into the carriage. Even as the twosome watched from their rented room, Darcy climbed in after his sister.

"It is time," Wickham said, grabbing a bag containing various accouterments for an abduction, and hurried out the door with Mrs. Younge in pursuit.

/

"We will back in less than two hours," Darcy said to his coachman. The man bobbed his head respectfully and carefully directed his horses to move off the rough road which ran parallel to the beach. Darcy gave one glance around him and noted, absently, that two horses were approaching from the direction of Ramsgate, though he was too far away to see the riders clearly. He was a trifle surprised that anyone else was using the trail today. During their past trips to Ramsgate, they had rarely seen others while enjoying the sights and studying the birds. With his party disappearing down the path toward the beach, he hurried to catch up with them.

/

"Do you think Mr. Darcy recognized us?" Mrs. Younge asked fearfully as Wickham directed his horse onto a narrow trail that led toward the ocean.

"No, of course not, or he would have chased us down in outrage," Wickham answered irritably, though he kept his voice low. "Henrietta, my dear, you need to get hold of yourself. We will tie the horses along the path and proceed to the treeline near the ocean. We will hide amongst foliage until Georgiana wanders by and then drag her into the wood. By the time Darcy realizes she has disappeared, we will have her on my horse and will be on our way."

"She may not wander this far north," Henrietta murmured.

"If she does not, we will try again another day," Wickham said patiently. "You know how much the girl likes this beach. This will not be her only trip here."

Mrs. Younge blew out a breath and struggled to calm her racing heart. This was their only chance of escaping the dreary poverty of their lives. They would not, *could not*, fail.

/

The trail which led to the water was narrow, and Elizabeth, tugging at her skirt to free herself from a drooping branch, congratulated herself once again for bringing several older gowns for her journey to Ramsgate. Mrs. Bennet had been horrified, of course. She always wanted her daughters dressed very well when in company, but Elizabeth had insisted that Georgiana would likely want to visit places with mud and weeds.

The path opened out into open sea and sky, and Elizabeth gaped in awe. She had been greatly impressed with the beach at Ramsgate, but the shore here was wild and free with blue sky overhead, interspersed with a few wispy white clouds, with rough grasses at her feet, pools and rivulets of water flowing across wet sand, and strange mossy clumps which decorated the beach area.

"Is it not marvelous?" Georgiana asked, her eyes glowing with pleasure.

"It is absolutely incredible!" Elizabeth replied joyfully. "Do you not think so, Miss de Bourgh?"

"I do," Anne said softly. She had missed the trip to the beach the day before and found herself almost unable to speak for wonder. The soft breezes caressed her cheeks within her bonnet, and even as she watched, a wading bird some ten feet away lifted its head from the water with a shell its beak.

"What kind of bird is that?" Colonel Fitzwilliam asked.

"It is a black tailed godwit," Georgiana said. "They have strong beaks and can burrow into the sand for worms and mollusks to eat."

"Look over there!" Elizabeth cried out, pointing at a medium sized brown bird with very red legs standing near the edge of the rippling waves.

"That is a redshank," Georgiana declared. "They wade in search of little fish, but they also forage on land for insects, spiders, and tadpoles. Is he or she not beautiful?"

"Do the males and females look the same, then?" Elizabeth asked.

"The females are supposed to have slightly lighter upper parts," her young friend said, "but I can never quite be certain. Peafowl are far easier to tell apart as the peacocks are so very different from peahens."

"Look at those cliffs!" Anne said, waving an excited arm toward the city of Ramsgate. "I had no idea they were so tall, nor so striking!"

"They are marvelous," Darcy concurred, squinting towards the white cliffs which flanked the main harbor of the town. "I have heard that Dover also has incredible cliffs."

"The white cliffs of Dover are far taller, actually," Richard commented. "They are a full three hundred and fifty feet high and can be seen from miles out at sea – on a clear day, anyway."

"Georgiana, whatever are you doing?" Anne asked in astonishment.

Her young cousin, who had seated herself on a convenient rock, looked up in surprise and said, "I am taking off my shoes and stockings. I always wade in the waters here; it is quite private, you know. Will you not join me?"

"Oh, I could not!" Anne cried out, turning startled eyes on Elizabeth, who blushed rosy pink.

"It is entirely reasonable for you to do so, Georgiana," Darcy said carefully, "since you are with family and a female friend. It is not the same for the other ladies."

"Is it not?" Georgiana asked in a disappointed tone. "That truly is unfortunate, as the water is delightful. It would be … inappropriate?"

"Very inappropriate," Elizabeth said firmly, though she bestowed a warm smile on her friend. "I did, however, wear mitts today and will enjoy dipping my fingers in the pools and the rippling waves that wash up on the beach. I assure you that Miss de Bourgh and I will enjoy ourselves very much without wading. This place is as breathtaking as you said it would be."

"Indeed it is," Anne said and was aware of a strange twinge of envy at the sight of her young cousin rising to her feet, lifting up her skirts, and walking into the shallows. Her whole life, she had been wrapped in lambs' wool, sometimes literally. Her mother had never permitted Anne to get dirty, or wet, or tanned. Here, surrounded by the cries of unknown birds and the rustling of the grasses and trees, she felt a sudden, deep, heartrending desire for freedom from the limitations of her life.

"If you look carefully, you may find some sea shells!" Georgiana suggested, beginning to wade north along the shore.

"There are also crabs, so watch your toes, Georgiana," Darcy said in amusement, though his gaze was on Elizabeth.

She smiled happily at him and wandered closer to say, "This really is an incredible place, Mr. Darcy, do you not think? It is peaceful, but also so full of life. I adore it."

"I am glad that you do," Darcy murmured, his eyes fixed on the beautiful face of the woman he loved. "I wonder if you would enjoy looking at the tidal pools. There are often small fish and snails within."

"Oh, that does sound marvelous!" Elizabeth said, looking around eagerly. "What is a tidal pool, exactly?"

"It is a pool which changes depth depending on the tide," Georgiana explained and pointed one arm toward the north. "There is a tidal pool in amongst those rocks right there; I remember it from our trip last summer! Brother, you should take Elizabeth's arm so she does not trip. The ground is a little rough."

Darcy chuckled at this minatory order and turned to Elizabeth. "Shall we investigate the tidal pool?"

"I would enjoy that very much," Elizabeth said, reaching out to take her companion's arm. Under the gentleman's coat sleeve, she felt powerful muscle and sinew, and suddenly felt herself strangely shy in such close proximity to this man whom she admired more every day.

"Miss de Bourgh, Colonel Fitzwilliam, would you care to join us?"

Anne cast a warning look at the colonel and said, "I think I will walk along the shore a bit. Perhaps I will see additional birds or other wildlife."

"Perhaps you will," Richard said with quick understanding. "I confess that I am more interested in relaxing than walking, so will find a convenient mossy spot to rest. You may not know this, Cousin, but military men are notorious for napping at every opportunity."

Anne chuckled and began walking northward along the shore.

/

Ten minutes later, Anne de Bourgh looked back along the shoreline with contentment. Darcy and Georgiana were some fifty yards behind her now, and her younger cousin was up to her knees in the ocean waters. Beyond them, Anne could just see the recumbent form of Colonel Fitzwilliam, who had found a comfortable mossy place to recline. They were all of them dressed rather simply today, and Anne marveled again at how comfortable, how relaxed, how freeing it was to be out in nature with patient, generous, charming friends and family.

She felt comfortable, safe, and accepted. She never wanted to go back to Rosings, though it was her home of birth. She wanted to be where she was not forced to wear elaborate clothing, where she could be herself…

She sighed and then flashed a smile at Elizabeth Bennet, who, after speaking with Darcy for several minutes, had decided to follow Anne northwards along the shore. Anne had long admired Miss Bennet for her vigor and her energy, not to mention her well-bred determination to never bow to the dictates of the autocratic Lady Catherine. Anne heaved a satisfied sigh. She had known for many years that she and Darcy were not a good match, in spite of Lady Catherine's insistence that the heir of Pemberley and the heiress of Rosings were destined for one another. Anne was thankful that her cousin had found a far more compatible woman as a potential bride.

Anne turned toward the water and took a deep breath to fill her mouth with moist, gently salted air. She had not felt so well in many a month. Indeed, she generally felt sickly at Rosings in the summer, though she knew not why. Perhaps she could convince Lady Catherine to take a trip here next…

In a sudden, terrifying instant, a hand clapped itself over her mouth, even as an arm grabbed her around the waist and lifted her off the sand. Anne froze in confusion and horror, too bewildered to so much as think.

/

In later years, Elizabeth was quite certain that an angel from heaven above had warned her of Anne's predicament. She had enjoyed her time with Darcy as they studied small creatures in the tidal pool and then, when that gentleman had gone to check on Georgiana, she had started wandering down the shore toward Ramsgate in search of beautiful shells. She had been walking with her eyes down on the sand, when something prompted her to lift her head, just in time to see a sturdy male form drag Anne de Bourgh into a clump of bushes some ten feet from the water's edge.

"Stop!" Elizabeth screamed at the top of her voice. "Help! Stop! Miss de Bourgh! Struggle! Fight!! Help!!"

Wickham, who had been feeling pleased with his efficient capture of Georgiana, felt a surge of flummoxed horror at these words, even as the lady in his arms began to thrash around wildly. Henrietta Younge, who had rushed to his side with a scarf in order to gag their captive, took one horrified look at the woman in Wickham's arms and cringed. "George, you fool! That is not Georgiana!"

Wickham cursed and turned his captive sideways, only to have his eyes flare wide. "Anne de Bourgh! She is also an unmarried heiress, Henrietta. Quick, gag her, and we will…"

"There is no time!" his accomplice yelped, though she rushed forward to force the scarf into Anne's mouth. "Someone is coming..."

"Stop!" Elizabeth Bennet screamed, rushing into the woods and, heedless of the danger, throwing herself upon Wickham. "You villain, let her go! Let her go! Anne, bite down!"

Anne, who had been wriggling madly in Wickham's harsh grip, obediently chomped viciously on the hand near her mouth, causing Mrs. Younge to scream and reel back in agony.

Wickham fell to the ground with Elizabeth on top of him, thrashing and punching while Anne, out of breath, rolled free.

"Kick him!" Elizabeth wheezed as she fought Wickham's harsh embrace. The man was panting, his eyes crazed, his teeth pulled back in a furious grimace. Anne, galvanized by the danger to her friend, obediently rolled to her feet, aimed, and kicked the man directly between his legs.

Wickham screamed in anguish and released his hold on Elizabeth just as Darcy and Colonel Fitzwilliam tore through the brush, their faces twisted with fear. Mrs. Younge, recognizing that all was lost, dropped her bag, took to her heels and fled toward her horse and potential escape.

Chapter 32

Fitzwilliam Darcy looked down on his captive, and his face turned red in fury. "Wickham!"

The man in question, still supine, lifted his hands protectively and croaked, "Now Darcy, just relax. I can explain…"

Colonel Fitzwilliam stepped forward and planted one booted foot on Wickham's neck. "We are not particularly interested in your explanations at the moment, Wickham. Darcy, you should fetch Georgiana."

"I am here!" Georgiana exclaimed, pushing her way into the small clearing where they had gathered.

"Miss de Bourgh, it is all right, you are safe," Elizabeth said, embracing the fragile heiress and handing her a clean handkerchief. "You are entirely safe."

"I know," Anne panted out, struggling to regain some semblance of calm. "Thanks to you. Are *you* all right, Miss Bennet?"

"I am well," Elizabeth assured her and turned her gaze on Darcy, whose distressed expression caused her own heart to flip oddly. "Truly, I am well. Do not worry."

"I am very glad," he said, his eyes slightly wet. "If something had happened to either one of you, I would never have forgiven myself."

"Mr. Wickham?" Georgiana cried out, having finally recognized the man lying on the ground with a brown boot to his neck. "Why is he here?"

"Apparently he decided to attempt an abduction of another heiress," Darcy said grimly, staring down at his father's godson.

"No, they were trying to capture Georgiana," Anne explained, releasing Elizabeth and wobbling a little. Darcy quickly wrapped an arm around her slight form.

"They?" Darcy asked sharply.

"There was a woman here as well," Elizabeth declared, glancing down the trail which led to the main road. "I did not recognize her, but she was about five and thirty, two or three inches taller than me, and she had black hair."

"She knew Georgiana by sight, and called her by her Christian name," Anne murmured. Now that her terror was over, she felt faint.

"Sit down, Anne," Darcy ordered, guiding her over to a handy tree trunk which was lying nearby.

"I am wearing your dress, which will be soiled," Anne protested, looking at Elizabeth.

"It is of no concern," Elizabeth said warmly. "Indeed, I will sit with you if you do not mind. I am quite winded myself."

The two ladies took their places on the log, and Elizabeth said, "The unknown lady had blue eyes and a mole on her left cheek next to her lips."

Georgiana and Darcy exchanged shocked looks and Georgiana said, "It sounds like my old companion Mrs. Younge, but she has red hair, not black."

"She was doubtless wearing a wig!" Darcy declared. "Of course, it *would* be Mrs. Younge. I suppose she is too far to capture now, but I promise that we will deal with her later."

"You should tie up Mr. Wickham so that he cannot run away," Georgiana stated, staring angrily down at the man who had tried to elope with her a year previously.

Darcy, who was caught between belated terror, relief, and fury beyond what he had ever known, looked at Richard, who said, "Georgiana is correct."

"There is no reason to…" Wickham began, only to be cut off when Richard increased the pressure on his captive's neck.

"There is the scarf with which they tried to gag Miss de Bourgh," Elizabeth said, pointing toward the ground.

Darcy nodded, and after retrieving the scarf, knelt on the ground and tied Wickham's hands very firmly together. He then motioned to his older cousin, who removed the boot from Wickham's neck and lifted the man bodily to sit against a tree.

"Well," Wickham said with an unpleasant sneer, "now that you are all comfortable, perhaps we can discuss the situation at hand. It may not have worked quite like I hoped, but you will, I am certain, agree that we need to come to some sort of agreement here. I have laid hands on two delightful young unmarried ladies in the last few minutes, and when word gets out that I embraced them close to me, and pressed a kiss on their lovely lips..."

"You did not!" Elizabeth snarled suddenly.

"My dear Miss Bennet," Wickham said with a facsimile of his charming smile, though his eyes were whorls of anger, "I confess that I am quite disappointed in you. I thought we were friends back in Hertfordshire."

"We were," Elizabeth agreed as she stood up, her eyes blazing. "We were before I learned the truth of you, that you are a vile, lying, cheating, selfish, debauched travesty of a man. I despise you!"

A tic formed in one of Wickham's cheeks but he merely said, "That is a pity, since I hold your reputation in the palm of my hand. I suggest that you…"

"No, you do not," Darcy interrupted angrily. "You attempted the abduction of Miss de Bourgh of Rosings. That is a matter for either transportation or hanging!"

Wickham's smile faded away to blank astonishment and he stared at this childhood friend in disbelief. "Nonsense, Darcy. I am George Wickham, godson of … in any case, things do get out, you know. Miss de Bourgh really has no choice, you know. I will tell everyone that she agreed to meet me here, that we kissed, and then we did even more than that, and…"

Darcy's closed fist smashed into Wickham's face, causing the bound man to stop speaking. The master of Pemberley then turned to look at Anne, who was staring in horror at her former captor, her face white as her fichu.

"Is he … he is right, is he not?" she gasped brokenly. "If word gets out…"

"It will not get out," Colonel Fitzwilliam said coldly. "As Darcy said, this is a capital offense."

"Is not the situation very dangerous?" Georgiana asked, her blue orbs glittering with unshed tears. "My brother says that a lady's reputation is very fragile, and if someone were to gossip…"

"Richard?" Anne said, rising to her feet and turning toward her military cousin.

"Yes, Anne?"

"May I speak to you in private for a few minutes?"

Richard, startled, looked at Darcy, who nodded and said, "We will watch Wickham."

"Good," the colonel said, guiding Anne some twenty feet down the path toward the main road. Once they were away from listening ears, he looked down and asked gently, "Anne, what can I do for you?

"Will you marry me?"

The colonel's expression shifted from benevolent to incredulous. "What?!"

"Will you marry me?" Anne repeated, and lifted a restraining hand. "Please, before you say another word, kindly listen. You know that there is a chance that what happened this hour will escape into society and that it would be best if I were wed quickly. I know that *you* wish to marry a wealthy woman. You are a fine man, Richard – genial, outgoing, but also a leader of men and quite able to go toe to toe with my mother and Wickham and emerge the victor. I realize my only attribute is my wealth, and if that is not enough, do not hesitate to refuse my suggestion. I merely think that … I believe we could be happy together at Rosings, and…"

She trailed off miserably and found herself twisting her handkerchief between wet hands as her throat tightened.

Richard stepped closer to her and took her hands in his own. "Anne, I am truly honored, and I think we would deal well together. I merely wish to know – I presume that you do not require a love match? I do like you, and care for you, but I am not in love."

"I am not in love either," Anne said firmly, "and I assure you I do not expect any such passion between us. I am not like Darcy or Miss Bennet – I wish only for a comfortable, safe home and a kindly man who will be patient with my weaknesses. But again, if you do not wish…"

"Anne," Richard interrupted her. "You are entirely correct that I do need to marry for money, and I can think of no other heiress of my acquaintance whom I would rather wed. Would you do me the honor of becoming my wife?"

"I will," Anne said and beamed up at her cousin in relief. "I will."

/

George Wickham was, at heart, an actor, with an actor's ability to adjust his expression and words to meet any situation regardless of what was actually going on in his mind.

Thus he sat against a tree, his hands tied in front of him, his posture casual, his expression winsome, his eyes calm, even as his mind worked busily on the question of how best to turn this to his advantage. He would happily marry Anne de Bourgh, but it was frankly unlikely that Darcy would agree to such a thing. However, a lady's reputation was extremely fragile. He ought to be able to wring a substantial sum from Darcy in exchange for his own silence. The question was how much Darcy would be willing to disburse to protect the family name.

His eyes drifted casually to the log where Elizabeth Bennet and Georgiana Darcy were now sitting side by side, arm in arm. He had known that Miss Bennet had accompanied the Bingleys to Pemberley earlier in the summer, but he had never imagined that she would befriend the Darcys in such a way. It was exasperating and frustrating. He had thought Elizabeth a true friend, but it seemed that even the independent Miss Bennet had been swayed by the wealth and influence of the Darcys.

For a moment, he considered making a sarcastic comment to that effect, but a glance at Darcy convinced him that he should refrain. He had seen his old playmate angry before, of course – indeed, the previous year at

Ramsgate, the master of Pemberley had physically tossed Wickham out the door when he had discovered Wickham closeted with his precious sister. Right now, with Darcy's expression thunderous, with his fists clenched, with Wickham's face swollen and angry from being punched, well – best to be silent for now.

The sound of steps caused everyone to turn just as Anne and Richard, arm in arm, entered the small clearing.

"Anne has just done me the honor of accepting my offer of marriage," Richard said, beaming. "Thus we need not concern ourselves about Wickham's threats regarding her reputation."

Wickham's jaw dropped open in surprised horror, and Elizabeth leaped to her feet, her face wreathed with smiles. "Oh, Miss de Bourgh, Colonel Fitzwilliam, I am so happy for you!"

"Please, will you not call me Anne?" the lady asked. "You saved me from abduction, after all."

"Of course, Anne. Please call me Elizabeth."

"Do you love one another?" Georgiana asked, her face fixed in a worried scowl.

Darcy winced slightly at this intrusive question, and Anne looked puzzled, but Richard, who understood his young cousin, said, "No, my dear Georgiana, we are not in love, but we do care for one another. Anne would like to be married to a reliable gentleman, and I would like to be married to a kind heiress. We both will benefit greatly."

"Furthermore, my marriage to the colonel will negate any possible concerns regarding Wickham's threats to gossip about me," Anne said, shooting a steely look at Wickham.

The man's mouth was hanging open in surprise, but at these words, he snapped his mouth closed, breathed hard through his nose, and said, "Even if that is true, there is still Miss Bennet's reputation to consider. I held her in my arms, after all…"

He trailed off as Darcy took a menacing step toward him, and Elizabeth said briskly, "Nonsense, Mr. Wickham, nonsense! You will shortly be locked up for abduction, and we are in Ramsgate, not Meryton. The Darcys and de Bourghs are of high society and well known in London, but the Bennets are minor gentry in Hertfordshire. There is nothing you can say here that will have any effect on my reputation at home."

"My dear Miss Bennet," Wickham purred, "I assure you that as the godson of George Darcy, I can…"

He stopped abruptly as Darcy stepped closer to him, his fists tight.

"Is it necessary for us to listen to his threats and lies?" Georgiana asked in genuine confusion.

"No, it is not," the colonel said, striding over to pick up a blue canvas bag which was lying near a tree. He opened it and his expression grew fierce as he pulled out a coil of thin rope.

"I see you came well prepared," he said icily, walking over to kneel by his captive. With swift movements, Richard tied Wickham's arms together with rope, removed the scarf from the man's wrists, and jammed the scarf into his prisoner's mouth.

"Darcy, we should get Wickham back to town, and I will report to the local authorities. I hope there is some sort of jail and that the local magistrate is a sensible fellow…"

"Colonel Fitzwilliam?"

"Yes, Miss Bennet?"

"Mr. Wickham was a member of a militia company in Meryton until a few months ago, whereupon he departed with his fellows to Brighton. It seems likely that he is a deserter from his company, and I am aware that Ramsgate has a substantial army presence. Perhaps it would be better to turn him over to the local military authorities?"

At these words Colonel Fitzwilliam produced a feral grin and looked down at Wickham who, in the face of such a threat, could not entirely maintain a sanguine countenance.

"That, Miss Bennet, is a marvelous idea," Richard said.

/

Ramsgate

"Fortunately, Miss Bennet was nearby and tackled Mr. Wickham, and I was able to wiggle free," Anne explained, taking a sip of tea fortified with brandy. She was curled up on a comfortable padded chair in her private sitting room, and her mind was a mixture of delight and belated anguish over what had come to pass.

Mrs. Jenkinson's faded blue eyes filled with tears and she said, "Miss de Bourgh, that is entirely dreadful! I am much at fault for failing to accompany you! I do not know what Lady Catherine will say."

Anne sat up slightly and grinned in a rather unladylike manner. "It does not matter what she has to say, because I asked Richard Fitzwilliam to marry me, and he agreed. As soon as we are wed, Lady Catherine will be relegated to the Dower House."

"My dear Miss de Bourgh, I am delighted for you!" her companion exclaimed. "The colonel is a charming, genial man, while also entirely able to manage your mother."

"Yes, he is," Anne said joyfully. "I do hope you are willing to stay on at Rosings, Mrs. Jenkinson. You have been a loyal and faithful comrade."

The older lady looked downcast and said, "I know I have been annoying at times, hovering over you and constantly offering you shawls and moving screens in front of the fire…"

"Because my mother insisted that you do so," Anne interpolated. "That will stop, of course, but I do beg you to believe that I consider you more than a paid companion. You have been a true friend."

Mrs. Jenkinson, who had indeed felt alarmed at the thought of finding a new position at her age, relaxed and smiled. "In that case, I would be honored and pleased to continue on at Rosings. Now I promise I will not hover too much, but I think you ought to take a nap after your ordeal. Or would you rather eat something first?"

"I am rather hungry," Anne said. "Perhaps you could ask someone to send up some toast, and then I will rest."

Chapter 33

"What will happen to Mr. Wickham?" Georgiana asked solemnly.

Elizabeth, who had changed out of her dirty gown into a fresh one, had been pacing up and down the drawing room, unable to relax after her recent ordeal. At this question, she stopped and sank down next to her young friend, her brow furrowed. "I am not certain, Georgiana, though his attempt of abduction could earn him a death sentence."

"And it should!" Mrs. Annesley exclaimed. Georgiana's widowed companion was usually a placid soul, but the news of Wickham's attempt to abduct her charge had turned the lady into a virago of fury. Elizabeth found it rather charming, if truth be told. It was wonderful that Georgiana had several passionate protectors.

"What do you think?" Georgiana inquired, her blue eyes fixed unnervingly on Elizabeth's brown ones. "Do you think Wickham should die?"

Elizabeth blew out a breath and sighed deeply.

"I … believe that I do," she said, though rather reluctantly. "The other obvious option is that he be transported to the Australian colonies, but he is such a rogue, and I fear that given his proclivities, he would eagerly take advantage of women elsewhere. I hate the thought of such a thing."

"As do I," her young friend said. "If he is hanged, will he be able to meet with a man of God to talk about his eternal soul?"

"Yes, he will," Mrs. Annesley declared. "I have a distant cousin who is a rector, and he provides spiritual instruction and comfort to condemned prisoners at Newgate. Wickham will have an opportunity to make his peace with God."

Privately Elizabeth wondered if Wickham, a man who had heartlessly plotted to abduct his own godfather's daughter, would submit to God's authority, but perhaps when faced with death, even George Wickham would seek forgiveness.

"Then I am at peace with a death sentence," Georgiana said, breaking into her thoughts. "He is an evil, dangerous man."

"He is," Darcy agreed, causing all three ladies to turn toward the door in surprise.

"Brother!" Georgiana exclaimed, rising to her feet and hurrying toward him. "Is Wickham locked up now?"

"Yes, and he is being held by the military authorities who have agreed to hold him for desertion and attempted kidnapping. Richard is working with the man in charge, a

Colonel Mueller, to ensure that Wickham does not escape."

"Good," Georgiana said in relief. "I am glad we are safe from him. What of Mrs. Younge?"

"Colonel Mueller has sent out men to search for her, though if she has any sense at all, she will have fled Ramsgate."

"One thing I do not understand, Mr. Darcy, is why Wickham attacked Anne instead of your sister," Elizabeth said. "Georgiana is a few inches taller than her cousin."

"Wickham explained that he made the mistake because Anne and Georgiana were wearing nearly identical bonnets," Darcy explained. "Mrs. Younge, who was familiar with Georgiana's preferred headwear, misidentified Anne because she was turned toward the sea, and in their rush, they did not realize that Anne was too short to be my sister."

"Such a vile man, and a horrible woman too, to plot against a girl like Georgiana," Elizabeth said in disgust.

"They are, but we will soon be rid of Wickham and Richard has promised to track down Mrs. Younge," Darcy said. He paused and added hesitantly, "Miss Bennet?"

"Yes?"

"Would you care to walk down to the beach with me?"

Elizabeth blushed and said, "Yes, Mr. Darcy, I would be delighted."

"May I come too?" Georgiana asked eagerly.

Darcy turned and put his hands on his sister's shoulders. "Another time, Georgiana. I would like to speak with Miss Bennet alone."

Georgiana stared in confusion, and then her face cleared. "I understand, Brother! Have fun!"

Elizabeth's face felt like it was on fire, but she managed a shy smile at Mr. Darcy. "I am certain we will."

Elizabeth was thankful for the crisp air blowing in from the ocean. She and Darcy had silently walked arm in arm from the red brick house down the street to the sandy beach. Now, with her cheeks cooled and her heart beating steadily, she turned to look upon her companion and said, "I love Ramsgate."

"I love *you*," Darcy said bluntly, which caused Elizabeth's traitorous skin to flush pink again.

"Mr. Darcy…"

"Please, allow me to speak further. I confess that the day I met you, I had no idea how quickly you would capture my heart. You are a beautiful lady, Miss Bennet, but I have known many beautiful ladies. No, I have fallen in love with you because of your courage, your intelligence, your wit, and your kindness to my dear Georgiana. By the time your party left Pemberley, I was strongly drawn to you. In these last few days, my attachment has grown only more robust. Today, when you bravely rushed to save Anne, well – I confess I was greatly alarmed when I heard your cries for help. If I had lost you … oh Miss Bennet, the threat of your loss has forced me to realize how I adore you! My dear Elizabeth, would you do me the honor of becoming my wife?"

He halted and stared down at her, his heart beating rapidly. He had not intended to declare himself so quickly, but then he had never imagined that within a day of their arrival at Ramsgate they would be subjected to an attack by George Wickham. When Elizabeth had cried out for help in the marshlands, Darcy had truly been frightened for her sake, and even now, though she bore herself with her usual strength, he felt a deep desire to pull her close and comfort her after such a terrifying ordeal.

Elizabeth had been thinking deeply as well. She loved Mr. Darcy, she knew that. But…

"You have not forgotten, sir," she said with some difficulty, "that I have relatives in trade, and that my mother and young sisters are not entirely as well-mannered as…"

"It is nothing to me," Darcy insisted with a rather wild wave of his hands. "I love you, and I love your parents for raising you, and the younger Misses Bennet because they are your sisters, and I hope, soon to be mine as well. I have not come to this decision lightly, I assure you."

Elizabeth's eyes were suddenly filled with joyful tears, and she nodded ecstatically. "In that case, yes, Mr. Darcy, I would be honored to be your wife."

"Oh Elizabeth!" the gentleman murmured, "Oh my dear Elizabeth!"

Elizabeth Bennet, who had thwarted an abduction attempt today, found new heights of courage as she lifted herself up on her tiptoes to plant a firm kiss on Darcy's mouth.

He returned the kiss with passionate enthusiasm, and they only broke loose when a cheerful male voice commented, "Well, it seems that more congratulations are in order."

Both breathing heavily, Elizabeth and Darcy turned smiling, bashful faces on Richard Fitzwilliam, who had been walking back toward the brick house when he spied his cousin locked in a firm embrace with Miss Bennet.

"Yes, Elizabeth has agreed to be my wife," Darcy said, beaming.

"I am very happy for you both," Richard declared.

/

"Thank you, Priscilla," Anne said to her maid, taking one last look in the mirror. She had a slight bruise on her cheek, but her face was otherwise unmarked. Her body was another matter, as she had contusions across her torso where Wickham had held her in his harsh grip.

She shuddered slightly, which provoked her maid to ask, "Are you well, Miss de Bourgh?"

"I am well," Anne answered quickly, and then added, "I am more than well. Colonel Fitzwilliam offered for my hand in marriage, and I have accepted."

"Oh, I am so happy for you!" the girl gushed. "Colonel Fitzwilliam is such a wonderful gentleman."

"He is," Anne agreed, passing out of her bedchamber into the corridor, down the stairs, and into the drawing room, where her cousins and Elizabeth were assembled.

All rose as she stepped into the room, and Richard rushed forward to grasp Anne's hands in his own large ones. "Anne! How are you feeling, my dear?"

She smiled at her fiancé's affectionate words and said, "I am well enough, though sore. Miss Benn... Elizabeth, are you well?"

"I am a little bruised but essentially unharmed."

Anne released her grip on Richard, though she remained close to his comforting bulk, and turned toward Miss Bennet. "I do not remember if I thanked you previously, Elizabeth. You were so very brave. Thank you for saving me."

"You did thank me," Elizabeth assured her, "and truly, I need to thank *you*. You were also brave, Anne. You fought and struggled and even bit Mrs. Younge to escape, and you kicked Wickham hard enough to make him let me go. You were marvelous."

Anne blushed at the reminder of her own kick at Wickham's nether regions, but she said in wonder, "I suppose I was rather brave. It is quite astonishing, really."

"It does not astonish me in the least," Richard said fondly. "But come, there is other news that will bring you much joy."

Georgiana, finding she could no longer hold back, cried out, "My brother and Elizabeth are engaged to be married!"

Anne's face lit up, and she turned toward her wealthy cousin. "Darcy! Many congratulations to you! Elizabeth is perfect for you."

"I quite agree," Darcy answered, his gaze fixed on his fiancee's vibrant countenance. "I prayed that God would bring me the right bride, and He has done so."

"Elizabeth and I will soon be sisters!" Georgiana said ecstatically.

"How soon?" Anne asked, her own eyes turning to fix on Richard's face.

"We were just discussing that when you came in, my dear," the colonel said, guiding her toward a comfortable couch so that they could both seat themselves. "I am inclined to think it would be best for us to marry quickly, the better to deal with Lady Catherine, though of course I will not press you if you wish for more time."

"The sooner the better," Anne agreed firmly. "The sooner that you gain control of Rosings, the sooner we can work to make the estate our home as opposed to my mother's."

"As for Elizabeth and I," Darcy said, "we too wish to marry soon, but I must ask for Mr. Bennet's blessing first. We will likely marry in Hertfordshire by common license as soon as we have arranged for the settlements and the like."

"Anne, we will need to speak with the lawyers regarding the specifics of Sir Lewis de Bourgh's will and your mother's jointure," Richard said, "and I must sell my Army commission. It will not take long. I imagine we can be married within a fortnight."

"That is marvelous," Anne began and then trailed away at the sound of an unwelcome, imperious voice in the outer foyer of the house. "Where is Darcy? Where is my daughter, Miss de Bourgh? Take me to them at once!"

Anne shot a horrified glance at Richard, who said, "Do not worry, darling. Darcy and I can manage Lady Catherine."

"Indeed we can," Darcy said grimly.

"I suggest that we should avoid telling Lady Catherine about Mr. Wickham's attack," Elizabeth said. "It would only upset her."

"You are right, of course," Darcy agreed. "Georgiana, do not say anything about Mr. Wickham, please."

"I do not wish to say anything at all to Lady Catherine," Georgiana said, her face twisted in distress.

"She frightens me, and she is going to be very angry when she hears that my brother and Elizabeth are engaged."

Elizabeth glanced at Mrs. Annesley who proposed, "Perhaps Miss Darcy and I should leave by the servant's door to avoid Lady Catherine?"

"That is an excellent plan," Darcy concurred with a grateful look at this sister's companion. He had chosen Mrs. Younge very poorly, but Mrs. Annesley was a treasure. He watched with satisfaction as the older woman shepherded Georgiana out of the room, and then he turned to Elizabeth. "My dear, my aunt may well be abusive towards you. Do you wish to leave?"

"Not at all," his lady declared. "My courage always rises with any attempt to intimidate me."

"Anne, you should leave if you are not ready to speak to your mother," Richard said.

"No, I will stay. I feel safe with you here."

The door opened, and the butler entered and said, "Lady Catherine de Bourgh."

Chapter 34

The lady entered with her head held high, her posture rigidly straight. Elizabeth found herself suppressing a smile at their unwelcome guest's hat, which was an elaborate turban decorated with tall peacock feathers. It was absurd headwear for a long trip in a carriage, but Georgiana would probably find the feathers interesting.

The woman looked around at the two couples standing in wait, and she scowled at the sight of Darcy, who was standing close to Elizabeth.

"Darcy, what is the meaning of this? I expressly ordered you *not* to bring Miss Bennet along with you to Ramsgate, and I told you to halt at Rosings for a few days on your way here."

Darcy clenched his teeth, but a quick glance at Elizabeth's dancing eyes quenched his temper. "Lady Catherine," he said, "I am not one of your lackeys to jump to your orders. I am my own man."

His aunt turned her attention on her daughter. "Anne, what did you mean by sneaking out of Rosings like a thief in the night while I was in London? I am most seriously displeased."

Anne, to her surprise, felt herself undismayed by her parent's obvious anger. She had always been intimidated by her mother, but in the wake of Wickham's attack, Lady Catherine seemed more a grotesque, even pathetic, figure.

"I was invited by Richard and the Darcys, Mother," Anne said simply, "and I am extremely thankful that I accepted their suggestion that I come here. We have wonderful news!"

Lady Catherine's irritable expression faded away and was replaced by obvious satisfaction. "You are finally engaged!"

"I am," Anne began.

"It is about time!" Lady Catherine cried out.

"To Richard!" her daughter finished loudly.

The older woman stared at her daughter, then at Colonel Fitzwilliam, who was grinning openly, and then back at Anne. "No! No! I forbid it! A mere second son? It is absurd."

"I am sorry that you are unhappy, Lady Catherine," Richard said, his eyes twinkling, "but I asked Anne for her hand in marriage, and she has accepted me. There is nothing you can do about it."

"Nonsense! Anne has the right to break an engagement, and she will do so. She will marry Darcy…"

"I fear Mr. Darcy does not have that option," Elizabeth interrupted in a clear voice. "A few hours ago,

Mr. Darcy asked for my hand in marriage, and I accepted. We are engaged."

Lady Catherine's pupils dilated in shock, horror, and then fury. "You ... you cannot be ... Darcy would not..."

"Indeed, I have," Darcy declared, reaching out and entwining his arm with Elizabeth's. "Miss Bennet has done me the honor of accepting my offer of marriage, and I could not be happier."

"No! You cannot be serious! Darcy, you are engaged to Anne! You cannot marry this ... this..."

"Take care how you speak about my intended bride," Darcy snarled, releasing Elizabeth and stalking forward to loom over his aunt. "I assure you that I will have no hesitation in throwing you out of the house if you insult Elizabeth."

Lady Catherine had indeed been preparing further invective, but the look on her nephew's face suggested that she had best try a different argument.

"Darcy!" she croaked. "Surely you must see ... your dear mother wished for you to marry Anne. You would not disregard her last desire..."

"My mother is dead," Darcy said coldly. "Even if she did wish me to marry Anne, there were never any formal papers signed regarding the match. I am in love with Elizabeth, and Anne is..."

"Love?" his aunt shrieked, her outrage sweeping away any semblance of restraint. "Love?? You are nephew of an earl and a lady, and master of a great house. You are not a peasant to think of the carnal desires of the flesh. Miss Bennet is not worthy of you! She is but the second daughter of a country gentleman, and her elder sister is married to a man whose fortune comes from trade! Are the shades of Pemberley to be so polluted?"

"Richard, will you assist me in escorting Lady Catherine to her carriage?" Darcy asked, his jaw tightening ominously.

"With pleasure," the colonel said, stepping forward. The two gentlemen lifted their aunt up by her arms and began carrying her toward the front door of the house. Lady Catherine was so shocked by this unexpected action that she grew rigid and silent for a minute. It was not until her nephews had carried her bodily out of the house that she began to wriggle and protest. "Unhand me, both of you. How *dare* you?"

Lady Catherine's carriage was drawn up in front of the house, and Darcy wrenched open the door with his left hand, whereupon he and Richard shoved their aunt into the enclosure.

"Lady Catherine," Darcy said, ignoring the shrinking maid who was inhabiting the rear facing seat of the carriage, "I warned you not to insult Elizabeth. You are not welcome here. Go home."

"Go home?" the lady repeated in a stupefied tone. "I certainly will not! You cannot throw me out! I am your near relation!"

"I do not care," Darcy said bluntly. "There should be substantial moonlight tonight; I recommend that you order your coachman to drive back to Rosings."

"If that is unpalatable," Richard said, "you can stay in the boarding house around the corner. I stayed there myself before embarking for the Continent two years ago. It is quite clean..."

"A boarding house? Me? Lady Catherine de Bourgh, mistress of Rosings? Are you mad?"

"You will not be mistress of Rosings much longer," Richard said with a sweet smile and slammed the carriage door closed.

/

"Is she gone?" Anne asked eagerly as the gentlemen reentered the drawing room.

"I believe she is cogitating in her coach as to what to do next," Richard said with an amused smile. "Darcy threw her out and informed her that she is not welcome, and we have ordered the servants to keep her from entering. You need not worry about her."

"I am not worried," his fiancée said gravely. "After today's frightening events, I find my mother less intimidating than usual."

"She is all sound and fury but with little bite," Elizabeth said, "for us at any rate. She does have substantial power over her tenants."

"Yes, and Richard and I will make certain that she is stripped of that power quickly," Anne said with determination. "Darcy, I know you are of the view that my mother has not been a good mistress of Rosings."

"I fear she has not. She, like many of her fellow landowners, has wrested money from the estate without plowing necessary money back in. For example, I have often tried to convince my aunt to pay for better cottages for the tenants but she always refuses."

"We will look into that as quickly as possible," Richard promised with a fond look at his intended bride.

"When should we leave Ramsgate?" Elizabeth asked. "I know that Georgiana will be disappointed, but given the situation perhaps we had best cut this trip short?"

"I think we should," Darcy agreed. "Lady Catherine may lower herself to stay in town so that she can continue to harass us, and the sooner I meet with Mr. Bennet, the sooner we can marry."

"That sounds wonderful," Elizabeth said. "Perhaps you and I should talk to Georgiana now and explain the situation?"

/

"I am not disappointed in the least," Georgiana said. "Yes, I love Ramsgate and the birds, but we can come back another time. I want you to marry Elizabeth as soon as possible, Brother."

Darcy reached out, pulled Georgiana into his arms, and kissed her blond head. "My dear sister, I know Elizabeth will agree with me that you are partially responsible for our engagement. It was your friendship with Elizabeth that first drew my heart and mind toward her."

Georgiana returned the embrace with fervor and smiled at her brother's betrothed. "Elizabeth is the best friend I have ever had. I am so happy."

/

"Yes, Lady Catherine," the landlady said nervously. "I have several rooms on the second floor, including a corner room looking over the adjacent courtyard as you requested. It is quite fortunate as the couple staying in that room departed in a hurry this morning and…

She trailed off under her new guest's basilisk glare, and Lady Catherine said, "I care not about any previous tenants. I assume the chamber has been well cleaned?"

"Oh yes, my lady, yes, with fresh, ironed sheets. I am certain you will be very comfortable."

Lady Catherine was positive that she would be absolutely miserable, but desperate times called for desperate measures. Darcy, Anne, and Richard had lost their collective minds, but she would make them see reason. In order to do so, it was necessary for her to stay in this hellhole of a boarding house.

"Take my trunks upstairs," she ordered her footmen and then turned to the landlady. "I will take dinner in my room in half an hour."

The woman opened her mouth in protest, and then shut it. Her noble guest was paying very well, and naturally had no desire to mingle with the mere commoners who would soon gather in the dining room.

"Of course, my lady, it will be as you wish."

Colonel Mueller of the 20th Foot Regiment stepped into his secretary's little room which led into his own, larger, workplace.

"Good morning, Lieutenant," he said to the young man.

Lieutenant Simpson stood up and saluted. "Good morning, sir. Colonel Fitzwilliam is waiting for you within."

Mueller nodded and strode into his own office, whereupon he exchanged salutes with Colonel Fitzwilliam.

"Good morning, Colonel," Richard said courteously. "I apologize for visiting so early, but I plan to depart Ramsgate today with Miss de Bourgh and wished to discuss Lieutenant Wickham's fate."

Mueller gestured toward a chair and took his own seat behind his desk. He pulled a notebook out of his coat, glanced at it, and said, "What is your wish regarding Wickham, Colonel Fitzwilliam?"

"I spoke with my cousins, Mr. Darcy and Miss de Bourgh, at length yesterday regarding this deplorable situation. We believe that his attempt to abduct Miss de

Bourgh is a capital offense and that he deserves the death penalty."

Mueller nodded, read a few lines from the notebook, and then looked up at his fellow officer. "I concur. I met with Wickham last night in the holding cell, and the man is an arrogant fool. He confessed, nay, he *boasted*, that he laid hands on Miss de Bourgh with the intent of forcing her into marriage. More than that, he claimed that before her rescue, he…"

Mueller trailed off at the thunderous look on Fitzwilliam's face. "I daresay you have a good idea of what was said about Miss de Bourgh. I need not say more."

"My cousin is also my fiancée," Richard said grimly. "As the daughter of Lady Catherine de Bourgh, and niece of the Earl of Matlock, her reputation is of great concern to our family. I hope that Wickham's guards are discreet men?"

"You need have no concern about that, I promise you. I have arranged for four of my most reliable men to watch over Wickham, and they will pay no attention to his lying mouth. I will arrange for the court martial as quickly as possible, and he will be executed in short order."

"Do you need me to be present as a witness?"

"No. The man has openly confessed to attempted abduction, along with admitting that he deserted his militia regiment in Brighton. I suppose we should be thankful he is an idiot."

Richard grimaced and said, "He is not a simpleton, but he is supremely arrogant. Wickham, a mere steward's son, was fortunate enough to win the favor of Mr. George Darcy, my uncle. Wickham has long presumed on his position as godson of his father's patron and has been in the habit of lying, stealing, gambling, and whoring without fear of repercussion. It has finally caught up with him."

"Indeed, it has."

/

"My lady?"

"What is it?" Lady Catherine demanded irritably. To her surprise she had slept long and hard and thus was breaking her fast later than expected. She had assumed she would be awake at dawn, if not all night, which would have given her more time to determine how to coerce her younger relations into submitting to her will.

"My lady, two carriages are being prepared for travel in the courtyard."

Catherine cast aside her piece of toast and rushed over to the window, where her maid had been watching the adjacent house.

"Tell my coachman to prepare for a journey," she ordered, "and pack up my clothing."

"Yes, my lady."

/

"I hope we will see one another soon," Anne said, embracing Elizabeth as the two ladies approached their respective conveyances in the courtyard.

Elizabeth returned the hug and said, "I hope so too, but if not, I promise to write frequently."

"Elizabeth," Darcy said, "perhaps you should step inside the carriage with Georgiana. I see my aunt approaching, and I do not wish to expose you once again to her insults."

Elizabeth glanced over to observe Lady Catherine, with two footmen in her wake, marching rapidly toward her. She had no fear of the lady, but she also knew that her beloved would be more comfortable if she was out of sight. She deliberately rose to her toes and planted a kiss on Darcy's mouth, then accepted his helping hand into the carriage. She sat down next to Georgiana, who looked rather alarmed, and said, "Do not worry, my dear. Lady Catherine can do nothing but squawk, you know. Perhaps it would help if you imagine her to be a loud, rare, type of bird."

This brought a smile to Georgiana's face and she settled comfortably into her seat.

"What are you doing?" Lady Catherine demanded shrilly as Richard closed the carriage door behind Anne. "Where are you going? I demand to be informed of your plans!"

"We have no intention of telling you our plans," Richard said in his blandest tone. "You have no authority over me, Darcy, or Anne, Lady Catherine. The sooner you accept that the better!"

"I am your aunt, and Anne is my daughter! You may not care about ruining your own lives, but I will not allow you to destroy Anne's life, do you hear?"

The door to the Rosings' carriage swung open at these words, and Anne surged out, her usually pale face flushed with anger. "Darcy has been a wonderful, kind host, and Richard will soon be my husband. Neither of them has tried to ruin my life – *you* have, with your insistence that I do exactly what you want and marry the gentleman you have chosen for me. This ends now,

Mother! I will marry Richard within the month, and you will be sent to the Dower House. Do you understand?"

Lady Catherine stared at her only child in wonder, her mouth gaping open. What was Anne saying? Everything she had ever done was for Anne's sake! The girl was far too sickly and fragile, and frankly stupid, to manage a great estate, and as for Colonel Fitzwilliam, an army man, a second son, he was in no way prepared to administer Rosings. It was completely absurd…

"My lady."

She turned in confusion toward her footmen, one of whom repeated urgently, "My lady, you should move out of the way."

She did move, numbly, as the two carriages were set into motion and her two nephews, and niece, and daughter, and their accursed guest, Elizabeth Bennet, rolled away smoothly toward a nearby road. She felt like screaming and shouting and howling, but there was no reason to do so, was there?

She had lost.

/

Longbourn

Two days later

Mr. Bennet was happily reading one of John Home's plays, *Douglas*, when a loud shriek jerked him out of his contentment. He sat up in concern and leaned forward just as the door to the library was flung open, and his wife rushed in, her face suffused with delight.

"Mr. Bennet, oh, Mr. Bennet! Such wonderful news…"

"Mama," Elizabeth chided, hurrying in after Mrs. Bennet, "you should not…"

"Lizzy!" her father exclaimed, rising to his feet in order to embrace his favorite daughter. "My dear, this is a delightful surprise. Given your happy countenance, I assume that nothing is amiss, but I am confused; why have you returned from Ramsgate so quickly?"

"Well, as to that, Father, Mr. Darcy has a question for you," his daughter said, turning an arch smile on the gentleman from Derbyshire, who had quietly stepped into the library.

Mr. Bennet's brows lifted, and he looked at Elizabeth, who was blushing, and his wife, whose smiling cheeks were indicative of her joy, and said, "Please do come in, Mr. Darcy."

"Ten thousand pounds a year," Mrs. Bennet squealed, "and a large estate in Derbyshire! Oh Lizzy, Jane is nothing to you! Oh, I shall die of happiness!"

Lydia, who had descended from her bedchamber in response to all the noise, stared incredulously at her second sister and said, "You are truly marrying Mr. Darcy, Lizzy?"

"I am," Elizabeth said.

"How can you do such a thing, when Mr. Darcy was so unkind to poor Mr. Wickham?"

"Now Lydia, you will hush *now*!" her mother ordered, casting an anxious glance toward the drawing room door. "It matters not what happened between Mr. Wickham and Mr. Darcy. The lieutenant is poor, and Mr. Darcy is rich, along with being handsome and tall."

"Nor is Mr. Wickham a good man," Elizabeth said firmly, grateful that Georgiana had elected to stay back at Netherfield with Mary and Kitty, who were currently helping Jane. "He has a reputation for leaving unpaid debts, you know."

Naturally she would not tell her family about Wickham's thoroughly evil acts at Ramsgate, but his less scandalous crimes could be discussed with ease.

"That is true enough," Mrs. Bennet admitted. "I heard that several officers left unpaid debts when they left Meryton, including Mr. Wickham."

"If Mr. Darcy had given Mr. Wickham the church living, the lieutenant would not be so poor!" Lydia flashed back.

Elizabeth caught her mother's eyes and shook her head, causing the Bennet matron to subside, muttering irritably.

"Lydia, why do you care so much about Mr. Wickham?" Elizabeth asked gently.

Lydia champed her jaw angrily and said, "He is so handsome and charming, Lizzy. If I had gone to Brighton with the regiment as I wanted to, I think that maybe..."

She trailed off and Elizabeth leaned forward, her eyes boring into her sister's. "Maybe what?"

"You think that Mr. Wickham liked you, Lizzy, did you not?" the girl said, tossing her dusky curls. "Well, before he left, he said that he greatly admired me. Perhaps if I had gone to Brighton, Wickham and I would be married by now!"

Elizabeth paled and was actually thankful when her mother cried out, "Marry Mr. Wickham, Lydia? A penniless steward's son? Do not be ridiculous! With your elder sisters married to wealthy men, there is an excellent chance that you will find a rich man of your own in time…"

Elizabeth allowed the words to wash over her as she contemplated the potential disaster of Lydia becoming involved with Wickham. The latter would not, of course, marry a woman with no dowry, but Lydia was probably too stupid to realize that. If Wickham had succeeded in seducing the youngest Miss Bennet, it would have been a catastrophe for the entire family.

"Lydia," Elizabeth said suddenly, breaking into her mother's diatribe, "Mr. Darcy gave Wickham three thousand pounds to give up all rights to the living, and at Wickham's request."

Lydia stared at her sister in wonder. "Three thousand *pounds*?"

"Yes. I am afraid Lieutenant Wickham was not an honorable man in spite of his endearing appearance."

The door to the drawing room opened, and Mr. Bennet stepped in with Darcy behind him.

"Mrs. Bennet," the master of Longbourn said, "you will be pleased to hear that Mr. Darcy has offered his hand in marriage to our second daughter, and I have granted him permission."

"Oh, Mr. Darcy! I am so very happy," Mrs. Bennet exclaimed rushing forward.

"I am as well, Mrs. Bennet," Darcy replied courteously and pressed a kiss on the matron's gloved hand. "Your daughter is a treasure."

Mrs. Bennet had found her second daughter thoroughly bewildering, and often exasperating, for many years, but she could only agree. "Yes, my Lizzy is absolutely wonderful. Now, we need to start preparing for the wedding!"

Chapter 35

Ramsgate

George Wickham was lying on the dusty mattress of his cell when the solid wooden door creaked open and Colonel Mueller entered, accompanied by an elderly man whose black cassock and white preaching bands marked him as a clergyman.

Wickham rolled sullenly to his feet and stood at some semblance of attention. He had already spent three days in this disgusting place, and while he no longer considered himself a member of the military, he would go through the appropriate motions in the hopes of leaving soon.

"Lieutenant George Wickham," Mueller said formally, "at ten o'clock this morning, a military court heard testimony about your crimes of desertion and attempted abduction of a lady. In view of the heinous nature of your actions, you have been sentenced to death by firing squad. Said punishment will occur at four hours past noon today. Mr. Clarke has graciously agreed to spend the next few hours with you in the hopes that you will find peace with God. Do you have any questions?"

Wickham stared at him blankly, his mind a sudden whirlwind of disbelief, confusion, and horror.

"Death?" he repeated numbly.

"Death, yes," Mueller said. "Both desertion and abduction are worthy of the death penalty."

Wickham shook his head slowly, then more wildly. "No, no! I am the godson of George Darcy. You cannot … there was no trial! I was not allowed to speak for myself! You cannot…"

"We can, and we did," the colonel answered icily. "I had no intention of allowing you to spread your lies about Miss de Bourgh in open court, Wickham, nor was there any reason for you to be present at your trial. Only yesterday, you spoke openly and shamelessly about your desertion of your regiment and your attempt to kidnap Miss de Bourgh, the niece of your godfather."

Wickham stared in horror at the colonel, then at the parson, whose aged face was full of compassion.

"No!" he cried out, collapsing onto his smelly mattress. "No!! No!!!!"

"May God have mercy on your soul," the colonel said gravely.

"Mr. Darcy, I do hope you will do us the honor of having dinner with us tomorrow," Mrs. Bennet said eagerly as Darcy rose to leave. "I am certain Elizabeth can tell me what dishes you particularly enjoy."

Elizabeth looked startled at these words and cast an uncertain glance at her love, who in turn grinned at her before turning back to Mrs. Bennet and saying, "I am most grateful for the invitation, but I intend to leave for London early tomorrow morning so that I can meet with my solicitor regarding the marriage settlements."

"Oh," the older lady exclaimed, fanning herself with her hand, "the settlements. Oh yes, of course!"

"Elizabeth, perhaps you should walk Mr. Darcy out to his carriage," Mr. Bennet suggested with a broad wink at his daughter, who promptly grasped her beloved's arm and guided him out the drawing room, down the corridor, into the vestibule, through the main door, down the stone steps, and onto the main carriageway, whereupon she wrapped her arms around him and kissed him thoroughly.

He responded with enthusiasm, and when they finally broke apart, he said huskily, "I think we should marry very soon, do you not think?"

"I do," Elizabeth answered fervently. "Partly because I am eager to become your wife, and partly because I want to avoid weeks of my mother obsessing over the wedding breakfast."

Darcy chuckled and said, "I understand that completely, and eagerly look forward to serving you in this matter by marrying in haste."

"How long do you think the settlements will take?" Elizabeth asked practically.

"They should take no more than three days, and I will obtain a license while in Town. Perhaps we can plan on wedding a week from now?"

"That sounds wonderful."

/

Matlock House

London

"No, I do not know where Richard is," the Earl of Matlock said absently, his eyes fixed on the plaster moldings adjacent to the ceiling above his head, "nor do I care."

Lady Catherine, who had been stalking angrily up and down the parquet floor of her brother's study, turned and stared at him in outrage. "Not care? Not *care*? Have you listened to a word I said? Richard has proposed to

Anne, and she has accepted him! You must stop this travesty!"

"Stop it?" the earl demanded, peering at his sister with obvious amusement. "Why should I? My second son will soon be master of a great house. I am absolutely delighted, Catherine!"

"But … but Anne is to marry Darcy! Matlock, if you do not interfere, our wealthy nephew will wed a mere country gentleman's daughter, a woman of inferior birth, with no fortune and pitiful connections!"

Matlock stood up from his chair and waved a languid hand. "I do not particularly care, Catherine. Darcy has always been a resolute soul, and while this woman may not be ideal, he is hardly likely to change his mind based on my arguments."

The door opened and Lady Matlock entered, looking puzzled, and said, "You wished to see me, Husband?"

"Yes, my dear, my sister has brought wonderful news. Richard is engaged to Anne!"

"Oh, Catherine!" Lady Matlock cried out. "How absolutely wonderful! My dear son will not have to return to the Continent, and will be master of a wealthy estate. How delightful!"

Lady Catherine stared at her sister-in-law, then at her own brother, and howled in frustration.

1

London

"Madam?"

"Yes, Sally?" Mrs. Younge said distractedly as she kneaded a large lump of bread dough.

"There are some men to see you in the vestibule," the servant girl said nervously.

Henrietta scowled with irritation. After the disaster at Ramsgate, she had rushed back to her boarding house and was now catching up on all the duties left undone while she was away in Kent. Fortunately, she was too busy to dwell overlong on her disappointment. Wickham, who always fell on his feet, had doubtless extracted a substantial sum from Darcy in exchange for his silence, but it would not be thirty thousand pounds, nor was there any likelihood that Wickham would share his largesse with her since she had sensibly run away. It was a great pity that they had mistakenly snatched Anne de Bourgh instead of Georgiana Darcy.

She hastily took off her apron, wiped down her hands, and hurried into the front entrance hall as she scowled in annoyance. She did need additional renters, but interruptions meant that she was even farther behind…

She turned the corner and halted in dismay at the sight before her. Sally had neglected to inform her that the leader of the men was an army officer wearing a red coat, and that his four fellows all had an indefinable air of officialdom.

"Mrs. Henrietta Younge?" asked the officer in charge.

"Yes?" she answered fearfully.

"I am Colonel Richard Fitzwilliam, son of the Earl of Matlock and cousin to Mr. Fitzwilliam Darcy. You are under arrest for attempted abduction."

Mrs. Younge took a step backwards, and then halted. There was nowhere to run.

"I … I do not," she began, "please, I meant no harm."

Even though his eyes were dark with anger, the colonel kept his voice soft. "You and George Wickham attempted to take a gentlewoman by force, Mrs. Younge. That is a hanging matter, but if you cooperate and keep Miss de Bourgh's name out of any legal proceedings, I will arrange to have you transported instead of executed."

Henrietta swayed in place and reached out a hand toward a handy chair so that she did not fall over in her distress. "Transported? *Executed*?"

Colonel Fitzwilliam nodded, his expression grim, and said, "Wickham is slated to be executed shortly, Mrs. Younge. You can be thankful that our family considers you of less importance than Wickham, and thus, if you do not cause any trouble, you will at least have the chance to make a life for yourself in the Australian colonies."

Mrs. Younge stared at him in horror, her eyes filled with terrified tears. How could she have been such a fool as to involve herself in Wickham's schemes?

/

Ramsgate

George Wickham stood upon the grassy knoll, his hands tied behind him, his eyes covered with a white scarf.

Mr. Clarke stood a safe distance away, reading the Prayer for the Condemned Malefactor.

"Justly by man condemned to die, Jesus the desperate sinner's friend, Out of the deep regard our cry, And O! Let hope be in our end..."

When he had finished, Colonel Mueller glanced at his troops, then at the condemned man, and said, "Ready! Aim! *Fire!!*"

/

Longbourn

Elizabeth sat on her bed in her bedchamber, her mind tumultuous. She had lived in this room since she had graduated from the nursery, and everything about it was familiar, from the creaky board near the entry door to the way that the west window stuck after a rain. In the last few years, she had often been away for weeks at a time while visiting friends and relations, but in the past she had always known that she would come home to this room. But this was different. She loved Darcy very much and eagerly anticipated becoming his wife, but it was still a trifle melancholy to realize that she would never sleep here after her marriage. Her mother, who was still loudly ecstatic about her second daughter's incredible capture of a wealthy man, would put the Darcys in the best guest chamber when they visited.

There was a soft tap at the door, and Elizabeth called out, "Come in!"

Kitty and Mary entered, both looking flummoxed. Elizabeth leaped to her feet, rushed forward to embrace them, and said, "My dear sisters! I thought you were spending the night at Netherfield with Jane and Charles!"

"We asked Charles to send us home in his carriage so that we could speak to you," Kitty said. "Is it true, Lizzy? Are you and Mr. Darcy engaged?"

"We are!" Elizabeth exclaimed happily.

Her sisters looked at one another, and Kitty said, "Oh, Lizzy, I know that Mr. Darcy is very wealthy, but do you truly love him?"

"I do love him," Elizabeth said firmly. "I love him very much."

"But are you certain you know him well enough after a relatively short acquaintance?" Mary asked worriedly. "My dear sister, with Jane well married, we need not fear the hedgerows. I beg you not to accept an offer for merely pragmatic reasons."

Elizabeth looked at her in surprise. Even a year ago, Mary would not have considered whether compatibility was of any importance in marriage.

"I have not known him long," she admitted, "but I am well enough acquainted with him to know that we are perfect for one another. He is a wonderful brother, a diligent master of his estate, intelligent, kind, and…"

"Not to mention tall, handsome and rich," Kitty said with a giggle.

Elizabeth turned pink and said, "Yes, those things as well. Do not worry, sisters. We will be very happy together."

/

London

"Mr. Darcy, sir," the clerk said.

Darcy stepped into one of the meeting rooms of Mr. Newman, Solicitor, and halted at the unexpected sight of his cousins, Colonel Fitzwilliam and Anne de Bourgh, who were seated on a comfortable leather chairs across from a massive desk.

"Darcy, fancy meeting you here!" Richard said with a welcoming wave of his hand.

"I apologize for intruding," Darcy replied, casting an uneasy look at the papers spread out on a writing surface.

"Not at all, Cousin," Anne said. "When we heard you were waiting outside, we requested that Mr. Newman's clerk bring you here immediately. Are you willing to help us look over my father's will, along with the other papers regarding the disposition of the estate?"

"Please do," Richard chimed in. "I have no doubt you are more aware of the particulars of the estate, since I was frequently overseas these last years…"

"And Mother kept me entirely in the dark," Anne finished irascibly.

Darcy pulled another chair over to the desk and began looking through the documents, though he kept shooting surreptitious glances at Anne. His cousin looked very well with her cheeks slightly tanned, her body clad in a comfortable day dress of muslin, and her expression one of genuine interest in the documents before her. It was obvious that her engagement suited her.

"I assume you are here about your own marriage settlements?" Richard asked after a few minutes.

"Yes," Darcy agreed, his lips curving upwards in delight. "Elizabeth and I intend to wed exactly a week from today."

"Oh Darcy," Anne said contritely, "I am sorry for dragging you into our business when you have your own need to meet with Mr. Newman."

"There is plenty of time," Darcy assured her, glancing at the clock which showed it was just a few minutes after noon. "I am pleased to help you sort out any legal issues regarding Rosings. I can discuss my own marriage settlements with Newman in an hour or two."

"I presume you will be in Town for a few days waiting for the paperwork to be completed?" Richard asked.

"Yes," Darcy agreed, though a little sadly. He missed Elizabeth.

"In that case, I hope you will stand up with me at our wedding tomorrow?" Richard said.

"Tomorrow?!"

"Yes," Anne concurred with a saucy grin. "My mother is driving everyone nearly insane with her complaining about our betrothal, so my uncle Matlock has arranged for us to wed tomorrow. Once the ceremony is complete, we can send Lady Catherine to the Dower House and get to work."

"I would not miss your wedding for the world!" Darcy declared.

/

Netherfield Hall

"Elizabeth!" Jane exclaimed, pulling her sister into an embrace. "I thought you were planning to stay at Longbourn for the day!"

"I was," Elizabeth replied with an expressive grimace, "but Father had mercy on me and allowed me to borrow the carriage so I could flee here. Mother is driving me quite mad with her frantic preparation for our wedding breakfast. I do not care at all what we eat, and as for trying to find a pineapple for a table decoration, it is nonsense!"

Jane wrapped an arm around her sister and said peaceably, "Mother is naturally excited that her second child is marrying into great wealth, but I quite understand your frustration."

"I miss Fitzwilliam as well," Elizabeth admitted. "I know he only left this morning, but I can barely wait until he returns."

"That is because you are in love," her sister said fondly. "Now come, I know you do not like to be idle. Would you care to assist me in attaching lace for my baby's dresses?"

"I would be delighted."

/

St. George's

Hanover Square

"Dearly beloved, we have come together in the presence of God to witness and bless the joining together of this man and this woman in Holy Matrimony. The bond and covenant of marriage was established..."

Anne de Bourgh, arm in arm with Colonel Richard Fitzwilliam, gazed up into the face of the clergyman who was proclaiming the stately words from the Book of Common Prayer.

Flanking the couple were Darcy, on Richard's left, and Richard's sister, Lady Rebekah, on Anne's right.

St. George's was a large cathedral, but the pews had only a sprinkling of guests, all of whom had direct ties to the de Bourgh and Fitzwilliam families. One individual was very much not in evidence. Lady Catherine de Bourgh, furious to the last, had refused to attend the wedding ceremony of her only daughter.

Lady Matlock, seated at her lord's side, watched the ceremony with delight mixed with some anxiety. There was one section of the liturgy which was of concern...

"If any of you can show just cause why they may not be lawfully be married, speak now; or else for ever hold your peace."

Darcy stiffened at these words and cast a fearful glance at Richard and Anne, both of whom also looked nervous. Two or three seconds passed in apprehensive silence, and then the clergyman continued, "I require and charge you both, here in the presence of God…"

Everyone aware of Lady Catherine's opposition to the match heaved out a deep sigh of relief, and the ceremony continued.

As it came to an end, with Richard and Anne officially husband and wife after signing the marriage register, Darcy hurried over to congratulate his cousins even as one thought was uppermost in his mind. In six days, it would be his turn to wed his beloved Elizabeth.

/

Meryton

Six days later

The sky overhead was a mass of swollen gray clouds eager to drop rain on the earth. The wind, too, was brisk, such that Darcy had to clutch his hat as he stepped out of the carriage and hurried toward the front door of the church.

He cast an absent glance skyward before entering the church, and sent a hasty prayer heavenward that the rains would delay until Elizabeth and her family had arrived.

Not that his bride would care if her hair was wet and her wedding gown disarranged, but Mrs. Bennet would, and Darcy preferred to have Elizabeth's mother as calm as possible on this exciting day.

"Darcy!" Bingley exclaimed, standing up from his chair in the vestibule of the church. "I fear it is not a particularly propitious day outside, but I daresay you do not care."

"I do not," Darcy agreed, pulling his watch chain so that he could check the time. It lacked twenty minutes until ten o'clock, the time that the wedding was to start.

"I have been cast out of the sanctuary while Jane, her mother, Miss Darcy, and the Misses Bennet deck it with flowers, but since you are the groom, it would be best if you…"

He broke off as the door into the sanctuary flew open, and Lydia Bennet, dressed in her festive best, rushed into the room.

"Mr. Darcy!" she exclaimed, her handsome face flushed with excitement. "You must come in, sir. Lizzy will be here soon, and you should not see her before the wedding begins!"

Darcy found himself chuckling as the girl grabbed his arm and tugged him into the main body of the church, where Elizabeth's sisters were running around adjusting flowers, and many of the gentle inhabitants of Meryton were already seated on the pews. He was not a man who enjoyed being the object of mass attention, but somehow in this moment, with his wedding finally here and his darling bride on her way, he felt entirely at peace as various ladies and gentlemen smiled and shifted excitedly at the sight of his tall form walking quickly down the aisle with Bingley in pursuit.

Within a few minutes, there was the sound of voices in the antechamber, and a minute later the doors opened to reveal the sight of his Elizabeth on her father's arm. Darcy felt suddenly short of breath. She was dressed in ivory with a soft green overdress and a straw hat, with an attached veil that cascaded down her shoulders. Her hair, her glorious chestnut hair, becomingly framed her lovely, joyful face, and he watched in awe as she walked down the aisle, whereupon Mr. Bennet carefully took her hand and placed it on Darcy's own.

Darcy turned toward the rector, Mr. Allen, though he took a moment to smile at Georgiana, who was seated on the front pew. He knew, as did Elizabeth, that Georgiana had brought the two together. How fortunate he was to have such a wonderful, unusual, and peculiar sister.

"Dearly beloved," Mr. Allen began, *"we have come together in the presence of God..."*

Epilogue

Chapter 1

May, 1815

Ramsgate

Kent

Richard Fitzwilliam, husband of Anne, master of Rosings, looked out over the swelling seas and took in a deep breath of contentment. He was delighted because the breeze, though cold, was invigorating, and he was relieved because he no longer faced arduous journeys across the water to Europe, where even now armies were forming and shifting as the Allies prepared to battle Napoleon for supremacy after the Corsican had fled Elba, marched across France, and taken the throne from the hapless Louis XVIII. Fitzwilliam feared that the upcoming war would result in great loss of life, but his only part now was to pray. He was a husband, a father, and a master of a great estate. His duties were in England.

"Seez!" a little voice squealed. "Dada, seez!"

Richard wandered a few yards farther down the beach to where his two Darcy cousins were watching over Miss Arabella Darcy, a robust child of almost two years old.

"I see the seals, darling," Mr. Darcy said, crouching down next to his small daughter. "They are so big and gray!"

"Bi!" Arabella agreed, waving one chubby fist toward the dozen seals lying on the sand some fifty feet away, looking like so many plump lumps.

"I think we ought to retreat a little," Georgiana said. "I see pups among the seals, and we would not want to disturb their feeding."

Darcy nodded and hoisted his little girl up onto his shoulders, which caused her to shriek in delight. "Where would you like to go, Georgiana?"

"Let us walk toward that marsh over there," his sister answered, pointing toward the south. "I see spoonbills hunting for food, and I think I glimpsed a curlew flying in that direction a minute ago."

"Very well," Darcy said, deliberately bouncing his daughter to make her giggle. "We should return to the carriage in about thirty minutes, as Bella will be getting hungry."

Georgiana smiled up at her little niece and said, "I will also be hungry."

"Me too," Richard agreed.

/

London

"Has Lydia left her bedchamber yet?" Kitty asked eagerly as she bounced into her eldest sister's favorite sitting room.

Jane Bingley looked up from needlepoint and shook her head. "It is not yet ten o'clock, and you both were up late last night at the ball. She is almost certainly fast asleep!"

Kitty wrinkled her nose and said, "She promised me that she would get up in time so that we can both go to the British Museum with Mr. Banfield."

Jane set her work on a nearby table and said, "Kitty, do sit down, please."

Kitty obediently did so, though she looked puzzled and nervous.

"Kitty," Jane said carefully, "you have been spending a great deal of time with Mr. Banfield, and many of our friends are taking notice. Do you care for him?"

Kitty looked at her sister as if she was insane. "Care for him? I *love* him! He is wonderful! He is kind, and generous, he loves art, he is godly, he..."

"Is a second son," Jane finished. "I do not mind that, of course, I promise you. Mr. Banfield receives a reasonable allowance from his father, and he has taken Holy Orders, so if he can find a position, that will bring in additional income."

"He was just awarded a position as a curate in St.Albans," Kitty declared, "which will bring in an additional seventy pounds per year."

"That is wonderful, and it is likely that, if you wed him, Mr. Darcy can find a more valuable living for him in time. I merely wish to be certain that you have thought through the financial aspect of a possible marriage with Mr. Banfield. You will not be able to afford a house in Town, nor will you be able to purchase as many gowns as you are used to."

"Mary wed a clergyman, and you said nothing to *her* about money!" Kitty said truculently.

"I did not, but Elizabeth did," Jane said calmly. "Mary is very happy with Mr. Allen, and while their income is not great, at least Mr. Allen was awarded the living in Meryton after his father retired. Truly, my dear, I am not trying to discourage you. I merely wish you to be certain of the situation."

Kitty glowered in a way that was quite adorable on such a pretty face. "I love Mr. Banfield. I *adore* him. I would go in rags in order to be his wife!"

"I am certain that will not be necessary," Jane said affectionately. "Kitty, I think you have chosen a fine young man. But it is vital that you are prepared to live on far less than you are accustomed. It would not be fair to Mr. Banfield if you accepted his offer of marriage and then complained about having little money."

Kitty considered this gravely and then said, "I understand, Jane, and I promise you that I will be content. I am not like Lydia, you know. I do not need an exciting life, nor do I need expensive trinkets and the like. I wish for an honorable husband who shares my interests, and I have found that in Mr. Banfield. Of course," and here she sighed piteously, "he may not offer for me."

"I believe he will, and soon," Jane replied, picking up her needlepoint and returning to her work. "He spoke to Charles only yesterday on the matter."

"Oh!" Kitty cried out in joy just as the door opened and Lydia entered with a nursemaid and young Adam Bingley at her heels. Following them all was a black puppy, who began cavorting eagerly around the room, barking enthusiastically.

A few minutes later, Charles Bingley stepped into the doorway of the sitting room with young Mr. Banfield at his heels. The room was a cacophony of noise and movement, with Jane helping their noisy little son build a tower of blocks, Lydia petting the wiggling, yipping dog, and Kitty sitting back with stars in her eyes.

"Kitty," Bingley said with a smile, "Mr. Banfield has requested the honor of speaking with you in private. Are you willing?"

"Oh yes!"

/

London

May 2, 1815

My dear Amelia,

Yes, I am fixed in London for the present. Lord Hayward is spending a few weeks in Brighton as a number of his friends are there, along with the Prince Regent, of course. My sister, Louisa, is delighted to host me here in London for the Season. As the wife of a baron, many doors are open to me, and she is most pleased to have opportunities to meet with such exalted company.

My brother Charles is also in London, though he and his wife have not attended many parties this Season. Jane is increasing again and has been making a grand fuss about it. I saw her last week, and she said she was feeling somewhat better.

Louisa, too, is increasing again. I hope this one is a boy, though I will say that my little niece, Emma, is quite an attractive child.

I expect you are enjoying yourself in Scarborough. I have heard that the waters are excellent, and the sea waters most healthful, though of course the company cannot be as elegant and refined as here in Town.

Sincerely,

Lady Caroline Hayward

There was a soft tap at the door, followed by the entrance of Louisa Hurst with her little daughter Emma in her arms.

"Caroline," she said cheerfully, "I have been going through my wardrobe, and there are so many gown that I know I will never fit in again, or at least they will be entirely out of fashion by the time I am thin enough. My dresser is going through them, and we wondered if you would care to see if there is anything you would like."

Caroline sucked in a pained breath but managed a grateful smile. "Yes, Louisa, that would be wonderful. Thank you."

"Excellent. Now I need to take Emma upstairs for a nap, but I will join you in my dressing room in ten minutes."

Louisa rushed away and Caroline stood up and walked to stare into a nearby mirror. To her relief, her outward façade was calm in spite of the turmoil in her mind and heart. It was utter humiliation that she, the highest ranked female in her family, was currently dependent on the financial support of her sister and brother. She, Lady Caroline Hayward, married to an actual baron…

A childless baron who was forty years old and had made her his second wife after his first wife died in childbed and the babe with her. A baron who was a spendthrift and a gambler, who had run through all of Caroline's dowry in short order, and was even now drinking and carousing with the Regent while she stayed in Town with her sister. A baron who was always selfish, and, when in his cups, cruel.

A tear formed in Caroline's right eye, and she wiped it away.

/

Ramsgate

"Miriam is finished, Mrs. Darcy," Ruth said, wrapping her baby daughter in a blanket and placing her in a basket at her side.

"Will you please feed Andrew?" Elizabeth requested, gesturing toward her four month old son who was lying in his cradle, his hands eagerly grasping his little feet.

"Of course, Madam," Ruth said, standing up to fetch the heir to Pemberley.

Elizabeth looked down at her younger son, Stephen, who had been born twenty minutes after his brother, and pressed a kiss on the fuzzy head. Her pregnancy with the twins had been challenging, and she was thankful that both she and the babes had survived the delivery. It was unfortunate that she was not able to provide quite enough milk for both infants, but together she and Ruth, her wet nurse, were managing to keep the twins and Ruth's little daughter well fed and healthy.

"When you are finished with Andrew, I can take him," she said to Ruth, who nodded as she brought the little Darcy to her breast.

The door to the nursery opened and Anne de Bourgh entered with her own infant son in her arms. She greeted her cousin by marriage, sat down, and began to suckle her own child.

"How did you sleep last night, Anne?" Elizabeth asked once Baby Lewis was feeding well.

"I slept very nicely," Anne responded brightly. "There is no doubt that Ramsgate agrees with me. Lewis was also kind to his Mama and slept a full eight hours."

Elizabeth lifted Stephen upright, patted his little back until he burped copiously, and then handed him to a nursemaid so that his nappy could be changed.

"That is very kind," she said with amusement. "My little ones woke up at two hours after midnight and were determined to be fed. Miriam also slept through the night, so it was only my rascals keeping us awake."

"They were born a little early, Madam," Ruth said in a propitiating tone. "It is not surprising they need some extra nourishment in the middle of the night."

"Oh, yes. The twins are effectively younger, though they were born a week earlier than Lewis and Miriam," Elizabeth said, walking over to take Andrew from the wet nurse. The two had discovered that while neither had enough milk to feed two babies, together they could feed three, and thus all three infants were satisfied.

The door opened and a maid slipped in to say, "Mrs. Fitzwilliam, Mrs. Darcy, the gentlemen and Miss Darcy asked me to inform you that they have returned from the beach."

"We will be downstairs in a few minutes," Elizabeth assured her.

/

"Mama!" Arabella squawked. "Mama! See seez! See seez!"

Elizabeth handed Andrew to her husband and reached down to swing her daughter into her arms. "What did you say, darling? See...?"

"Seez! Seez!" her daughter burbled.

"Seals, my dear," Darcy said at Elizabeth's bewildered look.

"Oh, seals! How wonderful, Bella! You saw big seals?"

"Yes, and there were some pups too," Georgiana said gravely. "They are not very lively creatures, but it was quite interesting."

"I am certain they are!" Elizabeth declared. "Have you seen seals here before?"

"Yes, though never their young," her sister-in-law explained, walking over to take Stephen from a nursemaid. Georgiana kissed the baby on the nose, who gurgled

461

happily, and then continued, "I am thankful that you were not well enough to stay in London for the Season, Elizabeth. We have never been at Ramsgate so early in the year, and I am so excited that I was able to see seal pups!"

Three years previously, Anne Fitzwilliam would have been horrified at such a speech, but she knew Georgiana well now. Her cousin did not mean any harm, though sometimes her words sounded impolite.

"I think," Elizabeth said gently, "that you mean that you are enjoying being here in Ramsgate in the spring, and that you are also thankful that I can rest and recover here by the sea, which is most healthful."

Georgiana's brow furrowed, and her lips moved as she silently repeated Elizabeth's words, and then she said aloud, "I understand. It is unkind to say that I am glad you are unwell. I did not mean to be rude."

"I know," Elizabeth said fondly as she turned to her husband. "Shall we not take the children into the drawing room and have some tea?"

Darcy, his heart full at the sight of his wife, his sister, and his three precious children, could only nod in happy agreement.

Chapter 2

Green Havens

Pemberley

April, 1822

"Jane, my dear?"

Jane Bingley, who was studying the accounts for the household, looked up fondly at her husband. Charles had grown a trifle stouter in the decade since their marriage, but he remained the handsome, kind, generous gentleman who had won her heart.

"Yes?" she asked.

"Hurst and I are taking Hubert and Samuel out so they can practice riding a pony, and Adam and John are coming with me. We will be back by dinner time."

"Have a wonderful time," Jane said with a wave of one slender hand. He grinned at her and strode off, and she began doing sums again.

Five minutes later, she heard familiar feminine voices, and she found a bookmark, marked the spot in the ledger, and closed it just as Mrs. Bennet, Mrs. Hurst, and Lady Hayward entered the room.

"Mother, sisters!" Jane said, reaching over to ring the bell for a maid. "Would you care for some tea?"

"Oh yes, that would be quite pleasant, my dear," Mrs. Bennet said. "It is a little chilly today, though I am certain it will warm up soon."

"I am certain it will. Shall we all sit down?" Jane suggested. A maid appeared, and she gave the necessary orders for refreshments.

"I understand that the boys are going riding this morning," she remarked, turning to look out across the west lawn which led to the stables.

"Yes," Louisa agreed. "Emma was quite indignant that she was not invited, but I explained that she would be quite bored, as the young ones are learning to ride small, gentle creatures."

"Your Emma is as vigorous a horsewoman as Jane was," Mrs. Bennet commented. "Jane was riding horses by the age of nine, which I confess terrified me at times."

"Yes, Emma is a marvelous rider," Louisa said, "though I would say in many ways she is more like Elizabeth than Jane. She loves to climb trees and jump in mud puddles."

"Oh yes, my Lizzy was always coming home at that age with her petticoats dirty and her stockings torn," Mrs. Bennet said, shaking her head. "I quite despaired of her, only to have her successfully capture Mr. Darcy, with all his wealth!"

"Elizabeth is perfect for Mr. Darcy," Louisa said comfortably. "Am I correct that you are going to Pemberley tomorrow, Mrs. Bennet?"

"Yes, and Jane and her children are coming with me. In truth, I was not pleased when Mr. Bingley gave up Netherfield in favor of Green Havens, but now that Mr. Bennet is gone and the Collinses have stolen Longbourn, I find it most convenient to have three of my daughters living within twenty miles of one another in Derbyshire. I do not enjoy traveling as much as I used to. It was *very* kind of Mr. Darcy to give Kitty's husband the Kympton living. The parsonage is lovely, and Kitty has done wonders gardening the glebe! It is a charming place to raise her children, and so near to Pemberley."

"I do not enjoy traveling as much I used to either," Louisa commented, "though we do intend to travel to London in a month for part of the Season. Mr. Hurst's youngest aunt, who just returned from many years on the Continent, wishes to meet our children for the first time."

"Are you also going to London, Lady Hayward?" Mrs. Bennet asked politely.

Caroline managed a slight smile and said, "No, Charles and Jane have offered to host my son and me for the near future, which is very kind of them. I would not be

465

able to enjoy myself anyway given that I am still in half mourning."

Mrs. Bennet sighed deeply. "I quite understand, Lady Hayward. It is a terrible thing to lose a husband, especially when your son is still young. I hope you have a good steward for your boy's estate."

Caroline swallowed hard and turned a beseeching look on her sister-in-law. Her husband, Lord Hayward, had died of an apoplexy only seven months previously, leaving her a widow with a seven year old son, Samuel, who was, of course, the new Baron. Unfortunately, her husband had also mortgaged all of his property to fuel his dissolute lifestyle, leaving Caroline and her son with only three hundred pounds a year in income from her jointure, thus forcing her to live off the generosity of her brother and his wife. She had been so proud of herself when she had captured a member of the nobility a decade previously; now, she knew titles were nothing compared to kindness, stability, and respect in a marriage.

To her grateful relief, Jane turned the subject by saying, "That reminds me, Mother, I received a letter from Mary only this morning. She says that she visited Charlotte Collins a week ago, and that Charlotte has hired Mr. Wesley to be steward of Longbourn. I am certain he will do an excellent job!"

"Oh I daresay he will, though your father never found it necessary to have a steward!"

"No, but Charlotte is now a widow, and it would be too much for her to oversee the mansion itself, look after her three sons, and care properly for the tenants."

Mrs. Bennet grimaced. "Yes, I suppose that is true. I still think it ridiculous that Mr. Collins inherited the estate instead of Jane, but I am most thankful that all my daughters have made good marriages!"

"Have you heard from Mrs. Vincent recently?" Louisa asked with interest.

"Not in more than a month," the older lady said, "but then my Lydia was never a great writer. She is doing very well; her husband was promoted to general last year, you know, and Lydia is proving a most gifted hostess to the British diplomatic families in Paris. She has not yet conceived a child, and I do worry about that, but she has only been married for three years, and for part of that time, her husband was stationed elsewhere."

"It sounds like she is happy," Caroline said, finding it hard to keep the bitterness out of her tone. To think that she, with her excellent education and large dowry, had made a far poorer match than all the Bennet daughters, including the boisterous Lydia!

"She is very happy," Mrs. Bennet said cheerily.

Rosings

"Anne!" Richard Fitzwilliam cried out, surging into the nursery where his wife was nursing their youngest child and only daughter.

"Yes?" Anne asked, eyeing the letter her husband was waving around eagerly. "What has happened? Is something wrong?"

"No, everything is right! This is a letter from my mother, and she tells me that Tony's wife gave birth to a healthy son two days ago!"

"Oh, Richard!" Anne exclaimed, "that is absolutely wonderful!"

"It is," Richard responded, dropping into the chair adjacent to his wife. He reached over and stroked baby Esther's fluffy head and said, "I truly thought I was going to be stuck with the earldom given that Anthony sired five daughters before this little one."

Anne chuckled and caressed her husband's lean cheek with an affectionate hand. "Most men would be pleased to be heir to an earldom, darling."

"Well, I am not most men," Richard said decidedly. "Rosings is quite enough for any man to oversee, and I would despise having to care for the Matlock estates in Lincolnshire, especially since Tony is not as gifted an administrator as my father was, God rest his soul."

"I would loathe it too," Anne agreed fervently. "I feel much better now that I visit Ramsgate for many weeks every summer, and my mother is not permitted to cross the threshold of Rosings, but I still hate to travel long distances."

"I know you do," Richard agreed, kissing his wife on the cheek and then jumping to his feet. "I need to send a congratulatory letter to Anthony and his wife. I will include your good felicitations, if I may."

"I am indeed overjoyed for them and relieved on my own account, though you will not write about the latter, of course," Anne said with all sincerity. Her marriage of convenience to Richard had transformed into a union of genuine respect and camaraderie, and she had worried that when her brother-in-law, the current Earl of Matlock, passed on, Richard would be forced to spend substantial time away from her. Certainly there was no absolute guarantee that Richard would outlive his brother, but it seemed likely. Her Fitzwilliam was a hearty and energetic man, and the current Earl of Matlock was consistently delicate, but now the earldom would go to Anthony's son.

Yes, she was very relieved at this news.

/

Sydney, Australia

"Henrietta, here is the flour you need."

Mrs. Henrietta Brown, formerly Mrs. Henrietta Younge, looked up from kneading a lump of dough and said, "Thank you, Wilbur. I had just run out."

"Shall I send Alice to assist you with the bread?" her husband inquired.

Henrietta carefully dabbed her nose with the back of her mostly clean hand and said, "No, I think I am well enough for now. Thank you."

"You are welcome," her husband said courteously and scurried away, leaving Henrietta in charge of her kitchen.

Henrietta's sentence of seven years of labor had ended some two years previously, whereupon she could have returned to England. She had decided not to do so. There was nothing left for her in her land of birth, and here in Australia, she was a valuable commodity as there were far more men than women. She had chosen to marry Mr. Brown, who had left England some years ago with his family in order to make a living here in Sydney as a baker.

The first Mrs. Brown had died five years previously, leaving two daughters, and Henrietta now found herself stepmother to Alice and Barbara.

Her hair was now white, her face was wrinkled, and her clothing was practical instead of elegant. However, after seven years working as a washerwoman as a convict, she was pleased to have her own home, her own family, and to contribute to her husband's business.

Wickham was dead these ten years now, and Henrietta, while she deeply regretted her idiocy in taking part in his schemes, could only be thankful for what she now had.

/

Pemberley

Fitzwilliam Darcy swung off of his golden mare, handed the reins to a servant, and asked, "Is Mrs. Darcy still here?"

"Yes, sir," the man said. "She, Miss Darcy, and the children are up at the pond, sir."

"Thank you. Kindly provide water for Firefly and allow her to graze."

"Yes, sir."

Darcy glanced around with interest as he strode toward the path that would take him to the pond. Five years ago, Georgiana, along with Mrs. Annesley, had moved from Pemberley into the Lodge, the better to continue her peafowl experiments. Miss Darcy's attempts at breeding white feathered peacocks and pea hens had been remarkably successful, such they had all agreed that the walled garden near Pemberley was not large enough for her work. To his delight, she was receiving substantial attention and praise from other avian enthusiasts in the British isles.

He strode down the path which led to the back yard of the lodge, now transformed into a myriad of coops and runs, with plenty of open space for the birds to roam in good weather, and protective spaces when the winds blew hard and the snow fell. He grinned at the sights and sounds of the birds who were wandering to and fro, clucking and gibbering, posturing and occasionally even scuffling.

He began walking the path toward the goldfish pond, his heart pumping, his lungs pulling in the crisp April air. It had been a long and hard winter in Derbyshire, and he was even more appreciative of spring than usual, though he always loved spring, when the new plants pushed themselves above the dirt, when the sheep gave birth, and the cows and horses enjoyed frolicking in the pastures after a long winter in their stalls.

Darcy passed through the last stand of oak trees and halted at the sight before him. The sun was shining in a clear blue sky, and the waterfalls, flush with melted snow, poured vigorously down from the upper pool to the lower. It was beautiful.

Even more lovely, however, was the sight of his beloved wife, who was sitting on a convenient rock, holding some small object in her hand, with her children gathered around.

They made a charming picture; dark haired Arabella, now nine years old, took after both her mother and her aunt in that she was an extremely vigorous child who adored animals of all kinds, especially cats. The twins, Stephen and Andrew, now sturdy seven year olds, were nearly identical in features but different as night and day in personality. In spite of this, they were the very best of friends and were almost always together. Another son, Elias, age five, was blond like Jane Bingley, and shared his aunt's calm temperament. Last came little Phoebe, age three, a vigorous red haired child with a will of iron. Given that both Darcy and Elizabeth were strong willed individuals, the little girl's determination was no great surprise, but she did keep her parents and nursemaids on their collective toes.

"Papa!" Stephen called out, drawing the attention of everyone. In an instant, the children and Elizabeth were racing toward him, and then his offspring were hugging him while his wife took the opportunity to plant a hasty kiss on his lips.

"My dear, how was your trip?" Elizabeth asked when the children had subsided.

"It went well, but I am relieved to be home," Darcy answered. He had been forced to visit a subsidiary Darcy estate some two days away in order to deal with the sudden death of a steward. The older he got, the less he liked being away from Elizabeth, but it had not been practical for her to come with him on short notice because of the needs of the children, Georgiana, and the estate.

"We are happy to have you home as well," Elizabeth assured him, bestowing another quick kiss on his lips.

"Mama, do not squish the frog," Arabella said worriedly, which caused Elizabeth to grimace and lift her closed right hand. She opened it to reveal a tiny, exquisite frog, thankfully still unharmed.

"Thank you for reminding me, dear," Elizabeth said. "Can you return him to the pond?"

"Yes, Mama."

Not surprisingly, the five Darcy children wanted to watch the frog return to its home and rushed off, which allowed their parents to indulge in a longer kiss, though Elizabeth first assured herself that the two nursemaids in attendance were hovering near the children to make certain that no one fell into the water.

"Elizabeth, Brother! I caught him!"

Darcy disengaged from Elizabeth and waved a hand at his sister, who was just emerging from the tree line beyond the pond with a peacock in her arms.

"Georgiana!" he called back, and watched happily as she approached him on rapid feet, her blonde hair escaping from her simple straw bonnet, her blue cotton dress slightly smudged from her battle with the peacock, who was in turn regarding his captor with beady eyes.

His sister would never marry, Darcy knew that now. She was still unusual, even peculiar, still fascinated with birds and disinclined to be in the company of strangers.

He also knew it did not matter. Georgiana was happy as she was – sister to Darcy and Elizabeth, aunt to the Darcy children, who adored her. She did not need a husband, nor was there any reason to force her into society; there would always be someone at Pemberley to love Georgiana.

"Mercury escaped his enclosure this morning," she announced when she was close enough to speak with ease. "I am so glad that I found him! He is the peacock with the most white feathers of all my peafowl, you know."

Darcy put his arm around his wife and beamed down at his beloved sister. "I am very thankful that he is safe, my dear."

The end

Please Write a Review

Reviews help authors more than you mig
you enjoyed *Peacocks of Pemberley*, please <u>review it on</u>
<u>Amazon</u>. A 5-star rating means you think others should
read it. Thank you!

Thank you for reading *Peacocks of Pemberley*! If
would like to hear when my *next* story is published, sign
up for my newsletter. You will also get a FREE story just
for members called *A Busy and Blessed Day*. You will also
be among the first to hear about special promotions, get
insights into my writing, etc. <u>Click here to get your free</u>
<u>book.</u>

Here is the link in case you need to manually type it in:
<u>www.subscribepage.com/s1p4z6</u>

Sneak Peek of *Darcy in Distress*

Mr. Darcy is rich, well-connected and handsome, but he is also exhausted, broken-hearted and afraid. Can Darcy and Elizabeth Bennet find happiness together?

Assembly Hall in Meryton

October 15th, 1811

Elizabeth Bennet smiled at her close friend, Miss Charlotte Lucas, and said, "Come, my dear friend, you must give me your latest knowledge about Mr. Bingley and his party from London. Do you know how many gentlemen and ladies we can expect for this evening's assembly?"

Charlotte chuckled and shook her head. "Indeed, Eliza, I truly do not know. The last I heard, Mr. Bingley will be accompanied by his five sisters and a cousin, though I have no knowledge as to whether the cousin is a gentleman or a lady."

"'Tis far too many ladies," Elizabeth responded with a comical twist of her lips. "There are not enough gentlemen already without adding five or six more potential female partners to the mix."

"I hope Mr. Bingley will make up in his person and character for such discourtesy as having five sisters."

"Well as to that, you are entirely correct. We are indeed blessed to have a wealthy, eligible, single gentleman now installed at Netherfield Hall; I hereby forgive him for having five sisters, or ten, or even twenty, so long as he graces us with his august presence before the end of the night."

There was a sudden flurry at the entrance to the hall as several newcomers entered, and Charlotte turned her head and said, "I believe that is Mr. Bingley and his party now! Mr. Bingley is the one in the blue coat, and there are three more gentlemen and only one lady!"

Elizabeth laughed and declared, "I like him already, my dear Charlotte, but come, I see your brother approaching, and I promised him the first dance."

Charlotte watched wistfully as her friend departed; she was seven and twenty years of age, plain, and poor, and she was rapidly dwindling into an old maid. She did not fault Elizabeth for being handsome, intelligent, and charming, but she wished that some man would gaze upon her with the admiration she saw in her own brother's face as he looked down upon her friend.

/

Fitzwilliam Darcy, master of the great estate of Pemberley in Derbyshire, reluctantly followed his friends into the large room where an assembly was in progress. He ought not to be here, he knew that. He should be back in Netherfield Park ensuring that his beloved mother and sister were settling in well. It was not fair to the people of this little town for him to intrude upon them so; they did not know that his very name was the subject of scandal and gossip in the great houses of London. He was tainted by his blood; his father had left his wife and children in anguish, and now his uncle, the Earl of Matlock, sought to destroy the fragile bonds which were welding the Darcy family back together again.

"Darcy?" Bingley asked softly. "Are you coming?"

Darcy grimaced as he observed a stout man of some fifty years, his countenance alight with welcome, waiting a few yards away.

"Mrs. Hurst," Darcy said hastily to the only female member of the party, "might I have the honor of this dance?"

Mrs. Louisa Hurst smiled sympathetically and nodded. "Of course, Mr. Darcy."

He grasped her hand and bestowed a grateful look upon the lady. He was thankful that Bingley and his married sister and her husband had welcomed the Darcys with open arms, even in the midst of dishonor and turmoil. He led her out to the dance floor as the music struck up for the next dance.

/

"Charlotte!" her father's voice said heartily from her left. "Please allow me to introduce Mr. Bingley and his party."

Charlotte turned and curtsied toward the group, which was composed only of three gentlemen since the tallest of them all, a dark haired, exceptionally handsome man, was leading out the lone woman of their party to the dance floor.

"Charlotte, Mr. Bingley, Mr. Hurst, and Mr. Wickham. Gentlemen, my elder daughter Charlotte."

"Good evening, sirs," Charlotte said politely. "It is wonderful to meet you all."

"It is our pleasure to be here," Mr. Bingley returned, a smile filling his handsome and cheerful face. "Miss Lucas, might I have the pleasure of the next dance?"

Charlotte nodded and held out her hand, "I would be honored."

/

Elizabeth had been acquainted with Samuel Lucas since they were both children. She knew he was passionate about hunting and horses, and thus she was able to keep up an inconsequential conversation through their time together while also observing Mr. Bingley and his party.

The new master of Netherfield had invited Charlotte Lucas to dance, which Elizabeth approved of tremendously. She knew that her friend sat out many dances because gentlemen were scarce and Charlotte was not pretty, though she was sensible, intelligent and kind.

Of the four other newcomers, one was a finely dressed, pretty woman of some five and twenty years, another a plump man with a rubicund complexion, and the remaining two men were a startling contrast in male beauty. The one dancing with the lady of his party was tall, dark, and grim while the other gentleman, who was currently circling around Charlotte's younger sister, Maria, was of medium height, blond, blue-eyed, and wore a winsome smile on his fair countenance.

Elizabeth chuckled aloud at her mother's likely response to this deluge of handsome male humanity at the assembly, though of course it remained to be seen whether the Mr. Bingley's companions were single and wealthy; both were vitally important to Mrs. Bennet of Longbourn, who was most eager to find rich men as husbands for her five poorly-dowered daughters.

/

George Wickham looked down happily at his partner. He had been working hard for many weeks and, as a friendly soul, was delighted to spend a pleasant evening dancing with comely young ladies. His current partner was one of five Bennet daughters, four of whom had inherited their mother's considerable beauty.

"I do enjoy London very much, Miss Elizabeth," he said cheerfully, "but the country has its own pleasures. Do you visit London often?"

"I generally visit my uncle and aunt in Gracechurch Street at least once a year," Elizabeth answered as her feet glided through the familiar steps of the cotillion. "I enjoy London, though I love my home as well."

"I understand completely," Wickham said heartily. "My childhood home lies in Derbyshire, on the great estate of Pemberley, and I always feel at peace there, though I relish traveling to other places as well."

Elizabeth twirled in place and asked, "Pemberley? Is it a large estate?"

"A very large estate, yes, whose owner is propping up the wall of your assembly room even now."

Elizabeth followed her companion's glance toward the dark haired, handsome gentleman and lifted an inquiring eyebrow. "I assume he is a friend of Mr. Bingley's?"

Wickham nodded and said, "Yes, that is Mr. Darcy, master of Pemberley, whom I am honored to call my friend as well. We grew up together, you see, though I was but the son of the steward and he the heir of the estate. He has been very kind to me."

Elizabeth cast another long stare at the gentleman and turned her attention back to her partner. "He has a very fine figure, Mr. Wickham, though he is not quite as handsome as you are."

Wickham managed a slight bow in the midst of their rotation around one another and said, "Why thank you, Miss Elizabeth; most ladies find my friend more appealing."

"No doubt due to his wealth?" Elizabeth inquired archly. "Does that explain his disinclination to dance with any of the local ladies? I daresay he is used to being feted and flattered and fawned over at the parties in London."

A shadow crossed Mr. Wickham's face, and he shook his head. "No, Miss Elizabeth, my friend is quite a ... a humble personage, truly. I suspect he is not asking any of the fine ladies to dance because he is not certain that he is an acceptable partner for such beautiful young women."

Elizabeth curtsied as the dance came to an end, and she smiled up into Wickham's face. "I am certain your friend is a most acceptable partner, at least so long as he does not trip over his toes or worse yet, mine."

"He is quite an accomplished dancer," Wickham assured her. "Might I introduce him to you?"

"Certainly!"

Lady and gentleman walked in perfect amity toward Darcy, only to realize that Mr. Bingley, the new master of nearby Netherfield Hall, had similar thoughts.

"Come, Darcy," he insisted from his position next to his taller friend, "I must have you dance. I hate to see you standing about by yourself in this stupid manner. You had much better dance."

The tall master of Pemberley ducked his head and murmured something too quietly for Elizabeth to hear, and Bingley responded indignantly, "Nonsense, my friend, nonsense. You are not making an offer of marriage, but merely asking..."

He broke off as Wickham arrived with Elizabeth at his side. The lady considered the unknown gentleman with interest; now that he was standing directly in front of her, she realized that he was even more handsome than she had discerned from across the room, blessed with height, wavy black hair, a tall, muscular form, and dark brown eyes which at the moment were filled with worry.

"Miss Elizabeth," Wickham said, "may I please introduce you to my friend, Mr. Fitzwilliam Darcy. Darcy, Miss Elizabeth Bennet."

The lady curtsied and the man bowed before saying hesitantly, "Might I solicit your hand for the next dance, Miss Elizabeth?"

"Certainly, Mr. Darcy."

"Is this your first journey to Hertfordshire, Mr. Darcy?" Elizabeth asked courteously as the pair twirled in a country dance.

"I have never stayed in Hertfordshire," Darcy responded, "though I have ridden through it on occasion. It seems a pleasant area."

"It is," Elizabeth agreed.

Silence fell again as Elizabeth considered her partner. He was rich, along with being an excellent dancer. It was most peculiar that the gentleman seemed so uncertain of himself. Perhaps he was shy? Elizabeth enjoyed analyzing the characters of new acquaintances, and it seemed that Mr. Darcy would prove an interesting study.

"Mr. Wickham tells me that you have an estate in Derbyshire," she said a few minutes later. If the poor man was bashful, she would do her best to give him easy conversational topics.

"I do, yes," Darcy answered, and lapsed into silence again.

Elizabeth suppressed an irritated groan. Pulling conversation out of this man was like trying to squeeze blood from a turnip.

"What is the geology like, sir?" she tried. "I enjoy rocks and mountains and hills and forests."

The man's gloomy countenance lightened a little at this, and he finally managed to speak more than a few words. "It is very different from here in Hertfordshire, Miss Elizabeth. My estate is not far from the Peak District, which is renowned for its mountains, rivers, and gorges."

"It sounds delightful," Elizabeth said with an encouraging smile. "Is much of your estate forested?"

"Approximately half of the demesne is covered with trees..."

George Wickham, who was dancing with Miss Kitty Bennet, relaxed as he and his partner swirled by Darcy and Miss Elizabeth. It seemed that the lady had managed to entice Darcy to speak, which was encouraging.

He sighed inwardly as he looked down at his fair partner. His poor friend had indeed suffered these last months, and Wickham hoped that here in Hertfordshire, Darcy would find both rest and friendship in the kindly locals.

/

I hope you enjoyed this excerpt from *Darcy in Distress*! The complete book is approximately 390 pages and contains 31 chapters plus 2 chapters of epilogue

and multiple happily ever afters! It is <u>now available on</u> <u>Amazon and Kindle Unlimited</u>.

- Laraba

Regency Romance Books by Laraba Kendig

Available now on Amazon and Kindle Unlimited!

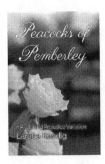

Peacocks of Pemberley

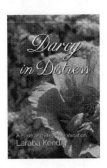

Darcy in Distress

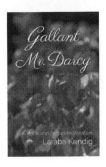

Gallant Mr. Darcy

Longbourn's Son

The Golden Daffodil

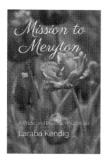

Mission to Meryton

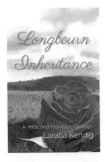

Longbourn Inheritance

The Enigmatic Mr. Collins

Darcy Sails After Her

A Fortuitous Fall

The Banished Uncle

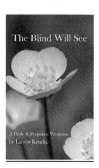

The Blind Will See

I am Jael

<u>I Have Been Jaeled</u>

Available now on Amazon and Kindle Unlimited!

Note from the Author

A year after my husband and I were married, we went on vacation to the Upper Peninsula of Michigan, in the so called Rabbit Ear which pokes into Lake Superior. I went there for my undergraduate studies at Michigan Technological University and wanted to show the area to my husband. One day we went on a hike which ended on the shore of Lake Superior, and my favorite straw hat was blown into the water and started drifting away. My husband, like Mr. Darcy, did not leap in after it. That was a good call as the water of Lake Superior is dangerously cold, and it was just a hat ... and the wind was quickly blowing it away from the shore. But it was my favorite hat.

Peafowl! They are fascinating birds, are they not? I have never owned peafowl and never will, as a horde of children is quite enough work. I did purchase several books about peafowl so that I could write about them with some level of authority. One book, *Why Peacocks*, by Sean Flynn, gives a first person account of a writer who acquired a few peacocks here in the United States. In spite of the harsh winters and in spite of the fact that the common peacock originates from warmer climates, his peacocks thrived. So yes, peacocks would be happy in Pemberley.

Also, there *are* entirely white peafowl now, though I found no record of such a bird in the Regency times. They are not albinos, oddly enough, but they have a genetic mutation called leucism. They have normal eye color, where as an albino creature has no pigment at all. In the wild, I would guess a white peafowl would attract predators because it would not blend into its surroundings, but in a safe environment, they thrive.

Lastly, I hope it was clear that I was writing Georgiana as being on the autism spectrum. I am not an expert in this area and ask forgiveness for any errors in my portrayal of Georgiana. I did read much of the book *Autism in Heels* by Jennifer Cook O'Toole; she was diagnosed late in life with autism, which explained a great deal about her struggles as a child, teenager, and young adult. I also was inspired by Temple Grandin, who has a remarkable ability to understand animals.

Again, thank you for reading my book. I hope you enjoyed reading this story as much as I enjoyed writing it. ☺

Don't forget ... **to sign up for my free monthly Regency Romance Newsletter.** When you sign up, you will get a FREE story just for members called *A Busy and Blessed Day*. You will also be among the first to hear when my next book is released, about special promotions, insight into my writing, etc. Click here to get your free story.

Here is the link in case you need to manually type it in:
www.subscribepage.com/s1p4z6

Dedication

As usual, my husband was a tower of strength through the writing of this book. I am "the talent" in that I write the stories (and a tongue-in-cheek joke between us!), but he manages the editing, the book cover design, and all the hoops that Amazon has for us to jump through in order to publish our books. He also works full time to provide for me and our large family. In addition, we had a second round of COVID-19 in September and October, so it was a crazy time! Honey, you are amazing and I love you!

Copyright © 2022 by Laraba Kendig

Made in the USA
Columbia, SC
02 February 2023

11474946R00272